DEAD LIST

A THRILLER

JOHN CORWIN

RAVEN HOUSE

BOOKS BY JOHN CORWIN-

PSYCHOLOGICAL THRILLERS

The Family Business

AMOS CARVER THRILLERS

Dead Before Dawn

Dead List

Dead and Buried

Dead Man Walking

Dead by the Dozen

Dead Run

Dead Weather Days

Dead to Rights

Dead But Not Forgotten

CHRONICLES OF CAIN

To Kill a Unicorn

Enter Oblivion

Throne of Lies

At The Forest of Madness

The Dead Never Die

Shadow of Cthulhu

Cabal of Chaos

Monster Squad

KILL OR BE KILLED

Amos Carver is just minding his own business when a woman falls to her death right around the corner from where he's working.

At first it seems like a senseless tragedy. An accident. Carver can't help but investigate. When he does, he realizes this was no ordinary woman. She was a trained killer. And she was looking for him.

There's a contract on Carver's head. But who's behind it? The Brazilians? His former government unit, Scion? The military company, Breakstone?

Running isn't an option. If they tracked him to his new city, they can track him anywhere. Some problems are best met head on. Especially when the prey is a trained killer himself. The game becomes survival of the fittest.

But it doesn't matter how many assassins Carver kills if he can't find out who's funding them. It's a simple numbers game. They'll keep coming. Carver will get tired and eventually slip up. Then a bullet or a blade will put him six feet under.

Carver will have to stay in the shadows. Strike when he can. Find allies if possible. Follow the trail of money and bodies to the top.

And cut the head off the snake.

— • —

CHAPTER 1

SATURDAY NIGHT

A body hurtled groundward.

It slammed into a dumpster in an alley. A club entrance was just around the corner. The twenty-somethings waiting to go inside shouted in unison when the dumpster rang like a gong. Some jumped. Others scattered like frightened deer.

Carver was also just around the corner. He wasn't going into the club. He was a bouncer. He'd been working at Club Periclean for a few months. He'd broken up fights. Dragged out drunks. Strongarmed troublemakers. But he hadn't heard a ruckus like this before.

His first instinct was to take cover. He didn't jump. Didn't shout. But he did back up a few steps behind the safety of a concrete wall. A moment later he registered two things. One: The sound wasn't a gunshot. Two: It came from the alley.

He walked around the corner into the alley. The streetlamp highlighted a horror scene. He saw blood. Saw an arm dangling over the side of the dumpster. Carver jogged over. Looked inside. Saw a crumpled body. The clothing was casual. Jeans and a t-shirt. The face was a bloody mess, but the long, blond hair hinted at a woman. The bone structure in the face confirmed it. Even with all the blood he could tell she was young. Maybe early thirties.

She didn't have a purse. A phone. Nothing that Carver could see, anyway. No bulges in the jean pockets. Nothing near her hand. It was possible she'd been holding a phone. If she had, it was somewhere in the dumpster. Probably smashed to pieces.

Carver looked up. The club was in the bottom of La Playa, a high-rise condominium. This one was thirty stories tall. She could have fallen from anywhere. The roof. Maybe the single illuminated balcony about twenty stories up. It was hard to say. It was nearly one in the morning on a Saturday. Most condo residents were probably asleep.

Some of the people waiting in line wandered around the corner. Cell phones recorded. Gasps of disbelief. Cries of horror. One girl bent over and threw up.

"Holy shit. What happened?" A guy rushed over and looked inside the dumpster. He reeled back. Stumbled. Probably never seen a dead body before. Definitely not one broken and tangled like this one. He doubled over and vomited.

Carver had seen plenty of bodies in worse shape. Blown up. Burned. Incinerated. Run over by a tank. He hadn't seen many that had fallen from tall buildings, though he'd certainly introduced a few targets to gravity.

The other bouncer, Jeff, ran around the corner. "What the hell was that?"

"Someone fell." Carver didn't try to stop the crowd from looking inside the dumpster. "Call the police."

Jeff saw the arm. He waded through the gathering crowd. Looked inside. Quailed. "Oh, shit. Oh, God."

There was a lot of that going around. A lot of curious people suddenly wishing they hadn't been so curious.

Carver went back to the unguarded club entrance. The line was a lot shorter. Most of the crowd had gone for a look at the body. He wondered if the woman had jumped. If it was an accident. If someone pushed her.

Jeff came back around the corner. Phone to his ear. Talking. "It's horrible. Please get someone here immediately." He nodded a few times. Ended the call.

"I'll be right back," Carver said.

Jeff nodded. He was shaken. Eyes distant. Mind clouded.

The club entrance was near the main entrance to the condos. There was a horseshoe drive for the club, and one for the condos. They were separated by a strip of bushes. Cars pulled in. A valet took the car. There was no self-parking on the premises for the condo or the club.

The difference between the club and the condo entrances were the elevators. The club was only two levels. Level one had a bar and dance floor. Level two was the VIP lounge. There were stairs and two elevators. But they only went to the second level. There was no way to access the higher floors in the building from the club. Not as far as Carver knew.

The condo entrance led to an elevator lobby. Two elevators shuttled residents and guests to higher floors. There was a service elevator around the back near a loading dock. It was used when residents moved in. Carver knew this because he liked to know the layout of a place if he was going to be there a lot. Entrances, exits, escapes were important.

There was a side entrance to the condos just inside the parking garage. You could slip in the door. Creep to the elevator lobby. Go to any floor. He'd done it before. He'd gone to the roof for a bird's-eye view of the surroundings. From there, he'd mapped out his escape routes.

Some might call it paranoia. Carver called it being prepared. It was just as normal to him as brushing his teeth. Curiosity was also normal to him. It sometimes conflicted with the paranoia. One side of him was saying to stay put. The other side wanted to have a look. To see if there was more to this than an accident.

This time the curiosity won.

Carver jogged around to the condo entrance. Slowed his pace. Stood within view of the exit. It had been two minutes since the woman landed in the dumpster. That was a lot of time for someone to come down the elevators. At this hour not many people would be using them. They were slow for a building this tall, but not so slow that someone couldn't get out of the building in two minutes.

But that was under normal circumstances. Carver had seen the elevator repair van sitting in the drive earlier. One elevator was out of service. That left one elevator for thirty floors. Even at this hour the lift was getting some use. It was Miami, after all. Plenty of night owls of all ages.

The main condo entrance was all glass. Carver could see the elevator lobby from his position. He saw an older couple exit. They were dressed up. Laughing. Staggering. They stopped to talk to the concierge. Greetings were exchanged. They all laughed about something. The woman pointed at the valet station. Nodded. Waved goodbye.

Another man exited the elevator a moment later. He wasn't smiling. Wasn't staggering. He walked slow, like someone trying to look unhurried. Unworried. He wore black jeans. A dark shirt. He had a thick mustache. No beard. A thick head of hair combed to the side. He was young. Probably in his late twenties.

The look in the man's eyes set off all kinds of alarms in Carver's head. He wasn't just some resident out for a late-night walk. He wasn't just some young guy, either. He had that dead look in his face. Like someone who'd seen too much for anything to bother him. He also left via the parking garage door. Slipped out quiet as a ghost.

It was possible that man had something to do with the woman's death. It was also possible Carver was reading too much into his body language. Sometimes you'd see what you wanted to see. But his gut disagreed. It told him he was right. The other thing his gut said was that it was none of his business.

Don't get involved.

The man walked to the street. Leaned on a palm tree next to the sidewalk. Took out a phone and started tapping on the screen. Carver moved so the bushes hid him. He kept watching. The guy kept messing with his phone. He didn't smile. Didn't laugh. Didn't react to anything he saw on his screen. Just kept the same dead expression.

A vape pen appeared in his hand. He took a long draw. Kept tapping on his phone. Another draw. More scrolling on the phone. He tucked away the vape. Stared long and hard at something on the screen. Turned and walked back toward the condo building. But this time he was headed to the club.

Carver was starting to think his gut reaction was all wrong. Police sirens wailed in the distance. They were on the way. The guy didn't seem to care. He kept coming. Tires screeched. An unmarked police cruiser peeled around the corner. Pulled into the mouth of the alley. A middle-aged man in a cheap suit got out. Started shouting at the crowd.

Another guy got out of the other side of the car. He talked to the first guy. Nodded a few times. Started shooing people back from the crime scene. He and the other guy looked like plainclothes cops. Maybe detectives.

The mustached man saw the cops. He didn't falter. Kept walking straight toward the club. Not a worry showing on his face. No curiosity either. Like the appearance of two detectives was of no concern. Carver backed up. Kept the concrete column between him and the guy. He walked back to the club entrance. Jeff was outside talking to the night manager, Preston.

"Hey, Clint." Jeff waved him over. "Can you get the crowd back in line?"

"Why didn't you bar them from the alley?" Preston looked from Jeff to Carver. "The last thing we want is social media flooded with videos about a dead woman outside our club!"

Jeff looked pale. "I nearly lost my shit when I saw the body. I'm sorry."

Preston sighed. "Clint, get that crowd cleared out. The police are going to be pissed."

The detective was still trying to push back the onlookers but wasn't having much luck. Carver waded through the crowd. Got to the dumpster. Folded his arms over his chest and gave a cold look at the club-goers. "I need everyone back to the line. This is a crime scene. Anyone who doesn't go now will spend the night in jail."

People exchanged worried looks. Women tugged their friends' arms. Dragged them away. Some of the men followed. There were a few stragglers, but they turned tail when Carver came for them.

The cop threw up his hands. "Why wasn't that done first thing? This crime scene is going to be dirty as hell."

Carver walked back to the mouth of the alley. He saw the guy from the condo talking to Jeff and Preston. They were both shaking their heads. The guy motioned toward the door. Said something else. Preston shook his head. Pointed to the line. The guy took out a wad of money. Preston looked tempted, but he pointed to the line again.

The guy looked around. Saw Carver. Saw the detective. He got in the back of the line and stood there.

The detective was staring at the arm dangling out of the dumpster. "What happened?"

"I heard a loud crash. I came around the corner and saw that." Carver poked a finger at the dumpster. "I took a look inside. Female, late thirties. Burgundy jeans and a white t-shirt."

The detective gave him a curious look. "You a cop in a former life?"

Carver shook his head. "No."

"Okay, so what were you, then?"

"I watch a lot of detective shows." Carver shrugged. "That's about the extent of it."

The detective grunted. "Yeah. Everyone thinks they can solve crimes after watching one season of CSI."

"Not me. Too much work."

"Hey Hughes!" The detective called to his partner. "Walk the perimeter for me?"

The other detective nodded. Started walking around the side of the building.

Blue lights flashed. Two more patrol cars veered around the corner. The uniforms got out of the cars and the detective started barking orders.

Carver started to leave, but the detective stopped him.

"I'm going to need a sworn statement."

"I told you all I know."

"Put it on a piece of paper and sign it." The detective gave him a card that said Bill Leach on it. "Call me if you think of anything else."

"Sure." Carver went to the door entrance. Preston was gone. Jeff was turning away a group of older women. They weren't taking the rejection well. One of them shouted at Jeff. Grabbed his arm.

The guy from the condo walked around the line. Straight up to Carver. "Are you Carver?"

Carver frowned. "Who?"

"Amos Carver."

Carver shook his head. "I'm Clint. I don't know a Carver."

The guy looked him up and down. "Funny. I was told there's a big guy who works here. Name of Carver."

"Got a picture?"

"No."

"Description?"

The man shook his head. "No, I'm a friend of a friend. I just need to give him a message."

"From who?"

"A concerned citizen."

Carver shrugged. "Write it down. I'll give it to office manager."

He shook his head. "I've got to deliver it straight to him. Can you find out if he works here?"

Carver turned to the side. "Hey, Jeff, you know a big guy by the name of Carver?"

Jeff glanced back. He was letting a group of girls through the rope. "Who?"

"Carver."

Jeff did a doubletake when he saw the condo guy. "I told you there's no one here by that name."

"What's your name?" Carver asked. "Maybe he's one of the kitchen staff. I'll go tell them you're looking for him."

"Can you get me in?" The guy flashed a wad of money. "Make it worth your while."

Carver took the money. "Yeah, come on in." He opened the door. Let the guy go in. Then he walked back over to Jeff. Stared down a pair of guys who were giving Jeff some lip. They saw Carver and backed down.

It was curious. The guy might have just pushed a woman to her death. Then he came from the condos, straight to the club and asked for Carver. He didn't have a military look to him. Didn't look like someone who'd done time in the service. He didn't look like a Brazilian drug cartel member either. As far as he knew, those were the only two groups of people who might want him dead.

Carver didn't like that his name might somehow be connected to the dead woman in the alley. But he also couldn't simply go into the club and follow the guy around.

He had been on the other side of the state. Resting and relaxing in Clearwater. He'd had enough money to get by on. He could've had more, but he'd given most of it to Paola. She'd gotten tired. Wanted more from him. He wasn't the kind of guy to settle down. To give her what she wanted. So, she'd decided to leave. To start a new life somewhere else.

He'd given her two bags of cash stolen from her former employers. She'd cried. Told him she wished things could be different. Wished he felt the same way she did. And that was the problem. He had feelings for her. He'd wanted her to stay. But that wasn't good for anyone, especially not her.

Paola had left. Then he'd left a few weeks later. Used his money to buy fake IDs, moved to Miami, became a bouncer under the name Clint Wilkins.

The fact that someone had traced his real name to this location was concerning. It meant his fake identity might be compromised soon. That just wasn't going to work for him. It was time to move on. To find a place so remote they'd never find him.

First, he had to figure out how he'd been traced here. He hadn't told a soul where he was going. What he was doing. He'd gone to a trusted contact for the fake ID and documents. They were good. They'd given him a new life with social security number, history, and everything. He hadn't told them where he was going either.

So, why was someone here asking for him by name?

CHAPTER 2

WEDNESDAY AFTERNOON

Who is Amos Carver?

The words hung on the laptop screen. The cursor blinked behind the question mark. Elena Diaz hit the enter key and moved it down a line. She had barely scratched the surface of the Morganville story. No matter how hard she dug, she kept hitting roots.

None of the local cops would talk to her. The feds had swept in and thrown a blanket over the whole thing. But even the feds were fighting among themselves. They might try to keep everything secret, but sitting in the local diner was a real eye-opener.

There were FBI types. NSA types. Military types. The CIA might even be in the mix, but they were hard to tell apart from the others.

Elena sipped her coffee and watched a pair of the military types eating sandwiches. They were easy to identify with their buzzcuts, demeanor, and stride. They were also in better shape than most.

Three FBI agents sat at another table. They looked with suspicion at the military guys. They were in decent shape. A couple wore cheap suits and had facial hair that wouldn't pass muster in the military. Or maybe it would these days. The standards had fallen far since her father had served.

There were no locals in the diner. Morganville had been on its deathbed for decades. It had gone from a graveyard to a slaughterhouse. Now it was about to become a graveyard once again. Maybe this time for good. The mayor and his son were dead. The wife and daughter had returned to bury the other half of their family.

Elena had interviewed them. They'd been shocked. Devastated. They were also in acute denial about the activities of their male family members. The sex trafficking, their relationship to the massive drug ring in the paint factory, and the deaths of dozens of women at their hands.

The feds were focusing their investigation on that. The official statements all read the same. A local sex and drug trafficking ring had been put down with assistance from Breakstone, a private military company. Federal agencies had assisted.

Jasper Whittaker had been at the center of it all. He'd been the ringleader. Overseen drug and sex trafficking and every crime in the entire county if the feds were to be believed. There had been a Brazilian connection, but the feds said it was all on Jasper.

And he was conveniently dead.

But there were multiple crime scenes across the county. Dead inmates at the county jail. A burned down house with multiple bodies inside, including two guards from that jail. A roadside motel where dried pools of blood had been discovered. The mayor's hilltop mansion massacre, and the paint factory where twenty plus bodies had been piled up like so much refuse.

The only reason anyone knew anything was because the locals had discovered the crime scenes first. Gossip had spread word far and wide on the wings of social media. But now everything was being quashed.

Gilbert sat down across from Elena. "FBI is getting ready to release a joint statement with the local PD in twenty minutes. I've got the crew waiting."

"Whoopty-fucking-do." Elena sipped her coffee. "It's just more bullshit. Why was the CEO and founder of Breakstone found dead across the road from the mayor's house? Why isn't anyone talking about Chad Dorsey?"

"Mayor Morgan hired security personnel from Breakstone. One of his guys put out a high alert and I guess Dorsey decided to personally check in on it."

"More bullshit!" Elena hissed it quietly. There were more fed ears in here than at Quantico. Some of them were looking at her. She looked right back at them. "Care to comment about it?"

The military types looked at her. One of them grinned. "Over dinner?"

The FBI agents regarded her with dead stares. Then they went back to eating.

Elena gave Gilbert a knowing look. "They're tossing us rotten scraps. The real story is being covered up."

"I think they're just working through a mountain of stuff."

Elena stared at the question on her laptop screen for a moment. Then she closed it. She slid the laptop into her backpack and picked it up. "Guess I'll see you at the news conference." She left.

The streets outside were empty. An old man walked his dog down Main Street. He was the same old man who'd discovered three bodies in an ancient boiler behind the equally ancient electric company building. She'd interviewed him and discovered he knew nothing of importance.

She hurried around the corner before he saw her. Every time he saw a reporter, he'd talk to them. Try to extend his fifteen minutes of fame. He didn't seem to understand how small and insignificant his role had been in the grand scheme of things in Morganville.

The only name of note was spoken in hushed whispers. She'd overheard one of the cops saying the name. When she'd asked about it, they'd closed down real fast. But it was obvious from the looks on their faces that they were conspiring to keep it quiet.

"I agree with you."

Elena nearly jumped out of her skin. She turned and saw a middle-aged woman standing near the back corner of the building. "I'm sorry. What?"

"They're covering it up." The woman spoke softly. "My cousin saw those women that were being trafficked up at the old Whittaker mansion. She was part of the cleaning crew that tidied up the place about once a month. She was going to stop by one evening and take a look around to see what needed cleaning, but the lights were on. She looked inside a window and saw a whole mess of women inside. They looked rough. Beaten up."

"She didn't call the police?"

"There was a cop inside with them. Holly Robinson."

"She didn't knock or ask what was going on?"

The woman shook her head. "She figured Jasper must have let them use the place for something. She was just with the cleaning service, so she left."

"All those abused women were staying in Jasper's mansion?"

"Yeah, and the strange thing is, it was days before all hell broke loose and the feds swarmed this town."

"Has she been out to the mansion since then?"

The woman nodded. "She says a couple of women are still hiding out there. Like they decided to just stay. Maybe one of them will tell you what really happened. I ain't no conspiracy theorist, but you don't get this many federal agencies and the military poking around if there ain't something huge going on."

"I agree." Elena smiled. "Thank you so much. What's your name?"

"I ain't saying and keep me out of it." The woman smiled back. "Good luck, young lady. You're going to need it."

Elena shivered with excitement. This might be the one thing that broke the story wide open. Or it might be another dead end. She'd spoken to Deputy Robinson a few times and had been convinced the woman was stonewalling her. Now she knew for certain that was the truth.

Gilbert and Twila were waiting outside the police department for the news conference. Elena wanted to skip it, but she didn't feel like losing her job. It had taken years to work up to being an on-camera reporter. She'd worked hard to keep her body in good shape. To maintain her good looks.

Ten years ago, that alone would have landed her in front of the camera out in the field. These days nobody wanted to be accused of hiring someone based on looks or other physical features. She'd had to fight off three men for the job. Only her tenacity and willingness to go above and beyond had landed her ahead of them.

Twila handed Elena a list of questions. They were the same questions everyone was already asking. The same questions the investigators routinely ignored or glossed over.

Chief Ritter spoke first. "First, I want to thank Agent Beauregard and his team for their top-notch expertise and assistance. Second, I'd like to thank federal government for supporting the investigation as much as they have."

Agent Beauregard was the tough old piece of meat standing next to him. He looked like a man who'd survived the kind of stress that would kill most people. He just smiled and nodded as Ritter spoke. Then Ritter finished his piece and motioned Beauregard to come talk.

"Thank you, Chief Ritter." Beauregard set a tablet on the podium. A pair of large screen televisions turned on and displayed a map of the area. On it were several dots and lines connecting them.

It was the same map they'd been using to tie together the multiple crime scenes. Information had been filled in little by little. Now weeks later, all the dots had something associated with them.

The agent spoke for a while, reviewing everything they'd mentioned before. He went over tidbits of new information. Then he surprised everyone with his next words. "We have now concluded the investigation. Only cleanup remains."

Agent Beauregard looked down at the tablet and brought up another image, a timeline of events. "This is the timeline we've assembled." He tapped on the first event. "Late Chief Rhodes was investigating the paint factory. She requested assistance from former military acquaintances who were then working for Breakstone. The cartel discovered this and killed her. Late CEO of Breakstone, Chad Dorsey, sent two squads of his people to investigate. He did this free of charge at the request of Rhodes's former squad mates, Tony Menendez and Sam Rocker."

He tapped down to another point on the timeline. "They traced the cartel to the paint factory. They confronted Jasper Whittaker. A firefight broke out. There were multiple casualties. Meanwhile, another cartel attack happened at the mayor's mansion. The Breakstone personnel there sent an emergency call to their headquarters. They were short of personnel since many were out of state training. Dorsey organized a small squad consisting of himself, Menendez, and Rocker. They left Atlanta and drove to Morganville to assist."

Beauregard went to the next item. "They were ambushed upon reaching the mansion. They were all killed as was everyone at the mayor's mansion. In conclusion, it is our finding that Jasper Whittaker colluded with a Brazilian drug cartel to distribute drugs and women across the southeastern states. Morganville was one distribution hub. This investigation should lead us to others."

He cleared his throat and continued. "Mayor Morgan was a user of the sex trafficking, not a distributor. He aided and abetted Jasper Whittaker's criminal enterprise."

"It's a lie!" Allegra Morgan, the late mayor's wife, stood at the back of the crowd. "They're all lies! My husband would never do any of this."

Agent Beauregard went quiet and watched while a pair of deputies escorted the sobbing woman away. He spoke somberly once she was gone. "I know this is very hard to hear. Friends and neighbors of the community were doing horrible things behind the scenes. We have a complete list of accomplices, including two security guards from the county prison. We will disseminate our findings to the press at the end of this conference."

"I'm sure it'll be useful," Elena muttered.

"Finally, Chad Dorsey and Breakstone were not liable for any of the activities. The guards who aided the mayor and kept the secrets of his criminal activities were not acting in accordance with Breakstone rules and regulations. Breakstone is hereby cleared of any wrongdoing. With that, I am going to allow the current CEO of Breakstone to make a statement." He stepped aside.

A young, fit man stepped up to the podium. He offered a somber smile. "I'm Leon Fry, the new CEO of Breakstone. Our hearts go out to the community for the tragedies that occurred here. It was Chad Dorsey's sincerest hope that Breakstone could help overextended police forces keep law and order across America. That includes fighting small time criminals and large-scale organizations like cartels."

He looked around the crowd. "I'd like to say that despite the extreme disparity in numbers, our highly trained operatives were able to overcome and defeat a huge cartel operation. This despite us not knowing what we were up against. Chad Dorsey believed in his mission so much that he died for it. I'm happy to say that Breakstone will continue his mission. We will recover and grow stronger. Morganville marked a major milestone for us, and we hope that this will encourage other communities to put their faith in us."

He left the podium and stepped down.

Agent Beauregard returned to the microphone. "And with that, I will now take questions."

Elena raised her hand along with the other reporters. There was more press here than on a good day in the White House briefing room. The story had captured national attention. It had seemingly involved a massive conspiracy that included Breakstone. But the FBI and others had put in overtime to make them look like innocent victims.

Of that, she was sure.

Beauregard took questions from ten reporters. Every single question was a softball he hit out of the park. Elena took note of the reporters he chose. She didn't recognize a single one except for two from national news outlets. Even they didn't ask hard questions. It probably wouldn't have done any good anyway.

Elena still tried. She took a deep breath and shouted, "Who is Amos Carver? Why is the FBI orchestrating a coverup for Breakstone?"

Nearby reporters looked around for the source of the question. But other reporters were shouting questions of their own. Desperately trying to squeeze one more answer out of the lead agent.

Leon Fry was the only one who looked concerned by the name. He stared at her for a moment then started talking to his assistant.

Beauregard kept talking like no one said anything. "This will be the last press conference. We are packing up and heading out. Thank you for your patience as we investigated and made sense out of a very complicated series of events." Then he turned and left as other reporters clamored for his attention and shouted questions.

Chief Ritter was the only one who didn't plaster a smile on his face. He looked pensive. Maybe a little sad. He knew the truth and he didn't like what was happening. But Elena had tried interviewing him. He'd given her the same runaround as all the other cops.

"Boss wants us back in Atlanta tonight," Gilbert said. "I'm going to the hotel room to pack."

"I need the car." Elena held out her hand for the keys.

Gilbert gave her the keys. Ten years ago, they would have rolled up in a broadcast van. Now everything could be done with a laptop. Live broadcasts went over the cellular network. No need for the giant antennas anymore.

She was turning to leave when Leon Fry stepped in front of her. He looked even younger up close, but his eyes told a different story. "What do you know about Amos Carver?"

Elena raised an eyebrow. "What do you know about him?"

"I'm just looking for loose ends like everyone else." He smiled, but it didn't reach his eyes. He handed her a scrap of paper. "This is my personal cell number. Feel free to call if you find out more about him."

"What's your interest?"

"I've heard the name several times. No one knows who he is." Leon shrugged. "I'm curious to find out."

"So am I." Elena put the number into her phone. "If I find out more, will you agree to an interview?"

"Sure." Leon's smiled grew friendlier. "I will warn you that I'm new to my leadership position. I still don't know everything about Breakstone."

"I'm sure whatever you have to say will be interesting." Elena noticed that others were watching them talk. The feds looked suspicious. They didn't like this.

Leon's assistant took his arm. "Sir, we have to get back to Atlanta. You have another appointment."

"Okay." Leon nodded at Elena. "Have a good day, Ms. Diaz." He left.

Elena watched him leave. Wondered why he was so interested in Amos Carver. Hopefully, she could find out. She went to the parking lot behind the only hotel in town. Walked to the rental car, a plain white sedan.

She searched the maps app and found the address for the Whittaker mansion. It was apparently considered a landmark of Morganville even though it was a couple miles outside of town. She reached for the door handle.

"Elena!"

Elena opened the door halfway and turned around. A woman was weaving between parked cars toward her. She was blond. Pretty. Wearing a navy-blue pantsuit reserved for women twice her age. She had a press badge hanging on a lanyard around her neck just like all the other news hounds.

The badge had flipped around so the name wasn't visible. Elena closed the car door. "Can I help you?"

The other woman was panting when she reached her. "I was trying to catch you but, my God, there are so many people out here today." She had a genteel southern accent. The kind you only heard in movies.

Elena remembered seeing this woman a day or so ago. But she'd looked different. She certainly hadn't been wearing a pantsuit. "I'm sorry, who are you?"

"Oh, where are my manners?" The woman flipped the badge around. "I'm Melinda Gross with the Washington Post. I was born and raised one county over. I never thought Morganville would be a hot spot for national news."

Elena felt bad for anyone who worked for a newspaper these days. They relied heavily on their internet paywalls and online advertisers rather than the actual paper that was their namesake. "How can I help you, Melinda?"

"That name, Amos Carver. I've heard it mentioned before. But nobody can tell me anything about the person it belongs to. If you have more information about this mystery man, maybe we can pool our resources and find out who he is."

Elena had already asked other reporters if they'd heard the name. A few had. None of them thought it was important. Had she finally found someone who believed the same as her?

"As long as the pooling of resources is equitable, yes. I'll be upfront and tell you that all I have is a name and several people mentioned seeing a drifter by that name here before the town turned into a warzone." Elena decided to keep her cards close to her chest until Melinda proved she had useful information. "That's all I know."

"I'm in the same boat as you." Melinda sighed. "The local police are playing dumb. I've interviewed dozens of locals and only a few remember a big guy by that name."

"Feels like the entire town is stonewalling us." Elena reached for the door handle to the car. "If I find out anything, I'll let you know."

"I'd be willing to share a byline with you if we could cooperate closely on this." Melinda handed her a business card. "That's my cell number. You can reach me anytime."

Elena didn't have a business card. They were old-fashioned. "I'd certainly love a byline in a big newspaper like yours." She opened the car door. "I'll be in touch."

"Great!" Melinda waved. "Talk to you soon."

Elena slid into the car. Closed the door and started the engine. She nosed out of the parking lot and onto Main Street. Cut down a sealed chip road that rumbled beneath the tires. She hit seventy miles per hour in the fifty zone, but all the cops were back in town sniffing each other's asses and celebrating the end of the investigation.

The iron gate to the circular drive was open. She drove around, parked right in front. Walked to the front door. She twisted the knob. The door opened. Elena walked inside to a huge foyer. There were big staircases leading to the east and west wings. An office. More rooms along the wide hall.

One was probably a dining hall. A living room or den. But there were too many to fit all the normal room names. This was a real mansion. A place with more rooms than most people had sense.

Faint music trickled from somewhere in the back. She followed the music. Entered a ballroom. It looked like something out of the 1920s. Ornate metal panels on the ceiling. Big chandeliers. Black and white checkered marble. Ornate wallpaper. The room was a work of art.

A thin young woman was dancing by herself. She spun on her toes. A ballet dancer, maybe. She gasped and froze when she saw Elena. Turned off the music.

Elena smiled reassuringly and hoped this was someone with answers.

CHAPTER 3

SATURDAY NIGHT

Carver felt hunted.

It wasn't a new feeling. He'd been hunted plenty of times. He'd been a fugitive in other countries. Hidden in the forest. Survived on the land. Eventually made his way out of the country and back to relative safety.

Just because it was something he'd experienced before didn't mean it was pleasant. That it was okay and didn't affect him. It was a gnawing sensation in the pit of his stomach. A tingling on the back of his neck. Like he was being watched. Followed. Being preyed upon by something unknown and unseen.

The guy asking about him was out in the open. That didn't mean he was a known quantity. Just because the danger was in front of you didn't mean you were any safer. This guy was probably just the tip of the iceberg. A worker bee. Doing the bidding of some unknown adversary. Or maybe he was something else. Something unexpected.

Carver had two options: investigate or leave. The problem was, he had barely enough money for a new identity. His various secret bank accounts were running low. Months ago, he'd had millions in cash. But most of that had been given away or left behind. Carrying around that much cash was too hard. He'd been satisfied with a couple hundred thousand, but most of that was now with Paola.

Leaving seemed like the best decision. He'd have to trash his fake ID. It was a huge waste of fifty grand. And now he'd have to drop another fifty on a new one. But the question still lingered. How in the hell had they found him?

The club crowd was thinning out fast. The police presence was driving away newcomers, and some who'd been in line had left. Preston looked devastated. Saturday nights were the biggest moneymakers. A dead woman had ruined his evening. Now he'd have to explain it to the club owner, Vince Fabiano. He wasn't a man who took disappointment well. He was also probably a Cuban mobster. There were a lot of those in these parts.

Carver waited for the last people in line to get through. Then he talked to Jeff. "I gotta take a leak."

"Yeah, sure." Jeff looked worried. "I don't think it'll get much busier."

Carver went inside the club. He went to the bathroom. It was packed with drunks. One guy was hunched over the sink emptying his guts. The sober men cleared a path when Carver came inside. The drunk ones were too lost in the haze to care.

Carver went to the guy puking in the sink. "You need to call a ride. You can't be here anymore."

"Dude, I'm fine." The drunk guy heaved into the sink again.

Carver lifted the man's phone from his back pocket. Held it in front of him. "Unlock the phone. I'm getting you a ride."

"Dude, I'm—"

"Say you're fine one more time, and your ride will be in the back of a cop car."

That seemed to get through the drunken haze. "Fine." He put his thumb on the screen. Unlocked it.

Carver took the phone. "Okay, meet me outside the bathroom in five minutes."

The man splashed his face with water. "I'll be there."

Carver stepped outside the bathroom. Used the man's phone to call a Clearwater number. It rang four times. Went to voicemail. Not surprising considering how early it was. He left a message. "This is Carver. Call me back ASAP."

He went to a rideshare app. Scheduled a ride for the drunk. The app said it was five minutes away. The phone rang. Carver answered it.

A female voice spoke. "Carver?"

"Amy?" Carver couldn't remember if that was her name or not. "I need to talk to Holland."

"He's dead." She whimpered. "They killed him three days ago."

Carver went still. "Tell me everything."

"I'd just come in through the back door. I heard a commotion. I heard someone asking about you."

"Male or female?"

"Female." Her voice cracked. "I grabbed a gun. Ran up front. There were two shots. A bullet punched through a wall and hit my shoulder. I went down."

"What did Holland tell them about me?"

"I don't know."

"What happened next?"

"I picked myself up. Ran to the front. He was bleeding out on the floor. Some of his fingernails were gone. I think they started torturing him before I got there. He died before I could ask him anything."

"Does he keep client information on a computer?"

"He doesn't keep normal records and he doesn't put anything on a computer. All he keeps is a paper list of new names with their new social security numbers. But it uses a cipher so nobody can read it but him."

"Was the list missing?"

"Yes."

Someone had deciphered the list. Someone had found Carver's fake social security number. They'd traced it to his job at the club. That meant they had access to government resources. But if that was the case, how hadn't that guy known his fake name was Clint? And how hadn't he known what Carver looked like?

The drunk guy staggered out. He had puke on his shirt and looked ready to pass out.

Carver kept talking to Amy. "Is there anything else you can tell me? What the woman looked like?"

"No. She was gone when I came out." She sobbed. "Who in the hell is looking for you, Carver?"

"Amy, this isn't my phone. I'll try to call you again sometime from another number." He ended the call. Deleted the records from the call log.

The rideshare car arrived. Carver dumped the drunk in the backseat and tossed his phone into his lap. Closed the door. The driver wrinkled his nose and drove away.

Running was out of the question. Carver didn't have another contact for high-quality documents. He now knew that running would be futile. The people after him had traced him to Clearwater. Traced him to Holland's. Traced him here. They'd find him wherever he went. He didn't feel like looking over his shoulder constantly.

So, he went back inside the club. If that guy was still here, then he was going to answer a few questions. Either that or Carver was going to extract a few answers. Together, they were going to establish who was after him and who he needed to kill to stop it.

Carver checked the bathroom. Checked the VIP area. There was no sign of the guy. He stopped at the main bar and asked the bartenders if they'd seen him. Sure, they'd seen a lot of guys who looked like the man he described. It was no help.

He went back through the kitchen. Out back through the service entrance. There was clattering. Something slamming into metal. Carver looked down the line of dumpsters in the back. Saw movement in the darkness. He ducked and hustled down the service road. Just outside the condo service entrance he found the guy he was looking for.

The man was gasping and holding his side. He was also bleeding out. Carver knelt and pulled up the guy's shirt. There was a nice long Z cut in his abdomen. A professional job.

Carver grabbed the guy's head. Turned it toward him. "Who are you? Who's the dead woman?"

The man blinked. Shuddered. "You Carver?"

"Yes."

The man took a shivering breath. "Elena Diaz. Assassin...kill..." His blood ran out before he finished the sentence.

"Unhelpful." Carver laid the man back down and grimaced at the blood on his hands. This was messy. And who in the hell had killed him? What in the hell was going on here?

He stayed low and peered around the dumpster. Not a soul in sight. Then he checked the man's pockets. Nothing in them. Not even spare change. Either the killer emptied them, or the guy was following protocol. His cell phone was on the ground. Smashed to bits. Like someone stomped it.

Carver didn't touch anything else. The last thing he needed was his fingerprints and DNA at a murder site. Considering how much he'd touched it might already be too late. Telling the police also wasn't an option. Not unless he wanted to be under a magnifying glass. This night was getting more complicated by the moment.

Glass shattered. Carver looked up and saw a man standing outside the service entrance. He wore a janitorial uniform. A broken bottle and spreading pool of liquid were at his feet. His mouth hung open. He looked from the corpse to Carver.

"I didn't do this, if that's what you're thinking." Carver stood. "I just found him like this."

The man was backing toward the door.

Carver kept talking. "The police are already here. Someone fell off the roof earlier right around the corner."

That didn't sway him. The janitor ran inside and slammed the door behind him. It looked like Carver wasn't going to have a choice in the matter. He looked at his bloody hands. There was no good way to clean them. He was going to have to talk to the detective. The biggest question was whether he was going to keep pretending to be Clint Wilkins or come clean as Amos Carver.

The dead man had been looking for him. If Carver gave up his real name, then anyone else coming after him would have an easier time finding him. On the other hand, using his fake name hadn't helped all that much. Now that they had his fake SSN, this identity was burned.

But keeping the fake identity might muddy the waters. It might make it just confusing enough that the next guy didn't know Wilkins was Carver. That might give Carver enough time to react.

Carver took the long walk around the back of the building. The alley was roped off around the dumpster. Detective Leach was standing in the middle of it, watching a crime scene unit work on it.

Leach glanced up. Saw Carver. Carver held up bloody hands. Motioned him over. The detective put a hand on his service piece. He motioned his partner, Hughes, over. Pointed at Carver.

"I found another body," Carver said.

"What?" Leach approached, hand still on the hilt of his gun. "Is that why there's blood on your hands?"

Hughes drew his piece. Held it low.

Carver nodded. "I heard a commotion in the back alley. I went to investigate and found a guy. His abdomen is all cut up."

Leach gave Carver a good long look. "Lead the way."

Hughes kept his piece drawn. "Keep your hands visible at all times."

Carver took Leach and Hughes down the alley to the body. It was still there. A radio barked. Hughes answered it. Spoke in code. Got a message back. He turned to Leach.

"A janitor just called this in on 911. Said he saw a big guy next to the body."

"That would be me," Carver said. "He was still breathing when I found him. I checked the wound and saw it was hopeless."

"Looks like your simple statement just got more complicated," Leach said. "I need you to tell me everything."

"It's not that complicated." Carver rubbed his fingers together. Felt the blood turning sticky. "I want to wash my hands."

Hughes knelt next to the body. Examined the wounds. "Jesus. Someone did a job on him. Stabbed him in the lower right abdomen. Twisted and slashed up at an angle."

Leach turned to Carver. "Don't wash your hands just yet. I want them photographed."

"I didn't do this."

"Didn't say you did. But it makes the woman in the dumpster a lot more interesting." Leach looked over the crushed cell phone. "Hughes, get a uniform to tape this off. Don't let anyone near it."

"You got it." Hughes spoke into his radio.

"Clint, come with me." Leach headed back the other way.

Carver followed him. Mulled over how much he should say. Tried to piece together what had happened tonight. Had the dead man pushed the woman off the building? Or had someone else done that? And who had killed the dead man?

The man had gone inside. Presumably looked around for Carver, not knowing what he looked like. For some reason, he'd gone out the service exit. Maybe he hadn't wanted to draw more attention to himself. Or maybe he'd been lured outside.

There was a lot in motion tonight and Carver was getting caught between the gears. He was going to get crushed if he didn't figure out what was happening soon. The only thing he knew for sure was that it had to do with him. His enemies were hunting him. They'd almost found him. If he didn't play his cards right, they'd find him for sure.

Carver had made enemies all his professional life. He'd made more enemies just a few months ago in a dead little town called Morganville. Most of his enemies had the resources to track him down like this. There wasn't much else he could do to narrow down the possibilities. Not until he knew who the man and the woman were.

Leach took him back to the dumpster. He got his CSI folks to take pictures of Carver's hands. Extract residue. Examine the skin. Look over his face and body.

Carver let them do what they needed to do. "What are you looking for?"

"The dead man's knuckles were bruised. Scraped. He didn't go down without a fight." Leach stared at Carver. "I don't see any bruises or indications you were in a scuffle. I just want them to confirm it."

One of the techs finished his examination. "He looks clean."

"Okay, good. Wash his hands."

The tech produced a bottle of solvent and some paper towels. He gave them to Carver. "Go clean up away from here."

Carver took the bottle. Went outside the police tape to a strip of grass. He poured the liquid over his hands. It washed off the blood real fast. He tossed the bottle into the garbage. Wiped his hands off with the paper towel. It didn't feel as clean as using soap and water, but it was good enough for now.

He went back to the dumpster. Stayed outside the police tape. He looked up. Light was still shining from the window he'd noticed earlier. It was the only lit balcony on this side of the building. That didn't necessarily mean anything. In fact, why keep a light on if you planned to push someone off a balcony? It'd be better if it was dark.

A uniformed cop brought Carver a clipboard. "Fill out your statement and sign."

Carver wrote down the simple version of facts. Left himself out of it. The only problem was that Jeff might give a statement too. If he saw the dead guy, he might mention other facts. That the dead guy was looking for Carver. That he also talked to the man he knew as Clint. That Clint let the man inside the building.

It was likely that Jeff wouldn't find out about the other body. Or Leach might round up all the witnesses to the dumpster dive and show them the dead man. Carver wasn't a detective. He didn't know what Leach would do.

Once he finished the statement, Carver went inside the club. He washed his hands with soap and water. Then he went back outside. Went to the condo's office. The concierge looked up at him.

"Are you with the police? Jorge told us about the body."

"Do you have cameras out back?"

"No, I'm sorry. Only in the parking deck, the elevator, and on the different floors."

"Good enough. Where can I view the footage?"

"Um, one second." The woman got up and opened a door behind her. Inside was a monitor and a computer. She motioned him around the concierge desk.

Carver went into the security room. The woman sat down. Opened a program. A grid of camera views appeared.

"What do you want to see?"

"Show me the elevator about thirty minutes ago."

She clicked on one of the views. The elevator footage filled the screen. "It uses motion detection so it's not always recording." The first clip showed the old couple getting on the elevator.

"Not that one."

She clicked another clip. There he was. The dead man. Getting on the elevator on the thirty-second floor.

"Can you find footage of that guy getting on the elevator on this floor?"

She tried more clips. Found him on the third. He was getting on the elevator. With him was the dead woman. She was staggering. Drunken. Hardly able to keep her head up.

She was only minutes away from flying off the building.

— · —

Chapter 4

WEDNESDAY AFTERNOON

The woman standing before Elena looked thin. Malnourished. Her eyes were haunted. It was the same look Elena had seen on the faces of other sexual abuse victims.

Elena didn't know what to say to her, so she started simple. "Hello, I'm Elena."

The woman bit her lower lip. Dirty blond hair hung over her pale face. "What do you want?"

"I just want to ask you some questions."

"I don't have any answers." She shivered and hugged herself. "Please leave."

"Camilla, who are you talking to?" A darkhaired Latina entered the room. She narrowed her eyes when she saw their visitor. "Who are you?"

"Elena."

"What do you want?"

"Answers. I want to know who Amos Carver is."

The blonde flinched. The Latina smiled. "A reporter."

"Yes. The FBI and local PD just finalized their investigation. They said that Breakstone is innocent and nailed everything to Jasper Whittaker. But some witnesses mentioned a name they'd heard. Amos Carver. They described a big man. Said he was always nearby when there was trouble."

"Amos Carver." The Latina's smile grew. She walked across the room. "I'm Becca."

Elena shook her hand. "Nice to meet you. I take it you know Amos?"

"Carver." Becca laughed. "Just Carver."

Camilla kept hugging herself. "We're not supposed to talk about him, remember?"

"I've been following the news." Becca's smiled soured. "Breakstone is taking the credit. That's not right."

"Carver wouldn't care."

"They were up to no good too. They tried to kill him." Becca bit her lower lip. "We don't know much. They didn't tell us much. But Carver's the one who killed off the cartel. He's the one who freed us. Chad Dorsey from Breakstone was part of it too, but they never told us exactly how."

Elena took out a notepad and started writing. She preferred it to typing on her phone. "They said Dorsey died in a gunfight with the cartel."

"I don't know for sure, but I don't think that's what happened." Becca motioned her over to a table. There were red leather chairs around it. This section was carpeted. There had probably been more tables here at one time. A place where onlookers could watch the dance floor.

Elena sat across from Becca. "Chad Dorsey, Sam Rocker, and Tony Menendez were all killed right across the road from the mayor's house. Breakstone said they were responding to an emergency."

"I heard Holly, Paola, and Carver talking about Breakstone," Camilla said. She took the last chair. "They were in the study. I tried to listen, but it was hard to hear them."

"The mayor had Breakstone security guards." Becca rolled her eyes. "Don't tell me Dorsey didn't know the mayor was raping women."

"Any hard evidence?"

Becca looked at Camilla. "Tell her about the hotel room."

Camilla's pale skin grew even paler. She swallowed hard. "They asked some of us to come clean up a hotel room. The whole place was spattered with blood, guts, brains." She shuddered. "There was a truck nearby. It was sagging from the weight of something in the back. There was blood dripping from the tailgate."

Elena's mouth dropped open. "Who is they?"

"Holly, Paola, and Carver." Camilla rubbed her forehead. "They were at the center of everything. Always conspiring about something."

"Of course, they were." Becca laughed. "They were killing a whole lot of bad guys, Camilla. Vigilante justice isn't exactly legal."

"I know." Camilla looked down. "I just hated feeling like they didn't trust us."

"This is why they couldn't trust us." Becca sighed. "Because we're talking to a reporter."

"Yes, but this is about making sure Breakstone is held accountable." Elena put down her pen. "I'm convinced there was a huge conspiracy between the cartel and Breakstone. If we don't find the truth, then Breakstone is going to come out of this smelling like a rose."

"I agree." Becca touched her hand. "I just watched the live news conference. It made my blood boil. These people need to burn."

"Carver mentioned Rhodes a few times," Camilla said. "I think she was something special to him."

"That's the former chief of police?"

Camilla nodded. "I didn't know that until after Carver rescued us. I'd been a prisoner for months."

Becca shuddered. "Most who stayed that long didn't survive. Jasper killed some girls."

"Carver killed him. Cut him open on his bed." Camilla smiled. "Fat bastard got his just desserts."

"Tell me more about this hotel room," Elena said. "Who was killed there?"

"There was a military helmet and rifle that belonged to one of the dead guys." Camilla stared at the table. "Whole place stank of blood and gun smoke. The walls looked like Swiss cheese."

"The helmet belonged to one of the dead?"

Camilla nodded. "The helmet looked just like the one that was in Dorsey's truck. The one that they found his body next to."

Elena nodded. "It looked like Breakstone equipment."

"Yes."

"You think there were bodies in the back of the pickup?"

"Yeah. A lot of them." Camilla met her eyes. "I heard them say something about a mine. We cleaned up the room, the sidewalk and even a bloody patch of grass behind the motel. Then they took us back here."

Elena clenched her fists to hold in the excitement. "Do you have any other details about Carver? Who he is? Where he's from?"

"Nothing." Becca shook her head. "He never said much. Paola, on the other hand, she said a few things about him."

Camilla scowled. "Paola worked for the cartel."

"She was a prisoner like the rest of us." Becca put her hand on Camilla's. "Just because she wasn't being raped doesn't make her a criminal."

"I know. But it wasn't fair."

"Drug cartels aren't exactly known for being fair, my friend." Becca patted her hand. "Paola rejoiced just as much as the rest of us when Jasper was killed."

Elena jotted it down. "It's funny, but there wasn't a single mention of a Paola from any of the investigators."

"Because the local police repressed it. Carver asked them to never mention his involvement and never to mention Paola." Becca folded her hands in her lap. "Holly agreed to it. She knew Carver and Paola would probably end up in jail if the truth came out."

Camilla laughed mirthlessly. "I think Holly would've gone to jail too. The feds used that to blackmail her and the other local police."

Becca nodded. "They did what they had to do. They're good people, Elena. But I have a feeling that if Breakstone stays in operation, then they'll try to hunt them down and kill them."

Elena frowned. "For revenge?"

"I think it was more than that. A lot more." Becca shrugged. "Carver didn't talk about it, of course. Holly said Breakstone tried to frame Carver for killing Rhodes. She said someone from Breakstone killed Rhodes."

Elena almost dropped her pen. "You heard this straight from Deputy Holly Robinson?"

"She brought Ritter out here to meet us and figure out how to handle the aftermath." Becca leaned forward. "I overheard them talking about it. Ritter was overwhelmed. So was Holly. I asked them if I could help, but they stopped talking."

This story was getting juicier with every passing moment. She turned to a blank page in her notepad and jotted down the important bits.

Breakstone killed Sheriff Rhodes?

Carver knew Rhodes. Maybe served together.

Possible kill squad from Breakstone sent after Carver.

Find any abandoned mines in the area.

The tidbits she'd gleaned from Becca and Camilla were great, but the payload was with Carver or Paola. Maybe Holly Robinson would talk now that Breakstone had been cleared. Maybe Elena could approach her with this new information and promise that she could break the story and still protect Carver and Paola.

She moved on to the next big question. "Any idea where Carver or Paola are now?"

Camilla nodded. "Paola said something about Clearwater. I think she and Carver were sleeping together."

"They definitely were," Becca said. "You could see it from the way Paola looked at him."

Elena wasn't surprised. "Did Carver look at her the same way?"

"Carver always looked the same. Quiet. Watching." Camilla shivered. "Scary."

"He's tall, big, and muscular," Becca said. "On the surface he's handsome. Looks nice. But he's impossible to read. I talked to him one time and he just looked at me and listened. I felt like he was really hearing me, you know? But then I wasn't so sure he cared."

Elena stopped writing. "What were you talking to him about?"

"About how Jasper nearly choked me to death." Becca flinched. "I can still smell that pig. His rancid body odor trapped under layers of fat. And the spittle around his face. Him licking his tiny lips. Then casually choking me out and smiling. The only thing that saved me was a phone call."

"You told Carver about this?"

Becca took a deep breath. "Yes. I was thanking him for killing Jasper."

"What did he say?"

"He smiled. Put a hand on my shoulder. Said I'd be okay." She wiped a tear from her cheek. "He looked sincere. But underneath it all, I felt like he was dead inside. Like killing didn't faze him at all."

"Same," Camilla said. "It was a normal day in the office for him."

Elena figured that was true. The body count had been over twenty. That was a lot of killing. It was more than most serial killers. Not that she was equating him to a serial killer, but he certainly had a similar mindset.

She moved to the next question. "You said Paola mentioned going to Clearwater?"

Becca nodded. "I think Carver likes beaches. I got the feeling he'd been in Florida before he came to Morganville."

It sounded like a good next place to go. Elena asked more questions, but the women didn't have more answers to give. She ended on a personal note. "Why did you decide to stay here? Doesn't this place give you bad memories?"

"I like it here," Camilla said. "Ritter seized the property for the city since he said it was used for crimes."

"It was?"

Becca shook her head. "No, but he did it so we could stay here. Then he split up the seized funds from the paint factory and gave us and the families of other victims money."

"That's very generous."

"Paola asked him to do it," Becca said. "There were millions of dollars in cash stored under the paint factory. They could have kept it, but I think Paola got Carver to back up her idea."

Camilla smiled. "They were all afraid of him. They did whatever he said."

Becca laughed. "I'm afraid of him."

Elena asked a question that would be important if she ever found Carver. "Do you think he would have hurt any of you?"

Camilla shook her head.

Becca shook her head too. "I don't think he did anything out of a sense of right or wrong. I think he just wanted to be left alone. But they were trying to cover up Rhodes's murder and blame it on him."

Elena wrote that down. "So, he's a live and let live kind of guy. But if you cross that line, then you're going to die."

"That's exactly how I'd describe him." Becca reached over and touched her hand. "If he thinks your story might cause people to start looking for him again, then..." She trailed off. Shrugged.

Elena felt a chill of fear. "You really think he'd kill me?"

"I think you should just be careful." Becca patted her hand. "The only reason we're telling you all this is because Breakstone needs to be held accountable. I think they might wait a while and then start killing off those of us who were involved."

Elena had little doubt of that. Breakstone was well connected politically. Dorsey had testified in a private hearing with Congress just hours before being killed in Morganville. He'd had powerful friends.

News organizations had sent several FOIA requests to Congress about that hearing, but had been refused because it was considered classified. Elena had called in all her favors. No one had been able to find out anything.

There was no telling how far up this reached. Dorsey had publicly spoken about making the military smaller, leaner, and cheaper to run. There were old interviews where he'd said it was time to get rid of the bureaucratic ruling class and replace it with civilian oversight.

That sounded like the kind of thing Congress would never agree to. But maybe something had changed. Maybe he'd made inroads and they'd been preparing to do something big with Breakstone.

There was an awful lot to unpack. A lot to research. She'd studied a great deal about the paint factory cartel. She'd traced it back to Brazil. But the trail had ended at Brilhante Tintas, a Brazilian paint manufacturer. The company was privately owned. There was no trace of a cartel owning any part of it.

The feds had revealed that the drugs were shipped in containers of paint. That the paint was so thick it tricked x-ray machines and scanners. Dogs couldn't sniff out the drugs because they were inside plastic bags suspended in the paint.

They'd assumed the paint was being shipped from Brilhante Tintas, but the packing slips had possibly been forged. Their conclusion was that the Brazilian company had nothing to do with the cartel.

As for the identity of the cartel, there hadn't been anything identifying them at Whittaker Paint factory. Anyone who could have answered questions was dead. In the end, the only criminal organization identified had been Whittaker Paint.

They'd thought Jasper Whittaker was the mastermind. The one trafficking the cocaine. The one trafficking the women. The one running his own mini cartel in the heart of Georgia. Like most things about the investigation, it didn't add up.

"Thank you so much for your help." Elena stood and walked toward the front door.

Camilla remained seated. Becca stood. Took Elena's hand and walked with her to the front door. Elena felt oddly touched and a little uncomfortable.

They stepped outside. Becca hugged her tight. Kissed her on both cheeks. Then she stood back, still holding both of Elena's hands. She looked at her for a long time, tears pooling in her big brown eyes.

Elena cleared her throat uneasily. "What's wrong, Becca?"

"I just want to remember you, the brave girl who's chasing death."

The bottom of her stomach felt like it dropped out. "I'm not chasing death. I'm chasing the truth."

Becca blinked and tears spilled down her cheeks. "I know, Elena. I hope you survive to find it. Because if Carver doesn't kill you, the people who want him dead might."

CHAPTER 5

SATURDAY NIGHT

Carver was still looking over camera footage at the condo.

He replayed the one where the woman who'd fallen into the dumpster was riding up the elevator with the man Carver found sliced up moments ago. She looked drunk. Hardly able to walk.

He turned to the concierge. "Can you show me camera footage from the floor they got off on?"

"Yes, of course." The woman found the video files. The man guided the woman off the elevator. Half-carried her because she could barely walk. He took a keycard from her. Used it to open room 30042. It wasn't the room with the lit balcony. But it was close.

"Who owns that room?"

The woman checked the computer. "It's a rental. The occupant's name is Jane Smith. A real estate company owns it, but we handle the rentals."

"The name sounds fake."

"We require an ID and credit card." The woman stared at the name. "I can print out the info if you'd like."

"Yes, please." Carver watched her press a few buttons. A moment later, she handed him a printout. Jane Smith of Phoenix Arizona. The credit card info was under the business name, Floral Decorations. There was a copy of the picture ID. It was definitely the woman from the dumpster.

"I mean, the name does sound fake now that I think about it," the woman said. "But we get hundreds of rentals a week. Nobody stops and thinks about the names."

Carver didn't care. "I need to get into that room."

"I'll show you right up." The woman grabbed a keycard, and they went to the elevator. Took it to the thirty-second floor. A moment later, they reached the door. She opened it.

Carver flicked on the lights. The den was empty. The kitchen showed signs of use. A cup of cold coffee. Some grease in a pan. Dirty dishes in the sink. Otherwise, it was clean.

He went into the bedroom. A suitcase was open on a chair. The clothing was normal. Jeans, t-shirts, socks, underwear.

He didn't touch the suitcase. Maybe there was more inside of it, but he didn't want his fingerprints on it.

"Oh, my." The woman stiffened.

Carver saw the same thing she did. Another open case. This one packed with handguns and ammunition. A pair of long knives. A sketch of someone resembling Carver was next to it.

The woman looked from the sketch to him. Her face went pale. "What's this about? Is that a drawing of you?"

"No. But it looks like she was here to kill that person." He blew out a breath. This wasn't getting any simpler.

"Oh, my."

"Yep." Carver went back to the den. The sliding glass door was open. The curtains were tangled. He looked around for cameras but didn't see anything. "No cameras in the rooms?"

"These are private spaces. Unless they have their own surveillance, of course."

They didn't. But it looked like the man had brought the woman in here with her own keycard. He'd escorted her to the balcony. Shoved her over the railing. A table and chair were knocked over. It looked like there had been a struggle.

Carver stepped onto the balcony. Looked down. It was directly over the dumpster. This was the spot. "Can you step out of the room? I don't want to pollute the crime scene any more than necessary."

"Of course." She backed out of the door. Watched from the hallway. "Should I email the footage to you?"

"No, you'll send it to Detective Leach. He'll talk to you himself." Carver gave the room a good onceover. He examined at the case of weapons. Glock 43s. There were no serial numbers. The metal was smooth where they should be. Like nothing had ever been engraved in the first place. He figured the other two serial number locations looked the same.

The knives were carbon steel. Ridged bone handles. There was a blank slot in the case. One of the larger knives was missing. They looked sharp enough to gut a man. Just like the mystery man from the alley. But the weapons looked unused. Untouched. Why would he bring the woman back to her room, toss her over the balcony, and just leave the weapons here?

He retraced the man's steps in his mind. Tried to figure out where this had started. Where the woman had been before he reached her. They'd come up the elevator just minutes before her plunge. The man hadn't wasted any time. He'd brought her up, tossed her over. Had he opened the weapons case or was it already open? Had he taken the missing knife?

The man hadn't been wearing gloves. If he'd touched anything, maybe his prints were in here. The scene wasn't even staged to make it look like an accident. The man hadn't been careful. Hadn't cared about the cameras. He'd made a lot of mistakes. As if he didn't care about being seen. It looked like sloppy work.

Carver would have covered his face. Taped over the elevator camera. Tossed empty alcohol bottles around the room. Taken the weapons case. That would have made it look like a drinking accident. The woman certainly looked like she was intoxicated in the camera videos. Maybe the man had slipped her something. It just didn't add up.

He returned to the hallway. "Can you print pictures?"

"Sure." The woman looked around him at the room. "Find anything?"

"Only more questions."

They returned downstairs to the security room. The concierge printed a picture of the woman's ID. Carver had her print a picture of the man and the woman together in the elevator. An image of the man alone in the elevator. Then he had her open footage from earlier in the day. Jane Smith had checked in just after lunch.

She'd gone up the elevator with the same suitcase he'd seen in the room. The weapons case wasn't with her. She took the elevator down thirty minutes later. Returned to the building at eight in the evening. This time she had the weapons case with her. Her face remained the same in all the footage. Unsmiling. Serious. Deep in thought.

Other people also used the elevator moments before the accident. An elderly couple. A darkhaired woman. A woman and her child. A family of four. Another darkhaired woman. None of them had exited at the thirtieth floor.

The concierge looked from the footage to Carver. "What do you make of it, detective?"

"Thanks for your help. Detective Leach or Hughes will be here soon." Carver left. Folded up the pictures and tucked them in his pocket. He passed by Leach who was on his way into the condo lobby.

Leach stopped him. "Don't go anywhere, Wilkins."

"I thought I'd go home and get some sleep."

"I mean don't leave town." Leach looked around. "Where are you staying?"

"Motel down the road."

A motel?" He frowned. "You don't have a house?"

"Don't have one. Don't want one."

"You prefer living in a motel riddled with drug dealers and hookers?"

"It's better than having a mortgage." Carver looked around. He wondered if the person who killed the man was still around. "I told the concierge to expect you."

Leach was already walking again. He stopped midstride and turned around. "What do you mean?"

"She's preparing the camera footage. Got some real good shots of the killer."

Leach stormed over to him. "Who do you think you are poking your nose into police business?"

"I'm a guy who found a dead man. The same man who probably pushed a woman out of a building." Carver shrugged. "I'm helping you. Saving you time. You can thank me later."

Leach's lips curled into a snarl. "You're interfering. You're a bouncer, not a damned detective." He pointed a finger at Carver's chest. "Keep it up and I'll put you in jail for obstruction."

"You're welcome." Carver turned and headed for the club. It was already emptying out. The police were questioning everyone. Asking for statements. Taking names. Carver skipped past them and went inside. He went to the bar. Gina and Crystal were already cleaning up and closing out.

"I didn't even make half the usual." Gina slumped against the bar. "I can't believe the cops shut us down early."

Carver took out the pictures. Unfolded them and put them on the bar. "Either of you recognize these people?"

Gina looked up. Saw Carver. Smiled. "Who?"

He tapped the pictures. "Here."

She looked them over. Nodded. "Yeah. I remember them."

"Me too." Crystal picked up the one of the dead man. "He came in here. Asked if I'd seen a blond woman with a scar on her cheek. I told him no, even though I saw her sitting in Candy's section."

"He asked me the same thing," Gina said. "I got a creepy vibe, so I said no."

"Either of you talk to the woman?"

Gina looked up at Carver. "Is that the woman who fell off the building?"

"It is."

"Did this guy have something to do with it?"

Carver nodded. "I think he pushed her."

"Holy shit!" Crystal teared up. "That bastard!"

"Did either of you talk to him much?"

They shook their heads.

"Where's Candy?"

Crystal pointed to the employee entrance. "She's closing out her tips."

"Thanks." Carver started walking that way.

"Hey, Clint."

Carver turned to Gina. "Yeah?"

She touched her collarbone. "You have a little blood on your shirt."

He looked at the collar of his t-shirt. There was a dark spot on the gray material. "Thanks." He went through the employee door. Back to the counting room. Preston was counting tips. Dividing out the house cut, and the wait staff cut. Some of the girls cleared two thousand in a night with bottle service and other VIP nonsense. But they usually took home only a fraction of that.

Carver didn't understand how it worked. Why the house took such a big percentage. They made money on the food and alcohol. It seemed unfair to take a cut of tips. Carver was dead certain that the first time Preston tried to take a cut of his tips, he'd pick him up by the shirt and slam him against a wall.

Preston looked up at him. He looked confused. "Can it wait, Clint? I'm trying to get these girls home."

"I'm not here to talk to you."

Carver saw Candy. She was sitting in a chair. Most of the girls didn't go home until they watched their tips get counted and divided. They didn't trust management. Carver didn't blame them.

He sat next to Candy. Took out the pictures. "This woman was in your section?"

Candy blinked. "Huh?" She looked at the images. Nodded. "Yes, why?"

"Was she with anyone?"

"Yeah, a woman with black hair. They both had water to drink. I told them they had to buy alcohol or food or leave the table." She looked up as if deep in thought. "They ordered steaks and margaritas. But they didn't eat or drink. They just sat there, looking like they were angry with each other."

"Did they say anything to you?"

"No, they just talked to each other from what I saw." Candy's forehead pinched. "Who are they?"

"This one is dead in the dumpster outside." He pointed to the woman in the picture.

She gasped. "That's the dead woman?"

Carver nodded.

"Who? I want to see!" The other girls started crowding around.

Preston groaned. "Keep it quiet, okay? I'm counting."

"I saw that guy!" Brandy pointed at the picture of the man and woman in the elevator.

"Yeah, I remember him," Candy said. "The darkhaired woman left. Then that man started hitting on the blonde. She looked pissed. Next thing I knew, they were gone. The darkhaired woman came back and asked where her friend was. I told her she'd been talking to some guy and then she left. She looked angry. She made me describe the man and then ran off."

A clearer picture was forming in Carver's head. "You didn't hear anything they talked about?"

Candy squinted hard. Like she was pushing herself to the limit. "Wait, I do remember one thing. The blonde was showing the other woman a drawing. Like a police sketch. I didn't get a good look, but it had a big, muscular man in it." She frowned. "Kind of looked like you."

Carver was getting a real clear picture now. "Did the dark-haired woman come back?"

Candy shook her head. "No. She never came back."

Preston was looking through receipts. "They also didn't pay the bill." He held it out. "That's coming out of your tips, Candy."

"The woman was pushed off a building," Carver said. "She couldn't pay the bill."

"Her friend could have."

"Just take it out of my check," Carver said.

"That's a hundred twenty and change, Clint." Preston shrugged. "Whatever."

"God, you're not even going to give him the employee discount?" Candy huffed.

"Management don't give a shit," Brandy said. "Whole club could catch fire and they'd take their cut."

Carver turned to Candy. "Describe the darkhaired woman."

"Black hair. Pale skin. My height. Kind of old. Like thirties, I think. She looked the same age as the other woman. In fact, they looked a lot alike except for hair color. The blonde also had a tan."

"Like twins?" Carver said.

She shook her head. "No. Something about the noses and eyes. Maybe they're sisters?"

It was possible. Or it might just be that Candy wasn't very observant. "When did they arrive?"

"It was just after nine. They were my first table."

"They wouldn't have been let in after eleven," Brandy said. "Too old."

Anyone could get into the club before ten thirty. Once that time hit, Jeff roped off the entrance and became the judge of who would get inside. Carver hadn't even arrived until ten. He was normally there earlier, but the bus had been running late.

"Do you remember when the darkhaired woman left?"

Candy squinted. "Around eleven. I think she went to the bathroom, but I'm not sure. I don't think she could've gotten back in if she left the building."

"How about when the man and blonde left?"

Candy wrinkled her nose. "Eleven twenty. I remember because I couldn't stop watching him hit on her. It was disgusting."

"Did anyone mention the name Elena Diaz?"

She shook her head. "No. Maybe that's the blond woman's name."

"Maybe." It certainly wasn't Jane Smith.

Carver left the copies of the pictures with the girls. "If anyone remembers anything let me know."

"What are you asking questions for, anyway, Clint?" Preston looked up from the receipts. "That's not your job."

"I'm club security."

"No, you're a bouncer." Preston laughed. "Big difference, buddy."

"Who's club security?"

Brandy laughed. "You're it, Clint. Preston sure as hell isn't."

"He's not security," Preston said. "Just let the cops do their business, okay?"

Carver stood. Leaned his fists on the table in front of Preston.

The other man looked up. Shrank back. "What?"

"If anyone remembers anything, they come to me, okay?"

Preston gulped. "Whatever."

Candy giggled. "Jesus Christ, you're scary sometimes, Clint."

"Sexy scary," Brandy said.

Carver left the room. The blonde and the brunette were a team. They'd been looking for him. The man had been following them. The women might have known he was a bouncer. But they didn't know he'd be standing outside, not inside. They'd arrived early. They hadn't checked outside that he knew of.

When the man took the blonde, he must have taken her through the back door. There was a back deck area where patrons went to smoke. There was a locked gate. It wasn't much of an obstacle to a pro.

And Carver had no doubt in his mind that a professional had been sent to kill him.

Chapter 6

Elena wondered if she'd be dead by week's end.

Becca's semi-prophetic warning still echoed in her head. She was chasing death. Carver and the people looking for him were dangerous. Elena was just a canary in a coal mine. She'd be the first to die and serve as a warning to others that chasing the truth was potentially deadly.

Despite that, she felt excited to be on the trail. She'd left the mansion and driven down the road to the hotel Becca and Camilla had talked about. The place was closed. There was a *For Sale* sign in the front.

She parked out front and called the realtor. No one answered, so she left a message. "I'm interested in the Shallowford Motel. I'd like to speak to the owner about its history first."

Clearwater was somewhere down her list of next items. First, she wanted to find out more about the motel massacre. She ran an internet search for a local abandoned mine. There was mention of a coal mine in one corner of the county, but it was still operational.

She ran down the search results. Changed the query to look for quarries. There was a granite quarry in the mountains. It was also still in operation. The search results mentioned abandoned quarries in other counties, but none here.

Elena gave up after an hour of reading. The internet might not have the answers, but there were other reliable sources she could use. She drove back toward town. Stopped at a busy diner outside of town.

This one wasn't full of tourists like the one near the Morganville Hotel. This one was where the locals ate. She looked around. Noted the oldest people in there. Walked to the table of an elderly couple.

Elena put on a smile. "I'm sorry to bother you, but I was wondering if you could help me."

"Eh?" The old man cupped his ear. "What'd she say?"

The elderly woman took the man's hand. "Albert, turn on your hearing aid."

He blinked a few times. Reached up to his ear and tapped a small device inside.

The woman looked apologetic. "He likes turning it off when I start talking to him."

Elena grinned. "I'm sure it's not for that reason."

"Sure, it is," the old man said. "She starts talking about knitting or local gossip and I just want some peace and quiet."

The woman smiled adoringly at Albert then looked up at Elena. "What can we help you with, young lady?"

"Someone told me there was an abandoned mine or quarry in these parts. I'm looking for it."

"Never heard of one," Albert said.

"Me either." The woman smiled apologetically. "Then again, we only moved here five years ago. We live in a small retirement village a mile down the road. Most of us moved here to get away from Atlanta."

"Oh." Elena clasped her hands together. "I'm so sorry for bothering you."

Albert stood up and looked around the diner. Then he pointed to a young man on the other side. "Go ask Charlie. He's been here all his life, or so he said." He spoke loud enough to raise the dead, probably because his hearing aid volume was set too low. Nearly everyone, including Charlie, looked at her and Albert.

Elena wasn't fazed. Being a TV reporter had cured her of being embarrassed for the most part.

"He works at the retirement village," the woman said. "Landscaping."

"Thank you so much." Elena walked over to Charlie. He watched her the entire way, a smile on his handsome face.

"Albert said I could help you with something?"

Elena smiled. "How did you ever know?"

"I could have heard him from three counties over." Charlie motioned toward the chair across from him. "Have a seat."

"Thank you." Elena sat down. "I'm looking for an abandoned quarry or mine in these parts. Albert said you might know what I'm talking about."

"Yeah, the old Granby Mine. It's out on route twenty-four, down a long gravel road, and up a mountain. There's an old quarry in the middle of the woods and tunnels leading into the mountain."

"I wonder why that didn't show up in any online searches."

"It's been abandoned for nearly a hundred years and it's a scary place." Charlie took a sip of his coffee. "Back in the sixties, some high schoolers had a party out there. One person got drunk and fell off the cliff into the quarry. They died. Sometime in the seventies, some adults went hiking in the tunnels and got lost for three days. The state added the area as a reserve. They boarded up the mine and chained off the road."

"Sounds like a death trap."

He nodded. "It is. I wouldn't recommend going out there. You can get around the chain easy enough, but the road is in bad shape. There's a hairpin turn and a cliff and parts of the road are washed out."

It sounded like the perfect place to hide bodies. "Any way you can show me where this road is on a map?"

He pressed his lips together. "I don't want to sound condescending, but you really shouldn't go out there."

"Please. It's for a research paper."

Charlie drank some more coffee. "How about I take you there? I've driven the road a few times. I just don't want to tell you and hear that some tourist died out there again."

"Again?"

"Some off roaders were out in Muddy Gulch. They went off the approved trails to do some rock driving and ended up on the gravel road. They took the curve too fast and went over the cliff."

Elena didn't want a local tagging along. She had the sense he was also hoping for something more. But he seemed nice enough, and she was comfortable turning men down for dates no matter how nice they were.

"Are you sure you have time to drive me out there now?"

He checked the time. "Yeah, I've got an hour." He put some money on the table. Waved at a waitress. "Thanks, Fran. See you next time."

The waitress winked at him. "Maybe see you and the young lady."

Charlie laughed. "I highly doubt that."

Elena wondered why he said it like that. Like he was the one who wasn't interested.

He walked outside and over to a Jeep. It had a slightly elevated suspension. Medium-sized tires. A bar with an array of LED lights on it. It wasn't stock, but it wasn't outrageously modified either. He opened the passenger side door. Elena hopped in. He went to the other side. Climbed in and started it.

An audiobook started playing on the stereo. Something about a wizard assassin. Charlie turned it off quickly. "Sorry. I don't care for music much. I'd rather listen to a book."

"Me too." Elena showed him her phone and the list of audiobooks. "I'm more into true crime though."

"You and every woman out there." He laughed. "My ex watched murder documentaries all the time. Then she'd switch over to a baking show like it was nothing."

"I don't like cooking shows."

"So, just murderers for you then?"

Elena laughed. "Yeah, I guess so."

Charlie pulled onto the road. He eased up to the speed limit. Adjusted his rearview mirror. Left one hand on the steering wheel and set the other on the armrest. "It's about seven miles up the road. Shouldn't take too long to get there."

"Great, thanks." Elena checked her phone. Gilbert had messaged her. He wanted to know when she was coming back. She replied. *Working a lead. It'll be a while.*

His reply was prompt. *Dude, you're a TV reporter, not an investigative journalist! It's time to go home.*

Elena tapped out an angry response. Deleted it. She didn't need to antagonize her crew. She'd started in the newspaper biz. She'd been an investigative journalist. She'd brought corrupt local politicians into the light.

She'd investigated mistreatment of workers. Uncovered child labor. Revealed a pedophilia ring at a local school. Her life had been threatened more times than she could remember. She'd been a newsroom star, all by the young age of twenty-five.

But the newspaper had long overstayed its welcome in the realm of new media. It had been hanging on by its fingernails for nearly decade. It couldn't hold on any longer. A billionaire bought the newspaper. New management laid off half the staff. Cut budgets across the board.

What had once been a hard-hitting paragon of journalism turned into a joke. Instead of investigating and finding the truth, the newspaper printed rumor and intrigue. Lives were ruined. The newspaper was sued.

There were more layoffs. The newspaper became little more than a glorified lifestyle section. It just reprinted what all the other news outlets were already reporting. Anyone who didn't submit at least one story a week was let go.

She'd seen the writing on the wall. There was no future in the newspaper industry. Where there had once been only a few national news outlets, the internet now hosted hundreds. Everyone had an equal voice, and the truth was drowned out in political rhetoric.

A girl had to make a living. So, she'd started working in television news. She was supposed to be a pretty face regurgitating whatever was on the teleprompter. But it was hard letting go of what she really loved.

Elena texted Gilbert the location of the car. *It's not far outside of town. I'll find another way home.*

"Trouble on the home front?" Charlie was still watching the road, but he'd probably seen the expressions on her face.

"I'm supposed to be back in Atlanta tonight."

"And you're not excited to get out of this Podunk county?"

"Not while there's still something to be investigated."

He raised an eyebrow. "I thought they ended the investigation today. Sounded like old Jasper Whittaker was one hell of an evil guy."

"He was, but he also wasn't the only one."

"And you think something might be up at the mine?"

Elena realized she'd been talking too much. She was upset at Gilbert's remark. She had something to prove. Getting this local involved had been stupid. She should have just driven here herself. "I just thought it sounded like an interesting place to visit."

Charlie chuckled. "I'm sure that's it."

"You don't have to take me there. Maybe it's best if you take me back to my car. I can find the mine on my own."

"Doubtful." He shrugged. "Look, I think it's pretty admirable for a journalist to go the extra mile these days. Seems like most news is just rumor and people shouting each other down. Nobody's out there looking for the truth like Fletch, you know?"

A laugh burst from Elena. "You've seen Fletch?"

He grinned. Nodded. "One of my favorite movies of all time. It might be a comedy, but it was still the golden age of newspapers. Can you imagine a reporter going undercover for weeks at a time these days? Or flying all over the country to hunt down a story? Pretending to be the mattress police?"

"My dad hated that movie." Elena's smile faded. "He didn't really admire anyone. He just kept his head down and did his job."

"What did your dad do?"

"He was a cop and made it to detective in his early thirties. There was a murder, and a lot of the upper brass were obstructing his investigation. Witnesses started disappearing." Elena had been just a kid, but she remembered it like it was yesterday. "He was approached by a newspaper journalist who was also looking into it. He thought one of the mayor's rich friends was involved."

"Wait, is this the Mary Matthews murder?"

Elena nodded. "She was just some teenager. She'd been raped and beaten. The body was found in downtown Atlanta. All the clues pointed to a local ex-con. But my dad thought it was too perfect. It smelled like a setup."

"Okay, I remember that story. They traced DNA evidence back to a bodyguard for William Lawson, the construction mogul." Charlie turned down a small, paved road that curved through the mountains. "Turned out he was involved in some kind of sex-trafficking ring."

"That investigation brought down two city councilors, the Lawson Construction Company, and the mayor. The police chief resigned too. But my dad was persona non grata after that. Once the heat died down and a few months had passed, he was bucked down to traffic."

"Oof."

"Yeah. So, he quit and went to work in the newspaper business."

"Nice." Charlie slowed and looked at the bushes on the side of the road. A cluster of them were broken and flattened. "Hmm, looks like someone's been through here recently."

"How recently?"

He shook his head. "Past few days. The weeds and bushes usually pop back up after a couple of weeks of being run over."

Elena considered the timeline. If Carver and his accomplices had come out this way months ago, then the bushes would have been fully recovered. Someone had been out here since then. That didn't necessarily mean anything.

Charlie drove over the bushes and navigated down the gravel road. It was bumpy and rutted. The overgrown weeds on the side brushed against the outside of the Jeep.

"I hope this doesn't scratch your paint."

Charlie laughed. "Wally's been through worse, believe me."

She raised an eyebrow. "You named your Jeep?"

He grinned.

"You're one of those people, aren't you? A Jeep fanatic."

"Guilty as charged." He trampled bushes on the left to avoid a washed-out section of road on the right. "I have a winch and everything."

"Then I should be in good hands."

"That's debatable."

She laughed. "Great."

Charlie slowed as they came to a sharp bend. The gravel road hugged a mountain on the left. To the right was a steep drop into treetops. Elena opened the window and looked over the ledge. It was a couple hundred feet to the bottom.

Charlie got them around the curve and onto a straightaway through a forest road. "What newspaper does your dad work for?"

Elena rolled up the window and stared straight ahead for a moment. "He's dead."

"I'm sorry to hear that."

"He was looking into misuse of government funds by the mayor's staff. He vanished for a few days, and someone found him in an alley with a bullet in the back of his head."

"Oh, God. That's awful."

"The FBI got involved since local law enforcement couldn't be trusted. They had a suspect but didn't have the evidence to prosecute."

"Sounds like your dad had a lot of run-ins with politicians."

"I guess because politicians don't know how to behave when they get into power."

Charlie slowed. They exited the forest and entered a large open space. The terrain went from gravel to dirt and solid rock. To the right was a sheer drop-off into a blue lake at the bottom of the old quarry.

He navigated past the gaping maw and to a rock face with massive wooden doors. They looked like they were made of railroad ties or something similarly thick. The Jeep slowed and stopped. Charlie put it in park.

"Here we are."

Elena slid out. The air felt cool. Smelled sweet. Birds sang and insects chirped. She felt about as far from civilization as she could get. She walked toward the doors. A heavy chain was looped tightly through the metal handles.

She tugged on a handle, but there was no give. They'd come all this way for nothing.

CHAPTER 7

SATURDAY NIGHT

Carver felt certain that professional killers were after him.

No ordinary citizen carried around a briefcase full of weapons. No average Joe could track him down even with a fake identity. It had the smell of government all over it. That business in Morganville should have blown up into something big.

Instead, it looked like most of the scandal had been swept under the rug. The politicians who'd been supporting Breakstone were still in power. The military leaders who wanted to privatize black ops were still working behind the scenes.

Even a guy with two braincells to rub together could see the writing on the wall. Someone powerful wanted Carver dead. Even though he'd told the others involved not to mention him, someone had. There had been too many mouths to silence. That was why Carver decided moving on was best. Why he'd invested in a new identity.

And now that was shot to hell.

This was a big problem. A huge one. He couldn't just kill his way to freedom. He didn't even know who to target or how many targets there were. His group, Scion, had been just a small part of SOTFOR—Secret Operations Tactical Force. There was no telling how many secret operations commanders there were.

Any number of them could have been assisting Breakstone. Maybe even SOC Holt, the guy calling the shots for Scion. The one Rhodes had taken her orders from. She'd never met the guy. Didn't even know where he was stationed. At least that was what she'd told him and the others.

Rhodes's death had started the entire mess in Morganville. It had become a noose around Carver's neck. He'd killed enough people to loosen the noose, but now it was starting to tighten again.

He had to find the brunette. She was the only one who could tie together the events of the night. Finding her was a dangerous proposition. If she was partnered with the dead woman, then it meant she was also trying to kill him. That still left another question wide open. Who was the dead man? Had he been looking for Carver so he could protect him, or had he also been looking to kill him?

Maybe there was a bounty on Carver's head. Maybe there were multiple bounty hunters looking to score. That scenario made more sense. The context jibed with the events of the night. So, what was he going to do about it?

There was no clear-cut answer, so Carver left the building. He hooked right, skirted the first crime scene. Headed through bushes to the neighboring condo property, La Playa. Miami was thick with high-rise condos. It was like the whole place was covered in them and strip malls. He walked down the sidewalk. Crossed a side street. Entered a strip mall parking lot.

The buildings got shorter the more he walked. He entered the older section of the island. Lots of vintage motels, colorful buildings, fewer strip malls. He was staying in a hostel at the far end. It was about as cheap as it got around these parts. Even the motels were over a hundred a night.

There was something strangely comforting about sleeping in a room full of other people. It reminded him of the old days. The barracks. A group of strangers thrown together for boot camp. Except with the hostel, it was like a turnstile. New strangers every night. There were a few regulars, people who'd been there for weeks.

Carver only knew them by sight. He hadn't talked to anyone. He preferred to keep to himself. It was better that way. He continued down the sidewalk. The bus that ran this route wouldn't be along for another twenty minutes. He didn't mind sitting and waiting, but he was in a hurry.

This would be his last night in Miami. He'd catch some sleep then leave midmorning. Maybe it was time to visit the west coast. They had beaches. They had swarms of homeless. He could fit right in. Camp anywhere his heart desired.

He was about a block from the hostel. Something caught his eye. A silhouette. A glimpse of movement. It was hard to say, because it was in the corner of his eye. He cut into an alley. Crouched.

The streetlights were spaced about a block apart. They alternated from one side of the street to the other. That left a lot of dark spots. A lot of places for people to remain unseen. It wasn't unusual to find people in those dark spots even at this time of night. Sometimes homeless people. Sometimes a drunk staggering home. Sometimes a drug user on a high.

This wasn't a usual night. Carver remained still and focused on the dark area across the road from the hostel. That was where he'd caught a glimpse of someone. But the streetlamp between him and that area made it impossible to see what was over there.

He cut across the road. Detoured down the back alley. Made his way through the darkness until he was behind the building across the road from the hostel. There was no alley here, so he continued to the road. Hooked a right. Eased up to the corner. Peeked around it. Nothing was there.

Carver slipped around the corner. He leaned against the building and studied his surroundings. If someone had been here, they were gone. Maybe his eyes were playing tricks on him. It wasn't unusual to see things that weren't there. Especially when your senses were on high alert. But it was better to be safe than dead.

He crouched and waited. Fifteen minutes came and went. He let ten more go by. Then he got up and walked to the hostel. Went inside. The night manager was asleep behind the window. She was snoring gently, a book in her lap.

Carver had already paid in advance, so he walked past. Entered the stairwell. Climbed to the second floor. He was in room thirty-eight, bunk three. Two of the six bunks were taken, or they had been last night. It was dark, so he couldn't tell. He could hear breathing. Heard someone shift in their bunk.

He left the room. Went to the row of lockers in the hallway. Opened his locker and pulled out the duffel bag. Inside were a few pairs of clean clothes. Mostly black t-shirts and black jeans. Dress code for the club. He didn't keep anything of value inside the bag. At this point, he didn't have much of value.

Carver went back to the room. He stripped down to his underwear and climbed under the covers. His senses were on high alert. His mind was racing. It was hard to calm down. To go to sleep. It normally wasn't a problem for him. Civilian life was making him softer with every passing day.

He finally shut it off and drifted to sleep.

SUNDAY MORNING

CARVER'S EYES SNAPPED open a few hours later.

He sat up. Looked around. Whoever had been sleeping in the other bunks was gone. He grabbed a towel from the shelf and went to the bathroom. He showered, dressed, and stuck his duffel bag into a locker. Then he went down to the dining area. The remnants of the free breakfast were still there. Bagels, toast, eggs, bacon. It was already eight in the morning, so most of the food was gone. He'd need a supplement from a diner.

Carver went outside. A police car was parked on the curb. It was unmarked, but the color scheme was a dead giveaway. It was a black Charger with base wheels and small hubcaps. He knew it was there for him, but he pretended not to see it.

"Hey!" Hughes hopped out. "Clint Wilkins, you need to come with me."

Carver stopped. Turned around. "Can it wait?"

"No."

"I'm hungry."

Hughes shrugged. "Not my problem."

"Okay, by me. You can wait."

"I'm not waiting. You're coming with me."

Carver turned and walked to the diner a block down.

Hughes followed him. "Stop and come with me."

Carver didn't stop. He wouldn't stop. Not until he had a decent cup of coffee and more food.

He entered the diner. Sat at the bar. Got a coffee in short order. Hughes sat next to him. Also ordered a coffee.

Hughes was short. Slim. He had a gnarled nose and purple veins in his nose. He was probably in his fifties, but a hard life and hard drinking made him look much older. It was a wonder he didn't have a pot belly.

Hughes saw him looking. "I could arrest you for obstruction. For not following the instructions of a police officer."

"You could, but do you want to?"

The man narrowed his eyes. "Damned kids these days don't respect cops anymore." He stared at his coffee. "Do one wrong thing and you end up on social media. Face plastered everywhere like you're pure evil."

Carver didn't have an opinion on that. He ordered sausage, eggs, and grits. "Leach wants to see me?"

"Yep." Hughes sipped his coffee. "Your statement was slim on details."

"Not many details to state."

"You witnessed two murders, so I'd say there's a lot."

"A woman fell into a dumpster. A man got cut up. I found both bodies. End of story."

"He has questions for you."

"I don't have answers."

"Oh, he thinks you will." Hughes' phone rang. He answered. Listened. "Yes, right next to me." He nodded a few times. "Got it." Ended the call.

Carver polished off his coffee, got a refill. His second breakfast arrived, and he demolished it in short order.

Hughes got up. "Ready?"

"I'm not paying for your coffee."

Hughes dropped a twenty on the counter. "Fine. Let's go."

Carver followed him outside. Went to his car. Climbed in the front.

Hughes looked like he wanted to say something but didn't. He nosed into traffic and drove a few blocks to a big, fancy building. He steered around back. A metal gate lifted and allowed them into the parking deck. He found a spot and parked. Got out and led Carver to the elevator.

They took it down a floor. Took a door into a department. Cubicles divided the area. There was an office at the end. A sign on the door said *Director Ramirez*. Phones rang. People chattered. The room sounded full. Busy.

Hughes steered Carver into a cubicle with Leach's name on the outside. Leach was inside behind the desk. Hughes mocked a salute and left. Leach was on the phone. He pointed to a chair. Carver sat down.

The desk was shaped like an L. The front part was larger. Covered in files, loose papers, fast food wrappers. There was a computer monitor on the side section. Cables ran through a hole in the back. A picture of the woman from last night was on the screen. It was the same picture from the security footage. There were other pictures below it.

Carver leaned closer and looked at the other images. They looked like part of a police record. Leach glowered and turned off the screen. He hung up the phone and kept glowering at Carver. Then he slid a sketch across the desk. The sketch from the dead woman's weapons case.

Carver picked it up. Looked it over. Slid it back to Leach. "What's that?"

"You."

Carver shook his head. "Doesn't look like me."

"A guy that big has to be you."

"Jeff is about my size."

Leach laughed. "The other bouncer? He's half a foot shorter than you."

"I'm six four. There are plenty of guys that height."

"Who's Carver?"

Carver didn't hesitate. He'd made up his mind. Decided how to handle this. "I don't know. The dead guy was asking for him."

"So was the dead woman, apparently. She asked the people at the bar. Asked her waitress too."

Carver played stupid. "What's that have to do with this drawing?"

"That's obvious. The guy in the sketch is supposed to be Carver." Leach examined the sketch. Looked from it to Carver. "Looks an awful lot like you."

"Looks an awful lot like a lot of people. How do you know the guy is tall? There's no size reference. Plenty of muscular guys in Miami, too." Carver shrugged. "Is that why you brought me here? Because you have a drawing of a generic muscular man?"

"You stuck your nose in a lot of places last night. You saw this sketch. You saw the weapons case. The condo concierge told me all about it. I don't think you'd get so involved if this wasn't about you."

"I'm in charge of security at the club. I needed to know what happened."

"You're a bouncer, not club security." Leach smirked. "I checked with your manager."

"A bouncer is security. I keep people out. I let people in. I kick people out. I keep people safe."

"That doesn't make you club security. It sure as hell doesn't give you authority to get camera footage from the condo."

"Is there a law against me investigating?"

"There's a law against obstructing a police investigation." Leach leaned his elbows on the desk. "I could hold you for that."

"I didn't obstruct. I facilitated." Carver crossed his arms. "What did you find out about the woman?"

"I'm not telling you anything. You're a person of interest in a double homicide."

"Meaning you have proof I did something?"

Leach worked his jaw back and forth. "Don't test my patience, Wilkins. I'll let you cool off in a jail cell for twenty-four hours."

"You know I didn't do anything. There are witnesses. But if you tell me more about the woman, maybe I can help."

"You were a cop, weren't you?" Leach looked him up and down. "Law enforcement, maybe even military."

"Let's just say that I can't talk about it, okay?"

Leach snapped his fingers. "I knew you were in the service. You look awfully young to be out of the game, though." He turned on his monitor and pulled up Carver's fake driver's license. "Says here you're twenty-eight."

"I enlisted when I was eighteen."

"I figured as much. Problem is there isn't much else about you. No military record, nothing."

"That's by design."

Leach leaned back. Took a long draw from a vape pen. His stare went distant. "There's a lot about this that doesn't add up. A lot of variables that don't fit together. You're one of those variables."

Carver wanted to tell him some of the truth. It would be nice having the police help him for once. But telling the truth exposed him to the events of Morganville. He'd left behind a warzone and enough bodies to put him away for good. Civilians didn't treat killing the same way.

Kill an OPFOR in war, and you were a hero. Kill a criminal in the civilian world and it made you a criminal. Carver didn't feel like putting his fate in the hands of the police. Even the good ones would throw someone to the wolves just to close a case. They didn't care about the people caught in the crossfire.

He'd dealt with the military police enough times to know there wasn't much difference between them and their civilian counterparts. Nothing stood between them and an investigation except maybe someone higher up the chain of command. He didn't blame them. They were just doing their job. Just like he used to do his job. Nothing got in the way of completion.

And that was why he couldn't trust them. Just like someone shouldn't trust him when he was on mission. You have an objective. You do everything in your power to complete the objective. Nothing gets in the way unless a commander tells you otherwise.

The next objective was finding out what was in that police file. Without inside help, there was only one way to accomplish that.

Carver would have to steal the information.

CHAPTER 8

Charlie leaned against the Jeep.

"Here we are, the Granby Mine. There's a hiking trail going to the bottom of the quarry. There's another trail that goes to the mountain peak. You can find the cabins the workers used to live in a short distance away too. What would you like to do first?"

Elena tugged on the chain. "I want to go inside."

"Unfortunately, it's off-limits." He checked the time. "I'd better be getting back."

"You don't know of a secret way inside? Another cave or something?"

"Why are you so hellbent on getting inside?"

"I just want to see what it looks like."

"Mhm." He spread his arms. "Not much we can do about that."

She took pictures of the chain. "Okay, I'm ready to go."

"You plan to come back out here with bolt cutters or a hacksaw?"

"No, of course not." Elena noticed deep tracks in the dirt. It looked like something with beefy tires had made a U-turn. "I've got to get back too."

Charlie followed her gaze to the tire tracks. "Wow, someone ran a Hummer out here." He knelt and put a hand into the tracks. "It'd take a really heavy vehicle to sink that much into the dirt."

"These tires look even wider than the ones on your Jeep."

Charlie frowned and nodded. He took out his phone and tapped on the screen.

"What are you doing?"

He pointed to the tree line. "The state installed trail cams. Me and my Jeep friends found them."

"Jeep friends? Like a cult?"

"Basically." He fiddled with an app. "The state puts the cameras midway up a tree then runs a solar charger to the top branches. It's a pretty cool setup. Zero maintenance. But whoever set them up didn't change the default login."

"That's not too bright."

"It's typical, though." He frowned. "Weird. There's a new camera out here. The app is showing the serial number, but the default login isn't working."

"Well, at least someone knows how to change the password."

Charlie chuckled. "Yeah. I'll just login to the older camera." He entered a username and password and the app switched to an image of them. "Smile, you're on Candid Camera."

Elena waved and the figure on the video waved. It was an overhead view, angled down to watch the entire area around the giant doors and the quarry.

Charlie tapped the screen and the live image turned to a series of thumbnails. "It only records when there's movement."

"How far back does this go?"

He scrolled to the end. "The oldest clip is from a month ago. Most of these recordings have deer, coyotes, and other animals." He continued scrolling up. "Some tourists drove up here and had a picnic three weeks ago."

"How romantic. How do you know they're tourists?"

"The license plates are from DeKalb County." He stopped and tapped on another one. "Whoa."

"Whoa, what?" Elena watched the image. A strange truck like nothing she'd seen before wheeled into view. It had huge tires like a Hummer, but that wasn't what it was.

"That's a Rezvani. It's basically a tank on wheels."

"I've never heard of those."

"It's a heavily modified Jeep Gladiator." He shook his head. "No wonder the treads were so deep."

Four men in black fatigues stepped out of the vehicle. One went to the large doors and tugged on them. He shook his head. Another guy pulled a rifle from the car. Aimed it at the padlock. The others waved him off.

A fifth person got out. He was chubby and balding. He wore jeans and a flannel shirt, but Elena recognized the shape of his head. It was one of the local cops. Maberly. He pulled out a keychain. Selected a key. Unlocked the padlock.

The men tugged on the giant doors. Swung them open. The camera angle didn't show inside the opening. The men switched on flashlights. Walked inside. Maberly paced around outside for about twenty minutes.

The men returned. Closed the doors. Chained them together. They looked animated. Angry. The trail cam audio was spotty and distorted. The microphone wasn't meant to capture sound from so far away.

Maberly climbed into the back of the Rezvani. The other men spoke for a while. One of them got something from the vehicle. He pointed to the trees and walked out of sight.

A few minutes passed and the man returned. Then all the men piled into the vehicle. It wheeled around and left.

Charlie frowned. "What was that about?"

"Probably had to pee." Elena pointed to the other thumbnails. "Can you play those?"

The next one was two days later. A black SUV parked in front of the doors. The Rezvani came into view moments later. The SUV driver got out and unlocked the chains. The men from the Rezvani tugged open the doors.

The SUV drove inside. The Rezvani went in after it. The image blinked off a minute later. The next video was thirty plus minutes after the vehicles went inside. The SUV rolled out. The rear end was sagging.

The Rezvani came out. It was towing another SUV, identical to the other one. They were using a chain, so someone was behind the wheel of the towed vehicle to steer and stop it. Behind that came a Jeep Gladiator. The rear bumper was coated with black streaks. As if liquid had leaked from beneath the tailgate.

When the vehicles were clear of the doors, the men shut them. Chained them tight. The Rezvani pulled the SUV out of sight.

The video ended.

"What in the hell?" Charlie stared at the screen. He played the next video, but he and Elena were the stars of that one.

"Can I get a copy of those videos?" Elena asked.

"You knew something was in there, didn't you?"

"I thought there might be something."

Charlie tapped a bar at the top of the camera app. A dropdown menu opened. There were two long numbers listed. "I wonder if that other trail cam has video."

"Probably just the same footage." Elena looked up at the trees but didn't see another camera.

"Yeah." He tried to login to the other one again and failed. "I wonder why the rangers would change the password on the new one but not the old one."

"Probably because someone else installed it."

"Yeah, probably." Charlie went to the Jeep. Opened the armrest. He pulled out a key. Walked to the padlock and unlocked it.

"You've had a key this entire time?"

"Yeah. Got it from my ex-girlfriend." He unwrapped the chain. Tugged it off. It dropped to the ground with a clatter.

"Why did she give you a copy?"

"I asked her if I could make a copy. She said yes."

Elena pulled on the metal bar that served as a door handle. The massive, tarred timbers were heavy. The hinges were stiff. Charlie helped and they opened the door. It was wide enough to drive a dump truck inside.

"Why did she have a key in the first place? Is she a ranger?"

He shook his head. "No, she's a cop."

There was only one female on the police force. "Holly Robinson?"

"Pretty easy to guess with all those clues." He climbed into the Jeep.

Elena hurried after him and got in. "You're driving inside now? What happened to being careful and all that?"

"You can drive inside for miles. The tunnels get smaller, and there are mine cart tracks, but the Jeep fits."

"Sounds dangerous."

"If you know where you're going, it's not too bad."

Elena gave him a disapproving look. "All those warnings, and you're a big fat hypocrite."

He turned on the headlights and entered the darkness. The inside was huge. The light didn't even reach the other side. He flipped a few switches for the LED light bar and the entire place lit up bright as day.

A dark patch on the stone caught her attention. "I guess all those lights do come in handy."

"From time to time." Charlie parked in front of the dark patch and got out.

Elena hopped out and knelt in front of the stain. There was a black stain of engine oil. The rest was black, but not the same kind of black. It looked like the Rezvani boys had dumped cleaner over the stone. It smelled like chlorine. Bleach.

They hadn't done a very good job. If anything, they'd made it stand out even more. It wasn't hard to figure out the nature of the stains. It was blood. A lot of it. The Jeep Gladiator had been loaded down with bodies.

Blood didn't always coagulate post-mortem. Sometimes it remained liquid for hours after death. The bodies had leaked for a while after being brought here. The blood seeped through the tailgate. Pooled on the ground. Little rivulets spread out across the stone. Soaked deep into the pores.

The Rezvani boys had poured bleach all over the stone, but they hadn't brought enough to do the job. It was clear why they'd retrieved the bodies. The dead had once worked for Breakstone. Not only did they look like former military, but they were driving an expensive, heavily modified vehicle.

She photographed the area with her phone. Walked in a wide circle. Light glinted off something metallic. She walked back to where the SUV had been parked. Found a slug. It was still pointy.

Charlie examined it. "Hardened point. Five-five-six ammo. Armor piercing round."

"How do you know that?"

"Because I have ammo like that."

Elena gave him a knowing look. "You country boys like shooting, don't you?"

He shrugged. "Shooting, hollering, mud bogging. The usual."

"I grew up in the city. Redneck culture was kind of a shock the first time I encountered it."

"It's okay." He winked. "We feel the same about city folk."

She pocketed the slug. "I wonder how Breakstone found out about this place."

Charlie looked confused. "Breakstone? Those men were with the same company that supposedly beat the cartel?"

Elena nodded. "Except I don't think that's what happened."

"I'm all ears."

"How well do you know Maberly?"

Charlie's eyes narrowed. "I mean, he's big and lazy if that's what you're asking. I don't know him all that well, but he was always sitting at his desk snacking when I came to visit Holly at work."

"He's the one who unlocked the door for those men. I wonder why he didn't just give them the key."

"They probably needed someone to help them find the gravel road and get out here. It's not an easy place to find."

"True." Elena looked up and around. She envisioned Carver and friends driving the SUV in here. Leaving it and the bodies to rot. She wondered if she should tell Charlie that his ex-girlfriend was probably helping Carver. She figured it was best not to involve him too much.

Since the FBI had helped Breakstone clean up the mess so well, it probably wouldn't be hard for a few extra bodies to show up. They'd lump them in with the others who'd supposedly died fighting the cartel.

"This place gives me the creeps." Charlie motioned toward the Jeep. "Let's go."

Elena figured there was nothing else to find in here, so she got in. Charlie put his cell phone in the holder. He tapped on the map app. The phone buzzed. He frowned and tapped on a new notification.

"The trail cam app just started recording something else." He switched to it. A green Jeep was parked outside. It was the kind with the pickup truck bed on the back. The wheels were big, and it was jacked up a good foot higher than Charlie's.

"One of your friends?"

He shook his head. "None of my friends have a Gladiator that nice."

A pair of men emerged from the Jeep. They were dressed in black fatigues. They put on helmets with NV goggles attached to the top. They pulled military rifles from the back of the Jeep. Pulled some levers on them and opened lids on the scopes.

"Oh, shit." Elena stared at the equipment. "They're with Breakstone."

"What are they doing out here?"

Elena thought back to the first video with the Rezvani. The one where the man had run into the woods. He hadn't been going to take a leak. He'd been placing a trail cam. Breakstone had been watching the area ever since.

And now they'd sent people to investigate.

Charlie gave her a concerned look. "Okay, I'm no conspiracy theorist, but I have a bad feeling about these guys. Like, if we try to talk to them, we're going to end up at the bottom of the quarry."

Elena watched the live feed. The men were stalking forward, rifles aimed and ready. It looked like the live feed from Iraq when troops went door to door in the cities. These men were ready to shoot on sight.

That seemed awfully dumb. Did they plan to shoot every tourist who came out here? Or only the ones who went into the mine?

Charlie got out and walked around the back of the Jeep. He opened the trunk. Elena walked around beside him. He opened a long case. Pulled out a military rifle. Tugged on a lever and popped in a clip.

It was flat at the top like a normal clip, but the bottom was round. "How many bullets are in that clip?"

"It's a magazine, not a clip. Holds fifty rounds."

"Holy shit, that's a lot."

He opened covers on the ends of the scope. Peered through it. "Time to find out if these boys are friendly."

"You want to shoot your way out of this?"

He shook his head. "I want to show them that we're armed too. Just in case they get any bright ideas."

"What if they shoot the moment we step outside?"

"I don't think they will unless they're stupid. It's hard to cover up bullet holes. If they forced us off the cliff at gunpoint, then it would just look like an accident."

"You've been waiting for this moment all your life, haven't you?"

Charlie shook his head. "No. But I've been ready. Maybe it's better if you wait back here. I'll go talk to them."

"No! Do you have another gun?"

"I have a pistol. Do you know how to shoot?"

"Of course. My dad was a cop. He took me to the gun range."

"But you call a magazine a clip."

"I never claimed to be a specialist."

"Get in the Jeep. You drive."

Elena pointed to the tunnel. "Is there another way out of here?"

He nodded. "Five miles back. But it's partially caved in."

"Great." Elena hopped in the driver seat. Started the engine.

Charlie checked the live feed. The men were outside the big doors. Looked like they were about to come inside.

"I have an idea."

He raised an eyebrow. "An idea?"

She nodded. "Those are NV goggles on their helmets?"

"Looks like it."

"So, they'll be able to see the Jeep no matter how dark it is?"

"To a certain extent, yes. But not from a hundred yards off. They'd have to be close."

"How close?"

"Like thirty yards, maybe? I don't know."

Elena wheeled the Jeep around. She hugged the left side of the tunnel. The side with the door still closed. "Tell me when they come inside."

"They're still talking outside. Standing about twenty feet outside. Looks like one is on a cell phone. Probably getting instructions."

"Good." She moved slowly, trying to keep the engine from growling too loud. It was already loud enough in the tunnel. The men outside would hear it. She parked about thirty yards from the door. Angled the vehicle toward the right. Turned off the headlights and LED bar.

The engine idled. It wasn't exactly quiet, but it would have to do.

"They hear us. The guy on the phone just ended the call. He's pointing to the quarry. Made a pushing motion. Holy shit, I think they do plan to push us in."

"Are they coming in?"

"They're waiting." He rotated the phone screen so she could see it. "I think they're waiting for us—no, wait. They're coming."

The men headed inside. They pulled down their NV goggles. Aimed their rifles. They were coming to get them.

CHAPTER 9

SUNDAY MORNING

Stealing information was easier said than done.

Carver's former organization, Scion, provided gadgets to make things easier. There were devices that could copy data from a computer just by putting it into a slot. There were devices that could steal data from phones via bugs in network protocols. Name a problem, and there was probably a gadget to solve it.

These days, Carver was on his own. No gadgets to make covert operations easier. Even if he somehow broke into the Miami police building, he had no way to steal the data from a secure computer. The information probably wasn't even stored locally on Leach's machine. It was probably on a server somewhere. Maybe here, maybe in cloud storage.

He couldn't do this on his own. The question was, would anyone help him? He studied Leach's desk. There were no family pictures. Just a picture of an orange cat curled up in a chair. He wasn't wearing a ring or jewelry of any kind. He was about as plain as it got. Carver wasn't a great judge of clothes, but Leach's outfit looked like something right off the bargain rack.

The detective didn't have a lot of personal responsibility. He didn't have a lot of money or other things going for him either. This job was his life.

Carver gave Leach another try. "Do you want to close this case fast?"

"Of course."

"Do you think I have something to do with it?"

"No comment."

"Two people died on club property last night. I've been bucking for a promotion to head of security at the club. It'll make my resume look better. It'll mean I can finally move up to a bigger, better club as something other than a bouncer. If you share some information with me, I think we can help each other."

Leach pressed his lips into a line. He glanced at his computer screen. Back at Carver. "Are you holding back information?"

Carver had held back the name Elena Diaz. Maybe it was the name of the killer. Maybe it was the name of a cat. The dying man had mentioned the name and assassin in the same sentence. "Maybe I forgot something."

The detective pounded a fist on his desk. "Look here, asshole. I'm not playing games with you."

"I'm not playing games either." Carver leaned back in his chair and kept eye contact with Leach. "Help me and I'll help you."

"I'll help you into a jail cell is what I'll do." Leach stood. "In fact, I think that's what I'll do right now."

Carver stood and held out his wrists. "Fine. I could use a vacation."

Leach glowered. Clenched and unclenched his fists. He dropped heavily into his seat. "Not afraid of jail? You must have done time."

"I've been in prisons that make US jails look like a tropical resort." Carver shrugged. "That's what happens when you get caught on a mission."

"I supposed," Leach said.

"These people are pros. This is a very dangerous situation."

The detective nodded. "Maybe I could use your help. You know how to handle yourself. How to survive."

"Yep."

Leach wrote on a piece of paper. "I can't show you anything here. They'll buck me down to patrol in a heartbeat." He slid the paper to Carver. "Meet me here eight PM."

Carver was a little surprised by the sudden change of heart. "What changed your mind?"

Leach stood and pretended to stretch. He was actually looking around the room. Then he sat and leaned forward. "Some of the shit I found didn't make sense. This woman had a record. Minor stuff. There was a note saying she claimed to be someone's CI. She didn't name names. Didn't show any proof." He shook his head. "We found nothing on the dead guy. Nada. Not a thing."

"That doesn't explain why you changed your mind."

"Because that weapons case is something special. A custom design made for high-level assassins. That means I'm going to need someone around who can keep me alive while I investigate."

"Isn't that what your partner is for?"

"Hughes is ready to retire. I'd rather let him ride out the next two months on easy street."

Carver nodded. "I understand."

Leach cleared his throat. "Just meet me and I'll show you everything."

Carver couldn't argue with the logic. The weapons case itself was nothing special. He'd seen custom weapons cases that were much nicer. Some had hidden compartments and even quick slots on the top or sides to access a weapon in a hurry. Still, it was a hitman's case. Better to be safe than dead.

"I'll see you there." Carver drummed his fingers on the desk. "Can I go now?"

"Yeah." Leach stood. "Come on." He led Carver past the cubicles, down a hall, through a secure door, up to a secure checkpoint at the front entrance. "Later."

Carver watched him go. He studied the front area. The desk, the secure door, the lobby. There were six cameras along the way to Leach's desk from this route. It looked like he wouldn't have to break in after all, but having a Plan B was always a good idea. Whatever the plan, he wouldn't come in this way. The parking deck entrance was best. Fewer cameras. Fewer doors.

Hopefully it wouldn't come to that. Hopefully Leach really wanted to help him. Only time would tell. Since they weren't meeting until eight, Carver had plenty of time to kill. He didn't want to waste it, but there wasn't much he could do without more information.

Carver wasn't a detective. He didn't know what other steps he should be taking right now. He'd probably missed obvious clues in the camera footage. There was probably more to the assassin's weapons case that he'd overlooked. If he'd been a little more perceptive, he'd probably know where to go next and what to do.

There was one person who knew what to do. Leach. Sometimes the only course of action was to follow someone else. So, Carver walked around the block. Found a motorcycle scooter rental place. Dropped a few bucks for one. Electric scooters were everywhere but he wasn't about to use one of those.

He found a spot across from the parking deck exit. Settled in for a wait. About an hour passed before Leach's car poked out of the garage. It turned right. Carver put on a helmet. Started the scooter and pulled onto the road.

Leach drove for a while. He pulled into a rundown neighborhood and parked in front of a multi-unit house. He stepped out of his car. Looked at a piece of paper. Checked the number on the mailbox. Checked the paper again. Then he tossed the paper into the car. Unsnapped his holster. Put a hand on the butt of his gun.

Carver wasn't familiar with this area. The houses were older. Concrete exterior. Cracking paint. They were still probably worth a pretty penny.

Leach knocked on the door. Stepped back and waited a few seconds. No one answered so he knocked again. The door opened. Carver couldn't see who was on the other side. He drove the scooter down the road for a better look. But Leach stepped inside, and the door closed before he got there.

Carver kept going. He drove around the block. Circled to the other side. Then he parked. Put the helmet on the scooter. Walked between the yards of two multiplex homes. He saw the rear sliding glass door of the apartment Leach had entered. The curtain was drawn. No way to see inside from this angle. He went to the corner. Found a dirty window on that end. It looked into the kitchen. The kitchen led to a hallway. The hallway led to the room with the sliding glass door.

There was movement, but it was hard to make out. Someone shouted. More movement. A series of thuds. Leach was Carver's only link to the investigation. He couldn't afford to let him die. But he resisted the urge to smash inside. *Wait and assess.* His dead commander, Rhodes, valued patience over impulsiveness. She was usually right.

So, he waited and watched. It was hard to see anything through the window. The ruckus stopped. A door squealed open. Carver went to the front corner and peeked around. Leach pushed a scrawny old man down the sidewalk. The man was in handcuffs. His nose was bleeding. His arm was scraped. Leach looked no worse for the wear.

The detective shoved him in the back seat of the car. He hopped in the driver seat and gunned it down the road. Carver had a lot of questions. The most obvious was, did this arrest have anything to do with the investigation? It didn't look related.

There was only one way to find out.

Carver went around the corner. The front door was closed but it wasn't locked. Leach had just left it like that. Carver used his shirt to open the door. He went inside. The place stank. Body odor permeated the air. The place was tiny. Maybe five hundred square feet. A single bedroom with a mattress on the floor. A tiny kitchen. A small living area with sliding glass door.

The appliances were modern. Stainless steel. The bathroom was covered in gray tile. It had a large shower, no bath. The place looked recently renovated, but it was filthy. The kitchen trashcan was overflowing. The sink was full of dirty dishes. The toilet had a brown ring around the bowl.

Small crystals spilled on the bedroom floor explained it. Methamphetamine. Why had a homicide detective arrested a drug user? Police departments had vice squads for that. Maybe he was an informant. Maybe Leach thought he could provide information for the investigation.

Carver kept looking. He noticed an air vent on the wall in the bedroom. The paint around it was scratched. The screws were missing. He pulled on it and the register slid free. The duct behind was filled with small plastic bags of meth. He put the register back in place. Kept looking. The vent in the bathroom was the same. Bundles of cash were hidden behind it.

Having extra money never hurt, so Carver took them. He slid the register back in. Wiped it down with his shirt. He did the same for the other one he'd touched. Then he slipped out of the front door and closed it. Went back around the corner, through the yard to the other side of the block.

He hopped on the scooter and put on the helmet. He'd gained extra cash, but no useful information. There were still a few things he needed to do. He drove to the meeting spot, a small bar in North Beach. It was a no-frills sports bar in an old strip of shops.

The hostess looked him up and down when he walked in. "How many, sir?"

"I'll just sit at the bar."

"Sure, go right ahead." She motioned to the long bar along the back wall.

Carver went inside. The interior was large enough to get lost in if you wanted a private conversation. There was a separate section with booths and tables. Plenty of places to huddle and talk. He sat at the bar. There was a special for mangoritas. He didn't care for sweet stuff, so he ordered a whiskey. The bartender poured two fingers and set it in front of him. The top of the round barstool rotated, so Carver turned to face the room.

There was a camera behind the cash register. Another camera at the door. He couldn't see what was in the other section. That was probably where Leach would want to meet. Carver polished off the whiskey. Dropped some drug money on the bar. Went into the other section and walked toward the bathroom. Only one table was occupied. A man and a woman eating tacos. Carver didn't see any cameras.

He used the bathroom then walked out the back door. The alley was typical. A dumpster, a stream of foul water trickling into a grate, a line of back doors for other businesses. There was a concrete wall around a small parking lot. A delivery truck idled behind it. Just beyond that was a vacant lot surrounded by a chain link fence. This was a good way to come if things went south.

There was also a stack of old wooden crates. A couple of used tires. A few dented metal trashcans. Carver envisioned which way he'd run. What he'd do to trip up any pursuers. There was a lot of wide-open space. The concrete wall provided some cover, but there wasn't much else beyond that. He didn't want to get shot in the back trying to make it across the vacant lot. This would require some planning.

With the recon done, Carver drove the scooter back to the rental place and turned it in. He was getting hungry, so he ducked into a sandwich shop for lunch. Two sandwiches later, he was full enough, so he paid with the drug money and went to the bus stop. The bus took him to a storage facility.

It was an original building. Single story and large for the island, but small by most storage facility standards. It was relatively far from the hostel and close to the interstate bridge off the island. That was by design in case he needed to make a hasty get-away.

He went inside. His unit was in the middle not far from the front gate. He unlocked and opened it. Inside were two duffel bags. One was lumpy and full. The other was almost empty. The mostly empty one had held his cash reserves. Now he was down to a fraction of the last bundle.

Carver was interested in the lumpy bag. He unzipped it. It smelled like oil and gunpowder. That was because it was full of rifles, pistols, and ammo. He had an AK-47, an M4A1 classic, and an M4 carbine with optics and suppressor. He pushed them aside and pulled out a Glock 19. He considered taking off his shirt and putting on the shoulder holster. But his t-shirt wouldn't do squat to conceal it.

He chose the Glock 42 instead. It was slim, compact. It wouldn't help much in a firefight, but it might be enough to get him out of a bad situation. He strapped on the ankle holster and slid the pistol into it. With the pants leg down, the bulge was barely visible. Maybe that would be good enough, or maybe it was a mistake to not take one of the 19s.

Rhodes would know what to do. She'd have a clever but simple solution. Maybe she'd set up a drop near the bar. Hide two pistols and ammo under a dumpster. Or inside a flowerpot. If things got hairy, she'd execute an escape plan and probably draw her enemies into a trap.

No reason why Carver couldn't do the same thing. He picked up a pair of the Glock 19s and put them in a small satchel. A box of ammo went inside too. He locked up and left.

This was probably overplanning. He and Leach would talk. Leach would threaten him to extract information. Carver would push back. Eventually, they'd reach middle ground. Information would be exchanged. Maybe they'd even find the next clue in the case.

But Carver saw it all differently. He saw an unknown element in Leach. The guy might be on the level. He might be playing his own game. It was hard to say. Picking up the meth addict alone had been unorthodox. It rang an alarm bell in Carver's head. Until he knew better, it was best not to entirely trust Leach.

Because trusting the wrong person was a bad way to die.

CHAPTER 10

WEDNESDAY AFTERNOON

The armed men entered the mine.

They were off camera now. Silhouettes framed against the daylight seeping through the door. Then they became part of the darkness.

Elena laid her seat all the way back. "Duck."

Charlie ducked. "What brilliant idea do you have?"

"Nothing special. Just be ready to shoot."

"So far, I hate your idea."

Elena tried to imagine how far the men had come. They were walking slowly, steadily. The Jeep would come into view in a few seconds. She wondered if she should have turned off the engine. Kept it quiet. Or maybe left the Jeep idling further back in the cave as a decoy.

It was too late now.

She counted their steps in her head. Imagined them coming closer and closer. Rifles pointed. Fingers on the triggers. Her heart pounded. Hands began to shake. They were close. Monsters in the dark.

"You in the Jeep. Come out with your hands up!"

"Out now! Hands up!"

Elena flipped up the LED light switches and turned on the headlights.

Two men about twenty yards away shouted in surprise and shielded their NV goggles. Elena shifted into drive and gunned it. She veered around the man on the right. Angled for the big door. Gunfire erupted.

Splinters flew from wooden door. The Jeep burst outside into daylight. A bullet pinged off metal. Nothing else seemed to have hit them.

Charlie raised his seat upright and looked back. "Holy shit! That was a good idea."

Elena veered down the gravel road. The Jeep bounced over ruts. The steering wheel threatened to tear itself out of her grasp. It felt loose. Unresponsive.

"The modified suspension makes steering tricky," Charlie said. "Better let me drive."

She ground to a halt. He got out. Removed the magazine from the rifle. Ejected a bullet with the pull of a lever. Then he secured it in the trunk.

"You're taking too long!"

"I'm not driving pell-mell down a bumpy road with a loaded rifle bouncing around in the car!"

Elena was already buckled into the passenger seat. Charlie got in, buckled up, gunned the accelerator. The Jeep shot down the road. The big wheels bounced off the ruts. He wrestled with the steering wheel.

Pop! Pop! Pop!

Elena looked back. The Gladiator wasn't far behind them. One of the men was trying to fire a pistol out of the window, but the constant bouncing spoiled his aim. "All that rifle securing let them catch up to us!"

"Open the glove box. Load the pistol inside. Fire back."

Elena popped open the compartment. A big black pistol was bouncing inside. A clip—magazine was bouncing next to it. She took it out. Aligned the magazine. Popped it in. She remembered to pull back the slide to chamber the first round.

The Jeep bucked wildly from side to side. She held on tight and wondered how she was supposed to shoot back.

"We're coming to a smoother spot. Open the window and fire. You don't have to hit them. Just let them know we're armed, okay?"

Elena rolled down the window. The Jeep flew over a hump and hit a flat spot in the gravel road. The seatbelt had ratcheted tight. She couldn't lean out of the window. So she put her left hand out. Aimed back. Fired a few rounds.

The Gladiator's windshield spiderwebbed.

"I hit it!"

"Lucky." Charlie snapped his fingers. "Get your arm in. We're coming to the hairpin turn."

Elena tucked her arm inside.

"Put on the safety. I don't want you accidentally shooting your leg."

"Where is it?"

He tapped the side of the pistol. "There."

She flipped it.

The Jeep bounced hard. More shots popped off behind them. Something whined through the cabin and punched a hole in the windshield.

"Shit!" Charlie gunned it toward the curve. "I've only done this at speed a few times. If the bullets don't get us, the cliff just might."

Another bullet punched through the center console.

"We don't exactly have a choice!"

He turned the steering wheel The rear tires drifted across the gravel. They hit the ruts. Bounced. There was a sudden dip as one wheel went over the edge. The rear whipped out of control.

The front tires bit into the slope on the other side. The Jeep lurched forward. Tilted up and over the slope. It teetered on two wheels for a moment before slamming back down on all four. Charlie gunned it and they made it past the hairpin.

There was a loud screech. Elena looked back. The Gladiator spun out of control. Shot over the ledge. Vanished from sight. The treetops shook from the impact.

"They went over!"

Charlie hit the brakes. He took the pistol from Elena, got out of the Jeep, ran to the ledge. Elena got out and ran after him. She looked down. The Gladiator was upside down. Bent and mangled. There was no sign of the occupants.

"Oh, my God!" Charlie stared at the wreck. "Stupid assholes!"

Elena was shaking. She had to sit down. Take deep breaths. The adrenaline rush was dissipating and with it, all her energy. They'd nearly been shot. Nearly gone off a cliff. Somehow, they'd survived.

She got on her knees and looked over the ledge. There was no easy way down, but she wanted to search the Jeep. Search the men. If they had cellphones, they might have valuable information.

"Charlie, is there a way down there?"

"You're kidding me, right?"

"No, I'm not. We need to search their vehicle. They tried to kill us!"

He crouched. Put a hand on her shoulder. "Elena, you need to forget all of this. Go home. Be safe."

"This is just proof that Dorsey and his Breakstone goons aren't the good guys!" Elena pushed to her feet. Brushed the dirt off her pants. "I'm going to find a way down."

"What if these aren't the only people they sent?" Charlie looked down the road. "What if more are on the way?"

She clenched a fist. "We're armed. You can keep a lookout with your gun."

"No. Hell no." He shook his head. "I might be a good old boy with a gun, but I'm not suicidal. I'm going to report this to the police."

"The police?" She laughed. "If you think the sheriff or the Morganville police can do anything about this, you're crazy. The FBI or someone on the federal level will just quash it."

Charlie worked his jaw back and forth. "There's a way down there, but we have to go the long way around."

Elena blinked in surprise. "You're going to take me?"

"If I don't, you'll try to do it alone and end up dead."

"Probably."

He sighed. "Get in."

They got in the Jeep and Charlie drove back down the gravel road until they reached asphalt. He turned left. Opened the map app on his phone. Zoomed in on their location. He pointed to a blue line wending through the forest. "There's a dirt road that runs a ways along the creek. It dead ends about two miles from the crash site. Then we'll have to cross the creek and walk."

"That doesn't sound too bad."

"It's not as long as there's still a log going across the creek. Someone said it got washed away during a thunderstorm a few months back." He shrugged. "I haven't been down the creek trail in years."

Elena looked out at the forest. Everything was so surreal right now. She couldn't believe that only moments ago they'd been running for their lives. Her hands were still shaking. Charlie looked calm.

She turned to him. "Did you serve in the military?"

He nodded. "Army. I was eighteen and stupid. Figured I could serve my country. I ended up in the desert for most of those five years. Learned how to shoot. How to keep my head down when snipers decided to take potshots at us. I never saw any action, though."

"You ever hear of Amos Carver?"

Charlie frowned. "I've heard that name before. I think my uncle mentioned it."

"Who's your uncle?"

"Oscar Bennett. He's a lawyer. We met for beers and pool a few months back. He was talking about some crazy client of his named Amos Carver."

"What did he say about him?"

"Not much. Just that he was supposed to represent him, but then the cops had to let him go. Lack of evidence."

"So, he was in jail in Morganville?"

"I guess." Charlie shrugged. "He didn't say much more about it."

Elena didn't remember a single mention of an Oscar Bennett. It was possible Holly had warned him to be quiet. She didn't want Carver's role to be known. It probably wasn't worth asking Bennett for information. He'd probably keep quiet like everyone else.

Charlie slowed and checked the map. He took a sharp turn and drove down a shallow embankment into the forest. There was a creek to the left. It was about twenty feet across. The water looked clear and clean.

"Can the Jeep get across the creek?"

Charlie shook his head. "It's been done, but I'm not risking getting stuck out here."

"Yeah, not today."

The dirt road was mostly overgrown with ferns and short vegetation. It looked like no one had been on it in a while. At least it wasn't too rutted or bumpy like the gravel road.

Charlie pointed through the trees to a distant cliff. "That's where they fell off."

"Doesn't look that far."

"Distances can be deceiving when there are mountains involved."

Elena didn't know how to respond, so she looked out the window at the cliff. Ten minutes later, the road ended at a ledge. The creek flowed over the ledge and dropped about fifty feet into a small pond. Somewhere on the other side, the creek continued flowing downhill.

The creek bank was a little higher here. Maybe ten feet above the waterline. A log had once bridged the banks. Now one end had fallen into the water on this side of the creek.

Charlie looked down at it. "I guess it's possible to cross. Climb up to the other side."

The water looked about five feet deep. Even at four feet, it would be hard to cross with the strong current. Falling in this close to the waterfall would be bad. There was nothing to grab. No rocks or branches.

If she fell into the water, she was going for a long ride to the bottom. The pond below looked deep. Maybe she'd survive. Maybe she'd break her neck. It was hard to know. She dropped a rock over the side and watched it splash.

Charlie looked apprehensive. "Are you sure you want to do this?"

Elena checked the time. "We've been gone a lot more than an hour. Are you going to get fired?"

He shook his head. "It's my landscaping business. I have other people on the job."

"You don't have to keep risking your life. This is my choice."

He sighed. "Yep. I know. But I can't just let you get yourself killed."

"You'd rather die with me?" Elena laughed. "Is it because I'm a woman?"

"I'd rather not die at all. If you were a man, I probably wouldn't have come out here in the first place."

"You feel responsible for me?"

"A little." He shrugged. "I guess if a man isn't willing to die protecting a woman, then he isn't much of a man."

"Any woman?"

He fidgeted. "Probably not. Just an attractive one."

"At least you're honest."

He grinned. "It's one thing I've got going for me."

Elena went to the edge of the creek. Steeled herself. "Here goes nothing."

"Let me go first. I can lower you."

She nodded. "You're taller."

"You're what, five feet six inches?"

Elena nodded again. "Close enough."

Charlie turned so his back was to the creek. He got on his knees, then slid over the side. He dropped to the broad log below. Held out his arms to keep his balance. "Feels solid at least."

"I'm coming." Elena followed his example and slid backward over the side. Charlie grabbed her hips and lowered her easily. It sent a little thrill through her. These country boys were built strong.

Charlie had already turned and was walking up the log to the other side. His work boots had no problem gripping the surface. Elena's sneakers were barely up to the task. They were more for looks than hiking.

She got on her hands and knees and started crawling. Charlie looked back and laughed. "Converse ain't exactly good for this, are they?"

"No, they're not."

He shuffled sideways down the trunk. Reached out a hand. "Come on."

Elena took his hand. Stood. Her feet slid a little. The rubber had some traction, but the soles were flat. He took her by the waist and swung her around to his other side. She gasped in surprise.

"I wasn't expecting that."

"Seems easier to get you in front." He kept his hands on her waist and guided her forward.

"I swear I'm more capable than this. It's the shoes."

He chuckled. "I don't doubt it."

She reached the other side and stepped up. Charlie stepped up behind her. He looked back at the other side of the creek. "I just wonder how we're going to get back up that side."

"Easy." Elena pointed to the Jeep. "You lift me up, I'll use your winch to pull you up."

He nodded. "Good idea."

The next part of the hike took twenty minutes. They were almost to the fallen Gladiator when Charlie threw a hand in front of Elena. Pulled her behind a tree.

"What?"

He peered around the tree. Pointed to the cliff. "Ropes."

She followed his finger. There were two ropes dangling down the cliff. A pair of people in black were rappelling down. Another pair of people in black were already at the Jeep. They had stretchers with them. The kind used to airlift people to helicopters.

"How many people does Breakstone keep in these parts?" Charlie hissed. "It's Morganville for God's sake."

"It might be small, but they lost a big battle here. Maybe several big battles." Elena watched the men work. "They aren't taking any chances."

"Guess not." Charlie sighed. "Should I get my rifle and shoot them?"

Elena's eyes flared. "Are you crazy?"

He grinned. "Sorry. Gallows humor."

"You're one of those people?"

He nodded. "Always helped me when we were under fire. You never knew if a stray bullet would be the one that ends you. So, we'd joke about it. Guess it's still automatic for me even after all these years."

Elena wished she could laugh. What could have been a huge break for her was gone. Breakstone was in full control of Morganville. It was time to cut her losses and move on.

CHAPTER 11

SUNDAY AFTERNOON

Carver took the bus back to the bar an hour before the meeting with Leach.

Instead of going inside, he walked around to the alley. There was no one there. No sign anything had been moved. The old tires looked like permanent fixtures, so Carver chose them. He dropped a pistol into one, the other pistol into the next one, and the ammo in the third. Unless someone poked their head into the hole, they wouldn't see anything.

He walked to the opposite end of the alley. Circled the block and approached the bar from another direction. Just in case Leach had someone watching for him. He kept an eye for unmarked cars. For people who looked out of place.

Carver spotted Leach's car parked on a side street. No one was inside. He surveyed the main street. No sign of anyone watching the place. Just the typical mix of tourists and locals. He leaned against the corner of the building. Watched and waited.

A man in a business suit stood across the road. His eyes roamed the area. The suit was too nice to belong to a cop. A woman waved at the man. The man waved back. They held hands and entered a store.

After one last look, Carver went inside the bar. As expected, Leach wasn't in the front section. Carver found him in a booth tucked into the back. Arriving after Leach was a mistake. The detective had his back to the wall. He could see anyone entering this side of the restaurant. Carver would have to constantly look over his shoulder.

There was an upside. The backs of the booths were tall enough to hide the occupants. No one would see Carver or Leach unless they were almost standing next to the booth. This section was almost full of diners now. It was enough human camouflage to make Carver feel moderately safe.

He slid into the booth. Leach was nursing a whiskey and snacking on cheese fries. The detective frowned. "You're late."

"What do you have to share?" Carver asked.

Leach grunted. "This works both ways."

"So, let's work it both ways." Carver shrugged. "What've you got?"

"First you gotta give me something, anything to let me know you're not playing games."

Carver was ready for that ploy. "I have a name."

"A name?"

"Yep." Carver stole one of Leach's fries. "The dead man gave it to me before he died."

"Why would you withhold something that damned important?"

"I don't trust you."

Leach worked his jaw back and forth. "Fair enough."

"We're not enemies, we're not friends." Carver stole another fry. "Maybe we have a common goal. Maybe we don't."

"We have a common goal. We don't have to be friends for that."

"True." Carver reached for another fry.

Leach yanked the plate away. Then he raised his hand and got a server's attention. "Can you help my friend, please? He's hungry."

Carver ordered a burger and fries. Water on the rocks. Tonight wasn't the night to drink alcohol. When the server left, he got back to business. "What do you have on the dead woman?"

Leach slid across a slim file. "Not much. Just enough to create more questions."

Carver opened it. Nicki Jones, age thirty-four. Arrested for shoplifting two times. Alleged CI, confidential informant. No handler named. The address was an apartment.

"I looked up the apartment address," Leach said. "The manager said no one by that name ever lived there, and none of the people living in the unit for the past ten years match that description."

"No driver's license, no identifying documentation found anywhere?"

"None." He shook his head. "We found cash, no credit cards, no ID."

Carver stared at the pictures. The woman was moderately attractive. Ordinary. The kind of person who could walk right up to a target and knife them in the gut. "Is the name an alias?"

"Maybe. I've got her images going through facial recognition. Her prints are in the national search queue."

"What about the dead guy?"

"First, you gotta give me the name you've been holding back."

It was a fair trade. "Elena Diaz."

Leach wrote it down. "That's all you have?"

"There's one more thing to it, but I want to see the guy's file."

"Fine." He slid it across.

This file was thicker. Carver opened it. First thing he saw was a picture of the dead guy in a police uniform. Desmond Price, thirty. Joined the police at age twenty-one. Made vice squad in five years. Was known for several high-profile busts. Moved to the DEA two years ago.

"He was one of the good guys," Leach said.

"Then why'd he push that woman off the balcony?"

"He must've been arresting her. She put up a fight."

"You saw the same video I did?" Carver shook his head. "She was barely standing. I think your boy drugged her or something."

Leach went quiet for a moment. "I don't know what happened. It doesn't make sense."

"Makes sense if Price was crooked."

"Maybe."

"DEA agents follow some kind of protocol. Even if he was undercover, why did he take that woman up to her room? Why did he push her?"

"If he was undercover, he probably had to wait for backup."

Carver spotted a familiar face in the folder. It was the meth addict Leach had picked up earlier. He was Price's CI. "How'd you get this information without the DEA barging in and taking over the case?"

"I didn't." Leach scowled. "The information search pinged someone at the DEA. Now they're sending someone to partner with me and find out what happened to their agent."

Carver flipped through the pages. There were more informants, but they were in different cities. Most were associated with other cases. The case files only gave summaries. Most were closed. Some remained open.

"Okay, I gave you the file. Now tell me what else Price said."

Carver thumbed past another case file. "He said, Elena Diaz, assassin."

"She's an assassin?"

"Maybe it's the real name of the dead woman. Maybe it's the name of the other woman."

"Too many maybes." Leach dipped fries in ketchup and ate them. He wiped off his fingers then tapped on his phone. "Let me see what a search turns up."

"You can run a records search from your phone?"

"I can submit a request. Someone else handles it."

"Good enough." Carver closed Price's file and slid it back. "Jones met with another woman at the club. The server said it looked like Price was hitting on them. The other woman left. Price came back and talked with Jones again. A few minutes later they were on that elevator together going to the room. Jones fell. Price came to the club again. Started asking people about someone named Carver. I let him inside to look. Then I decided to go inside and see if he'd found Carver. Instead, I found him nearly dead out back."

"That summary was more useful than your written statement."

The server arrived with Carver's food. He put mustard and ketchup on the inside of the bun. Closed it up and took a bite. It wasn't the best he'd had, but it was good enough.

Leach realized he wasn't getting a reaction, so he started talking again. "Finding that other woman is the key. Otherwise, all we have is a DEA agent taking a drugged shoplifter up to her room and giving her a one-way ticket to the ground. Not to mention the weapons case with that sketch in it. It's a damned puzzle with no fitting pieces."

Carver ate some fries and thought it over because he was one of the pieces. How did he fit into this? Why were Price and Jones looking for him? Maybe Jones and the other woman were the ones looking for him. Price drugged Jones and got the name out of her. Then he went to the club and started asking around for Carver.

Leach finished off his drink. "Got something you want to add?"

Carver opened Price's folder and pulled out the file on the meth addict CI. "Maybe you should round up this guy and ask him some questions. He might know what case Price was working."

"Already done," Leach said. "I brought him in earlier and interrogated him. He said Price was working a couple of cases. One was for a meth ring, and another was for cocaine. Price was the handler for some undercover agents. The CI was just a low-level dealer."

"Still in custody?"

"No, I cut him loose."

"These women must be connected to one of the drug rings." Carver mulled it over. "Maybe the DEA can shed some light on it."

"What about the Carver fellow? Why have a sketch of him? Why bring hitman into this?" Leach fingered a fry. "Maybe he's a low-level dealer. A club is a good place to deal."

Carver had dealt with plenty of users at the club. Not because they were using, but because they couldn't handle themselves while on the drugs. He usually called them a taxi or rideshare and got them out of the club.

The reason there was no security inside the club was because the owner didn't want it. Carver had seen enough to know that the drug pushers were probably working for the owner. It was a nice little self-contained economy. People got whatever they wanted. The owner got richer. If anyone else tried to sell drugs, they got a rough boot from the club.

Despite that, Carver knew the owner wasn't running a drug ring. Judging from the variety of drugs the pushers offered, the owner was sourcing from multiple drug operations. The only class of drugs not offered were opioids. Heroin and related were too addictive and bad for business.

It made him wonder if the owner knew either of the women. Maybe they worked for suppliers. Maybe Price was onto the club's operations. It was a possible link, but he couldn't exactly track down the club owner and question him about it. Well, technically he could, but he didn't want to. He was already exposed. Dragging a mobster into the equation would only make things worse.

The supplier theory didn't hold water anyway. These people had tracked Carver from Clearwater. They'd found and tortured the guy who'd provided him with his fake documents. They'd come all the way to Miami to find him. They were out for blood, plain and simple.

If the women were assassins. If they'd traced Carver to Miami, traced him to the club, and searched for him there, then how did a local DEA agent like Price get caught up in it?

Leach was staring blankly at his fries. He was probably trying to reason through it too. But he was missing a crucial element—Carver. Without knowing that there were people who wanted Carver dead, he'd keep running in circles. He'd keep thinking it was a local drug thing.

For Carver, the most important thing was tracking down the other woman. Maybe she was Elena Diaz. Maybe Jones was just her assistant. None of the information provided by Leach was helpful for achieving that goal.

"I can't make head or tails of it." Leach dabbed a fry in ketchup. "I could put all these pictures on a corkboard and make a mess trying to thread them all together. But until I find out who this Carver fellow is, none of this is moving forward."

Carver considered telling Leach the truth. It would go one of two ways. He'd arrest Carver or he'd decide to help so he could solve the case. But that would open Carver up to a few dozen murder charges in Morganville. He'd have to trust Leach explicitly. And that just wasn't going to happen. There was another way to handle it. Another way to get Leach the information he needed.

It would require deceit and trickery. But it would shield Carver just a little bit. And unless he wanted Leach to keep chasing his tail, it was information the detective needed. Carver needed Leach to track down the mystery woman. That was the only way to find out who was hunting for Carver. Then he'd be able to assess whether it was possible to shut it down or better to keep running.

He sketched a few scenarios in his head. Worked them over for inconsistencies. The idea might work, but it still felt risky. Detectives were usually perceptive. Even a moderately gifted detective might see right through Carver's lie. Or maybe it just seemed obvious to Carver because he was the one inventing the ruse.

Rather than test it now, he tried a different tact. "Leach, what made you become a detective?"

Leach blinked a couple of times. "Why do you want to know?"

"Curiosity."

"Bullshit." Leach laughed. "You want to know what kind of man I am. You want to know if I got into this business because I'm pure of heart. If it's because I want to put away the bad guys and keep people safe."

"I think you're the type to do whatever it takes to close a case even if you have to frame someone to do it."

Leach's face turned bright red. "You don't fucking know me, Wilkins." His fists clenched. "Do you think I'd be meeting you here if I wasn't trying to get to the truth?"

"Maybe you're just looking for someone to take the fall."

Leach slid out of the booth. "Fuck you, asshole." He gathered his folders. "I'll figure this out on my own."

Then he left.

CHAPTER 12

Charlie and Elena made their way back to the Jeep.

Charlie lifted Elena. She grabbed the creek bank and pulled herself up. Then she used the Jeep winch to help Charlie up. He drove them back to the diner where Elena had parked her car. She was sweaty. Dirty. Tired.

Charlie walked her to the car. "Well, I think that was fun. It was certainly exciting."

She smiled. "Bet you never thought your lunch break would go like this, did you?"

He laughed. "Not in a million years."

She took his hand. "I'm so sorry for dragging you into this. I'm sorry your prized Jeep got shot up."

He squeezed her hand back. "I would ask you to stick around and go on a date with me, but I suspect you've got bigger fish to fry."

"Maybe some other time?" Elena blew out a breath. "Maybe something a little less exciting."

"You bet." He hugged her. Kissed her forehead. "Please be careful."

"No promises."

"Let me give you my number just in case."

She handed him her phone and he punched it in. Called himself so he'd have her number.

Elena stood on tiptoes and kissed his cheek. "Take care." She got in the car and wheeled it onto the road. Gunned it and headed back to town.

Gilbert and Twila had sent her nearly a dozen messages and called multiple times. She called Gilbert back.

"Hey, sorry. There was no cell reception where I was."

"Elena, we've been waiting around this God-forsaken town for three hours." Gilbert's voice shook with anger and stress. "Come get us now before I lose my fucking mind."

"I'm on the way. ETA fifteen minutes."

He ended the call. Probably to avoid screaming at her. Gilbert was a bit of a drama queen. This time she couldn't blame him.

When Elena drove into the hotel parking lot, Gilbert and Twila were waiting with their suitcases. They both looked tired. Irritated. Ready to kill her.

Twila looked her up and down. "What happened to you? You're filthy!"

Elena didn't answer. She ran into the motel, got her things and dumped the suitcase into the trunk.

Gilbert drove them back to Atlanta. Neither he nor Twila had much to say. Elena sat in the back and watched the video from the mine on her phone. She transcribed her notes onto her laptop.

Twila finally looked back over the seat. "How did you get so dirty, Elena? Where did you go?"

Elena had already decided to keep her investigation secret from them. They wouldn't understand. Neither would her boss. But once she had more proof, something closer to a finished product, then she would pitch it to her boss. Maybe to a major newspaper as well.

"An ex-boyfriend of mine lives here. He asked if I wanted to go on a short hike. Unfortunately, we got lost."

Gilbert stared at her in the rearview mirror. "Then why the hell didn't you tell us that?"

"Because it was embarrassing. I don't like discussing my personal life."

Twila gave her a forgiving half smile. "Just tell us next time, please. I can't wait to get back to civilization."

"I'm sorry." Elena returned the half smile and went back to typing. She used her phone as an internet hotspot and started searching the internet. Florida beaches was the first search. Maybe Carver went to Clearwater. Maybe he changed his mind and went down to the Keys, or Miami.

If he was a big fan of beaches, he'd choose the best ones. There were endless beaches in Florida, but the top three seemed like a good place to start.

She searched news organizations in Clearwater and Miami. She compiled a list of investigative journalists. Most ran their own websites or YouTube channels. Many were politically oriented, so she crossed them off her list.

Elena sent the same email to all of them. *I'm looking for a man named Amos Carver. 6'4. Muscular. Medium toned skin, maybe darker with a tan. If you have any information, please respond.*

She compiled a list of detectives in the area. Sent them the same email. Then she did the same for Miami. That one took longer. By the time she was finished, they were back in Atlanta. She got in her car and went straight home. Showered, and went to bed. It had been a long day.

THURSDAY MORNING

TWO EMAILS WERE WAITING the next morning.

One was from Doug Weaver in Miami. The other was from Lisa Gallagher. Weaver ran his own site, the Miami Sentinel. Gallagher was with a newspaper. Neither had anything to offer, but both had similar questions.

Who is he?

Why are you looking for him?

None of the detectives had responded. Sometimes they did. Sometimes, they liked to use reporters to gather information. If they hadn't responded, it meant the name hadn't come across their desk.

She suspected that if Carver was really such a killer, then he might commit murder or some other crime in another city. Maybe other people were looking for him too. Maybe his name had popped up.

The question now, was what to do next?

She took a shower. Ate breakfast. Stared out the window at the rising sun.

She logged into her company's website. Looked up her vacation days. She hadn't used any yet and had six weeks available. That was mostly because once you got a gig in front of the camera, it was risky to leave it. They might like the substitute better than you.

She didn't even know who would stand in for her. It would be a tossup between Todd, the traffic guy or Elizabeth, the unattractive but energetic special-interests reporter. Neither was much of a threat.

Even if they were a threat, was Elena willing to risk her job just to pursue a story?

"Yes." She said with conviction. "Absolutely." All the money in the world wasn't worth it if she was unhappy. Besides, it's what her dad would have done. It was why her dad was dead. He'd been a man of conviction. A strong person. And she had no doubt this story was huge.

Elena texted her boss, Richard. *I want to take a week off. I'm exhausted after being in Morganville for so long.*

He didn't respond right away. He was probably mulling it over. Wondering how much more he could get her to do before granting her leave. Richard squeezed everything he could out of people. It was his job, but he also seemed to enjoy the power trip.

His response was typical. *This is a bad week. How about the first week of next month?*

I'm sorry, but it needs to be this week. I've never taken a day off. I deserve a break.

The lag time for his next response was twenty minutes. It was a tactic he used often. Not because he wanted the recipient to think he was considering it, but to make them sweat it out.

Elena was already packed for the trip when he replied.

No can do. The governor is holding a conference about legislative priorities tomorrow.

Elena waited fifteen minutes before replying. *I'm sorry. I'm feeling sick. This is just a bad week for me.* She sent it and waited for the threatening text that would come next. Gilbert and Twila had both been through this when asking for time off before. It would be no different for her.

Maybe you don't realize just how good you've got it here, Elena. You can always be replaced.

She replied with company policy. *According to human resources, any employee is entitled to take vacation time at any point except for blackout dates. This week has no blackout dates.*

She hesitated before hitting send. This would be the true test of just how valuable she was to the organization. Was she hot enough? Skilled enough? Did she check all the boxes? Or did Richard think he could cast her aside and find someone else to take her place?

Elena hit send.

She imagined Richard gnashing his teeth. Calling her several choice words. Typing out a text saying she either showed up or she was fired. She stared out of her high-rise condo window. Downtown was just half a mile away. She could almost see the corporate office from here.

It took him several minutes to decide her fate. *Fine. Enjoy your time off. Hopefully your job will still be here when you get back.*

That was about as good as it was going to get. She packed quickly. Took the elevator to the parking deck. Tossed her bags in the car, and left.

Clearwater, here I come.

ELENA REACHED THE MOTEL by early afternoon.

It was a one-star accommodation. She could afford better, but she wasn't here for pleasure. She dropped off her things and headed across the causeway to the island. There were still a few hours of daylight left.

She'd spent the trip speculating about what kind of a man Carver was. He was probably the kind to keep a low profile. Probably preferred cheap motels. But if he'd made off with wads of cartel cash, maybe he'd upgraded his experience. Maybe he'd gotten a house.

It seemed unlikely. Becca said the guy was a drifter. That he didn't like to stay in one place for long. At least that was what Paola had told her. That seemed the most likely assumption to proceed with.

First, she parked and walked down the main drag strip. She'd looked up a local sketch artist. Without a picture, she'd need something to show people. This seemed like her best bet. She found the shop and went inside.

There were caricatures pinned to the walls inside. A few normal pieces as well. The artist emerged from the back when he heard the bell ring.

"What can I help you with?"

"I need a sketch drawn from a description. Can you help me with that?"

"Just a verbal description?" He nodded. "I do work for the cops from time to time."

"Okay, good. I don't have a lot to go on."

"Not a problem." He tapped on a rate card. "Fifty bucks for the work."

"Do you have time now?"

"Yep." He motioned to a table and chairs. "Have a seat."

She sat down. He sat across from her. Put a sketch pad down.

Elena watched him. "Um, ready?"

He nodded.

She described Carver the best she could. Becca had given her a thorough description, including a tiny scar on his chin and a bigger one on his forearm. The artist sketched her a real work of art. If Carver didn't look something like that, she'd be shocked.

He turned the finished sketch to her. "How's that?"

"It's perfect." She took a picture of it. Paid him.

He rolled up the sketch and put it in a tube for her. "Good luck finding him."

Elena left and headed to the beach. She started across from the big blue Hilton. Worked her way up the beach. She hit paydirt an hour later.

The weathered owner of a surf shop nodded. "Yeah, he used to work here. Had a real pretty girlfriend too."

Elena was confused. Hadn't Carver taken hundreds of thousands in drug money? "How long ago was that?"

"A few months ago. I think he and the girlfriend broke up." He sighed. "She came here when he was working. Started crying. He looked real, I don't know, confused, I guess. Like he didn't know what to say."

"She left him?"

He nodded. "She said this wasn't what she wanted for the rest of her life. Something about kids, and him not really caring about her. It was heartbreaking, if I'm being honest. Carver wasn't really one to show emotions. When Paola left, he just kept quiet. Then went right on to helping another customer."

Elena wondered if Carver was a psychopath. "How much does this sketch look like him?"

"It's close. But there's something in that man's eyes that a drawing can't capture." He shrugged. "What do you want with him anyway?"

"Normally, that's the first thing people ask."

He shrugged. "Guess I like to gossip."

Elena had an answer ready. "He helped two of my friends out of a tight spot. He literally saved their lives. Then he just vanished. They want to thank him. So far, I've tracked him here."

"Sounds like Carver. He just stopped talking to a customer one day. Ran out of the hut and into the water. Pulled this kid out of the water. Apparently, he was drowning, and nobody even noticed."

"So, he's a nice guy?"

"I wouldn't say that. He's a man who does what he wants, but he seems to have some kind of moral compass." The old man shrugged. "I liked him. I felt comfortable having him around. And he kept the riffraff away."

"Any idea where he went?"

"No, but I know someone who might." He cleared his throat. "Just don't tell anyone you heard it from me."

Elena frowned. "Why is that?"

"Carver asked if I knew anyone who could forge an ID. I didn't ask why. I just pointed him to someone who might know."

"Who is that?"

"A guy named Pete. Works down at the Sandpiper." He jabbed a thumb over his shoulder. "Tell him Roy sent you and he might give you what you want."

"What does he look like?"

"Real thin, about five feet tall. Looks like a kid, but he's almost thirty." Roy chuckled. "He's a bartender, so you'll know him when you see him."

Elena felt a small rush when she left Roy and started walking toward the Sandpiper. She felt like a tracking pro. Like she was getting closer to the mystery that was Carver.

The Sandpiper was right on the beach. People sat on the back deck drinking and eating. The bar was packed. She didn't see anyone who looked like Pete. She flagged down a woman behind the bar. "Is Pete here?"

"He's not working tonight."

"Do you know where I can find him?" The woman frowned. Looked her up and down. "You're not here for a drink, are you?"

Elena wasn't sure how to respond.

The other woman laughed. "Oh, we know Pete's a plug for a lot of people. But he's not in town. He probably had to leave town to meet with a supplier. He'll be back tomorrow night."

"Great, thanks." Elena blew out a breath. She thought about eating there, but it was too crowded. She stopped at a pizza place on the way back to the motel. Got it to go, and took it to the room.

She compiled a list of more detectives and reporters in the area and sent them the same email she'd sent to the others.

She'd just finished eating when her phone rang. She didn't recognize the number, so she answered with a simple, "Hello?"

"Bill Leach, Miami PD. I got your email."

Elena blinked. Getting a call from a detective was unusual unless her query hit paydirt. "Great! Do you have records of an Amos Carver?"

"No, but I think it might be connected to some homicides here. What's the background on the guy?"

"He was involved in the events of Morganville, Georgia."

He paused. "That big mess with Breakstone and a drug cartel?"

"Yes."

"How does that connect to Amos Carver?"

Elena had a short answer ready. "I think he played a central role in everything that happened in Morganville, but no one will talk about him. Some women he helped escape a human trafficking ring thought he went to Clearwater. So, I came here, asked around, and found out he moved on a few months ago. He might be in Miami or the Keys, but I don't know yet."

"He helped women escape a human trafficking ring?"

"Yes, but I think he might have also killed a lot of people doing it."

Leach whistled. "Sounds like a character."

"Yeah. Maybe he's extremely dangerous, or maybe he's a good guy. I don't know yet."

"What's he look like?" Leach asked.

She described him right down to the scars. "I can send a picture to your cell phone."

He went quiet for a moment. "I'll have to look through the records, but it doesn't ring any bells. I thought he might be connected to a pair of homicides here a couple of months ago, but the perp description was of a short male, not someone over six feet tall."

"That's definitely not him." Elena was disappointed but not surprised. Sometimes casting a wide net found that tiny missing piece of the puzzle. This time it hadn't. Carver might be in Miami, or he might not. She'd still have to talk to Pete.

"Yeah, well it was worth a shot. Have a good one...what was your name again?"

"Elena Diaz. Thank you, Detective Leach." She ended the call and stared blankly at her laptop screen before shaking her head and getting back to business.

FRIDAY MORNING

ELENA WOKE UP LATE the next morning.

It took monumental effort to get out of the rickety bed. She didn't know what to do with the day since Pete wouldn't be available until that evening. She had a late breakfast then decided to comb the area near the surf shop. Maybe more people remembered Carver.

It turned out that he frequented the nearby restaurants. People easily recalled the big guy. Said the sketch looked close enough to him that they knew it was him. A waitress said she overheard Paola talking about Miami. One at another restaurant said she remembered them talking about the Keys. Yet another mentioned California.

Nobody knew for certain.

Evening finally came and she made her way to the Sandpiper. Elena spotted Pete the moment she stepped inside. He was short. Looked like an underaged kid. The neon-green cap he wore made him look even younger.

It was his eyes that showed his true age. His calm demeanor. His casual way of talking. No kid would have that level of composure. Most adults didn't even have that. Elena had bartended right out of college. It was a job that taught you social skills, that was for certain.

The bar was a big circle. One side faced the interior, the other side served the back deck. Two other women were working, but they were focused on the deck crowd.

Elena squeezed up to the bar. It took a few minutes before Pete made his way over to her.

"What can I help you with?" His voice was deeper than expected.

"Roy told me you could help me find something."

"True." He wiped down the bar. "Too busy now, though. Better have a drink and wait."

"Okay." She found a table inside and ordered food and a margarita.

The crowd started dying down around midnight. Pete came over and sat down across from her.

"How can I help you, Miss?" He trailed off, waiting for the name.

"Elena." She cleared her throat. "I need new IDs. High quality."

"There's a finder's fee."

"How much?"

"Two Gs."

She blinked. "That's—"

"Outrageous?" He grinned. "Wait until you find out how much IDs cost."

Elena blew out a breath. If she asked him straight up for information, he'd still probably charge her. "I'm desperate."

"People usually are when they're looking for these kinds of services." He shrugged. "I just connect people to other people. It's what I do."

"Besides bartending?"

Pete shrugged again. "That's why I'm so connected. Well, that and I'm trustworthy."

"Is there an ATM around here?"

He pointed to the front door. "Right across the street."

Elena had the money, but this might be a dead-end lead. Even if she located the forger, he probably wouldn't tell her anything about Carver. Client confidentiality was the primary reason people used these services.

She felt like she'd hit a brick wall. A dead end. This might be the end of the road unless she played ball.

CHAPTER 13

SUNDAY EVENING

Carver reached out and grabbed Leach's arm. "I'm not being serious. I was testing you."

Leach yanked his arm away. Then he backed up and sat in the booth. "Insulting me is a test?"

The detective had seen through Carver's first question but been sucker punched by the accusations. He had a blind side at least. It might be enough to exploit. It might be enough for Carver to tell his tale. But he wasn't sure enough just yet.

"I like to know who I'm working with."

Leach glared at Carver for a few seconds. "Makes sense. This is dangerous business."

"Extremely dangerous." Carver dunked a fry in ketchup and ate it. "We're hunting a hitman, after all."

The detective relaxed a bit. "I've dealt with dangerous people, but this is new territory for me."

"Are your people running prints and analysis on the weapons case?"

"Naturally." He stared at his empty glass. "No prints. No markings to indicate where it was manufactured."

"The best are hand-made. Cheaper ones are modified from existing suitcases or brief-cases." Carver envisioned the case. "This one looked like a mod, not an original. If there's no visible insignia, then you might find one using a blacklight."

"You'd think people like that would want to brag about their work. It's not illegal to make weapons cases."

"Anonymity is best." Carver drank some water. "If the authorities track them down and ask questions, it's not good for business."

"You know an awful lot about this kind of stuff."

"I know enough."

Leach raised an eyebrow. "Because you've dealt with hitmen and assassins?"

"Among other things, yes."

"Because you're Carver."

Carver didn't deny it right away. He wasn't sure if he should or not. "What makes you think that?"

"I just connected a dot."

"Must be an awfully big dot."

Leach grinned. "I just recollected something from a few days ago."

Carver sat back and said nothing.

"I had a voicemail. I don't remember who sent it, but it was from a reporter out of Atlanta, I think. She asked if there were any arrests or records for someone named Amos Carver. She left the same message with all the detectives in the department."

"All the detectives? Wouldn't that be something you'd ask the clerk about?"

"For most people, yes. Reporters aren't most people." Leach tapped a finger on the table, gaze distant. "Good reporters cast a wide net in the hopes they'll get lucky and find the right person. In that regard, they're kind of like detectives."

"I suppose. Do you still have that voicemail?"

Leach nodded. "This was Thursday or Friday. Just before the incident at Club Periclean."

"Did you call her back?"

"Yep."

"Why?"

"Because I thought there was a miniscule possibility it might be linked to a homicide that happened two months ago." Leach shrugged. "Sometimes casting a wide net can yield results."

Carver ate another fry. "Did it yield results this time?"

"I'm starting to think so. Just not in the way I expected." Leach sipped his whiskey. "I called her back. She said it was related to Morganville, Georgia. I'm sure you've seen the news reports on that place. Lots of drugs, sexually abused women, dead bodies."

"Yeah, I think I read about it," Carver said. "A real mess." Except it looked like Breakstone had taken credit for shutting down the local drug and human trafficking ring.

Leach nodded. "She found two of the women who were sex slaves. They talked to her. Said Amos Carver was part of everything. That he'd gone to Clearwater."

Carver kept a straight face, but he wasn't happy with himself. It was always something stupid that got you tracked down and killed. And there was usually collateral damage. Somehow, he'd left a breadcrumb that led to Clearwater. Someone must have overheard him talking to Paola. He hoped she was far away and safe.

Leach kept talking. "The reporter was in Clearwater when I spoke with her. She'd talked to a surf shop guy who said Carver worked for him. But he'd left a few months ago. Maybe gone to Miami or the Keys."

"Maybe you ought to hire this woman as a detective," Carver said.

"Yeah, I wish." Leach pressed his lips together. "Her information had nothing to do with the homicides I was investigating, but now it has everything to do with another homicide. She was right. It was just a matter of time before someone like this Amos Carver causes trouble."

"Why does this make you think I'm Carver?"

"She described a sketch that was a little different than the one in the assassin's briefcase. The only major difference is that it highlighted one significant detail." Leach traced a finger along his jawline. "That scar of yours."

Carver had a lot of scars. The one on his jawline was barely visible. Apparently, it was visible enough. One of the women he'd saved remembered it. She'd described him to the reporter. And now it was giving Leach a positive ID.

"If I were this Carver fellow, what would you do about it?"

"I'd hear him out before making a judgment call."

"Not good enough. Sounds like something big went down in that small town." Carver watched him carefully. "Detectives solve crimes. There's no gray area."

Leach barked a laugh. "The gray area is a lot bigger than you think. Especially if the homicide involves drug runners and human traffickers."

"Cops use people. They hold them under their thumb. Blackmail informants."

"Yeah. People use people to achieve their goals." Leach tapped a finger on the table. "Bottom line is, I'm ninety-nine percent sure you're Carver. I can haul you in again, take prints, mug shots, and so forth and confirm it."

Carver kept quiet.

"But I'm not planning on doing that because you're going to help me solve this case."

"And then what?"

"I'm not stupid, Carver." He put emphasis on the name. "You're a guy who killed a whole lot of very dangerous men if that reporter was right. You don't look the least bit concerned that I know who you are. You look like you're quietly assessing a potential threat. Like it could go either way and you're prepared to deal with it."

"Maybe."

Leach laughed and shook his head. "You'll let yourself get pushed only so far before you react. I don't have the time or the inclination to test those limits. I'd prefer to solve this case and survive the process. We can shake on it, or verbally agree, but I don't think that matters much to you."

"I believe in self-interest." Carver sipped his water. "Self-preservation."

"Me too. I think you're as interested in getting to the bottom of this as I am. So, I think we've both got plenty of motivation to cooperate."

"I'm not admitting anything. In fact, all I'm doing is role-playing as this Carver guy to help us piece things together. Even if I answer to the name, it's only acting."

"Fine by me." Leach leaned back. "You made a lot of enemies. The Brazilian cartel and the US government are at the top of the list. Just behind them would be the families of the people you killed and the people who benefitted from Breakstone."

Carver agreed. "A lot of people."

"Killing off hitmen won't stop the flow. The person or people behind the scenes will just hire more."

"Solving the two homicides won't accomplish much. I need to capture that missing woman and find out who hired her."

"Obviously. So, what I propose is that I do my thing and you do yours. And if we find leads, we share them. I'm not going after a professional killer without you there to help me."

"Sounds fair." Carver picked up the menu and looked at the milkshakes. He hadn't had one in ages, and it looked tasty. He looked over the top of the menu at Leach. "I think our next lead will come from the DEA."

"The feds say they'll share and then they never do." Leach spread out a paper napkin and wrote on it. He put rectangles with names in them. Drew lines from one circle to the other. Some lines were dotted, probably because he wasn't sure of the connection.

The names in the circles were Nicki Jones, Desmond Price, Elena Diaz, and Mystery Woman. At the top was a square with a question mark in it. Two lines ran from it to Jones and the mystery woman. A dotted line to Elena Diaz. Another dotted line ran from Price to Jones.

Leach crossed out Elena Diaz. "Now we know how she's involved."

Carver frowned. "We do?"

Leach chuckled. "I didn't mention the name of the reporter, did I? Her name is Elena Diaz."

"Price wasn't warning me about Diaz," Carver said. "He was telling me there's a price on her head."

"And now we know why."

"Because she's looking for me." Carver sighed. "She's probably the one who led them to me in the first place."

Leach nodded. "Looks like it." He tapped the drawing. "So, all we got is a napkin with the names of two dead people, a reporter who's a target, and that darkhaired woman."

"It's a start." Carver looked at the names. "Diaz's wide net filled in a vital piece of info."

"Yeah. We know the darkhaired woman's name isn't Diaz. That mystery woman might be the piece that solves the puzzle." Leach clicked the pen. "I hope the DEA can fill in some blanks."

"You have that reporter's number?"

"I called her from a landline, so it's not on my phone." Leach looked him in the eyes. "Why? You plan to tell her to stop looking for you?"

"No. I just want to ask some questions."

"You got a phone?"

"Yeah." Carver gave him the number to his burner phone.

"I'll text it to you when I find it."

"Thanks." Carver decided not to order the milkshake. He put a twenty on the table and stood. "Let me know what the DEA says."

"I will." Leach didn't look ready to leave. He put the napkin in a folder and tucked away the other files. "Let me know if you find anything."

"I will." Carver went down the back hall toward the bathroom. He didn't go inside. He went out the back door. Looked up and down the alley. It looked empty. He knelt and retrieved the handguns and ammo from the tires. Then he remained in the dark for a count of one minute. No movement on the roof. No movement in the vacant lot.

He didn't think he'd been followed here, but no sense taking chances when professionals were after you. He stepped around the corner and walked across the road. Then he took the sidewalk to the road running along the front of the restaurant. He watched the area for a while before going to the bus stop.

Carver waited with his back against a building so his flank was protected. He glanced back and forth at the passersby. His only advantage was that the killer didn't have a picture of him. They didn't know exactly what he looked like. There were a lot of big guys who matched the sketch.

The problem was he didn't know what the killer looked like other than she was a darkhaired Caucasian. There were plenty of them in this area. None of the ones he'd seen stood out from the crowd. Plenty of people looked at him because of his size. That was normal. But he was looking for someone who looked particularly interested in him.

He wondered if she was a contract killer or if there was an open bounty on his head. It depended on how quiet the client wanted to keep things. Open bounties could get messy. Too many people competing for the same target. He hoped it was a private contract. One person would be easier to deal with.

The bus arrived. He stepped into the middle door and took a seat at the back. It trundled down the road and eventually reached his stop. He stayed on and disembarked at the next stop. Carver walked to a side street and hiked down. Turned down an alley and reached the road in front of the hostel.

Then he played the waiting game for a few minutes. Observed the area until he felt reasonably certain no one was hiding in the shadows. Then he went inside. Went back to his room. He looked inside the other rooms along the way.

Most had two or three occupants. None were full. People were settling in for the night. It would be lights out before too much longer. It seemed safe enough to stay another night.

Carver took a shower. Brushed his teeth. It was almost lights out and no one else was staying in his room. He shoved his duffel bag with guns and clothes under the bunk. Kept a Glock under his pillow.

Then he took a few precautions. Rearranged the bunks. Gave himself some breathing space. The lights clunked out in the room and then the hallway. Carver lay on his back and let his eyes adjust. Dim light from a streetlamp seeped through a window. The rest of the room was pitch black.

Carver rested lightly. It wasn't quite like sleeping with one eye open, but it was close. It was the same kind of sleep he got when waiting hours or even days for a high-profile target to enter the sights of a sniper rifle. Except this time, he was the one in the sights.

The rattling springs of a bunk bed woke him. His eyes blinked open, but he remained still. He turned his head. A silhouette stood over the bunk he was supposed to be sleeping in. He could see movement, but it was too dark to make it out. He pulled the gun from beneath the pillow. He also pulled out something else. He snapped the top and tossed it.

The roadside flare burned to life. The silhouette shrank back. Shielded its eyes. But it was too late. They were blinded. The person wore black pants and a long-sleeved black t-shirt. Black gloves and a black knit cap. They were slender. Their skin was white. Strands of black hair protruded from beneath the cap.

They held a knife identical to one of the knives in the weapons case. It was long, slender, and perfect for gutting someone. It was probably the same knife used to kill Desmond Price.

Because the person holding it was the mystery woman.

CHAPTER 14

FRIDAY EVENING

Two thousand dollars for a finder's fee was insane.

Pete raised an eyebrow. "Well?"

"I'll be back in a minute." She pushed back from the table. Went outside and across the street. The line for the ATM was six people deep. It seemed crazy to be so busy so late, but the main strip was still alive with tourists.

Thunder rumbled in the distance. There was a flash of lightning far out in the gulf. It was going to start raining soon. A large crowd was still gathered around a karaoke bar. A pizza place was doing stellar business. No one seemed concerned about the impending thunderstorm.

Elena could see inside the Sandpiper from here. Pete was back at the bar talking to a blonde. She was a good six inches taller than him. Judging from the look on Pete's face, she wasn't ordering a drink. She was flirting.

"Great," Elena muttered. If she didn't get the money soon, he'd be gone.

Two of the people waiting in front of her got impatient and left. The person at the front finally got their money and staggered off. The others completed their business within ten minutes. Elena glanced back at the Sandpiper. Pete and the blonde weren't there anymore.

She jammed her card into the machine. Quickly navigated the menu. She requested two thousand. The machine returned an error. *The withdrawal limit is $500.*

"Damn it!" She looked back at the Sandpiper. Saw Pete and the blond walking toward the beach. Just her luck that the little guy would find love the moment she needed his services.

Five hundred would do for now. She took the money. Grabbed her card. Ran across the street to the side of the building where she'd last seen Pete. The area around the restaurant was well lit. The beach beyond was dark.

The half-moon cast beachgoers in silhouette. She saw someone holding hands with a much shorter person. Elena ran up behind them. A mother with her child gave her an alarmed look.

"I'm sorry. I thought you were someone else." She looked around and spotted other couples walking hand-in-hand. It was impossible to see any details in the dark. Lightning flashed closer to shore. For an instant it was bright as day.

Elena saw Pete's neon green ballcap during the flash. She saw the blonde with him. They were walking toward the long pier. Pier 60. Thunder rumbled. Wind gusted. Droplets of water crashed into her face.

People gasped in surprise at the quickly approaching storm. They hurried for shelter. For nearby hotels. Lightning flashed again. Pete and the woman were hurrying toward the pier. Elena ran after them.

The deep sand made running hard. She tugged off her sandals. Hooked a finger through the straps to hold them. Running was easier barefoot. A group of teens ran from the water, laughing and shouting. A gangly boy ran right in front of her.

Elena crashed into him. Lightning flashed as they tumbled to the ground. The boy shouted apologies. Got up and ran after his friends. Elena pushed to her feet. Saw Pete and the blonde beneath the lights at the front of the pier.

Crowds of people were running from the pier toward nearby hotels. Not Pete or his date. They went under the pier. It was obvious what was about to go down. She wasn't even sure why she was still chasing them.

The last thing she wanted was to watch the little guy copulate with a full-grown woman. But she really needed to talk to Pete now. Maybe he'd take the five hundred as a down payment. She finally reached the pier.

Lightning crashed. Thunder shook the air. The rain started beating down on the beach. Elena stumbled under the shelter of the pier. She heard moaning. It wasn't moans of pleasure. It was pain. And it wasn't the woman moaning.

It was dark beneath the pier. She huddled behind one of the supports. Pete cried out in pain. He shouted something, but it was lost to the waves and the storm. Elena crept closer. Another flash of lightning revealed Pete. The woman's long blond hair hung like a curtain over her face.

The woman held what looked like a short sword. Thin and curved. Like a fancy carving knife. She had Pete's hand twisted to the side. A foot on his neck. The knife to a finger. Pete was shouting. Crying.

Elena slipped closer. She was just ten feet from them now. There was just enough moonlight to see the figures dimly. Elena resisted the urge to run. To shout for help. Who was this woman?

Pete's face was in agony. "Please! They'll kill me if I say anything!"

"I'll kill you if you don't." The woman traced a thin red line on Pete's pinky finger. "But I'll start by dismembering you a piece at a time."

"Please no!"

"Talk, you little bitch!"

"Okay! Okay!" Pete sobbed. "His name is Holland. He's in Belleair." Pete shouted an address.

"Did he say where he was going?"

"He didn't tell me. Holland said he asked how California beaches were. Maybe that's where he was headed."

"See? That wasn't too hard." The blond booted Pete in the back. His face plowed into the sand. She put her knee on his back. Slid the knife somewhere beneath her skirt. Something else was in her hand. It was too small to see.

The woman yanked off Pete's sandal. He struggled, but she pushed down harder with her knee. She jabbed him between the toes with a syringe. His cries were muffled by the sand. Seconds later, his struggles weakened. He went limp.

She dragged him closer to the water. Left him face down on the wet sand. Then she brushed off her hands and knees. Casually walked away. Vanished into the storm-swept night.

Elena was frozen in place. Was Pete dead? Had she killed him? Maybe the woman was still out there watching. It didn't matter. She couldn't just let him die. She ran to him. Rolled him over as the tide tried to drag him out.

She pulled him back to shore. He was still breathing. Still alive. He opened his eyes. Blinked blearily. Spoke gibberish. It was like he was drunk out of his mind.

"Pete, are you okay?"

He gagged. Started to vomit. Elena turned him on his side, so he didn't choke. He threw up what looked like a taco salad. Kept vomiting until green bile spewed out. Then he shivered violently.

Elena didn't know what the woman had injected him with, but she needed to get him medical attention. She gripped him beneath his armpits. Lifted, and tugged. It was a good thing he was so small. He probably weighed a hundred pounds soaking wet. And he was definitely soaking wet.

There was nothing and no one nearby. The park was empty. The cars were gone. Everyone had run inside to escape the storm. The Hilton was the closest place. She dragged him across the parking lot. Wind and rain whipped her face. Stung her eyes.

Lightning flashed in quick succession. A man was hurrying down the sidewalk in her direction. He was in flipflops and shorts. Looked like an off-duty lifeguard. His eyes widened when he saw her dragging Pete. He ran over.

"Is he okay?"

"I found him on the beach. I think he had too much to drink. He needs help!"

The man scooped up Pete like he was nothing. "Holy shit, it's Pete!"

"You know him?"

He nodded. "Yeah. Most locals do. You sure he didn't cross the wrong person?"

Elena wasn't sure what to say. "Um..."

He grinned. "Don't worry. World's worst kept secret that Pete is the plug for just about everything in these parts."

"A woman beat him up then injected him with something."

His grin vanished. "Poison?"

"I don't know. He threw up a lot. He's acting like he's drunk."

"Okay." He hurried down the sidewalk. Elena jogged after him. He stopped at the main strip. He crossed the road. Kept going down an alley. Went around the back of a residential building. Kicked the door.

A woman answered a moment later. Her mouth dropped open. "What happened?"

"Alcohol poisoning, I think."

"Get him inside."

Elena followed the guy in. He lowered Pete onto a table. It looked like a medical clinic. There were posters about drug abuse and alcohol abuse on the cinderblock walls. An old white refrigerator in one corner. A pair of locked metal cabinets.

The woman tested his vitals. She opened his eyes and looked at them. She took his arm. Found a vein. Slid an IV needle inside and taped it down. She hooked it to a drip. Then she put an oxygen mask over his face. Opened the valve on a metal cannister.

She turned to Elena. "What happened?"

"I think someone injected him with a drug. He threw up everything in his stomach. I saw bile."

The lifeguard man put a finger to Pete's neck. "What do you think, Giselle?"

She lightly slapped Pete's face. His eyelids fluttered. "Pete, I need you to stay awake." She slapped him harder. "Get me some ammonia, Jaden."

The man opened a wooden cabinet. Rummaged inside and brought back a vial. He opened the lid and put it under Pete's nose. Pete's eyes flashed open. He jerked back.

"Okay, that's a good sign." Giselle slid the oxygen mask off. Put a tube in Pete's mouth. "I need you to blow into it."

He blew weakly. She looked at the results. "He's at point one eight. Not lethal, but it's a hell of a dose for someone his size." Giselle turned to Elena. "How did this happen?"

"Pete was dealing with the wrong person," Jaden said. "Not the first time he took a beating."

"This was attempted murder." Elena sat down in a chair. "The woman threatened him with a knife. Then she injected him and put him face down in the water. She was going to make it look like he drowned."

"That's insidious." Giselle put the oxygen mask back over Pete's face. "He doesn't even drink. He's a smoker."

"Wouldn't take more than a shot to get him drunk. He's a lightweight." Jaden put a hand on Pete's forehead. "Don't worry, buddy. We got you."

Elena was exhausted. Soaking wet. She just wanted to sleep. Then she thought of what Pete had told the woman. "Pete told the woman about someone named Holland. He gave her an address. Do you know anyone by that name?"

Giselle shook her head. "Never heard of them."

"Me either," Jaden said.

"Well, their life is probably in danger."

"Doubtful." Jaden shook his head. "The people Pete deals with know how to take care of themselves. Pete is a lightweight, but the people he deals with most definitely aren't."

"Agreed." Giselle put a hand on Pete's forehead. "That blond bimbo is probably in for a rude awakening if she tries the same shit on this Holland person."

Elena couldn't shake the feeling that the blond was a lot more dangerous than they thought. She thought back to the lightning flashes. Seeing the woman holding that knife against Pete. There was something familiar about her. About her voice. She could almost place it.

"You're a tourist?" Jaden asked.

Elena flinched from her thoughts. "I'm a journalist. I've been tracking a story. I was hoping Pete could help me find a man who's vital to my investigation."

"Is it Holland?"

Elena shook her head. "No. I think Pete was putting him in touch with Holland for a fake ID."

"If he's a local we might know him." Jaden glanced at Giselle, then back to Elena. "Is he in trouble?"

"Looks like it. The woman who almost killed Pete seems to be looking for him too."

Giselle sat down across from her. "You have a name?"

Elena fished her phone out of her pocket. Pulled up the picture of the sketch. Showed them. "This guy. His name—"

"Carver." Jaden nodded. "I've seen him. He and his girlfriend Paola were here for a while. He's the big hulking quiet type."

"I saw him once or twice," Giselle said. "He and his girlfriend went to the Sandpiper a lot."

"Pete talked to them a few times. I'll bet he can tell you more." Jaden looked at the small man. "Maybe he'll be better in a few hours."

"Come back late morning," Giselle said. "If the person who tried to kill Pete is after Carver, then we need to warn him."

"Where you staying?" Jaden asked.

Elena told him. "I'm parked nearby."

"I'll walk you over." He stood. "What kind of story are you working on?"

"Apparently a very dangerous one."

He laughed. "I'll say. But if anyone is after Carver, I think they'll be the ones in trouble. I saw that dude handle a drunk in two seconds. He looks dangerous."

"He is." Elena stood and looked at her bedraggled state. "I'm a mess."

"You're a hero." Giselle touched her arm. "Thanks for saving Pete. It was very brave."

"Yeah." Jaden nodded. "It's actually insane what you did."

He walked her through the rain to her car. She waved goodbye and drove back to the motel. Took a short, hot shower. Fell onto the creaking mattress and was asleep in seconds.

SATURDAY MORNING

ELENA DROVE TO THE clinic the next morning.

It was after nine. She was starving, but she wanted to find out if Pete could talk. Find out if he'd survived the night.

She knocked on the door. Giselle answered a moment later. Beckoned her inside. Pete wasn't in the clinic. Giselle led her up a flight of stairs. There was a small apartment there. Pete was on the couch drinking Gatorade.

His face was a little green. He had dark circles under his eyes. But he looked alert. And he was alive.

"Looks like I owe you." He stood weakly. "You saved my life."

"Sit down," Giselle said in a stern voice.

Pete sat. Buried his face in his hands. "God, I knew it was too good to be true. Women don't like short guys."

Giselle rolled her eyes. "Pete, you're short and built like a kid. What do you expect?"

"Wow, that's uncalled for." Elena stepped between Giselle and Pete. "He almost died and you're flaming him like that?"

Pete chuckled. "She gives me hell all the time."

Giselle smiled. "I think it's sweet that you defended him. But my boy needs to put on some weight and muscle if he wants a chance with a grown woman."

"Too much work." Pete took another swig of Gatorade. "So, you need fake IDs? I'll give you a name."

"No, I don't really." Elena sat on a divan next to the couch. "Pete, I'm actually a reporter. I'm tracking down a guy named Carver."

The little guy wasn't fazed by the revelation. "You thought you'd squeeze Holland for information? Wouldn't work." His eyes flared wide. "Oh, shit. I need a phone!" He held out his hand. "Now!"

Giselle pulled a phone from her back pocket and handed it to him.

He dialed a number. Listened to it ring several times before disconnecting. He dialed another number. It rang several times but this time someone answered. "Amy? Are you with Holland?"

Pete listened for a moment. His face fell. "How did they get in? Past all his cameras?" He listened for a while. "Lay low. I'm so sorry." He ended the call."

Elena already knew what happened before anyone asked. "Holland is dead, isn't he?"

"He was tortured and killed." Pete's voice was just a shadow. "And it's my fault."

CHAPTER 15

MONDAY EARLY MORNING

Carver drew his pistol.

Walked steadily toward the assassin hovering over the other bed. "Drop the knife and get on the floor."

The woman dove out of the door. Carver ran to the door but didn't go out. He picked up a pillow and pushed it through the doorway. The knife plunged into it. It withdrew just as quickly. Footsteps tapped down the hallway.

Carver stepped out. Dim night lights illuminated the hallway. The woman was visible a few doors down. She was moving at a fair clip. He ran after her. It was a straight shot outside. No corners to worry about. Well, at least not until he exited the front door. She might try to stab him there.

He raced past the front desk. The clerk wasn't behind the glass. He was probably in his bedroom behind the office. The front door slammed shut. Carver booted it open then jumped out. The woman wasn't waiting. She was gone.

Carver ran to the corner and spotted her. She hustled down the road. Dodged into a side street. He didn't think he could catch her. He was faster, but there were too many places to hide. Too many places for her to ambush him. He'd been prepared enough to survive her attack, but not prepared enough to capture her.

He went inside. The clerk was standing behind the protective glass. "Did you slam the front door?"

Carver shook his head. "Did a darkhaired woman come by here earlier and ask about me?"

The clerk blinked a few times. "Yes. She said she was trying to find her friend. Said he was a big guy. Muscular. I thought it might be you, so I told her where you were."

"Thanks. If you see her again, tell her she owes me money."

The clerk stared at him. "Are you certain you didn't slam the door?"

"Positive." Carver went back to his room. The flare was still going. He picked it up and examined the bottom bunk closest to the door. He'd borrowed the pillows from the other beds and arranged it to look like a body.

The sheet was ripped. Pillow fluff lay on top. The woman had stabbed and gutted a pillow in one smooth movement. The knife was razor sharp if it could do that to something as flimsy as a pillow. She'd made the bottom part of the Z and angled up to the right before realizing it wasn't a body. She might be left-handed.

Carver put the pillows back on the beds and cleaned up the fluff. He retrieved his duffel bag. Dunked the road flare in the toilet to put it out. Then he went to the rear exit. It was possible the killer had circled back. That would be the smart move. People usually assumed that because someone ran away, it meant they weren't coming back right away.

It was a good way to surprise a target. A good way to kill someone who thought they were momentarily safe. He slung the duffel bag strap across his shoulders to free his hands. Held a Glock in one hand, keeping it low against his leg so it wouldn't stand out. He crossed the road. Ducked into a back street.

Rickety chain-link fences ran down both sides of the road. There were some old cars parked along the fences. Garage doors and driveways. The houses were old. Concrete. Covered in peeling paint. The few that were well maintained were painted in bright colors. Yellows, blues, greens.

This was the same road the killer had turned down. She could be hiding behind a car. Behind a trash can. Maybe in a yard. The streetlights were widely spaced. There were plenty of dark places, ideal for lying in wait. A violent thrust from the dark would be the last thing he saw if he wasn't careful.

Carver kept to the shadows. He stopped every few feet and peered into the dark. Tried to see if the killer was lurking. He wished he'd grabbed night vision goggles from the storage unit. It would've been a smart move. Now it was just hindsight.

He crouched. Picked up a pebble. Tossed it at the fence down and across the road. It pinged off metal. He waited and watched. There was no movement. Maybe the killer hadn't circled back. Maybe she was long gone. Sitting somewhere and plotting her next moves. That wasn't what Carver would have done.

Carver knew exactly what he would do. Maybe the killer was doing it right this moment. He went prone next to an old car and watched. This time he wasn't watching ahead, he was watching behind.

He envisioned what the killer had done. She'd run. Stopped in a dark place and waited to see if he followed. When he didn't, she circled back. Went to a nearby place where she could see the front and back doors. She saw him leave. Now she was shadowing him.

Waiting for the perfect moment to strike. Which meant she probably knew where he was hiding.

That was okay. Unless she had NV goggles, they were both blind. The street was narrow. The chain link fences hemmed in both sides. The only places to hide were the dark spots. The streetlamps highlighted the places in between. There was no way to sneak past the light.

The killer was waiting in the dark. Waiting for Carver to appear beneath the next streetlight. Then she'd move up. She'd have to pass through the light Carver had walked through a moment ago. Then he could confirm she was following him. Right now, she was waiting and watching. Probably wondering why he hadn't appeared yet. Then she'd become suspicious. She might realize he knew what she was doing.

Carver rose and jogged forward. He passed under the streetlight and kept jogging. Once he was in the darkness, he ducked behind a car. He watched and waited. Took a road flare from his pocket. She would have to follow soon. When she did, he'd double back. Toss the road flare at her. She might be good with knives, but he had guns.

He glanced behind him. It was pure habit. *Always watch your six.* A figure crept toward him. Carver popped the cap on the flare and threw it. The woman threw up her hands to shield her eyes. He raised the Glock and fired. She dove to the side. Bullets pinged off a car on the other side of the road.

The woman ducked behind a trash can. Carver fired into it. She was still moving. Running for a nearby car. He aimed low. Popped off one more round. It struck her calf. She cried out and went down.

Carver circled her. Tossed another flare at her side. She climbed to her feet. Tried to limp away.

"Hold it there." Carver stepped close, but not too close. "Drop the knife."

The woman was Caucasian. Slim. Straight as a pole. Her hair was dark black, but it looked dyed. She was pale. A large freckle on one cheek was the only distinguishing mark visible. The rest of her body was covered in pants and a long sleeve shirt.

She bared her teeth at him. Clutched her long knife in the left hand.

"I have questions. Answer them and I won't cripple you." He aimed at her other thigh. "Drop the knife."

She threw it to the ground.

There was more to worry about. Someone might have heard the gunshots. Called the police. Carver decided that was okay. If the police arrested her then Leach could ask the questions. But for now, she was his prisoner.

"Who hired you?"

"My clients are anonymous." She had a flat midwestern accent. "They pay half up front and the other half on delivery."

"How much are they paying you?"

She shrugged. "A lot."

"How much?"

"A million even."

Carver whistled. "Someone has a lot of money, or they want me dead real bad."

"Probably both," she said.

The Brazilian drug cartel and people in the government had plenty of money and motive. He figured it could be either of them. "What do you know about me?"

The question seemed to catch her off guard. "I know what you look like. Your name, Amos Carver. You have military training. You're dangerous. Someone wants you dead."

"Who is Nicki Jones?"

She stared silently at him.

"Did you kill Desmond Price?"

"I don't know who that is."

"The man someone gutted behind the club."

She looked at the knife. "Yes."

"Did he kill Nicki Jones?"

She didn't answer.

"What's your name?"

"Theresa Smith."

Carver had expected a fake name. He could tell that Nicki Jones meant something to the woman. A partner? A lover? Sisters? It was hard to say. Theresa Smith kept a straight face. She was in pain. Angry but calm. A dangerous person, to be sure. She was looking for a way out. Waiting for Carver to slip up so she could kill him and collect the bounty.

There were faint bulges beneath her pants. One on each thigh, and one on each ankle. Probably more knives. Some killers had a specific modus operandi. A signature killing method. Theresa's was the Z cut. That might make it easier to link her to other murders. It might produce a name, or it might not. She didn't seem the type to use guns.

Leach could have her DNA taken. Her prints. Her mug shot. If there was anything to find, he could find it. But Carver didn't hear sirens. Apparently, no one had called the police. That meant he'd have to do it himself. He didn't want to call 911. It would be better to text Leach.

Carver took out his burner phone. He texted the detective. It was after two in the morning. It seemed unlikely that Leach would answer. He dialed the number and called.

It rang four times and went to voicemail. It looked like he'd have to call emergency services after all.

Theresa shifted slightly.

"Don't move."

"My calf hurts. I can't stand still."

"I barely nicked it."

"It's still painful to stand." Her hands were at her sides. Close to her pockets. They probably weren't pockets. Just slits leading to the knives sheathed on her thighs.

The longer they stood here, the greater the odds she'd try something. He didn't want to have to kill her. She was valuable to him. Maybe she didn't know who hired her, but with enough information, anything could be tracked.

"Theresa, I know you have more weapons on you." Carver aimed the handgun low at her legs. "I'll do my best not to kill you because I need answers. That means I'll shoot your knees first. Shattered kneecaps are no joke, okay?"

She seethed silently.

"Now, to keep us both safe, I'm going to ask you to disrobe. Start with your shoes. Then your pants. Then your shirt. You will take off the weapons slowly and toss them toward me."

Theresa bared her teeth. "Pervert."

Carver didn't budge. "Don't try to make this about anything else. If you refuse, I'll take out a kneecap, okay?"

She glared at him, face reddening.

"Okay, sit down and take off your shoes."

Theresa hesitated. Looked at the gun. Slowly sat down on the asphalt and unlaced her boots. She took them off one at a time.

"Keep your hands visible at all times. I know you're a pro with knives. If I feel the least bit jumpy, I will shoot a kneecap."

"At this angle, you'll kill me too."

"No, at this angle, the bullet will hit your shin. There's a lot of bone there. It'll probably shatter and cause a lot of damage." Carver nodded at her feet. "Pull up the bottom of the pants and remove the ankle knives."

She pulled up the hem of the pants legs. Unstrapped a nylon sheath with four small knives in it. She did the same for the other leg. Tossed them toward him. Carver kept a visual on the sheaths to make sure she didn't slip a knife free.

"Stand up and remove your pants."

Wincing, she stood. Unbuckled her belt. Unbuttoned the pants. Slid them down to her ankles. Knives were sheathed to the outside of her thighs.

"Remove those and toss them toward me."

She unstrapped them and tossed them.

"Pants all the way off."

Theresa bent down and pulled the pants free of her ankles.

Shirt off next.

She tugged the t-shirt up and over her head. Dropped it on the ground.

"Hands up, rotate slowly so I can see your back."

She did. There were small knives strapped behind her shoulders. The sheathes seemed to be held on by adhesive. Theresa wasn't thin. She was lean and muscular.

"Lose the knives."

Theresa pinched the hilts between thumbs and forefingers then tossed them next to the other knives.

"Turn around. Remove your bra and underwear."

She turned around, face reddening. She was close to losing her temper. That was okay. The only way to interrogate some people was by keeping them off balance. Making them so uncomfortable that they lost their cool.

Theresa slid off her underwear. She unhooked the bra and dropped it. Gave him a sarcastic smile. "Enjoying the show?"

"Rotate slowly and face away."

"You like what you see, Carver?"

"Rotate slowly and face away from me."

Her fists clenched and her face turned redder. She turned around. She had a small bottom, but it was always best to be safe.

"Bend over and spread your cheeks."

"Are you fucking serious?"

"Do it."

"You bastard."

"You've been to prison before. You know the drill. Now, do it."

Theresa bent over and spread her buttocks. Something was taped to the inside of the right one.

"Remove whatever that is and toss it in the pile."

"Asshole." She peeled it off and tossed it behind her without looking.

The pile was about halfway between them. Carver went to it and knelt. He picked up the object she'd tossed. It was a tiny sliver of metal. It could be used to pick handcuffs. It might even be deadly. Anything was possible in the right hands.

Theresa turned. She was cleanly shaven. No pubic hair, so at least she didn't seem to be hiding anything there. A body cavity search would probably reveal at least one more weapon, but Carver didn't want to get close to her. Up close and personal was her forte.

He slid the weapons pile further from her with his foot. He did the same with her clothes except for the underwear. "Put on your underwear."

She picked up her bra and panties. "I hope you enjoyed the show."

There was nothing to enjoy. It didn't matter if she was attractive or ugly. This was about survival. She'd lost all her rights as a human the moment she tried to kill him.

Carver knelt and frisked the pants and shirt. The back pocket had a stiff slip of paper in it. He slipped it into his pocket without looking at it. He carefully massaged the seams in search of anything stiff.

It wasn't as good as an X-ray, but it was enough to ensure she didn't have more knives hidden in them. He tossed them back to her. "Put them back on." He felt inside the boots and examined the soles. The heels unsnapped. Inside the hollow beneath was a set of lockpick tools. The other one hid a folding razor blade.

"Clearly, I underestimated you," Theresa said.

Carver removed the weapons and tools and tossed the boots to her. "Put them on."

"What now?" She glanced at the shoes but didn't pick them up. "Are you going to take me somewhere and torture me for information?"

"I considered it." He dumped her gear into his duffel bag. "I don't like it when people try to kill me."

"I don't like it when a man with a gun forces me to strip—"

"I'm going to stop you right there. We both know you're trying to play to shame or sympathy. I guarantee you it won't work with me." Carver motioned at her boots. "Put those on."

"You're a psychopath, aren't you?" There was no accusation in her voice. Just fact. She put on her boots.

"That's a good question." Carver checked his phone. Nothing from Leach. That meant he either had to call 911 or babysit an assassin until morning.

Calling the cops would lead to a lot of questions. They'd take him in. He'd have to sit around, answer questions. He'd have to keep quiet about Leach. Pretend he didn't know the guy. It would put Carver in a bad situation.

Babysitting an assassin was just as bad. It was a deadly proposition. One that could get him killed because she might pull a knife from her asshole or somewhere else he hadn't searched. The only way to play it safe would be to kill her. But he couldn't do that. He needed answers.

So, for now, he'd had to play a deadly game and hope for the best.

CHAPTER 16

SATURDAY MORNING

It was no surprise that Holland was dead.

And now the blond killer was hot on Carver's trail. Elena gave Pete a moment to process, then hit him with a question. "Did Carver say he was going to California?"

"He just said it sounded like a nice place to visit. Maybe he just said that to throw off anyone who tried to find him." Pete shook his head. "Amy said they got Holland's client list. It's on paper, not a computer. It's protected by a cipher. But if he gave it up, then whoever has the list would know the fake social security number assigned to the clients."

"Which is enough to track just about anyone these days."

Pete nodded.

Elena leaned closer. "Does Amy have a copy of the list?"

"There are no copies. But the killer didn't take the list. She left it behind because she had the info she wanted." Pete buried his face in his hands. "I'm so damned weak. I gave up Holland and she hardly even hurt me."

"It's not your fault," Jaden said. "I would've folded too, man."

Giselle put a hand on his shoulder. "It's not your fault, Pete. But you definitely don't want this getting out, or the people you're connected to might see you as a big liability."

Elena pressed him for more information. "Can Amy give me Carver's fake social security number? I need to find Carver and warn him."

"I already got it from her." He got up. Found a pen on the counter. Wrote the nine digits on a scrap of paper. "I've got a guy who can look up employment records by the social."

"Can he give you the fake name Carver is using?"

"That information is masked for privacy. They keep everything in separate databases these days because identity theft is such a problem." Pete looked around. "Where's my phone?"

Jaden held up a bag of rice with a phone in it. "It took a bath in the ocean. I think it's dead."

"Man, I just bought that phone!" Pete squeezed his eyes shut. "Giselle, you have a computer?"

"Yeah, why? I don't want to get connected with your criminal enterprises, Pete."

"I just need to access my cloud storage to look up a number."

Giselle took her phone back. "You're not using my phone to contact anyone else. Last thing I need is an assassin coming after me." She walked away and returned with a laptop. "Only use it to look up the number."

"You can use my phone." Elena put her phone on the counter. "I've got a texting app that uses a different phone number than my main."

Giselle frowned. "You can text from your phone without using your real number? Why do you have that?"

"I was using dating apps. I didn't want a bunch of strange men having my number."

The other woman gave her a thumbs up. "Smart girl."

Pete took a few minutes to look up the information. He used Elena's phone to text his contact. A response came moments later. Pete groaned. "Damn it."

Elena took her phone and looked at it. "What a surprise. He wants money."

"How much?" Jaden leaned over and whistled. "A thousand dollars?"

"It's a bargain compared to Pete's finder fee." Elena decided this information was worth the money. She typed out a message. *I'll pay it.*

He sent the payment info and she used an app to wire the money. He sent the information over shortly after. There was an employment ID number, a social security number, and a company name: Sunshine Entertainment.

Elena frowned. "That's it? What a rip off."

"Florida doesn't have a state income tax. If they did, I could get the info from their tax collection agency, easy." Pete rubbed his eyes. "I used to have a guy at the IRS, but he got found out and fired."

"Good to know my personal information is available for sale," Giselle said.

Jaden shrugged. "Social media has more on you than anyone else and they don't even pay for it."

"Joke's on them," Giselle said. "I don't use social media."

Elena searched for Sunshine Entertainment. It was an umbrella company for night clubs, concert venues, and restaurants in Miami. It looked like California had been a misdirect. She was relieved she didn't have to book a flight to the west coast after all.

She still had a problem. Sunshine Entertainment owned a lot of businesses. How was she supposed to track down which one Carver worked at? And what would he possibly be doing at a nightclub? Bartending?

Jaden was a step ahead of her. "I'll bet he's working as a bouncer. If he's as big as you say, that'd be the perfect line of work for him."

"He's huge," Pete said.

Giselle mussed his hair. "Everyone looks huge to you."

Pete slumped. "Yeah. It sucks."

Jaden scrolled down the list of clubs on Elena's phone. "I think you can narrow this down to the five nightclubs. Restaurants don't use bouncers."

Elena looked at the list. "Thanks. That's a great idea." She headed for the door. "Thanks for your help."

"You're leaving?" Pete pushed to his feet. "Just like that?"

"The killer is probably already in Miami." Elena gave him a smile. "Just be glad you're not another victim."

"I have some things that could help you." He leaned on the counter. "I owe you my life."

Elena was mildly curious. "What things are you talking about?"

"Take me by my place and I'll show you."

"I'll come with you." Jaden helped Pete toward the door. "That way you don't have to give him a piggyback ride."

"I'll take any help I can get." Elena headed for the door.

"Drink plenty of water," Giselle called after them. "Stay hydrated, Pete."

"Yes, mom!"

Jaden helped Pete into Elena's back seat, then he dropped into the passenger side. Elena followed Pete's instructions and drove to a small house back on the mainland.

Pete looked uncomfortable. "Can you wait out here?"

Jaden grinned. "Why? You live with your mom?"

"Maybe."

Jaden helped him out of the back seat and to the front door. Pete went inside and emerged a few minutes later, a small black bag in hand.

Elena got out of the car. "What's in the bag?"

He opened it and put the items on her hood. One looked like a USB stick. The others were small cameras. "Someone gave me these as payment a long time ago. This is real spy stuff, okay? Pro gadgetry."

"Doesn't look all that pro," Elena said.

He held up the USB stick. "Put the leech next to a smartphone or computer. Turn it on. It'll download everything on the device." He held out a hand. "Let me see your phone."

Elena handed it to him.

He flicked a tiny switch on the USB stick. An LED screen on the front lit up. Pete put it next to her phone. Messages appeared on the LED screen.

Detected

Connected

Downloading 0%

The progress indicator reached a hundred percent within two minutes. Pete held up the device. "Put it into a computer like a normal USB stick and you can view the documents. Sometimes it can even show you the PIN to unlock the phone."

Elena looked at it dubiously. "You're telling me this thing downloaded gigabytes of data in two minutes?"

"All the documents." He used tiny buttons on the front of the stick and opened a menu. "You can also have it steal account information. But then you need another special computer to decrypt passwords. Apparently, that thing is worth a few hundred grand. But I'll give you the name of the guy who can get stuff like that."

"What about these cameras?"

"They're not cameras. They're trackers." He put one on the tip of his finger. "They're magnetic and use a watch battery for power. Download the Bugg app and hold them next to your phone to register them. As long as there's a cell signal, you can track them."

Elena put the items in the small bag. "Thanks, Pete. These will be very handy, provided I live long enough to use them."

"Good luck." He took her hand and squeezed it. "Thank you for saving me."

"My pleasure."

Jaden gave her his number. "Call if you need backup, okay?"

Elena put it in her phone. "I don't think you'd do much better than Pete did against this woman. I get the feeling she's a pro."

He nodded. "Yeah, you're probably right. Do your best not to die, okay?"

"No promises." She got in her car and backed out of the driveway. They waved goodbye.

Once she hit the highway, Elena worked down a checklist of items. She downloaded the tracking app and activated the trackers. Then she worked down the list of clubs and called them. Someone answered at three of them.

She asked if they knew someone named Amos Carver who was working as a bouncer. When they said no, then she asked if any of their bouncers had worked there for less than three months. One club had a new guy who'd been there almost exactly three months.

She had exactly one lead, and the name of the lead was Club Periclean.

Elena was three hours into the five-hour drive when an email from Doug Weaver arrived on her phone. She read it when she stopped for gas.

I have some very good information on Amos Carver. Send me what you have, and we can pool our resources. I think we can break this story together.

She'd only just discovered that Carver was in Miami. It looked like Weaver had somehow discovered that too. What else did he know?

She sent him a reply. *Do you know Carver's location? Have you seen him?*

Weaver replied quickly. *I'll tell you what I know, but I want guarantees in writing and I want to know what you know. Let's meet in person and discuss.*

It was an evasive reply. He might know a lot, or nothing at all. Elena had dealt with these kinds of people all the time in the newspaper business. During her rookie years, she'd been far too trusting and given up information only to find out the other person knew even less than her.

A competitor had broken a major story using her information. Elena's boss hadn't been happy, to say the least. It had taught her a valuable lesson, one that she would never forget. She would meet with Doug Weaver, but it would be on her terms.

She glanced at the small black bag on the passenger seat. Maybe this would be a good opportunity to test out Pete's spy bag. If Weaver knew something, it would be on his computer. She just needed to locate him.

Elena reached the interstate and put on the cruise control. Then she ran a search for the Miami Sentinel while steering with her knees. She got an address and looked it up on the maps app. It was a house.

Like a lot of modern "journalists" Weaver worked out of his home. That was perfect. He wanted to meet in person. She could arrange to meet him at home. Then she'd use the leech to steal his data.

She used voice to text to dictate a reply to his email. "I'll meet you at your company headquarters. What's a good time to meet?"

His reply arrived when she was at the outskirts of town. She read it with one eye on the road. *We will meet at a public place at a time of my choosing. You will come alone with no phone or any recording devices. I'll have to frisk you to make sure. I have very sensitive information and won't risk it falling into the wrong hands.*

Elena laughed derisively. "He's crazy!" What had seemed like a promising lead suddenly felt like a dead end. This guy sounded like a conspiracy nut. No way was she letting him frisk her. That just sounded like an excuse to grope.

She found the cheapest motel she could near the island and got a room. Took her things inside and rested on the bed. It was getting late. But maybe it was a good time to go check out the night clubs.

First, she pulled up the Miami Sentinel website. The design was professional. It looked as good or better than many major news outlets websites. There were also multiple contributors. Weaver himself had penned a few opinion pieces and news stories.

His stories were mostly about privacy and surveillance. He also had a few local pieces about corruption, police misconduct, etc. The usual fare for a local rag. He seemed to be pushing for fewer police and more of what he called citizen patrols.

Elena didn't see anything that blatantly painted him as a conspiracy theorist, but she also didn't feel like digging through years of stories to find out. She might have better options available.

If Carver was a bouncer, he could be inside or outside a nightclub. She hadn't brought any clubbing attire with her. She threw on a short dress that might do the trick. Hoped it would get her past the front door if necessary.

Weaver's house wasn't far from her motel. She decided to pay him a visit first. Just to scope it out.

It took ten minutes to find the house. Elena parked across the road. A red sedan was parked in the driveway. Light shone from a window on the front left of the house. The other windows were dark. The curtains were drawn but were slightly open in the front.

The nearest streetlight was out, making it pitch black. Elena walked up the driveway like she belonged there. No sense trying to slink around in a short skirt. She went to the window and looked inside. A man she presumed was Weaver sat with his back to her. He was facing a computer.

She couldn't exactly knock on the door. She wasn't about to try to break in. Instead, she put a tracker under his car. The strong magnet locked onto the metal. Elena walked calmly back to her car and got inside. Turned on the tracking app.

A blip appeared on the map. If Weaver went somewhere, maybe she could break into his house. It was probably the dumbest idea she'd had in a while, but it was time for desperate moves.

Next up was a stop at Club Periclean.

She drove to South Beach. The fancy part of the island. The nightclub was in the same building as Lay Playa, a high-rise condo. The building looked like most others in this area. Thirty stories high. Glass, balconies, probably filled with tourists.

There was a small strip mall across the road. She parked there. Walked across the street. It was early by clubbing standards. It was Saturday night, but the line in front was short. It would probably be easy to get inside right now.

Then she saw him. Tall. Hulking. Short hair, medium toned skin. All business.

It was Carver.

CHAPTER 17

MONDAY EARLY MORNING

Carver considered killing Theresa.

He considered it long and hard, because the longer she was alive, the more chances she had to kill him. He was missing an essential tool that would increase his odds of survival. Rope or cuffs to secure her hands and arms would have to be the next order of business. He had some at the storage locker. It should have been something he'd picked up with the weapons, but it hadn't crossed his mind.

Taking a prisoner hadn't been a consideration. Planning for all contingencies was a vital part of mission prep. He was soft. Civilian life had reduced his tactical awareness. It made him forget hard lessons learned in the field. Carver had made too many enemies in Morganville. Enemies with boundless resources and anger.

He'd disrupted major legislation. Derailed the privatization of military special operations. Politicians had resigned over it. Others had fought political headwinds and cashed in on favors to stay in office. The military chain of command had also suffered losses. But those in the black operations sector had probably remained at their posts, hidden and untouched. They could rain down unholy hell on those who crossed them.

But in their eagerness to privatize dark operations, they'd intentionally crippled their own forces. Shot themselves not in just one foot, but both. Despite that, they still had numerous assets to count on. Off-the-books contractors who could get the job done.

Theresa broke into his thoughts. "You're going to kill me, aren't you?"

"It depends on how useful you are to me. Some things can be answered whether you're dead or alive." He visualized the distance between here and his storage unit. What would normally be a thirty-minute walk would be a treacherous hike with her.

He examined the chain link fence. The edges were bound to the pole by thick wire. Too thick to be useful. But one section had been repaired with regular braided wire. It was long enough to do the trick.

Carver motioned Theresa toward the fence. "Untie that wire."

She hesitated. Walked slowly to the fence. Started working on the wire. It came free a few minutes later. Theresa dangled it in front of her. "Bondage now, huh?"

He kept the gun trained low toward her leg. Walked closer and held out a hand.

She dropped the wire on the ground. "Oops."

Carver backed up a step. "Pick it up."

Theresa worked her jaw back and forth. Bent over and retrieved it. Held it out again.

He snatched it. Backed up. "Turn around. Put your hands behind your back.

She raised her arms and put them behind her head.

"No. Put them low behind your back, hands gripping the wrists."

Theresa begrudgingly did it. It looked easy for her. She was flexible. Limber. She might be able to wriggle free, but at least this would slow her down.

Carver walked behind her. He put the gun against her lower spine. "Don't make me cripple you, okay?"

She trembled with anger but remained silent.

Using one hand, Carver wrapped the wire around the wrists. The wire was a little stiff but not too hard to bend. After two loops, he twisted the wire twice, then wrapped it again. It was too stiff to tie into a knot, so he twisted it again. Rinsed and repeated.

The wire was laced around the wrists and up the forearms. It looked solid. Solid enough to safely walk her to the storage unit. Since he couldn't take her to the hostel, that seemed the best place to keep her until Leach could come.

It would be tricky. A single passerby could call the cops. Then he'd have to explain why he'd kidnapped her. He plotted out a route that would keep to the backstreets as much as possible. It was a route he'd practiced several times in case he needed to make a run for it. It would work.

He took out the burner phone. Took pictures of her face and profile. She didn't want to talk. Maybe facial recognition software could help.

Theresa sneered. "Should I strip again? Want me to bend over?"

"Let's go." Carver prodded her forward.

Theresa started walking. They reached the intersection. Crossed the street and continued down another dark backstreet. A car turned down the street. Its headlights lit them up. Then it turned into a driveway and a garage door opened.

Carver held position until the garage door closed. He waited and listened. All was quiet, so he pushed Theresa forward again. There was more traffic on the road ahead. He watched and waited. When it was clear, he pushed Theresa ahead and they scurried across.

They kept going like that. Staying in darkness. Waiting for an all clear. Hurrying to the next spot of darkness. Theresa matched his pace. Not because she was eager to get where they were going, but probably because she didn't want the police involved either. Being arrested guaranteed she'd be tied to the murder of Desmond Price.

She was a contract killer. No one would bail her out of jail. That was why her clients remained anonymous. That was why she remained just as anonymous to her clients. It avoided loose ends. It also meant she was on her own. It meant she'd try to get out of this herself.

Carver remained vigilant. He put himself in her place. She knew he wanted her alive. That he was going through a lot of trouble to keep from wounding her. He wanted her healthy. Alert. Able to answer questions. He'd been staying in a hostel, so he didn't have a place to keep her. She didn't know where he was taking her, but she'd figure it out soon enough.

Then she'd make a decision. Fight and flee or go into the storage unit. They were made of flimsy metal. Escape was possible. But she knew he'd probably be nearby. Trying to escape would make a lot of noise. It might attract attention.

As long as it wasn't the police, she'd welcome the attention. It would put Carver in a tough spot. He'd have to take another prisoner or let the other person call the police.

Carver ran through scenarios. He wound them out to a conclusion. Figured out what he'd do in Theresa's situation. Most of them boiled down to attracting attention and using a civilian to call the police or run interference. But somehow, he knew that wouldn't be what Theresa chose. Her skillset offered her other methods of escape.

They reached the storage facility. Carver punched in the code at the pedestrian gate. There was a camera at the car gate, but not here. He guided Theresa inside the fence.

"This is a dumb place to keep me," she said.

"It'll do for now." Carver walked her down the road between the units.

Theresa waited until they turned the next corner to act. She spun on one foot. Her other leg whirled out. It was a textbook roundhouse kick. It was more impressive because her hands were still bound. She didn't have extra impetus or balance.

Carver had noticed something different in her body language when they neared the corner. She'd taken the turn tighter. So, he'd looped out a little wider. He had a gun. He could afford to keep some distance.

The kick missed by a mile. She stared at him for an awkward second. Turned and sprinted away. Carver chased after her. She abruptly reversed direction and thrust out a leg. It caught him in the chest. But there was a problem with Theresa's calculations. She was shorter. Very lean and muscular. Carver was tall. He was thick and muscular.

She'd braced on her back foot. Used that power to thrust her foot at Carver's chest. But it wasn't enough to overcome the mass problem. Carver was just too big and heavy, and he had momentum.

Instead of the kick knocking Carver back or down, his mass crashed into the flat of her foot. Her back foot wasn't enough to keep her standing. Without her arms to provide extra balance, she crumpled and fell.

Carver bent down to pick her up. Something shiny flashed. A blade extended from the end of Theresa's boot. Her leg swung. Carver jumped back. The blade nicked his throat. He caught her ankle with the other hand. Kicked her in the hamstring. She cried out.

He kicked her again. Stepped back from the deadly boot. Aimed the gun. "You really aren't going to be useful, are you?"

"Stop!" She struggled to stand. Her bound arms prevented her. "Don't shoot."

Carver touched his throat. A speck of blood was on his finger. He stepped on her ankle. She grunted in pain. The foot with the bladed boot was pinned. He looked at the other boot. Decided not to take a chance. He stepped on her other ankle.

She groaned. "Please, stop."

He unlaced the boot. Yanked it off. Inspected the blade in the light. Poisoned blades usually had a gleam to them. This one looked bare. He didn't know how he'd missed the blade. It had been cleverly recessed into the sole. There had probably been a piece of rubber that popped out when the blade was activated.

Carver stepped off her ankles. He wriggled the blade. It was securely fastened to something inside. He wasn't removing it without pliers. He pushed the tip against the asphalt. The blade went into the sole. It sprang back out when he released the pressure.

He backed up a step. "Roll onto your stomach."

Theresa regarded him with a hint of fear. "Why?"

"So you can stand back up."

She rolled onto her stomach. Carver gripped the back of her neck and pulled her to her knees. Then he stepped back and let her stand. He prodded her forward. They reached a storage unit in the back. It wasn't his but he'd noticed it was unlocked and empty.

Probably because it was right next to the fence. The other units nearby were also unused. People rightfully thought the fence wasn't much of a deterrent. Someone could slip in and break into the units closest to the fence without too much trouble.

Carver opened the end unit and pushed Theresa inside. He reached up and pulled on the light string. The bulb turned on.

Theresa looked around at the bare concrete floor. "What now?"

It was a good question. Carver didn't feel like waiting out the night in a confined space with this woman. He needed something to secure her to. He also needed a gag. He also couldn't leave her alone while he went looking for those things.

"Sit down in the corner."

She did.

"Desmond Price killed Nicki Jones. You killed him out of retribution."

"Is that a question or a statement?"

"Confirm or deny."

"I killed the man you call Price."

"Why are you being cagey when it comes to Jones?" Carver had given it some thought. Jones might not be a killer. Maybe just an accomplice? Maybe a friend? It was a mystery he wanted answered.

"I don't feel like answering."

Carver nodded.

She spoke again quickly. "And you can't torture me. Not if you plan to turn me over to the cops."

Carver noticed something about her shirt. Something he hadn't noticed earlier. The road flare had been bright but it hadn't illuminated her clothing like the light bulb was now. The shirt was black but there were dark spots in the fabric. Dark spots on her pants too.

He opened the duffel bag and pulled out her knife. It was almost long enough to be a short sword. Like a miniature katana. Carver knew knives but not these kinds of knives. He was more of a survival knife kind of guy. They came in all shapes and sizes, but he preferred them on the shorter side.

All he needed was just enough length to cut a throat. Open an artery. Cause some pain. This blade looked like something that could filet a bear. The handle was stout. Easy to grip. It was made for a smaller hand than his. A custom job. This woman had a lot of custom gear.

It meant she had money. It meant she was successful enough to make the big bucks. She had a few scars on her body. Two small ones on her stomach. Another one just beneath her left breast. Several on her hands and arms. But none were ragged. All had been made with precision blades. It meant she'd probably earned most of them during training. Years ago, and a lifetime away. Her life before she became a killer.

He found what he was looking for. Spots of dark crimson along the blade. Some on the hilt. A professional like her wouldn't leave her blade dirty. She'd clean it. Oil it. Sharpen it. She hadn't had time to do it before coming for Carver. She'd killed someone else before him.

Theresa laughed. "Don't look so concerned, Carver. It's no one you care about."

"Whose blood is this?" He knew the answer already. He just wanted confirmation.

"No one important."

"You're not the kind to kill randomly. You're too cautious. Which means you killed Price for a reason. You used your signature gutting move to finish him. It's a statement.

It's brutal. It was revenge." Carver put the blade in the bag. "There's a part of you that enjoys killing. There's a part of you that tempers that joy. That tells you to be careful."

"You're saying a lot of nothing, Carver."

"You had a reason to kill Price. That reason was Jones. The other person you killed tonight was also for good reason. But this one you had to be extra careful. So, you made it look different." Carver felt certain he knew who it was. And it meant he was on his own again.

Because Theresa had killed Leach.

CHAPTER 18

SATURDAY EVENING

Elena wanted to run to Carver.

She wanted to tell him he was in danger. That she'd braved countless dangers to finally find him. But as she hurried closer, something became evident. This wasn't Carver. He was big, muscular, and tall. But not quite tall enough. Not quite muscular enough.

He was smiling at the women. Joking with them. Flirting. From what Becca and Camilla had told her, Carver wasn't the type who joked a lot or flirted. Her elation drained. Maybe this wasn't the place.

She couldn't leave without going inside. Places like this had bouncers inside too. At least, she vaguely remembered that. It had been a while since she'd been clubbing. Her early twenties seemed like a long time ago.

The line moved quickly. No one was turned away. The bouncer smiled. Looked her up and down. "You must not be from around here."

"Is anyone really from around here?"

He laughed. "Not really. ID, please."

Elena gave it to him.

"Atlanta. Nice." He handed the ID back. "Have fun, Elena."

She smiled back. "You know my name. What's yours?"

"Jeff." His smile grew wider.

"You remind me of a friend of mine." Elena touched his arm. "He's big like you. He worked clubs in Atlanta, but I think he moved here. At first, I thought you were him."

"Really? What's his name?"

"Amos Carver." She studied his face. He didn't react. "Never heard of him." He patted her hand. "Enjoy the club."

"Thanks, Jeff." She squeezed his forearm and went inside.

It was cold inside. Music pumped, but it wasn't too loud. The crowd was small. Most people were huddled around the bar. There were stairs leading to what looked like a VIP area. A short guy in a suit guarded the rope. Definitely not Carver.

Elena went to the bar. She got the attention of a bartender. Ordered a vodka lime. The woman returned with the drink a moment later.

"Want to open a tab?"

"I'll pay cash." Elena handed her a twenty. "Is Amos working tonight?"

"Who?"

"Amos Carver? Real big guy. Always serious."

"I don't know anyone by that name, sorry." She took the money and returned with change.

"Really? He told me he worked here." Elena sighed. "We went to school together."

"The only big guys here work the door. The owner doesn't like bouncers inside. He thinks it makes people nervous."

Elena laughed. "Isn't that their job?"

The bartender grinned. "It has been at most places I worked. I'm sorry I don't know your friend. Maybe he works at another club."

"Probably. He's perfect for the job. He's the most serious looking guy I know. Never smiles."

"Sounds like our bouncer, Clint." The bartender rolled her eyes. "He's damned good looking, but he doesn't seem interested in anyone, man or woman." She hurried off to help another customer.

Who was Clint? Jeff had been the only bouncer outside. She walked toward the bathrooms. A darkhaired woman was sitting alone at a table near the back. A waitress was taking her order. The woman barely looked at the waitress. Her eyes darted around the club. Like she was looking for someone.

Normally, Elena wouldn't have noticed. But she was especially alert ever since someone tried to kill her. She glanced at the other club-goers seated at tables. Most were with other people. Drinking. Laughing. Talking.

Some looked around the room. But they were looking at other people. Men leering at women. Women watching people on the dance floors. Normal club activity.

The darkhaired woman was watching and waiting. Expecting someone or keeping a lookout for someone. She didn't seem to be having a good time. Didn't seem to be having a bad time, either. The waitress looked frustrated. Like she was talking to a brick wall.

Elena stood near the hallway leading to the bathrooms. It seemed like a good spot to watch from. She saw another waitress walking in her direction. She started walking toward the waitress.

They nearly bumped into each other. "I'm sorry." Elena smiled. "I'm so clumsy."

"It's okay." The waitress smiled. Started to walk away.

Elena put a hand on her arm. "Do you know if Clint is working tonight? I told him I'd come see where he works."

The girl frowned. "He's normally here by now. If you didn't see him when you came in, you might want to check outside again."

"Ah, okay. Thanks!"

The waitress hurried off.

Elena turned to look at the darkhaired woman again. The woman looked directly at her and held her gaze. Elena shivered. Looked away. She casually wandered toward the bar. Made her way back to the front door. Stepped outside and looked.

Another man stood next to Jeff. He was shorter. Softer. Definitely not Carver.

She went back inside. Went to the far end of the bar. Kept her gaze on the front door. People trickled in. It was still early. Not even ten yet. She finished her drink and went to the bathroom. The club wasn't crowded but there was still a line.

It took nearly twenty minutes to wait for her turn. The crowd was a little thicker when she went back to the bar. She went outside. There was a new guy. A big guy. Hard body. Serious face.

Men waiting in line glanced at him repeatedly. They looked a little afraid and a little jealous. That had to be Clint. And she felt certain that Clint was really Carver.

The line had grown substantially. She wanted to approach him but now was a bad time. She checked the time and sighed. It was going to be a long night. She went back to the bar. The darkhaired woman was still at her table but now she had a friend.

The waitress was talking to them. The darkhaired woman didn't seem to be paying attention. She was staring at the blonde like she was unwanted company. Maybe they were a couple. Maybe they were having relationship issues. Maybe that was why the darkhaired woman had such an icy glare.

Elena went back to her little nook at the back corner of the bar. She ordered another drink. Thought about how to approach Clint. She couldn't go up to him at work. It would be rude to out his real identity in front of coworkers.

She needed to keep it private. Approach him when he wasn't busy. Maybe ask him to step away for a moment. Tell him it was about Morganville. If Clint was really Carver, he might respond to that.

Movement caught her eye. A man was talking to the darkhaired woman and her companion. Looked like he was flirting with them. The darkhaired woman seemed colder than ever. The blonde was facing away, but her body language was stiff.

"What are you drinking?"

Elena blinked and saw a man smiling at her. He'd squeezed in between her and a group of women. He was medium build. Easy on the eyes. "Vodka lime, why?"

"Let me get you another one."

"My boyfriend would probably object." She patted his hand. "Thanks, though."

"Oh, yeah, sure." He sighed. "Lucky man." He raised a hand to get the bartender's attention.

Elena turned her gaze back to the table. The darkhaired woman was gone. The flirting man was gone. The blonde was sitting there. There were two drinks and entrees on the table. They looked untouched.

"Is your boyfriend here?"

Elena flinched and focused on the man again. He had two drinks. One was a vodka lime. "Does it matter?"

"One drink won't hurt anyone." He smiled. "I promise."

"You want me to cheat on my boyfriend?"

"I want you to have fun. He doesn't seem to be here."

"He's not inside."

"He's in line?"

Elena shook her head. "He works outside. You know, the big hulking brute who never smiles?"

The man gulped. "Your boyfriend is the bouncer?"

"Yeah. Want to ask him what he thinks about you buying me a drink?"

"I'm sorry." He took both his drinks and hurried away.

"Wow, what a dirtbag."

Elena turned to face the source of the familiar voice. Melinda Gross stood there. Elena glanced at the table. The blonde was gone. Melinda's hair was the same as the blonde. Silky. Wavy. Not hanging limp like in Morganville.

"Don't look so surprised, honey!" Melinda smiled and touched her arm.

There was a faint prick. Elena flinched. Jerked her arm away. "What the hell was that?"

"What was what, honey?" Melinda held up her hands. They were empty. She was wearing a ring on her right hand. A bracelet on her left.

Elena felt woozy. "It's you." She grabbed the bar for support. "You attacked Pete on the beach."

"Honey, I've been following you for a while. You've been asking a lot of questions people don't want answered." Her accent vanished at the last sentence. It was flatter. Almost neutral. "Most of the media is going along with the plan. Sweeping things under the rug. But you're one of the outliers. I guess the apple doesn't fall far from the tree, does it?"

"What's that supposed to mean?" Elena felt relaxed. Dizzy. Standing wasn't a problem, but her knees felt weak.

"I got us a room, sweetie. We'll make this quick and painless, okay? It'll be just like going to sleep." Melinda put Elena's arm over her shoulder. She started walking her toward the bathrooms.

A waitress stopped them. "Is she okay?"

"Just a little woozy." Melinda had her accent back. "I'm taking her to the bathroom and then taking her home, okay?"

"Okay. Just let us know if you need help."

"Help." Elena could barely talk. The music and ambient chatter drowned out her voice. She tried to reach for the waitress but couldn't summon the strength.

"You're so pretty." Melinda kissed her cheek. "Such a shame. But if it's any consolation, I do admire your spunk. But it's just dumb to go against powerful people and think there won't be consequences."

"Breakstone...paying you...kill me?"

Melinda put her ear closer. "More like Chad Dorsey's ghost." She guided her down the hallway. Past the bathrooms. "Amos Carver pissed off a lot of powerful people. He really stirred up the hornet's nest. And you're just collateral damage."

Elena summoned all her strength to talk. "I made copies. People will know."

"Copies of what? The only thing on your laptop says who is Amos Carver? And your notes aren't even coherent. Of course, people won't find anything on your laptop. Certainly no copies." They were far down the service corridor. Away from the crowd. Near the back door. "Fifteen minutes from now, you won't have a worry in the world, okay? Just enjoy the buzz while it lasts."

There was a thud. A gasp. A shout. Elena wobbled unsupported. She tumbled forward. Hit the wall. Bounced sideways and rolled on the floor. She was on her back. The man from earlier was fighting Melinda.

Melinda was trying to grab his neck. Her ring looked different. The bottom had a sharp point. The man twisted her arm. Jammed the pointy end into Melinda's neck. She cried out. He yanked the ring off. Threw it on the floor.

The man wrestled with her until she slumped. The drug Melinda had used on Elena was on that ring. Now she was suffering the effects.

"Help," Elena gasped.

The man looked down at her. "Fucking loose ends everywhere. I'll come back to you."

Melinda hissed something unintelligible.

"Sorry. All's fair in war." He eased her into a sitting position. Then he lifted Elena. Slung her over a shoulder like a bag of rice. He carried her down the hall, into a door.

Elena smelled chemicals. Saw a mop. A shelf with cleaners on it. He sat her up next to the shelf. She put all her effort into a sentence. "Who are you?"

"No one. I'll be back." He left and closed the door.

Elena tried to move. Her arms felt heavy. Her head felt like a concrete block. But if she didn't get out of this closet, that man would return. He would take her somewhere and kill her. There was no question about that.

The chemical odor was strong. It was the only thing keeping her awake. It might not be enough for much longer. She put all her effort into moving her right arm. She lifted it parallel to the floor. Lifted it higher toward the doorknob.

Her hand touched it. She twisted. Her grip was too weak. Her hand fell. She slumped. Everything went dark. She faded in and out of consciousness. The door thudded. Something crashed outside.

She heard the man from earlier shout something. Heard a woman talk back. She couldn't understand what they were saying. Another thud. Another crash. Footsteps running. Consciousness faded again.

ELENA JERKED AWAKE.

Her limbs felt lighter. Her head wasn't full of fog. She gripped the shelf. Pulled herself to her feet. She had a mild headache. Her knees still felt like jelly. But she could walk. She opened the closet door and looked into the hallway.

Stacks of boxes had been knocked over. There was a streak of crimson on the wall. She stumbled out. Leaned against the wall. Slid her shoulder down it as she walked. It was the only thing keeping her upright.

A glint of metal caught her eye. Melinda's ring was on the floor. She leaned down. Fell to her knees. It was still where the man had thrown it. It looked like a normal ring again. She picked it up and studied it. There was a small hinge. The bottom unfolded into a short, sharp needle.

The needle glistened. It was drugged. Elena blinked to clear her eyes. She looked closer at the ring, but she was too foggy. She folded the needle. Put the ring on her finger since her skirt had no pockets.

She regained her feet. Started walking down the corridor. Past the bathrooms. Out to the main floor. The club was almost empty. She wanted to check the time, but she didn't know where her phone was. It had been on the bar. Then Melinda had taken her.

A bartender was cleaning up. She looked surprised to see Elena. "Didn't your friend help you leave earlier?" She reached below the counter. "You left your phone."

"Oh, thanks." She leaned on the bar for support and took it. "Where is everyone?"

"Someone took a swan dive off the roof or something. Landed in a dumpster." The bartender shuddered. "Everyone ran outside to see. I don't want to haunt my dreams with a sight like that."

"Someone fell off the roof?"

She nodded. "All I know is she has blond hair."

Adrenaline shocked Elena's body. Gave her a rush. She took her phone and hurried the best she could toward the door. The waitress who'd stopped her and Melinda earlier was coming in. Her face was pale. She saw Elena and gasped.

"Your friend fell off the roof!"

"My friend?"

"That blonde woman! The one who took you to the bathroom!"

Elena shook her head. "I don't know her. She fell off the roof?"

The waitress wiped tears off her cheeks. "It's so awful."

She's dead? Elena could hardly believe it. Had that man killed her?

Elena stumbled outside. Pushed through a crowd of onlookers. Cops were shouting at everyone. Telling them to get back. She managed to squeeze to the front. Saw the dumpster. Saw a bloodied hand dangling over the side.

CSI was all over the scene. Taking pictures. Recording statements. Elena wasn't concerned with that. She still had one goal.

Find Carver.

But he was nowhere to be found. She was exhausted. Nauseated. The drug was still affecting her. She was so tired. So groggy. Somehow, she found her car. Drove it back to the motel.

She forced herself to throw up into the toilet. Drank water until she felt ready to burst. Then she fell into a deep, dreamless sleep.

SUNDAY MORNING

MORNING CAME HARD AND FAST.

Elena could hardly believe she was alive. Her mind was clear, and her bladder was ready to explode. She relieved herself. Went back to the bed and lay down. Her mind raced with the events of the night before.

Melinda Gross, whatever her name was, had been following her. She'd been using Elena to track down Carver. But not just Carver. There was a list. Elena's name was on it. Whoever was behind this wanted all investigations into Breakstone stopped.

It meant the people she'd emailed might be in danger. That would be a lot of people. Too many to kill. But they might target the ones who'd contacted her back. The ones who might know something.

That put Weaver on the list. She had to find him. Find out what he knew. Publishing everything she knew was her top priority. She needed to make sure it got out in case someone else like Melinda came after her.

She checked the tracking app. Saw Weaver was still at home. She cleaned up. Ate a very late breakfast. Since Carver wouldn't be back at the club until late tonight, she would spend the day following Weaver.

She would leech his laptop and take his information without him even knowing what happened. Then she'd return to the club tonight and talk to Carver.

Hopefully he wouldn't try to kill her too.

Elena went to Weaver's house. He left around noon to go to a café. She followed him there. He ate lunch. Worked for a few minutes. Packed up his laptop and went to the bathroom. Then he left and drove to Club Periclean.

The crime scene wasn't even taped off anymore. The dumpster was gone. The blood had been cleaned up. Weaver knocked on the door, but no one answered. He kept knocking. Still nothing.

Finally, he gave up and went home. Elena left and got dinner. She still felt a little nauseated from the drug Melinda had used on her. It must have been a powerful tranquilizer or paralytic.

At ten, she put on another skirt and went back to the club. Jeff was there, but not her prime Carver suspect. She reached the front of the line.

"Hey, you!" Elena smiled at him. "They have you all alone out here tonight?"

Jeff wasn't in a joking mood tonight. He looked harried. "Yeah, my helper didn't call out or anything. He's just a no-show."

"I'm surprised you're even open tonight, especially after what happened."

"Well, Sundays aren't the best, but money is money."

"Thanks." She went inside. Looked around. The place was dead. She hung around until midnight, but Carver never showed. She went back to the motel, tired and disheartened. It looked like she was never going to find the guy.

She checked the tracker again. Weaver was still home.

Elena cleaned up and went to bed. She'd start over again tomorrow. Follow Weaver. Go to the club to look for Carver. Wash, rinse, repeat. She'd keep doing it until she could get to Weaver's laptop and find Amos Carver.

Because finding him might be the only thing that kept her alive.

CHAPTER 19

MONDAY EARLY MORNING

The detective was dead.

Carver still needed Theresa to say it. To confirm it.

"You killed a cop."

"Like I said, no one important."

"You killed them first then came for me. In order of difficulty? Or convenience?"

"The detective got himself put on a list."

"A list? Because of me?"

"Because of you. Because of a nosy reporter."

"Elena Diaz?"

She didn't answer and her expression didn't change. "You and the detective were collaborating. That made him a priority."

"You used your blade. A good coroner will see the similarities to the wounds on Desmond Price."

"Not from a single killing thrust to the heart." She smiled innocently. "I don't even think he knew he was dead."

"Who is Nicki Jones to you?"

"Changing subjects won't get me to answer that."

"It's interesting that you're avoiding the answer." Carver studied her reactions. She was good at hiding her emotions. "Well, you don't know who employed you and you won't answer questions about your woman friend. I don't think you're useful to me anymore."

Her eyes twitched. "Might as well turn me into the police."

"I don't think so. At least not alive."

"Threats won't squeeze more answers out of me."

"I know." Carver slid the blade out of the duffel bag again. He walked within range. She was sitting cross-legged in the corner. It was an awkward position to react from and she knew it. She began to shift her position.

Carver pointed the gun at her. "Don't move."

"I'll answer all your questions."

Carver put the tip of the blade over her heart. "No, you'll lie. If the detective was still alive, I'd want you alive. But there's no point in letting you live now."

"There's more going on here than you realize. It's not a simple hit."

"Then what is it?"

"Give me guarantees and I'll tell you everything I know."

Carver lowered the blade. "Fine."

Theresa sprang upward. The top of her head slammed into the bottom of Carver's chin. The impact knocked him back. His teeth rattled in his head. He impulsively drove a knee up. It caught Theresa in the stomach. Her breath exploded with a grunt. Her hands whipped around, somehow free.

Carver fired the gun. Theresa slumped. Fell facedown. She groaned and tried to push herself up. Carver gripped the back of her shirt and rolled her over. Blood was seeping from a wound in her stomach. It wasn't normally fatal, but tonight it would be. He wasn't in a saving kind of mood.

He worked his jaw back and forth. His teeth ached. She'd really nailed him good. He'd never seen anyone jump from a cross-legged position so fast before. She was far more agile than he'd reckoned. And it nearly cost him.

Carver checked her hands for weapons, but she didn't have anything. Her thumbs looked strange. Dislocated. That had allowed her to worm her hands free. Enabled her hands to fold so small that the wire lost its grip.

Carver knelt a safe distance away. "For what it's worth, you're impressive. A work of art."

Theresa bared her bloody teeth. "Get me to a hospital, you psycho."

He shook his head. "I'm sorry. You're too dangerous. If you want to tell me what you know, now would be the time."

"I don't think so." She spat weakly at him.

"Stomach wounds are the worst. It's going to take you a while to die, and it'll be painful."

"Torture won't get me to help you, asshole."

"I know." Carver picked up the knife. Pressed it to her chest.

"No, please. I'll help you. I'll—" Her eyes widened as the blade slid into her heart. It went in smooth and easy, right between the ribs. Her heart stopped almost immediately. She was dead in seconds.

Carver cut a strip of her shirt. Dabbed it in her blood. He cut off some hair. Rolled it up in the shirt so the outside was dry. He didn't want her blood seeping into his clothes. He wiped the knife hilt with her shirt. Put it in her hand.

She had ligature marks on her wrists, so he left the wire where it was. Removing it wouldn't cover up the fact that she'd been bound. He wiped off her boots. Stood, and surveyed the scene.

The cops could figure it out. They'd figure out she killed Leach too. Now he was back to square one.

He pulled the slip of paper he'd taken from her pants earlier. It was a square piece of thick paper. A valet ticket. It wasn't from the condominium next to the club. It was for a hotel down the street. Theresa had relocated after the two deaths at the club.

It was strange that she'd have a valet ticket on her. Like most professionals, she wasn't carrying anything personally identifiable. No ID, no wallet. No keys, keycard, or anything else. She must have slipped the valet ticket into her back pocket and forgotten to remove it. Her front pockets were just slits. They gave her easy access to the knives sheathed to her thighs. This woman was proficient. Highly skilled. A master.

Even masters made mistakes. There had been a slew of them leading to this point. Jones falling to her death. Theresa gutting Desmond Price. Whatever her plan had been, it had been thrown off kilter by those incidents. It had created a chain reaction. Given Carver a chance to be prepared.

If she'd known exactly what he looked like, known who he was, she would have killed him. Carver had no doubt about it. Her reflexes were faster than his. Her razor-sharp blade could have gutted him before he even knew what had happened.

Carver took off his shirt. He wiped down the inside door handle. Lifted the storage unit door. It rattled up the tracks. He wiped off the outside handle. Retrieved his duffel bag and gave the unit a once-over. The floor was swept clean. No dust to leave tracks. Theresa lay in a slowly expanding pool of blood.

He left the door open. Left Theresa like she'd probably left so many of her targets. Dead and bleeding. He didn't like leaving the bullet inside her, but there wasn't much he could do about that.

Next stop was his hostel. It should be safe enough to stay there now. He needed a shower and some shuteye. It took half as long to return as it had taken him to get to the storage unit. He kept to the darkness. Kept off the streets as much as possible. He didn't want a security camera recording him. Cops relied on that kind of footage to build cases.

He entered the hostel through the back door. Showered. Slid beneath the sheets naked as a jaybird. He was running low on clean clothes. Tomorrow would be a shopping day.

CARVER WOKE UP after six solid hours of sleep.

It was ten in the morning. Still Monday. Late for him, but necessary. He had a lot on the agenda. The duffel bag went into a locker. He wore his last set of clean clothes—cargo shorts and a t-shirt. His casual shoes were getting pretty worn. Time to replace those too.

His first stop was breakfast at the nearby diner. A television hung in the corner. A morning talk show was on. Carver ordered eggs, bacon, and a big stack of pancakes. He drank coffee while he waited.

Leach was at the top of his mind. He wondered how long Theresa had stalked him before killing him. She must have seen them in the bar. She might have even been inside at a nearby table. Leach had been in the lookout position, back to the wall. He'd probably seen her.

Carver would have picked her out of the crowd. But he'd had his back to a killer the entire time. Goosebumps ran up his back, his neck. He should have forced Leach to move. Given Carver the lookout spot. The man was—had been a detective. He hadn't been cut out for this.

Breakfast arrived. The local news came on. Top story was about a dead cop. A picture of Leach appeared in the corner. Found dead in the back alley behind the bar. There were no witnesses. No one in the restaurant remembered him except the server. He'd been stabbed once in the chest. No murder weapon found. No suspects.

It made Carver curious. He considered going to the bar. Asking the servers if they'd seen a woman by Theresa's description. He even had a picture. If she'd been in there the entire time, a server would know. That might help the cops, but it didn't help Carver.

They'd have to make the connections on their own. He needed access to facial recognition software. DNA testing. A host of things that were hiding inside police headquarters. Without Leach, he had no access. No way to analyze the evidence he'd gathered.

The next story was about a body found in a storage unit. Police were on the scene. The body hadn't been identified. The person who'd found her spoke to the reporter.

"She had this really weird short sword in her hand." He shivered. "It looked like she committed ritual suicide. Seppuku, I think."

The reporter spoke next to a Detective Rodriguez who refuted everything the first guy said. "The victim was shot in the stomach and stabbed in the heart. She didn't do this to herself. She was murdered."

"Any connection to the stabbing of Detective Leach?" the reporter asked.

"Why would this be connected in any way to that?"

The reporter looked confused. "Because he was stabbed in the heart, same as her."

Rodriguez shook his head. "Let us do our job and don't make assumptions."

The reporter looked miffed when she turned to the camera. "If you have any information regarding these crimes, please call our crime-stopper hotline." She gave a number. "This is Wendy Hernandez reporting live."

Carver paid for his food and left. He went to a strip mall about half a mile down the road. He bought two more burner phones from a repair shop. But that wasn't the only reason he'd come here. This was one of very few places with a working pay phone. He picked up the receiver with a napkin and punched the numbers with another napkin.

A bored-sounding man answered. "This is Action News's crime-stopper hotline. Do you have something to report?"

"I have a message for Wendy Hernandez."

The man sighed. "You and every hot-blooded male who calls this number."

"I know who killed Detective Leach."

The man suddenly seemed interested. "Tell me more. There's a reward for useful information."

"Wendy Hernandez only."

The man sighed. "Hang on." There was on hold music and a moment later, a woman answered.

"Wendy Hernandez."

The voice sounded the same, so Carver was reasonably certain it was her. "Detective Leach was killed by the woman found dead at the storage facility."

"You know this how?"

"I'm a CI working with the detective on a highly sensitive case. I'm not telling you my identity because I don't want to die. But word needs to get out that this woman was a contract killer. Leach was close to uncovering a group of people who are killing people to silence them."

"Can we meet? I promise I never reveal my sources." Wendy sounded excited.

"Nope." Carver hung up. That was enough to get the wheels rolling. Maybe get enough interest in the local media to slow down whoever was hiring the killers.

It reminded him of England a few years ago. Scion's psyops team fed a local reporter information about a conspiracy. It was supposed to disrupt the election there so the governing party lost power.

But the reporter reached out to other reporters. This reached the ears of those in power. They made a dead list. Hired terminal agents to complete the dead list. Instead of election disruption, four people wound up dead in accidents and overdoses.

It had been a major setback for Scion. Rhodes had gotten an earful for not protecting the reporter and other assets. For Carver, it had been a teaching moment. It showed how one incident could blossom into wide reaching death.

That was what was happening here. Carver had started something in Morganville. Elena Diaz investigated it. She'd contacted a lot of people. A dead list had been made and all the loose ends were being tied up.

The payphone started ringing. Carver let it ring and walked away. Hopefully he hadn't just added more names to the list. He couldn't worry about that right now. He had errands to run.

The first thing to do was in South Beach. He took the bus to Collins Avenue. Got off in front of the Betsy Ross. It was a chic 1940s style hotel. Expensive. The prices online were close to a thousand per night. This was the source of the valet ticket.

Why had Theresa gone from a condo rental to a hotel? The rent at the condos were around two or three hundred a night. It was close to her target. Maybe she'd planned on staying for one night. She planned to identify Carver and kill him in one night. Then she'd enjoy a vacation in South Beach.

Carver was leaning toward the theory that Nicky Jones and Theresa Smith were either related or in a romantic relationship. Every time he'd asked about Jones, Theresa had twitched or stiffened.

Killing Desmond Price was revenge. That was why she'd brutally gutted him. Hadn't given him a quick death like she had with Leach. Everything pointed to that theory. But it wouldn't be the first time Carver had been wrong.

He'd been wrong earlier when chasing Theresa. He'd thought she'd circled back and was flanking him. The moment he'd turned his back, she'd come from the other direction. He'd thought Theresa was harmless sitting cross-legged on the floor. That had nearly cost him too.

It was almost shocking that he'd come out ahead. That she was dead, and he was still alive. He'd miscalculated her several times. Those kinds of mistakes against master assassins usually ended with another notch in their belt.

It seemed likely that Carver was making another mistake. At least now the assassin was dead. He could probably afford a few more mistakes. Or it was possible Theresa had been telling the truth. Maybe there was a lot more going on than met the eye. She might just be the tip of the iceberg.

The next mystery he needed to solve was where Theresa had put her hotel key. It was possible someone else was staying in the room with her. They would be available to open the door when she returned.

But it seemed unlikely. Master assassins didn't make a habit of taking people with them on assignments. Theresa was far too professional for that. She would have understood that romantic partners were the worst people to trust.

If there was a falling out, they might report her to the police. They might try extortion. They'd also likely end up dead before they had a chance to even make a threat. It seemed most likely that Theresa was like most in her field—a lone wolf.

If true, that snuffed the theory about Nicki Jones. Carver didn't really know which way to go on that theory. His new theory gave him the obvious answer for the location of the hotel key. It was a simple, elegant solution. It was a solution someone like Theresa would utilize.

It was time to find out if Carver was right. If he wasn't, it meant he might have someone else to deal with. Someone else who hopefully wouldn't be a master assassin.

—·—

CHAPTER 20

MONDAY MORNING

Carver walked toward the Betsy Hotel.

There were several valets in the semicircular driveway. They were grabbing tickets from guests. Running into the parking deck. Returning moments later with the vehicle. Taking another ticket. Running for another car. The activity was constant and fluid.

Some cars were expensive. Others looked like they'd come from a used car lot. The guests wore a wide variety of clothing. Some dressed expensively. Others looked like beach bums.

It was a good mix. It helped Carver fit right in since his clothing appeared to be from the cheaper end of the spectrum. He walked to the valet station and handed the kid the ticket.

The kid glanced at it. Ran into the parking deck. He returned moments later with a two-seater convertible. An Audi R8. The soft top was up.

Carver handed him a twenty. The kid tucked it in a pocket and ran to the next guest. Carver climbed in the car. Slid the seat all the way back. Pulled out of the driveway and went down the road for a spell. He pulled into a parking lot.

He turned up the air conditioning then opened the armrest compartment. A hotel key was inside. It wasn't inside the sleeve with the room number. That was an inconvenience, but not unexpected.

Theresa was the type to memorize the room number and take no chances. Carver confirmed that by searching the glove compartment and the rest of the car. There was a calling card for an exotic car rental agency. Nothing else.

He leaned back in the seat and took out his burner phone.

The hotel website showed him the different kinds of rooms. Some were poolside. Some had a balcony. Some had an ocean view. One room had everything. The penthouse. It was a cool fifteen hundred a night. The question was, what kind of a person was Theresa?

Carver pulled up the exotic car rental website. He looked up the car he was in. The rent was over a thousand a day. There was a daily hundred-mile limit. Past that it was five bucks a mile. That answered his question.

He drove back to the hotel.

This time he didn't use a valet. He used street parking just down the block. Got out and hoofed it to the building. He walked past the valets and inside. The hotel was small. Only three stories tall. Even if he'd had to try the key card from top to bottom it wouldn't have taken him long.

Theresa's extravagance already told him which rooms to try. He went to the elevator. Ran the keycard over the reader. Hit the button for the penthouse. The elevator went up. It reached the top and stopped. The door opened to a hallway.

There were two doors in the hallway. One for each penthouse. He went to the doors. Fifty-fifty chance he'd get it right on the first try. He tested the door on the right. The keycard reader blinked red. He tried the door on the left. The reader blinked green.

"Figures," he muttered to himself. He'd used up all his luck with Theresa.

Carver opened the door and went inside. It was every bit as luxurious as it looked in the pictures. Hardwood floors. White marble countertops. Stainless steel cabinets with glass doors. A fully stocked liquor cabinet. A large bathroom with a huge shower.

The sliding glass door went to the wraparound terrace. It looked out over the beach on one side. Looked down on the pool from the other side. There was a hot tub. A cabana. Everything for a person with the money to afford it.

That was enough sightseeing for now.

Carver went into the bedroom. There was an empty suitcase in the walk-in closet. Dresses hung from the rack. Other clothing was neatly folded on shelves. Expensive high heels were on shoe racks.

A blanket hung over something in the other corner of the closet. Carver removed it. Underneath was a black suitcase with a white diagonal stripe on either side. It looked ordinary. No one would glance twice at it. It was also unique. Carver had seen a lot of suitcases at a lot of airports.

He couldn't remember seeing a single one with a stripe like that. It was nothing fancy, but it stood out. It was locked with a six-digit combination. The outer material was hardened polymer. A thick metal zipper secured all sides. The zipper handles were locked in place.

There was a recessed button next to the lock. It was used to reset the combination. Carver doubted it worked. This was almost certainly a custom case. The simple zipper lock was probably a decoy. If Theresa spent top dollar for a rental car and hotel room, she surely had the dollars to afford a top-notch assassin suitcase.

He found a pen in the kitchen. Used the tip to depress the combo reset button. Nothing happened. He went to the internet for help. Watched some videos on the burner phone. None of the methods released the zipper locks.

He set it aside for later.

Carver searched every nook and cranny in the hotel room. Theresa had a large array of skincare items in the bathroom. None of it was in airplane carry-on sizes. She probably packed everything in the large suitcase and checked it. But how could she carry on a suitcase full of weapons?

It was legal to take knives on commercial flights, but the bag had to be checked. Plus, it would almost certainly raise the eyebrows of anyone in security.

Except Theresa wasn't the kind to take those chances. She probably didn't fly commercial. If she had the money for this hotel and the car, then she could probably afford to fly chartered. She was probably one of those high-class assassins who only took high-paying jobs like Carver and long dead lists.

Or she didn't even take the case with her anywhere. Some assassins shipped their weapons to the destination ahead of them. Cargo planes didn't have the same kind of security precautions that passenger planes did. It was easy to ship to a secure location and pick it up onsite.

Carver used the map app on the burner phone to see what stores were nearby. He located a hardware store that would have what he needed. It was on the mainland, but now he had transportation.

He picked up the room phone and called the front desk.

"Hello, Ms. Smith. What can I do to make your day wonderful?"

"This is Mr. Smith."

"Hello, sir. Can we do anything for you or your wife this morning?"

"I was thinking of extending our stay."

"One moment, please." She typed on a loud keyboard. "We have you down for seven more nights. We do have availability for up to seven more, but the room is booked for several weeks out after that."

"We'll take the seven more, please."

"Absolutely, sir." She typed away. "Is there anything else I can help you with?"

"Yes, my wife asked me to keep an eye out for some friends who might visit us. Has anyone come looking for us at the front desk?"

"Aside from Ms. Jones, no one else has inquired. I'll be sure to leave a note for the front desk staff. Do you have any names you'd like me to list as authorized visitors?"

Carver managed a wry laugh. "They're my wife's friends and I can hardly remember their names half the time."

The woman laughed back. "I can understand, sir. Shall we use the number on file to send you notifications?"

"You can just send them to my cell number. My wife has business meetings all day." Carver gave her a burner number. "I'm a kept man."

She laughed again. "That's good to hear, sir. Anything else?"

"That will do it for now. Thank you." Carver hung up.

He had things to do. Important, life-saving things. But it felt nice to be in such luxury accommodations. Carver grabbed a dark beer from the bar fridge. He went to the deck and pulled up a chair. The waves crashed into the shore about a hundred yards away. People strolled along the beach. Some were beachgoers. Others looked like beach bums.

It was a nice morning. It might be fall in the northern states, but here in Miami it was always summer. Even now it was creeping up into the mid-seventies. It was hard to beat southern Florida beaches, at least in the United States. Compared to the surreal landscapes in Thailand, they were nothing special.

He finished his beer and left the hotel. Slid into Theresa's rental and drove it toward the causeway. A black Charger about three cars back caught his attention. It was black with the basic black eighteen-inch wheels that pegged it as an unmarked police car.

Carver took a couple of extra turns to confirm the car was following him. Then he headed for the causeway. Crossed it and reached the mainland. The nearest hardware store was in Little Haiti. It was a small place with a tiny row of parking in front. He parked the Audi, careful not to crunch the low front bumper into the curb.

Three old men sat outside the shop, smoking cigarillos and talking in Creole. Or maybe it was French. Carver couldn't really tell. They looked him up and down when he unfolded himself out of the sports car. Carver pretended to check in the car for something and saw the black Charger parallel park a block down the street.

It seemed unlikely anyone would have known he was staying at Theresa's hotel. Maybe Leach had told Hughes about Carver. Maybe he'd left information in case something happened to him. It seemed doubtful. He and Carver had only just started conspiring when Theresa killed him.

Carver had banked on enjoying Theresa's hotel room for a few days. He hoped the tail wasn't someone who'd ruin that for him. Now wasn't the time to deal with it. He had an assassin's suitcase to open.

He went inside the hardware store. It was a small shop, but it had the tools he needed. He purchased rope, duct tape, and zip ties too. He might have to tie up whoever was driving the unmarked police car. If people kept coming out of the woodwork, he might need enough rope for several more people.

The shopkeeper didn't even look twice when he rang up the items. Given the local drug trade, they were likely very popular items. Carver paid with his stolen drug money and gathered the bags. The Charger was still sitting a block away when Carver came outside.

He dumped his bags into the tiny front trunk. Folded himself back into the front seat. The Audi certainly wasn't a comfortable car for someone his height, but it was better than walking. It might also come in handy if he needed to get away from the Charger.

Carver backed out of the parking spot and onto the street. He headed south back to the causeway. The Charger hung behind him but there wasn't enough traffic to cover for it. It seemed best to deal with whoever it was now rather than later.

He took the first exit off the causeway. Drove around a large medical center. Carver chose a large, mostly empty parking lot as a good place to take care of business. He parked in the middle, far from the other cars. Slid the compact Glock into his back pocket. Got out and leaned on the car.

The Charger entered the parking lot a moment later. It screeched to a halt when the driver saw Carver waiting on him. Carver waved it over. The car remained in place for a moment. The driver was thinking it over. Thinking it over hard.

The interaction wasn't what Carver had expected. He'd expected a detective to get out. Walk over to him full of bluster. Ask him some questions. Threaten him with jail. The usual. But this was something else. Something entirely different.

The car pulled forward. Parked fifty feet away. A guy with dark hair and light skin got out. He was five feet eleven inches. Lean and toned. He wore black jeans, shiny leather shoes, and a gray t-shirt. He was dressed to the nines for an undercover cop. That was because he wasn't local PD. He was probably a fed.

He looked vaguely familiar. Something about the nose. The eyes. Carver couldn't place it. He hadn't seen this face before, but he'd seen one similar. He thought about everyone he'd seen recently. None of them came close to matching.

The guy leaned against his own car. Looked Carver up and down. "Who in the hell are you?"

Carver remained in place. "You were expecting someone else?"

"I was." The man had a western accent. California, probably. "I was expecting a woman. They said it would be easier for her to remain undetected. And yet here I am looking at a man who would stand out in any crowd."

Carver shrugged. "I just go where the money is."

"Don't we all?" The man shook his head. "I don't know how we're going to make this work."

"Take it up with the front office if you have a problem."

"Very funny." He didn't laugh. "Why didn't you show up for the meet this morning? And what in the hell were you doing at a hardware store?"

"I didn't like the meeting place."

The man worked his jaw back and forth. Like he was thinking hard. "You're the one who arranged the meet in front of the Betsy Ross."

"No, my handler did. Something didn't feel right."

The man's jaw tightened. "I hate freelancers. You're all paranoid and think you don't answer to anyone."

"It's not paranoia if the danger is real." Carver couldn't figure the man's affiliation. He was law enforcement. Almost certainly a federal agent. But which agency? Had they hired Theresa to kill him and the others? If that was true, this guy would certainly be suspicious that Carver looked very similar to the target in the sketch drawing.

He stepped out on a limb to see if he could get a clue. "There's a reason you didn't send an agency asset."

"Yeah, no shit. This is highly illegal on all fronts." The man blew out a breath. "Either way, I'm stuck being your liaison. We will keep our distance unless absolutely necessary. You are only to call on me in case of emergency." He walked toward Carver. His hand vanished behind his back.

Carver pretended to stretch his back. Put his hand on the compact Glock.

The man's hand reappeared with a small black object in it. Carver released the gun. Stretched his arms to his sides to complete the fake stretching routine. He considered asking the man for his name, but it was too risky. He was skating a fine line. Any questions could make the man suspicious. The last thing Carver wanted to do was take a federal agent hostage.

The man held out the object. It was a USB-C drive. The whole thing wasn't much larger than the metal connector. Carver took it and pocketed it. It seemed like he was now working with the feds.

What in the hell was going on?

CHAPTER 21

The mystery man backed up a step.

Carver wanted to ask what was on the drive, but he decided that would be too suspicious.

Mystery man answered the unspoken question. "The dead list has become larger. These are additions to the previous list."

"That means the price keeps going up."

"Yes, your agency already told me that." He sighed. "The longer it takes for you to terminate the source, the more it metastasizes like cancer. So, make it fast."

"Hard to keep up with email and phone calls."

The man ignored that. "The drive is encrypted. The data will self-destruct in forty-eight hours. Trying to copy it will also trigger data destruction."

"What if I took pictures of the information on the computer screen?"

The man stared at him for a long moment. "Well, I guess that's a loophole, okay?"

"I'm not saying I will." Carver shrugged. "Just seems obvious."

"Let's hope your instinct for self-preservation is strong enough to resist that urge."

"I have a very strong sense of self-preservation."

"Good." The man backed up. "The number you can reach me at is on there. You will only refer to me as Dan."

"Lieutenant Dan?"

Dan didn't look amused. "You weren't hired for your sense of humor, so let's cut that out."

"Okay, Lieutenant Dan."

Dan mumbled something under his breath. "There's a secure website linked in the information. You'll need to go there and enter the bank account you want the funds wired to once the job is completed."

"I just opened a super-saver checking account with my local bank."

Dan's face reddened. He backed away until he reached his car. Climbed in and wheeled around with a screech of tires.

Messing with a fed marginally brightened Carver's day. If he had a dime for every time a CIA agent had interfered in an operation, he'd have a lot of dimes. This guy wasn't CIA. At least, he shouldn't be. They weren't supposed to deal in domestic issues. They also weren't supposed to sanction the things Carver and his team had done. But they had.

Theresa hadn't been lying. There was a lot more going on than what met the eye. The question was, what did Carver have to do with it? He thought back to Leach's diagram on the napkin. He tried to imagine where Dan's image would go. Maybe he was DEA like Desmond Price. Maybe a line would connect the two of them.

If that was the case, why had Theresa killed Price? Maybe Price found out that a rogue DEA agent had hired an assassin. It still didn't jibe with the little Carver knew. All the bits and pieces seemed random.

Only a few things were concrete. Theresa tried to kill Carver. She'd killed Price. She'd killed Leach. Carver had killed her. Price might have killed Nicki Jones. That seemed the most likely scenario. Unfortunately, Theresa hadn't filled in the missing pieces for him.

Rather than think about it too hard right then, Carver decided to head back to the hotel. It didn't feel quite as safe as it had earlier. Dan knew where he was staying. Maybe Theresa had told him where she'd be staying. It seemed like a dumb move for an assassin. Anonymity was your friend in the killing business.

He kept an eye on the rearview mirror the rest of the drive. Dan's car didn't appear. No one else appeared to be tailing him. Carver dropped the car with the valet and grabbed the bags from the front trunk.

He took the elevator back to the penthouse. Grabbed Theresa's secure suitcase and set it on the table. He pulled the bolt cutters from a bag. Slid the pincers over one of the zipper handles. Pushed the handles together.

The handles were thick. That was why he'd purchased the biggest bolt cutters he could find. The pincers closed slowly. The metal resisted. Carver pressed harder and they slowly sliced through the metal. He repeated the process with the other handle.

Even with them free, the handles wouldn't move. It seemed that there was another locking mechanism. Probably inside the case. He brought out the hammer and crowbar. He put the case on the side with the front zipper facing up. The pointy side of the crowbar pressed down on the zipper seam. The hammer delivered the driving force.

After a few hard blows, the crowbar pierced the zipper. Carver used a flat crowbar to work down the seam. Once he got it started, the zipper separated easily enough. The zipper handles were latched into place on the other side. He pushed the bolt cutter through the seam. It sliced through the narrow interior latch in short order.

The suitcase opened. The inside wasn't molded like the one at the condo. This one had elastic straps holding down a variety of knives. These knives looked identical to the ones in Jones' case. There didn't seem to be any guns.

Carver tugged on a loop. A panel of knives popped out. A small piece of metal unfolded on the back like a kickstand. Carver set the panel upright on the table. There was a similar panel below the first. He pulled it out, set it on the table. Beneath that was a small laptop and two phones.

A panel on the other side had syringes. A variety of vials with labels. Some were hard drugs like heroin. Some were sleeping agents. Some would create paralysis or make a subject intoxicated.

They were tools for staging deaths. Overdose, drunk driving, whatever the killer wanted. The paralyzing agent wouldn't leave a trace for the coroner to find. The others would leave the traces the killer wanted the coroner to find. It was quite a toolkit of death.

A passport, driver license, stacks of US dollars, and several credit cards were beneath the drug panel. They all had Theresa Smith on them. Theresa hadn't just purchased fake IDs, she'd purchased an entire identity.

The real Theresa Smith was probably dead. Her social security number and everything about her had been converted to use for the assassin. It was an extremely expensive option, but worth it for professional killers.

There was no sign of her true identity. No paper plane tickets. Nothing indicating where she'd originated. He doubted the two phones or the laptop in the case would tell him anything.

Carver turned on the phones. They booted to a screen without lock protection. Neither had any data on them. They were restored to factory settings. The laptop also didn't have a password. He checked it out and found nothing on it.

It was a field laptop like the ones he'd used on missions. This one had a hardware button on the side. Hold it down for ten seconds and it'd erase the computer and restore it to factory settings. Theresa had been a pro through and through.

Carver inserted the USB drive into a slot. A program started. A dire warning popped up on the screen in big red letters. *Do not attempt to copy the data. Do not attempt to remove the stick. Attempting either will cause immediate data destruction. The data will automatically destruct within forty-eight hours.*

A countdown started in the corner of the screen. This was CIA tech. No doubt about that. It still didn't mean Dan was CIA. The NSA and other federal agencies shared technology. It could be any number of them.

Carver clicked on the lone folder icon in the program. It opened a new screen with two file icons. They were numbered one and two. He clicked the first one. A dossier opened.

There were several pictures of a bearded man. A name, an address, known locations. Known activities. Instructions.

Terminate with extreme prejudice. Staged suicide or accidental death only.

The next target was a woman. She looked young. Long, brown hair, brown eyes. Caucasian. Identical instructions as the first. Neither of them looked dangerous. At least not physically. It was their professions that made them dangerous to certain people.

They were both journalists.

Carver read the dossiers twice over. He didn't know these people. He'd never heard of them. As far as he knew, they were in no way related to him. The disconnect was jarring. He mulled it over for a while. Then he took pictures of the dossiers with his phone.

Each target was worth three hundred thousand dollars. It was quite a payout. Someone really wanted these reporters dead. They were obviously working on something that a government faction didn't want them working on.

Carver had learned long ago that the government wasn't some monolithic thing. Government agencies weren't monolithic either. There might be an overarching culture, but every institution was broken up into smaller factions.

The CIA was a perfect example. The agency was supposed to be unified in mission. It was supposed to serve the best interests of the US abroad. Keep the homeland safe. But everyone had different ideas about how to do that.

The director was the one responsible for keeping it together. For keeping the agency actions cohesive. That was nearly an impossible task considering the covert nature of the agency. One side wanted peaceful methods. The other wanted war. Some preferred inaction.

Dan was likely part of a government agency. His faction was resorting to extrajudicial processes to handle a domestic issue. The question that mattered was, what was so dangerous that it warranted a double murder?

The two dossiers were the only things on the USB drive.

Carver's next steps were obvious. He had to meet with one or both of these journalists and find out what they were working on. Then and only then could he ensure that it had nothing to do with him.

With that information, he could safely disregard this job and focus on finding who hired Theresa. That might be impossible, but getting to the root of it was vital to his future health.

Doug Weaver and Lisa Gallagher were the two reporters. Weaver was local. Gallagher was from Tampa Bay. He decided to start with Weaver at the Miami Sentinel. An internet search said it was an online newspaper. It was founded by a small team of reporters from a large news organization after mass layoffs.

Why did Dan care about a small fry like this guy?

Killing someone was a method of last resort. It was much easier and better to discredit or frame then. Social media made the job a cinch in most cases. Scion's psyops had changed the course of elections domestically and internationally with few failures.

They rarely targeted national elections. It was far easier to target local ones. Shift the power in state legislatures, city councils, county commissioners. Start a rumor. Fake a story. Create some deepfake videos. It was so easy these days.

Sometimes it was impossible to take down a target with psyops. They might have too many fanatical followers. Their competition might be too weak. Sometimes they were running unopposed.

In those cases, death worked best. It was easy enough to stage a death. Harder to make it look like an accident. But that had been their specialty. Infiltration and termination. Accidental deaths were the best. It prevented martyrdom.

It was even better if it looked like they were up to no good. It cast a stain on their legacy. Made their followers doubt themselves.

Theresa might prefer knives, but her drug toolkit offered elegant solutions to tough problems. It made Carver think back to the video of Nicki Jones in the elevator with Desmond Price.

She looked drunk. What if Price hadn't been the one to drug her? What if it had been Theresa? Unfortunately, Leach's death closed that side of the investigation to him. The meeting he was supposed to have with the DEA would go on without him.

Leach's partner, Hughes, might handle it. Then again Hughes was close to retirement. They might hand it off to someone else. Whatever happened, Carver didn't have an inside angle anymore.

He studied the drug vials in Theresa's suitcase. They were labeled, nothing more. No instructions. No dosages. She had apparently been proficient in their usage. Carver had used some before, but he'd followed instructions. It wasn't something he'd memorized.

The heroin was easy. Just use the entire vial. The alcohol injection was relatively simple as well, though too much could cause premature death and leave clues for a coroner. Everything else required specific doses and applicators.

Syringes were okay for some uses but they left marks. Dermal patches were best for applying the paralytics. A faint trace of adhesive was the only evidence left by them. Theresa's toolkit was a masterpiece of death.

Carver felt a hint of remorse for killing her. Someone like Theresa trained relentlessly to be the best. She'd been an expert fighter. She'd known multiple ways to kill. She'd been successful at her work. Then she'd come for Carver. He'd had no choice but to kill her. And it was a shame.

In another life they might have worked on the same team. They might have taken down a political regime or stopped one from ever coming to power. Now she was in a Miami morgue. All that knowledge and ability gone forever.

Carver didn't blame himself. That was just the nature of the game. If you were good, you won, you survived. But there was always someone better or luckier than you. Always. That was why Carver didn't want to get back into the game. Theresa had almost been better than him.

His match was out there somewhere. Eventually he'd meet that person. Eventually, they'd kill him. Unless he managed to get out and stay out. Unfortunately, life wasn't giving him much of a choice.

It seemed a shame to work on such a nice day. He'd much rather sit on the balcony and drink. He checked the time and decided he could take an hour out of his busy schedule.

Carver ordered room service. They delivered a filet mignon and baked potato in thirty minutes. He ate it on the balcony and enjoyed another beer. Then it was time to get back to business.

He looked up the address for Weaver. It was the same as his business address. Apparently, he ran the Sentinel out of his home. There were multiple ways to contact him. A phone number, online messengers, and text.

Carver thought using any of them was a bad idea. Weaver was obviously being monitored. His house was probably bugged. Maybe even his cell phone. He needed to find another way to contact the guy. Get him out of the house.

The house was on the mainland. Across from the northern part of the island. Carver looked over the images on the map app. He studied the nearby roads. The stores. The houses. It was an older neighborhood. Traditional design. No backstreets. No alleys.

If the home was under surveillance, it would be a challenge to reach it undetected. Carver would need to study the area first. Find out if there was a human watching or if it was just cameras.

If Dan's agency discovered their hired assassin was visiting the target, that would set off all kinds of alarms. It would burn Carver's cover.

And a federal agency would rain hell down on him.

CHAPTER 22

Carver drove to his storage unit.

He parked down the street since the Audi would draw too much attention. It was doubtful the police could trace the rental or the hotel to Theresa. Unless they had her prints or DNA in a system somewhere, she would remain a Jane Doe.

Even if she'd had her fake ID with her, it would have only led the cops to the hotel and car rental. That ID had been in the suitcase with her other fake documents, so there was little to no danger.

It was still best not taking a chance and driving Theresa's rental into the same storage facility where she'd been killed. Carver used the pedestrian entrance instead. He went to his unit, grabbed a few things, and returned to the car.

He didn't wander anywhere near the unit where he'd left Theresa's body. There was still police tape blocking off the area. The police, however, were long gone. It was probably time to find a new place to stash his things.

Carver returned to the Audi. It was too flashy for a surveillance car, even in Miami. Renting another car wasn't an option. Carver had the fake Clint Wilkins ID, but he didn't have credit cards like Theresa.

Buying fake documents was one thing. Buying an entire identity was magnitudes more expensive. The Audi would have to do.

He drove to a thrift store next. Bought several changes of clothes. A hat. Sunglasses. Boots. He dumped the haul into the front seat of the Audi. Drove it to a parking deck and parked in an empty corner.

Carver got out and changed. He was too big to even try changing in the Audi. He removed the black cargo pants and t-shirt. Changed into his new clothing. Peach-colored shorts and a white button-up shirt. White tennis shoes and crew socks. He looked like a local now. Like someone dressed for golf.

He ducked back into the Audi. Drove to Weaver's neighborhood. Found a spot to park under a tree. The house was a block down from him, but this was as close as he could get in the Audi.

If a human was watching the house, they'd notice it. They'd report it. Dan would see the Audi and recognize it. Mission failed. The trick was getting close enough to the house so he could find the watchers.

If they were there, they'd see him. But they might not report the sighting if he looked normal enough. There were other people out and about. Kids on bikes. A woman pushing a baby stroller. Another woman walking a dog.

Carver put on the wide-brimmed hat and sunglasses. He pocketed a monocular and locked up the Audi. Then he started walking. The land was flat. There were no high points. No vantages for easier surveillance.

The best he could find was the shade of an oak tree on the same side of the road as Weaver's house. He slipped behind the wide trunk and used the monocular to scan the area. There were several cars parked on the road. They were all empty.

The houses were old. Mostly single story. The ones across the road had palm trees and fences in the front yards. They wouldn't be good for surveillance. Carver scoped them out anyway.

The blinds were closed on one house. The next one had old metal screens. He zoomed in and confirmed there weren't any cameras or other devices in the windows. The third one had filthy windows. Impossible to see into or out of.

There were cameras present. The house directly across from Weaver's had a doorbell camera. There was also a trail cam mounted on the fence. They were probably owned by the homeowner but that didn't mean anything.

The CIA or NSA could easily use them to watch the house. But it seemed unlikely they would. It was much more likely that the inside of the house was bugged. They probably didn't care about seeing the inside of the house. Listening was almost as good.

They could also intercept communications from Weaver's computer. They might have even installed keylogging software on it. The possibilities were endless. If they wanted this guy dead, they almost certainly had him under heavy surveillance.

That, of course, depended on which faction wanted him dead. If it was a rogue faction, there might be minimal surveillance. They wouldn't want anything to link them to Weaver. No software, no hardware.

If the faction controlling the agency wanted Weaver dead, then the sky was the limit. But that seemed highly unlikely. The controlling faction wouldn't resort to an off-the-books freelancer.

Carver swept the street. He took his time. Made sure he hadn't missed anything. There were no high points nearby. No spots for Dan's people to set up a long-distance camera. Once he felt secure with that, he walked to the other side of the road.

He repeated the process. It was hot. Humid. Autumn weather in Florida. This wasn't how he wanted to spend his free time. He didn't have a choice.

The other side of the road was clean. A few doorbell cameras, but nothing else that stuck out. He could probably knock on the front door if he wanted. But that wasn't going to happen. He just wanted to know what he was up against.

Carver looked at the picture of Weaver's dossier. He drove an old red Ford sedan. A blue Toyota was parked in the driveway. The Ford was gone. Weaver was out and about.

Weaver's known locations included two restaurants. He frequented a nearby cafe for lunch. It was too late for lunch. But he liked to stay there, drink coffee, write, and research. It was a good next place to look.

He ducked back into the Audi. Drove it to the café. Parked in a shopping center across the road. He scoped the area. The red Ford was parked out front. There was no sign of human surveillance.

Carver spotted Weaver in the window. The guy was sipping on coffee and staring at his computer screen. He had no clue someone wanted him dead. If Theresa was still around, Weaver would be dead in time for supper.

Maybe today would be his lucky day. Maybe it wouldn't. It really depended on how he reacted to what happened next. Initial contact would be difficult. It might trigger a flight response.

The tricky part was to not look like a threat. It was especially tricky for someone built like Carver. He was tall. Big. Slumping made some tall people look less intimidating. That didn't work for him.

He walked down the sidewalk. Cut across the busy road at a crosswalk. Took a meandering route toward the café. He went through the kitchen door at the back. A couple of people looked up, surprised.

Carver kept walking. He exited the kitchen. Entered a hall with the bathrooms. An older woman caught up to him.

"Sir, you can't enter through that door. That's for employees only."

Carver stopped. Turned. Looked down at her. "Sorry. I didn't feel like walking around."

She backed up a step. "Next time, please do. My insurance doesn't allow customers in the kitchen."

He nodded. "Okay."

The woman frowned slightly. Backed up and went into the kitchen. It would be a hassle going back out that way. It might cause someone to call the cops. Normally people wouldn't bother you if you acted like you knew what you were doing. Restaurant owners weren't normal people.

Carver saw Weaver. He was sitting in a booth. A laptop was open on the table in front of him. The remains of a sandwich were on a plate. A tall mug of coffee was in front of him. The man was staring at the computer screen.

There were plenty of covert ways to get someone's attention. Sometimes you could get a server to deliver a message. Sometimes you could drop the message on their table. Or sit down across from them.

There might be surveillance software on the laptop. The web cam might be recording everything and uploading it to the cloud. If Weaver opened a message, the camera would capture it. He'd look surprised. Glance around the room. Lock eyes with the sender.

It would alert anyone watching the video. They'd know that something unusual happened. That the target was tipped off about something. A Plan B would go into effect. Weaver would die another way.

Carver might be wrong. There might not be any spyware on the laptop. But he wasn't one to take chances like that. He'd have to figure out something else. Maybe wait for the big guy to go to the bathroom.

There was one other customer in the café. A young woman in yoga pants. She was sipping coffee and eating a muffin. She was also staring at a laptop screen.

He took a booth in the back corner. A partition hid him from the others in the café. But if he leaned just right, he could see them.

A server approached his booth. "Can I get you started on something, sir?"

"Coffee, black." Carver looked over the menu. "And a blueberry muffin."

"I'll have that right out, sir!" The server tapped the order on a tablet and left.

The coffee arrived a moment later, paired with the muffin. Carver sipped coffee. He pretended to read something on his phone. He watched and waited. Forty minutes passed. Weaver seemed to have an iron bladder. Or the coffee was dehydrating him.

Carver kept waiting.

Weaver finally closed his laptop. He slid out of his seat and went to the hallway with the bathrooms. Carver gave him thirty seconds. Got up and went to the bathroom. The reporter was in a stall.

Judging from the grunts, the coffee had gone through his system. The situation wasn't ideal, but it would do. Carver knocked on the stall door.

"Um, someone is in here."

"I know."

The grunting stopped. "Then why'd you knock? This is incredibly awkward."

"Because we need to talk."

"I swear to god if you're a stalker, I'm calling the cops. I have my phone with me."

"I'm not a stalker. I need to find out what stories you're working on. I need information."

"What?" Weaver laughed. "You followed me into a bathroom to ask me about a story?"

"I needed to make sure you weren't being watched or that your laptop is bugged."

"Oh, God, you're that lunatic who's been posting all over my social media, aren't you?"

"I never even heard of you before today."

Weaver laughed nervously. "Just my luck. Can't a guy use the bathroom in peace?"

"I need you to pay your bill and leave the café. Put your laptop in your car. Walk across the road and meet me in the thrift store over there. I'm in peach-colored shorts."

"Who are you? I didn't even see anyone else in the café except a girl."

"I'll tell you that at the thrift store."

"What's this about?" Weaver's voice was suddenly serious.

"You must be working on a story that has upset some powerful people. We need to talk about it so I can connect a few dots."

"I'm always working on stories that upset powerful people." Weaver sighed. "Look, unless you can give me a more compelling reason, I'm going to finish taking a shit and go back to work."

"Someone was hired to kill you. I killed them and took their place. You and another reporter, this one from Tampa, are on their radar. I need to find out why. I can explain more at the thrift store."

Weaver was quiet for a moment. "That's crazy. Someone was hired to kill me?"

"Yes."

"God, it must be that city council story I'm working on. I knew those assholes were corrupt."

"I don't think that's it. Meet me at the thrift store, okay? I'm leaving now. I'll see you over there."

Weaver blew out a breath. "This better not be a waste of my time."

"It won't be." Carver washed his hands and slipped quietly out of the bathroom. He wanted to leave via the back door but didn't want to cause a scene. He looked around the corner where the hallway went back to the dining area.

The girl in the yoga pants stood near Weaver's table. She picked up a small device near his laptop and hurried back to her seat. Then she plugged the device into her laptop. Carver recognized the device. He'd used similar ones before.

It used a close-range wireless signal to download the contents of a computer or mobile device. A leech. A tech had explained how it worked, but he didn't remember the details. It didn't really matter.

It meant that woman had just downloaded everything on his computer. It meant she had to be working for Dan. It seemed like a strange thing to do when the target was supposed to die soon. It indicated the laptop wasn't bugged.

They could have simply tasked the assassin with retrieving the laptop for them as well. Sending an agent to do something like this was unnecessary. It risked being caught in the act. Alerting the target.

It also made meeting with Weaver more difficult. The woman might follow him to the thrift store. If she did, that would be even dumber. She wasn't exactly dressed to blend in. Most men would notice her right away.

Maybe they just sent her in for a one-time data retrieval mission. Maybe she was a newbie. There were plenty of possibilities and Carver didn't have time to consider them. Weaver would come out of the bathroom in a minute and Carver needed to walk across the road to the thrift store.

He took the side door.

The girl didn't even see him. She looked flustered. Her face was slightly red. She stared at her laptop keyboard. Like she'd almost been caught doing something. Like she felt guilty about it. It wasn't normal spy behavior.

Strange.

Carver exited the café. He walked to the busy road. Looked both ways. Crossed it. He kept walking across the parking lot. The thrift store was much larger than the one he'd gone to earlier. This one was the size of a department store.

He went inside and grabbed a shopping cart. Then he went to a rack close to the door and pretended to look at women's raincoats. He looked out the window toward the café. A couple of minutes ticked past.

Weaver stepped outside. He opened his car. Dumped the laptop inside. Went to the sidewalk and looked both ways. Then he trundled across the street. He was slow. A couple of cars had to stop to let him finish crossing.

He made it to the parking lot. Stopped and put his hands on his hips. He stared at the thrift store as if reconsidering what he was about to do. Then he looked back at the highway he'd crossed. It must have looked more daunting from this side because he reluctantly started walking toward the thrift store again.

Weaver was almost to the door when the café door opened again. The yoga pants girl emerged. She looked inside Weaver's car. Then she looked across the road at Weaver. She stared at him for a moment. Then she started walking toward the road.

Carver picked up a purple raincoat and pretended to inspect it. He watched the girl dash across the road. She was in good shape, but she didn't look both ways before crossing. It was a good way to get herself killed.

Weaver pushed inside the thrift store. He was sweating. His face was red. He saw Carver and flinched. He opened his mouth to say something, but Carver made a zipping motion over his lips.

The girl was jogging across the parking lot. She'd be here soon.

Carver didn't want her disturbing them. He motioned Weaver to follow. They walked to the far back corner of the store. There was an employee's only sign in front of double doors. Carver poked his head through and looked around.

There were a lot of people sorting clothes. Everyone looked busy. They had earphones in. They were listening to music while performing a mundane task.

"What are you doing?" Weaver said.

"You're being followed." Carver nodded toward the sorting room. "We're going out back to talk."

"I'm not—"

"Fine. You can give up and die then."

"What in the hell is this about?"

Carver looked down an aisle. The shelving was high enough to block a view across the store. He didn't know where the girl was. He might have enough time to summarize the situation. "A top-level assassin was hired to kill you and make it look like an accident. The people who hired her—"

"A woman was hired to kill me?" Weaver laughed. "Fat chance." He patted a bulge under his belt. "I'm armed."

"Let's just say that you would be dead right now if I hadn't killed her."

"You're a kook, aren't you? Conspiracy theorist?" He rolled his eyes. "This is just a farce."

"Are you working on any stories relating to the federal government? Any corruption stories? Anything about big corporations?"

"Always and all the time." Weaver looked incredulous. "I'm a very busy man. Unless you have proof of something, I will be on my way."

Carver couldn't understand why anyone would pay a hundred grand to kill this guy. He was so full of himself no one would take him seriously. The news website had nothing on it that couldn't already be found on most major news sites.

There had to be a connection. "Tell me if anything I say means something to you." Carver looked down the aisle and didn't see the girl yet. She was probably walking around hunting for Weaver.

"Sure, whatever."

"Nicki Jones."

"Who?"

"Desmond Price."

Weaver frowned. "Never heard the name before."

"DEA, CIA, NSA."

"Duh, those are federal agencies."

"Lisa Gallagher."

"Yeah, she's a popular TV reporter in Tampa. Is she the other supposed target?"

Carver was running out of names. He tried one more. "Amos Carver."

Weaver flinched. "Yeah, I've heard that name." His eyes narrowed like he was thinking hard. "A girl from Atlanta called me. Said she was tracking down a guy by that name. She was chasing a story. I told her I'd look into it. I sent out queries to my local contacts. Gave them the description of the guy and the name. A couple said the name was familiar and one of my people said the description sounded a lot like this bouncer they'd seen."

"What was the girl's name?"

He pursed his lips. "Elena something. I called her back a couple of times to see if I could find out more about her story, but she said she hadn't found out anything."

Carver had a hunch. He knew why Weaver was being targeted. Probably why Lisa Gallagher was being targeted. It wasn't necessarily stories they were working on. It was because they were helping Elena Diaz track him down.

Morganville had been the origin. Elena Diaz was the catalyst for the dead list. She'd contacted dozens of people. Cast a wide net. Leach, Weaver, and Gallagher had been flagged for termination.

They were going to die because they'd replied to Elena Diaz.

CHAPTER 23

Weaver narrowed his eyes. He looked Carver up and down. Then he reached for his gun. Carver let him awkwardly tug it from the shoulder holster. Then he gripped Weaver's wrist. Squeezed. Weaver gasped. The gun dropped from limp fingers into Carver's other hand.

It was a compact .38. A midnight special judging from the poor quality. Carver popped open the revolver and emptied the bullets into his hand. He gave the gun back to Weaver.

"Don't do that again."

"You're Amos Carver, aren't you?"

"I am." Carver glanced down the aisle. He backed up and looked down the rows too. The girl was in here somewhere. He didn't want her to find them talking. "Now I know why someone wants you dead."

"Because of you?" Weaver looked stunned. "Why?"

"We need to talk out back. You're being followed."

"Fine." Weaver stuffed the pistol back into his shoulder holster.

Carver pushed into the stock room. He kept walking like he was supposed to be there. A couple of employees looked at him and Weaver, but no one said anything. They wouldn't make it as restaurant owners.

They went out the back door to a loading dock.

"Okay, we're here. In the heat and humidity." Weaver wiped sweat off his forehead. "Now, talk."

"What did you find out about me?"

"Not much. I might have given that reporter the impression that I knew more than I actually did. I thought maybe she'd give me a byline." Weaver shrugged. "What's so important about you?"

"I'm not important. Some people just don't like what I did to them."

Weaver nodded eagerly. "Well, tell me everything. Let's get you on the front page. Then they won't dare mess with you."

"That would be the opposite of what I should do." Carver pondered the offer. Publicity would only paint a bigger target on his back. He could do more from the shadows than in the open.

Elena Diaz was only painting more targets on more backs. Anyone who unwittingly responded to her was added to the dead list. She was like an angel of death and didn't even realize it. Anyone who'd ignored her calls was probably safe. Anyone who contacted her was another name on the list.

It seemed like overkill. Just because someone had contacted Diaz didn't mean they knew anything. Most dead lists were formed with careful consideration by informed analysts. Tremendous amounts of data went into making sure the list was precise. People weren't added on a whim or a gut feeling. An agent or analyst had to prove they belonged there.

This operation felt sloppy. Like the agent in charge didn't know what they were doing. Like they'd watched one too many spy movies and thought killing everyone was the answer. Killing too many people made as many problems as killing too few.

Dan had to be the one calling the shots. Nothing about their first contact felt right. It felt sloppy. Unplanned. The man had to be new to this kind of operation to let it veer so wildly out of control.

He hadn't even recognized Carver. Hadn't even looked at him funny. This despite the description and sketches of Carver Dan's people had been using to search for him. It reeked of ineptitude.

Carver benefitted from a modicum of anonymity. His military records had been purged the moment he'd joined his special division. No pictures were ever taken. No names were ever mentioned. Any records would have little to no information except for code names for the operatives.

The only pictures of him in recent memory had been taken for his fake ID. The other had been mug shots taken by Morganville police. Carver had destroyed them and his arrest record. The only thing available was a physical description.

That description had spawned a couple of sketches. One of them had been in Nicki Jones's weapons case. The sketch wasn't enough for a positive ID. Carver wasn't monstrously tall or big. He might stand out more than most, but not enough to verify his identity.

It meant even the people who put out the contract on his life didn't have a picture to go on. Whoever had tracked down the maker of his fake ID had only discovered a fake name. They hadn't even known about his scars.

Diaz's sketch and description were much closer. That was what helped Leach figure out that Clint Wilkins was actually Amos Carver. Without that critical information, there was no reason to expect someone to realize his true identity.

Maybe that was why Dan had been clueless. It still didn't explain why he was adding people like Weaver to a dead list without properly vetting them. With Theresa dead, Weaver, at least, wasn't in imminent danger.

Weaver clapped his hands. "Hey, are you going to tell me more or not?"

"Just keep your head low. Get your laptop checked for spyware and your home checked for bugs."

"Huh?"

"Just do it, okay?" Carver handed him back the bullets. "And get a better weapon."

Carver turned for the door.

"Wait! Please tell me what's going on." Weaver clasped his hands together. "We can work on this together."

Carver shook his head. "You'll only end up dead. Walk around the building, go back to your car, and leave."

Weaver worked his jaw back and forth. "And if I refuse?"

Carver clenched a fist and sighed. "Let's not go there, okay?"

The reporter backed up and almost tripped over his own feet. "Christ, man! No need to get violent." He backed up, turned, and hurried off.

Carver went inside the store. He walked the aisles to the clothing racks. From there it was easier to see across the store. He spotted the yoga pants girl in the shoes section. She was hurrying up and down the rows. Barely bothering to be inconspicuous.

It was no wonder that someone like Weaver was on the dead list. If this was the best spy Dan had to offer, then his operation was in trouble. And a lot of people were going to die.

Carver stepped back between shelves and started on an intercept course. She popped out three aisles down. He stepped behind a shelf. Waited a beat. Went back down the row. He waited at the end.

The girl sped around the corner and bumped into him a moment later. She looked up. Her eyes flared. She recognized him somehow.

"Hi," Carver said.

She gasped. Her lips moved but no sound came out. She was probably the worst spy Carver had ever encountered.

He narrowed his eyes. "What do you want from Weaver?"

The woman wore a backpack that probably had her laptop in it. It was one of the drawstring packs that looked like a sack. Her clothing blended in well. But her spying skills needed serious work.

"I just had a talk with Weaver out back. I recently discovered his life is in danger." Carver narrowed his eyes for effect. "Why are you following him?"

The woman finally found her voice. "Amos? Amos Carver?"

"Just Carver."

"Oh my God. Finally." She blew out a breath of relief. "I'm Elena Diaz."

The pieces fell into place. Carver raised an eyebrow. "You've been looking for me."

"Yeah, and that turned out to be a horrible mistake."

Carver nodded. "I know. You're getting people killed."

Elena stared at him for a while. "Somehow, I thought you'd be bigger. The women I interviewed described you as a giant."

"Maybe they were short. You look about five feet eight."

"They were short and that's my exact height." She sighed. "Never thought I'd find the man who ruined my life in a thrift store."

"We have a lot to talk about." Carver nodded toward the exit. "Let's go talk."

She hesitated. Bit her lower lip. "I guess things can't get much worse."

"Things can always get worse." He started walking.

Elena hesitated, then paced alongside him. She had long dark hair. Athletic legs, a slender torso. She looked like she kept in shape. That would be important.

"Do you jog?" Carver asked.

"I do."

"Lift weights?"

"Mostly lower body. Squats, hip thrusts, that kind of stuff."

"How would you rate your physical fitness?"

Elena looked him up and down. "Compared to you? A five. Compared to most people, an eight."

"Let's go with eight."

"Why?"

"I just want to know what I'm working with if we have to run or fight."

"We just met a few seconds ago and you're already evaluating me for hand-to-hand combat?"

Carver nodded. "Did you drive here?"

"No, I took a bus to the cafe. My car is at the hotel. I thought it would be more anonymous to take public transport."

"You have a cell phone?"

"I turned it off and left it in my car. I'm afraid they'll track me."

"Smart." Carver stopped next to the Audi. "You can ride with me."

Her eyes widened. "What in the hell is this? I was under the impression you didn't even have a car."

"I don't. This is a rental."

"You rented a supercar?"

"I didn't personally, no." He dropped inside and turned on the car. Cranked the air-conditioning to high.

She sat inside and put on her seatbelt. "Are we talking here or somewhere else?"

"Somewhere else. But we can talk on the way." He tapped the paddle shifter and pulled out of the parking spot. "You can start by telling me where you got a leech."

Elena produced the small, slender object from a thigh pocket. "It's not mine. Someone gave it to me."

"Who?"

"A guy named Pete. He gave it to me after a blonde assassin named Melinda Gross tried to kill him."

"Back up. Tell me how your journey to this moment started."

Elena took a breath. Sighed. "It started in Morganville." She told him about the investigation. How Breakstone came out smelling like a rose. How she'd first met Melinda there. She told him about the mine, the soldiers, the escape. Worked her way up to the present.

"That was the trigger," Carver said. "You started poking the bear on Wednesday. The bear almost found me Saturday."

"I didn't think about it that way." Elena stared blankly. "I led them straight to you."

"They just wanted me because they knew I could expose them." Carver stopped at a traffic light. "Or, maybe they decided to leave me alone since I'd gone silent." He shrugged. "You showed up at the mine. That proved to them that someone else knew about the bodies there. That put them on alert."

"Okay, but Melinda, the blond assassin, she talked to me even before that."

The light turned green. Carver accelerated. "You were on their radar. They wanted to see how much you knew. The killer decided you didn't know anything. Then you showed up at the mine. That changed everything."

"I think you're right." Elena sighed. "My God, I wonder if Charlie is okay."

"Don't try to contact him."

"I won't." She gritted her teeth. "I never thought searching for you would be so dangerous."

Carver shifted lanes to go around a slow car. "It's because they're protecting politicians and probably secret military programs that were supposed to go to Breakstone."

"Yeah, but it's strange so many federal agencies in lockstep. They're usually a territorial bunch." Elena's hand tightened on the door handle. "There's usually even infighting within agencies. I think they all have a vested interest in Breakstone. Either that, or someone powerful is calling the shots. Someone like the President."

"Did the military have people onsite during the investigation?"

She nodded. "I think even the CIA and NSA had representatives there. The FBI, DEA and ATF were most visible."

"That's a given considering the international drug trade." Carver glanced in the rearview mirror. "I think it's safe to say Weaver doesn't have any useful information."

"You spoke with him?"

Carver nodded. "He told me he acted like he knew more than he did so you'd give him a byline."

"I'm not surprised." Elena held up the leech. "We'll know for sure once I look at this."

"How many people did you contact?"

"I emailed dozens of reporters. I figured if you caused such a mess in Morganville then surely, you'd done something to stand out in Florida."

"Detectives too, apparently."

"Reporters, detectives, anyone who'd be close to the ground." Elena slid the leech back into her pocket. "Only a few replied. A detective from Miami called me back. Doug Weaver, Lisa Gallagher, and a few others whose names I can't remember off the top of my head."

"But you have the names."

She nodded. "I can show you the emails."

"Good. Because one or more of those people weren't detectives or reporters."

"Melinda Gross, to name one."

Carver turned onto the causeway leading to the island. He checked the mirrors and the rearview camera for tails. Traffic was heavier. A good tail would blend in. A good tail wouldn't drive an unmarked police car. They'd want something silver, white, or black to remain inconspicuous.

He'd counted four silver, twelve white, and eight black cars so far. None of them were still behind him. There was a red car that had been with him for a mile. It was a compact sports car. A Honda. The color was no good for tailing someone and maybe the driver knew that. Maybe they figured it was an ideal color because someone like Carver wouldn't expect it.

The Honda took a right turn off the bridge. Vanished down a side street. Just some ordinary citizen out for a drive. Not a highly skilled spy who knew how to blend in without blending in.

"Why did you go silent for so long?" Elena tried to look behind them, but the Audi's rear window was too small to be useful. "Is someone following us?"

Carver shook his head. "We're good." He kept quiet. Kept looking all the way to the hotel. He stopped at the valet.

The valet opened the door for Elena. Walked around and gave Carver another valet ticket. "Sir, we have a valet app if you don't want to receive paper tickets anymore."

"I didn't choose the Betsy because I like technology, son." Carver smiled. "Old school is the best."

The valet smiled and nodded. "I just wanted to make sure you knew, sir."

"Much appreciated." Carver took Elena's hand. "Come on, dear."

She flinched in surprise. Realized what he was doing and relaxed. "Sure thing, hubs."

They walked to the elevator lobby. Went inside an elevator. The doors closed and Carver released her hand. He slid the card over the reader, and they climbed to the penthouse. He led her inside.

Elena whistled and looked around. "You've got quite a hustle going on. Are you a traveling con man?"

"No, but that would be a good life." Carver went to the bar. "Would you like a drink?"

She found a light beer and took it. Put the cap on the edge of the granite countertop and hit it with the palm of her hand. The lid popped off.

"There's an opener right here." Carver picked up the ornate bottle opener and removed the top from his dark beer.

Elena raised an eyebrow. "The countertop will survive."

"It's a little disrespectful."

Her forehead pinched and her eyes narrowed. Like she couldn't decide if he was serious.

Carver went to the living room and sat on the couch. He set a coaster on the glass side table and put the beer on it. "Let's talk."

Elena went to the niche with the grand piano. Opened the lid and ran a finger across the keys without pressing them down. "I assume this room was also rented by your friend?"

"It was, yes. She had good taste."

Elena stiffened. "Had?"

"She's since passed away."

Her face paled. "What did you do to her?"

"Have a seat and let's talk."

"I shouldn't be surprised. If half of what the women told me is true, you killed an entire cartel."

"Not an entire cartel. Just their employees in Morganville."

She gulped and sat down in the chair across from him. Set her beer on the table. She took a tissue and wiped her forehead and upper lip. "I'm not cut out for this. I thought I could report on anything, but this is just too much."

"Relax and enjoy your beer." Carver lifted his and took a drink. "You're not dead yet."

Elena laughed nervously. A tear trickled down her face. "Not yet."

"Yep, so keep kicking. Maybe you'll make it to the other side."

"Other side? Like the afterlife?"

Carver smiled. "No, the other side of the raging river. You'll climb out cold, tired, beaten up. But you'll be alive. Everyone else will just wash right over the waterfall."

"Are you a good swimmer, Carver?"

He nodded. "So far. But sometimes there are things under the water that you don't see. A rock, a branch, a shark."

"Sharks don't live in rivers."

"They live in my rivers." Carver took another drink. "But maybe we each have some information that will help us see the dangers a little more clearly."

Elena wiped her tears away. Took a swig of her beer. "You're just like they described."

Carver didn't say anything. He sat back and enjoyed his beer.

She looked like she was waiting for a response.

He kept quiet.

"Yeah, just like that." She nodded. "You talk when you want to, do what you want to. It's like you're on this whole separate life plan from everyone else and that's okay by you."

"Once upon a time, I did what everyone told me to do. I had commanders. I had a team. Everything was timed to the split second. Everything had to be right, or everyone died." Carver crossed a leg and spread his arms over the back of the couch. "I enjoyed it. I liked having a rigid structure to keep me in line."

"And now?"

"I'm just winging it." He smiled. "That's the honest truth of it. I don't have a plan, and neither do you."

CHAPTER 24

There was no plan.

Only the will to swim across the raging river. Just like Carver said. Elena knew it was true. She'd been winging it since Morganville. The entire time she'd been a pawn for Melinda, and she hadn't even known it.

"You heard my story. I want to hear yours." Elena took out her notepad. "What really happened in Morganville?"

Carver took another sip of beer. "Let's get something straight. I'm not here to out myself with a news story. I'm not here to make your career. You're on the dead list just like me. I have a better chance of surviving than you do. Maybe I'll let you lay low while I figure things out, or maybe I'll preserve my anonymity the best I can and not lift a finger to help you."

"How in the hell did you ever have a girlfriend?" Elena shook her head. "Paola, right?"

"She wasn't my girlfriend. We slept together. Kept each other company for a while. She left. End of story."

"I don't know what she saw in you." Elena put her notepad away. "You're not anonymous, you know. People know who you are. They know what you've done. They're looking for you."

"And you led them right to me. You painted yourself as a target. Painted Doug Weaver, Lisa Gallagher, maybe that Charlie fellow."

Elena shuddered. "I didn't know that at the time."

"Well, relax, because I'm the assassin now."

She frowned. "What do you mean?"

"Let's talk about Club Periclean. You were there when Nicky Jones, aka, Melinda Gross died."

Elena nodded. "Yes."

Carver nodded back. "You said Jones was with a darkhaired woman. That she drugged you and was going to kill you in a hotel room."

"But the guy who'd been talking to her and the darkhaired woman earlier came along. They fought. Jones tried to drug him with her ring needle, but he turned it on her."

"That man was Desmond Price. DEA agent." Carver fit another puzzle piece into place. "Explains how she got drugged."

Elena nodded. "Price is the one who put me in the closet. Then he vanished with Jones. I think he came back for me later, but I heard him fighting someone outside."

"Must have been when he fought Theresa, the darkhaired woman."

"She and Jones were both assassins?"

Carver nodded. "Yep. Jones had a record for shoplifting. That was the only thing Leach found on her. I still don't know who Theresa really was."

"Leach was the detective I contacted. You knew him?"

Carver nodded. "He was investigating Jones' death."

Elena took out her notepad. "Can I write this down?"

"Yes. But keep my name and description out of everything."

It wasn't what she wanted, but she needed Carver to survive. She could still write a story. Maybe find another way to back up the facts. "Okay." She made a list of names.

Theresa Smith

Nicki Jones aka Melinda Gross

Detective Bill Leach

Desmond Price DEA

Besides her and Carver, these were the main players. The ones making the chess moves.

Carver picked up his beer off the coaster. "I've been working on a theory."

"Let's hear it."

"Nicki and Theresa knew each other. Theresa wasn't happy to see Nicki working the same contract. They also used similar kill methods. Knives, poisons, drugs. Jones also had guns. Theresa didn't. They also resembled each other in the face. Theresa was slender. Jones was bigger, more athletic."

Elena tapped her pen on her chin. "Teacher and student? Sisters?"

"Maybe both." Carver seemed to think it over. "Jones was in her late twenties, early thirties. Theresa was mid-thirties, if I had to guess."

"And they both went by the last name alias of Smith."

Carver nodded. "Jones was the little sister. Maybe she wasn't supposed to be a part of this. Maybe they were both hired, and Theresa didn't like it."

"What happened to Desmond Price?"

"Theresa gutted him in the alley behind the club."

Elena grimaced. "Oh, God." She drew a little skull and crossbones next to his name and Nicki Jones.

Carver pretended to grip a knife. He drew a Z over his abdomen. "Clean and precise."

Elena shivered and wrote it down. "That's really ballsy to gut a DEA agent."

"She came for me. I managed to take her prisoner. She wouldn't talk about Jones. Wouldn't say a thing. She tried to kill me a couple more times, so I put her down."

Elena put another skull and crossbones next to Theresa's name. "Maybe Detective Leach can positively identify her with DNA or biometrics."

"She killed Leach before she came after me."

Elena's mouth dropped open. "Theresa killed a Miami detective and a DEA agent. That woman was on another level."

"Yeah. She was a work of art."

Elena drew another skull and crossbones. Everyone on her list so far was dead. She was afraid to add another name to it. Like the list was cursed.

"Maybe the cops can find out who Theresa really is." Carver opened the beer and sat on the couch. "I don't think her identity will do me much good, though. The contract is anonymous. I don't know who hired her. I only know the fake name of the liaison, Dan."

"How much are they paying?"

"The dossier for Weaver and Gallagher lists them at a hundred grand each."

Elena whistled. "That's a lot of money for people who don't know anything."

"It is. It means if they're worth that much, I'm probably worth a whole lot more. Maybe five or ten times more."

"A million bucks?" Elena frowned. "They're throwing money at a problem. A problem they haven't even fully identified. Going after people like Weaver and Gallagher makes no sense. All they did was reply to my email. They didn't know anything useful."

"Exactly." Carver lifted the beer to his lips and drank. "They're not even bothering to vet the people they're adding to the dead list."

"Dead list?"

"Yeah." Carver ran a finger through the condensation on his beer bottle. "It's a hit list."

"And they're willing to spend as much money as it takes to terminate everyone on it."

Carver shrugged. "That's how the government operates. They have an unlimited supply of money. They don't even have to print it anymore. They can just add a figure to a computer somewhere and wire it. Free money."

"Printing their own blood money."

"Yep." Carver raised his beer. "And artificially increasing money supply causes inflation."

"Great. My death would raise the cost of living."

Carver offered a half smile. "By at least a tenth of a penny."

Elena leaned her elbows on her knees. "So, what do we do?"

"Theresa was hired anonymously, but she and the hiring agent were scheduled to meet in front of this hotel." Carver set the bottle on a coaster. "I'd just killed Theresa. I didn't know much of anything. He followed me. I confronted him. He thought I was the hired assassin."

"Does no one know what you look like or have a picture?"

"Nope, and I want to keep it that way." Carver took out a cell phone and handed it to her. "These are the assignments he gave me."

Weaver's face was in the first image. Gallagher was in the next. "Just these two?"

"He told me these were in addition to the others. I suspect he'd already sent over a list to the contract agency. He was meeting with Theresa to add Weaver and Gallagher."

"What's his name?"

"Dan."

Elena wrote it down. "That's not his real name."

"Nope."

"He's probably with a federal agency though." Elena considered the connections. "Maybe the DEA. Maybe that's how Price is connected."

"It's possible. Finding out more about Desmond Price might lead us to the source."

"Maybe more information on Theresa and Jones would be helpful too."

"Doubtful. They don't have trails. Nothing we can follow, anyway." Carver had thought it through plenty. "Even if they were alive and talking, they couldn't tell us who hired them."

"Or so Theresa said. Maybe she was lying."

"Maybe, but she's dead. Desmond Price and the DEA are the way to go now." Carver leaned back. "A DEA agent was supposed to talk to Leach today. Since Leach is dead, that agent is meeting with someone else at the police department."

"Leach's partner, maybe?"

Carver shook his head. "Doubtful. Leach told me his partner is retiring soon. They'll probably want to keep him out of the line of fire."

"Okay, so let's follow the DEA trail."

Carver nodded. "If we find out why the DEA was involved, it might be the missing link."

"Because the source has to be someone in the federal government, right?"

He nodded again. "No private citizen is going to carelessly throw around that much money. This is a person who's used to spending other people's money."

"A politician?"

"Possibly. But they'd have to be high up the food chain to have access to that much money."

Elena nodded. "Okay, so we have to find out who's meeting with the DEA. If that meeting even took place. Maybe they backed out after Leach's death."

"Some kind of meeting took place. Doubtful the DEA will help the Miami police, though. But maybe they will. Stranger things have happened."

Elena lifted the beer bottle to her lips and took a sip. "The feds are notorious for being unhelpful to local law enforcement. We still need to find out who they are and talk to them."

"Maybe we don't need to talk to them." Carver nodded at her thigh pocket. "You've got a leech. We just need to get it close to one of their computers or cell phones."

Her eyes widened. "You're right. But how are we going to get close to them?"

"First of all, we need to find out who they are and if they're still in town." Carver rotated the beer bottle on the coaster. "The only people who'd know that are the Miami police."

Elena slid a laptop from her bag. "Let's find out if Weaver had anything on his laptop. I doubt there's anything useful, but it's worth a shot."

"Don't use your own laptop." Carver went to Theresa's gear case and pulled out the laptop. "This one is safer."

"What is all that?" Elena looked over the knives and drugs in the case. "Is that an assassin's kit?"

"Yep. Nicki Jones had one similar."

"Creepy." Elena turned on the secure laptop and plugged in the leech. A list of files and folders appeared on the screen. It looked like Weaver kept his entire life on his laptop. "This is going to take a while."

Carver leaned over her shoulder. Pointed to a red icon on the desktop. It didn't have a label, but he recognized it. "Open that."

"What program is that?"

"It's an advanced search program. Makes it easier to find things quickly."

"I've never seen a program like that."

Carver shrugged. "I've seen it on military computers. I've seen a tech sift through terabytes of data to find the needle in the haystack."

She opened the program. Pointed it to the leech. "Okay, what now?"

"Search for DEA."

Elena typed it in. Hit enter. The program returned a dozen hits across three stories Weaver had written. They were old stories. None looked relevant. She searched for Carver and got no hits. There was one result when searching for her name, but it was just a note about meeting.

Carver leaned back on the couch and watched. He wasn't surprised that Weaver didn't have much of interest. It was another dead end. Maybe it was time to make some roads of his own. The trouble was figuring out where to start.

"I give up." Elena pushed the laptop away. "Leach's death must have been big local news. What have the local news agencies been saying about it?"

"There was a big story that day, but I haven't kept up with it."

"Really?" Elena grabbed her laptop and turned it on. She opened the websites for the local newspapers.

Carver let her do her thing and drank his beer. She read quietly, jotting down notes on a notepad every so often. He didn't know what useful information could be found from the local news agencies.

He'd been tasked with intel gathering plenty of times. But it usually involved finding someone. Infiltrating their house. Squeezing information out of them any way possible. He'd used leeches and a wide variety of data gathering methods. But he wasn't usually the one to sift through it.

The techs did that work. They separated the good information from the bad. The useful from the useless. They had powerful computers for decryption. For searching. For data capture. Entire teams took the information and formed it into a dossier.

It seemed unlikely that Carver and a reporter could replicate the work done by government agencies. Whoever was behind this knew all there was to know about them. If they didn't stay hidden, they'd be fish in a barrel.

"Got it." Elena circled a name on her notepad. "Detective Nadia Flores is investigating Leach's murder. They pinned it on Theresa thanks to your tip to Wendy Hernandez. But they're mystified about her death." She flipped back a page on the notepad. "DEA Agent Michael Turner met with local detectives about the death of Desmond Price. He had no comment about Price's assignment in Miami. But he's still in town and he's staying at the Faena at Mid-Beach."

Carver changed his mind. One determined person could find a lot of useful information.

Elena grinned. "You didn't think I'd find anything, did you?"

"Nope."

"More than anything, people love gossip. That's basically what news is. Some is factual, some is rumor." Elena underlined the hotel name twice. "If we find out which room he's staying in, can you get inside?"

"Probably. Depends on certain factors."

"Like what?"

"Is he alone? Does he keep his important items with him at all times? Does he leave the room during the day or work from there?"

"Make sense. I guess we need to stake it out."

"You have pictures of him?"

Elena pulled up an image on the screen. It was Turner at a news conference, flanked by local police. She played a video of him talking. Carver watched it carefully. He wasn't watching Turner so much as he was watching the people around him.

The camera panned across the crowd of reporters. Carver saw something. "Back it up."

Elena backed it up frame by frame.

"Stop." He stared at a face on the sidelines. It was Dan. "That's Theresa's liaison."

"You think he's with Turner?"

"I don't know." Carver studied the people around Dan. There were some cops, some people in plain clothes. Nothing that told him if Dan was associated with anyone else. He wished he had his old techs and facial recognition software. "Let's go find out which room Turner is staying in."

"How are we going to do that?"

"I'll figure it out when we get there." He picked up the leech. Grabbed Theresa's burner phones. Handed one to her. "You can use this."

She turned it on. "This is pretty nice for a burner."

"It was Theresa's. Same with the car and the hotel room. She was an extravagant spender."

"I'll say." Elena slid the phone in a thigh pocket.

Carver went to the bedroom. Looked in the closet. There were fancy wooden hangers permanently attached to the rod. There was also a drycleaning bag. He opened it and found what he needed inside. He folded it up and zipped it into a lower pocket on his cargo pants.

They left the hotel. Retrieved the Audi from the valet. Carver drove north about two miles to the Faena. There was a beach parking lot nearby. He drove around but it was full. That was a problem around here. Little to no parking.

He didn't want to valet it at the hotel. He wanted the car somewhere ready for a fast escape. A parallel parking spot opened on the side street next to the hotel. He nosed into it before a Porsche. The other driver gave him the finger.

Carver unfolded himself out of the car. The other driver sped off.

Elena sighed. "Wish I had that effect on people sometimes."

"A reporter wants people to be comfortable with them."

"Sometimes I want them to be scared of me." She waited on the sidewalk. "Now what?"

"Plan A." Carver walked down the sidewalk. Turned the corner. Entered the hotel. A hotel clerk was checking in a family. He got in line behind them.

A woman emerged from a back room. "Can I help you sir?"

Carver held up a finger. "One moment, please." He punched in a number on his cell phone. Handed it to Elena. "Call this number and ask for Michael Turner."

She frowned. "Huh?"

"Just do it." He approached the desk.

The desk phone rang. The woman smiled at him. "How can I help you?"

Carver nodded at the phone. "You can get that. I'll wait."

"Thank you, sir." She picked up the phone. "Hotel Faena. How can I make your day wonderful?" She nodded. "One moment, please." She put the call on hold. Dialed a three-digit number. Waited a moment. Ended the call and switched back to the caller. "I'm sorry, he's unavailable. Would you like to leave a message?" She nodded. "Thank you." Hung up.

And with that, Carver knew all he needed to know.

CHAPTER 25

"How much for a room on the fourth floor?" Carver asked.

The hotel clerk tilted her head slightly. "Do you have a reservation, sir?"

"No. Unexpected business trip."

Her eyes looked him up and down. Dark cargo pants and t-shirts weren't common business clothing. But this was Miami. "Let me check our availability, sir."

Carver nodded. "Thanks."

She typed on the computer and stared at it for a few seconds before shaking her head sadly. "I'm afraid we're booked for the night. But we do have condominium rentals across the road. Some of them might be open."

"Let me think about it. In the meantime, I might check out your restaurant."

"Please do. It's ranked as one of the best in Miami."

Carver left and went to the lobby. Elena was sitting in a chair. Looking around the area.

"Turner wasn't in his room. Is that what you wanted to know?"

"That was part of it." He sat down in the chair near hers. Looked back at the hotel clerk. She'd returned to the back room. "Let's go to the elevators."

He walked behind a column and entered the elevator lobby. Pressed the up button and waited. The doors opened. An older couple stepped out. Carver got in. There was a card reader, but it looked like it was for the upper floors. He pressed the button for the fourth floor. It glowed.

Elena got in. "Where are we going?"

"Turner's room. Four twenty-one."

"Did you sweet talk it out of the clerk?"

"Do I look like the kind of person who sweet talks anyone?"

She laughed. "No. More like frightens them into giving up their information."

"She dialed the room number when you called."

Elena snapped her fingers. "Smooth. I didn't even think of that."

The elevator dinged and stopped at the fourth floor. The doors slid open. They stepped out and walked down the hallway. The room door was unguarded. The hallway was quiet and empty. Carver stepped up to the door. Knocked loudly. Waited.

No one answered.

Elena gave him a look. "What now?"

His squad's techs could whip up keys for any hotel in seconds. The lock was a bigger barrier in the civilian world. That was if you didn't know a few simple tricks. He unzipped his pants pocket. Pulled out the twisted wire clothes hangar he'd taken from the dry cleaning bag.

Elena looked from it to the door. "You're going to pick an electronic lock with that?"

"Nope." He unfolded the wire hangar until it was straight except for the hook at the end. He knelt next to the door. Put the hook over the outside door handle. Pushed it about an inch higher. Then he bent the hangar ninety degrees where it met the floor. Bent the hook a little tighter.

The door handles in hotels were levers these days, not knobs. That was because of handicap laws and safety regulations. A lever was easier to use for disabled folk. Even if you didn't have a hand, you could push it down with an arm or leg.

If not for safety regulations, this would be a doorknob. It would also be next to impossible to do what he needed to do.

He bent the other end of the wire up. Formed it into a handle so he could grip it from this side. Then he laid the wire sideways. Slid the hook under the door. He slid it about even with the outside door handle. Twisted the hangar sideways. Felt the hook slide over metal on the other side.

Carver pulled his end toward him. He heard the hook clink against the handle on the other side. Felt the vibration in the metal. He pulled toward him and to the right. The hook latched onto the door handle.

He pulled slowly. Too far down and the hook would slide off the lever. Too far to the right and it wouldn't be able to pull down. He worked it slowly. There was a click. He pushed his shoulder against the door. It swung open.

"That was cool." Elena shook her head. "And simple. My god, we could break into anyone's room this way."

Carver gave her the wire hangar. "Go for it."

She held the bent metal in her hand. "Are you joking with me? I can't tell."

He didn't reply. He was already in the room. Looking around. Searching for a laptop. It smelled like aftershave lotion. The old kind his dad liked. He'd never forget that odor.

Elena bumped into him. "Why'd you stop, Carver?"

He walked into the bathroom. Barbasol shaving cream. Brut aftershave. It seemed old school for someone Turner's age. He looked like he was in his late thirties. Maybe his dad used the same shaving products too.

The odor was fine. But it triggered memories. Maybe even some emotions. None of them were pleasant. None of them mattered. What mattered was that Turner's laptop wasn't going to be in the bathroom.

"There's nothing here." Elena stood behind him. "He took his laptop with him."

Turner had a carryon sized suitcase. It was open. Inside were mostly jeans and button-up shirts. He didn't wear suits. Just street clothes. That seemed more acceptable to federal agencies these days. Helped them blend in with the populace.

"What now?" Elena pressed her lips together.

Carver considered the options. It depended on the kind of person Turner was. It depended on why he was in Miami. Was he just here investigating Price's murder? Was he here to assume Price's duties? Was he here for a short time or a long time?

"I think Detective Flores and Agent Turner are going to connect the cases," Elena said. "That is, unless Turner is here to prevent them from being tied together."

"Depends on what kind of a man Price was. Why was he hanging around with two assassins? He's with the DEA not the NSA or CIA."

"Maybe the killers were connected to drug cartels."

"Maybe." Carver didn't know. He couldn't even guess. Things were still too fragmented to make sense. He wondered what Rhodes would make out of all this. She'd probably spot a minor detail he'd missed. Solve the puzzle without breaking a sweat.

"We should probably leave." Elena tapped his arm. "In case Turner is coming back. It's almost dinner time."

"Yeah." Carver stepped into the hallway. Closed the door. Wiped down the handle with his shirt.

"You're so thorough."

"Habit."

They returned to the elevator. Returned to the lobby. Carver considered it for a stakeout, but anyone sticking around for hours would look suspicious. He went outside. Stopped at the valet station. A valet held out his hand for the ticket.

Carver ignored the hand. "Is self-parking allowed or only valet?"

The man withdrew his hand. "Just valet, sir. The charge is added to your hotel bill. Tipping isn't included."

"Thanks." Carver walked down the stairs to the sidewalk. He looked across the street. At the side streets. There was no good place to park for a stakeout.

Elena took out her burner phone and made a call. "Is Detective Flores there? Thanks." She waited. "Detective, is Agent Turner still there?" She nodded and ended the call. "I'm surprised that worked."

"Sometimes asking is the easiest way to get an answer."

"I think I caught her off guard." Elena smiled. "She said, yes, then almost immediately stopped and asked who I was."

"Good work." They went back to the Audi. Got in.

Elena's phone rang. It was the police station. Carver took the phone. Removed the battery. Got out of the Audi and dumped the phone in the garbage. He slid back into the Audi and gave her another phone.

She smiled sheepishly. "I guess I didn't think about them calling or tracing it."

"Asking for Turner raised a big red flag. It's okay. That's why I have a lot of burner phones." Carver edged into traffic. Drove to the police station.

Elena whistled. "That's one pretty building."

"It's Miami." Carver parked across from the parking deck exit and fed a meter. "Turner probably flew down from Washington. He's either got a rental or someone is giving him rides around town."

"There's only one parking deck entrance and exit. Maybe we can watch it?"

"Yep." Carver pushed himself out of the car. Sitting so low to the ground was hard on the knees and back.

He walked around the block. Stopped on the sidewalk across from the parking deck exit. Looked up and down the street for cameras. How long he was here would depend on what kind of a person Turner was.

Turner might be a workaholic. He might work through dinner. Order delivery. Send someone to get him takeout. He might not come out of the building until three in the morning.

Maybe Turner was a typical government employee. Maybe he didn't work that hard. Maybe he'd want to go out for dinner. Have some drinks. Relax.

Carver hoped Turner was the second kind of person. That would make this wait a lot shorter.

"That's a hotel." Elena pointed to the building across the road from the exit. "Maybe we could get a room and watch from there. It'd be less conspicuous." She nodded her head toward the cameras around the police building. "Someone will eventually notice."

"Good idea, but we'd have to get a room in the back corner. It might already be occupied." He looked at the neighboring building. There were multiple businesses inside. He entered the door. There was a lobby with chairs. No receptionist.

Other doors led to other businesses. They had lobbies of their own. He took a seat. Turned it to face the window. Sat down. A slim palm tree partially obstructed the view to the parking deck exit, but otherwise, it was perfect.

The metal gate rolled up. A patrol car eased out. Carver held his monocular to an eye. It gave him a clear view of the driver despite the sun reflecting off the windshield. He waited and watched. Counted the cars as they left.

Elena stood and stretched after an hour. "Want something to eat or drink?"

"Both." He gave her some cash. "A sandwich and water."

"I'll be back." She left and returned ten cars later.

Carver took a bag from her and unwrapped the sandwich inside. It was a turkey club. Nothing special, but it hit the spot. Elena ate hers. Watched cars for a while. Nodded off to sleep.

The forty-second car to leave the parking deck departed at seven thirty. The driver was Detective Flores. The passenger was Agent Turner. Flores turned right. Headed west. Carver nudged Elena.

She blinked awake. Bolted upright. "You see them?"

"Yep." Carver tucked the monocular into a pants pocket and went outside. Hustled around the corner to the Audi. Dropped into the driver's seat. Elena got in and closed her door. Carver performed a four-point turn to get turned around.

Flores was still driving straight. Carver accelerated after them. Slowed down about a block away. They turned north. He kept following. Maintained his distance. Too close and they might notice. Too far and he'd lose them.

The quarry pulled up to a valet at a Cuban restaurant. Turner got out of the car. Flores got out of the other side. Took the valet ticket.

"Is she really valeting a police car?" Elena gave Carver a confused look. "I didn't think you could do that."

"It's Miami," Carver said. There was a handicapped parallel parking spot right across the road. He took it.

"You keep saying that as if it answers all the questions."

"Parking is scarce, so if they want to eat, they have to valet."

"But you'd think the valets would let the cops park the car."

"She's a detective, not a patrol officer. That car doesn't have specialized equipment."

Elena nodded. "True. Probably just barebones inside. I just hope we don't get busted for parking in a handicapped spot."

Turner carried a briefcase. Probably a laptop bag. He wasn't leaving anything valuable in the car. It was smart of him. He and Flores went inside. The front wall was a big window so Carver could still see them.

There were no booths. A host sat them at a table for four. Turner took out his laptop and set it on the table. He talked to Flores. A server approached. Took an order. Carver watched with the monocular. Tried to read their lips. Their faces were angled slightly away so it was hard to make out much.

They ordered drinks. The server mentioned food. They shook their heads. The server left. Turner opened his laptop. Turned it on. He took out a tablet and tapped on the screen. Turned it toward Flores. She held it upright and looked at it. Nodded. Rotated it back toward Turner.

The screen faced Carver for a second. Long enough for him to see the sketch. The sketch of him. It was the same one Nicki had in her assassin kit.

"My sketch is better," Elena said.

"You can see it all the way from here?"

She nodded. "Not in great detail. It looks like a generic muscular guy. The sketch artist who made mine was better. I wonder why they're looking at it."

"They're probably merging the murder cases. Jones, Theresa, Price, Leach. They know someone by my description is involved."

"That's a lot of dead bodies." Elena shuddered. "Maybe they think you did it."

"They'd be twenty-five percent correct," Carver said.

Elena watched him uneasily. "You joke like killing someone is no big deal."

"It's not a joke and it's always a big deal." He kept watching. "Lives are connected in intricate ways. Socially, financially, physically. Remove that one connection and everything around it might collapse."

"Is killing a killer a good thing?"

"It depends. Are we talking professionals or murderers?"

Elena did a doubletake. "You differentiate?"

"One is for work. One is for fun."

"I imagine some do it for both."

"Some people enjoy their work." Carver lowered the monocular and rubbed his eye. "Theresa was skilled. She almost took me down a couple of times. She was impressive."

Elena gasped. "You admire her even though she was trying to kill you?"

"I admired her skill, not what she was trying to do with it." Carver kept watching. The car wasn't an ideal place to observe from. He had to keep his head turned. It was going to stiffen up after a while.

It was starting to get dark. The people inside couldn't see out, but he could see in just fine. There was a bus stop bench on the sidewalk. He pulled himself out of the car. Sat on the bench. Crossed his legs and got comfortable. Elena sat next to him.

Reading lips wasn't his strength. He could make out a few words here and there. Nothing important. It looked like they were talking about the food. Turner said something. Flores laughed. He smiled back.

"I think he's flirting," Elena said. "She's just laughing to be polite, though."

"How do you know?"

"Her back is stiff. The laughter doesn't reach her eyes. She isn't maintaining eye contact. I could go on and on."

"I see it now." Carver watched through the monocular. "What else do you see?"

Elena rattled off a list. "She keeps her hair in a tight bun. She's wearing a navy-blue pantsuit. Open carries her sidearm. She's all business. Not a light-hearted kind of person."

Carver went next. "Turner feels like a big man. Thinks being a fed makes him important. Thinks a local detective would look up to him. Maybe admire him a little. Enough to get lucky."

"You can tell all that from looking at him?"

Carver shook his head. "I know the type. FBI, DEA, ATF. Those types usually think they're better than their local counterparts. Something about working for the federal government inflates their egos."

"Sounds personal."

"I've dealt with all kinds of feds. You notice a pattern after a while."

"In this case, I think you're right. Turner's body language is very confident even though his looks don't back it up."

Turner picked up his phone. Put it to his ear. Spoke a few times. Nodded, and set the phone down. His smile faded. He talked to Flores.

She looked serious. Tense.

Elena leaned forward. "I wonder what that was about."

"Good question." Carver kept watching.

The answer arrived moments later. An unmarked car parked in front of a fire hydrant. The driver got out. Spoke to a valet. The valet nodded but didn't take the keys or the car. The driver went inside. Moved a chair from beside Turner. Set it on the side of the table so he could sit between him and Flores.

"Who's this guy?" Elena asked.

Carver knew it from the moment he saw the car. "It's Lieutenant Dan."

CHAPTER 26

Dan looked like the cat who ate the canary.

He swaggered in. Moved a chair. Sat to the side of the table even though it obstructed the aisle. The server looked irritated when they returned to the table. They didn't ask Dan to move, though.

Elena looked at Carver. "What does this mean? They're all in on it or they don't know?"

"Good question." Carver focused on Dan's lips. Thanks to his position, he was directly facing him. He couldn't make out much. Something about the investigation.

Elena got up and walked across the road. She knelt behind Dan's car. Put her hand beneath it. Got up, walked back over to Carver.

"What was that about?"

"I put a tracker on his car." She opened her hand to reveal small black objects about the size and shape of watch batteries. "More goodies I got along with the leech."

"I like it." Carver turned the monocular on the valet parking lot. He considered Flores' car. Wondered if it was worth tracking. Dan's certainly was.

Elena made the decision for him. She skipped across the road. Walked into the valet parking lot like she owned it. Knelt behind Flores' car and stuck a tracker to it. A valet parked a car and approached her. She smiled at him. Said a few words. He grinned. Nodded. Walked away.

She walked down the sidewalk away from the valet station. Crossed the road further down so the same guy wouldn't see her rejoining Carver.

Carver turned his gaze back to Dan. He and the others were looking at the sketch of Carver. It was generic. Almost useless. There was no scale for size. The face was plain. It could be anyone with a few muscles.

He'd only known it was him because Price had been asking for Carver.

Elena used the camera on her phone to zoom in on the sketch. "You'd think a pro like Jones would hire a better sketch artist."

"You seem good at reading people. You didn't pick up on anything when you talked to her?"

"Not a thing." Elena shook her head. "She seemed like just another news reporter looking for a scoop until she tried to kill me."

"Skill." Carver kept watching Dan. "You're lucky she thought you were useful in Morganville."

"I don't feel lucky."

"You're alive."

"Barely." Elena leaned back. "Finding the truth is a dangerous line of work."

"Yep. Probably not worth the money."

Elena stiffened. "It's not about the money. It's about exposing the unvarnished truth to the people."

Carver glanced at her. "There's pain behind those words. That kind of conviction comes from personal experience."

"My dad died doing what he believed in."

"He was a reporter?"

"A detective turned reporter." She bit her bottom lip. "He couldn't do anything about the corruption he saw in the police department. He went to a local newspaper. Nobody would bite. He tried other news organizations. They said they didn't believe him. That it sounded like a disgruntled employee trying to get revenge. Then the police chief called him in. Took his badge away. Told him to play ball and he'd get it back."

"Doesn't sound like he played ball," Carver said.

"He didn't. He quit. He learned how to write news articles. Found a small paper that was lean and hungry for real news. He gave them the article. The editor had some concerns about sourcing since my dad was the primary source. But my dad had secretly recorded several meetings."

"Other newspapers didn't think recordings were good enough?"

"They didn't want the story to get out because the owner was connected to politicians." Elena ran a hand down her face. "News organizations used to fight the machine. They kept people honest. These days they're part of the machine. They act in lockstep with politicians and government to spread propaganda, not truth. It's because they're more about entertainment than news."

"Most people want to avoid conflict, so they do what's easy." Carver shrugged. "It's human nature."

"You didn't do what was easy in Morganville. You did the right thing, albeit in the most violent way possible."

"No comment." Carver turned his attention back to Dan, Flores, and Turner. "It'd be nice if I could hear them."

"Maybe I could get near them."

"Bad idea. Dan knows what you look like and you're on the dead list."

"I just want to know if they're in cahoots or if Dan is using them." Elena stood. "It's worth the risk."

Carver held her wrist. "No, it's not. Be patient."

She sat down.

"What happened to your dad?"

Elena stared blankly at the restaurant. "His story barely caused a ripple. Politicians said it was disinformation. That the newspaper was a little local gossip rag that couldn't be taken seriously. Not long after, a big media company bought his newspaper. They fired the editor and put a corporate guy in his place. They told my dad to toe the company line or quit."

"Let me guess. He quit."

"Yep." Elena looked proud. "I was young, but I remember the bad years. He was gone a lot, investigating. I hardly saw him at all. I don't know how my parents scraped by. And then he faxed news stories to hundreds of different news organizations. Apparently, he'd spent those years finding rock-solid evidence, documented it carefully, and made the story irrefutable."

"His recordings weren't irrefutable?"

"No one openly admitted wrongdoing, so they weren't solid enough to be used as evidence." She pounded a fist on the bench. "This time the bastards couldn't deny it. He had everything. One big media empire ran the story because they politically opposed the mayor. Other news organizations finally picked it up and ran with it because they had no choice."

"He win the Pulitzer?"

She shook her head. "No. He wasn't even nominated. Two years later, he was found dead. Presumably murdered by a junkie. The junkie was shot and killed by police. It was all tied up very nice and neat."

"Drug addicts are excellent scapegoats." Carver lowered the monocular since Dan and the others were eating and not talking. "You want to be like your father?"

"Yes, except I want to survive."

"So far so good," Carver said.

"Except I've never uncovered anything major in my life until your story."

"You still haven't uncovered anything."

"And if I do, will you threaten to kill me?"

Carver shook his head. "No. Looks like Dan and his killer are already on the job."

"Except the killers are dead."

"Two are dead. Once they figure out I'm not an assassin, they'll find someone else."

"You're a target too. It would be better if you let me publish the truth about Morganville."

Carver shook his head. "Publish what you want but keep me out of it."

She turned sideways to face him. "Breakstone is part of a conspiracy covering up what really happened in Morganville. You can expose them."

Carver shook his head again. "Breakstone has friends in high places. In Congress. In the military. In federal law enforcement. Too many important people connected to that business to let it fail. Exposing them won't do squat."

"But why is Breakstone so important?" Elena threw up her hands. "It's a private security firm. There's nothing special about that."

"Their dearly departed CEO had big plans."

She nodded. "I went back and watched all his speeches I could find. He wanted to privatize some aspects of domestic security that are usually handled by the government."

Carver considered keeping his mouth shut. He considered keeping the truth from her. Whatever he told her would probably end up in the news. It was dumb to let her tag along with him. She'd eventually get a picture of him. Then his face would be all over the news. He'd be a wanted man. Even more wanted than he was now.

His biggest strength was his anonymity. Or at least the shreds of it he had left. Breakstone taking the credit for the cartel massacre was a gift to him. It meant only a select few knew what he'd done. They wanted to keep it that way. They didn't want the truth to get out. It would ruin a lot more than just Breakstone. It would ruin powerful people.

That was why they wanted to take him out quietly. That was why they wanted to kill Elena and anyone else who might have a shred of information. It was a lot of people to kill, but apparently it was acceptable in the big picture.

"You went quiet again." Elena sighed. "I was so excited about finding you. I thought you'd have so much to tell me. Finally, I'd be doing something important with my life. But it seems you're just as willing to let them get away with whatever they did."

"It's a matter of self-preservation. For you and for me." Carver turned to her. "You have a good job. Keep your head low. Enjoy your life. Don't spend it trying to bring other people down even if it's for a good cause."

"What a cynical thing to say." She huffed. "That's really rich coming from you, especially after what you did."

"I did what I did to survive. An old squad mate needed help." Carver clammed up before he said more. "Look at where this has gotten you. You're on a kill list right next to me."

"And I'd do it again if it meant bringing scumbags to justice."

Carver didn't see a point in arguing it. He turned back to the restaurant. Elena took the hint and stopped talking too. She rested her face in her hand and stayed that way for a while. Carver let her be. It was better that way.

Dan and company finished eating. He took out his phone and showed Flores and Turner a picture. In it was a middle-aged chubby white guy.

"You recognize that person?" Carver put the monocular in Elena's hand.

She flinched out of her sullen mood and lifted it to her eye. "I've seen him before, but I don't remember where."

Carver took the monocular back. He thought of something else. "Can you drive the Audi somewhere else? Park it out of sight? Dan's seen it before. We're lucky he didn't notice it on the way in."

"Sure." Elena took the keys. Got in the car. Drove it away.

Carver wished he had a spotting scope like the one he'd used on missions. It had a camera. He could have snapped a picture of the image on the phone. In those days he would have uploaded it for a facial recognition scan.

Those gadgets made life easy. Almost too easy. The kind of intel that had to be gathered in person in the old days could now be found with the stroke of a few computer keys. The old-school spies had better instincts. Better personal skills.

Elena returned. "I found a spot two blocks back." She gave him the keys. "Even though it's Miami."

"Thanks." He pocketed them. Went back to watching the restaurant.

Dan dropped some money on the table. He got up and left. Flores and Turner kept talking.

Elena watched Dan get into his car. "What now?"

"Let's hope the tracker works. We can't follow him in the Audi. He'll recognize it from a mile away."

"Should we keep watching these two?"

"What we need is to get your leech next to Turner's computer. I just don't know if it's better to try here or in his hotel room."

Elena pursed her lips. "I could distract them somehow."

Carver thought it over. Maybe they could wait for one of them to go to the bathroom. Distract the one left behind. The problem was, if they were working with Dan, then they might recognize Elena. They might recognize him.

Trying to leech the laptop in the hotel room would be a challenge too. There was no place to hide in there. No place to lie in wait. He'd have to get inside while Turner was asleep. Without a keycard there was no quiet way to do that.

The only thing to do was to be patient and wait. An opportunity would present itself eventually. Or it might not. If Turner was shuttling back and forth from the hotel to the police department, then it was highly unlikely.

Carver had the element of surprise. A lurker in the shadows. Stepping out of the shadows and trying to leech the laptop with a ruse would only reveal him. They'd know he was waiting and watching. They would become wary.

He just didn't see another way to do it.

Maybe it was best to go for Dan instead. Turner and Flores seemed guilty by association. Maybe they weren't Maybe they were just pawns. Dan was the most likely link to the top.

Elena showed Carver her phone. The map app was open. On it was a blip. "That's Dan."

He was headed for South Beach. Straight down Collins Avenue.

"Carver look." Elena pointed to the restaurant.

Turner was gone. Flores was sitting at the table alone. Turner's laptop was across the table from her. She looked toward the back of the restaurant. Toward the bathrooms. Turned the laptop around and started flipping through screens. She opened a file.

A picture of Doug Weaver appeared. She clicked the mouse. A picture of Elena appeared. Below it was a paragraph of text. Too small to read with the monocular. Next was a picture of another woman. Carver read the name aloud. "Lisa Gallagher."

Elena sucked in a breath. "I wonder if she's still alive."

Carver kept watching Flores. He couldn't tell if she was trying to look at the computer files without Turner knowing. She didn't seem to be in a hurry. There were more files. Pictures of Leach, Theresa, and Nicki. Leach was collapsed on the ground in the image. Theresa was in a pool of blood. Nicki lay broken in a dumpster.

They were crime scene photos. Nothing special. Nothing important. The images of Weaver, Elena, and Gallagher were different. There was no reason for Turner to have those pictures on his laptop. No reason except the subjects were targets.

The question was, did Flores know they were targets? Or had they connected them with the investigation? Maybe Leach had woven the threads together before he died in the back alley.

Turner returned from the bathroom. Flores kept reading the text next to the pictures. She was apparently authorized to look at the laptop. She pulled up the picture of Gallagher again. Spun around the laptop. Said something.

Turner nodded. Said something back. They spoke for a while longer. Flores left for the bathroom. Turner closed his laptop. Paid the check. Flores returned and they got in her car and drove off.

Carver stood and stretched. "You have a phone number for Lisa Gallagher?"

"Yeah. I copied it off my phone."

"Call her."

Elena dialed. Called the number. It rang a few times. Someone answered. "Hello, is Lisa there?" She put it on speaker phone.

"Who is this?" The voice was male. Sad.

"I'm a reporter from Atlanta. She and I are working on a story."

The voice sobbed. Carver knew what was coming next. Elena gave him a look. She knew too.

"Is something wrong?" Elena asked.

"Lisa—" He sobbed again. "Lisa took her own life yesterday."

CHAPTER 27

Lisa hadn't taken her own life.

Of that, Carver was certain.

Elena gave her condolences to the man, apparently Lisa's husband. She ended the call. Wiped tears from her eyes. "I got her killed with just an email."

"It wasn't the email that got her killed. It was the reply." Carver put a hand on her shoulder. "Not your fault. You were both just doing your jobs."

"Yeah, and someone else was just doing their job too. Probably Nicki Jones."

Carver nodded. "The timelines fit. She probably killed Gallagher the night she tried to kill Pete."

"That evil bitch." Elena banged her fist on the bench. "Why does she even have all those knives if she kills them with drugs instead?"

"The knives are for killing or compliance, whatever she needs." Carver made a finger gun. "Just like someone holding you at gunpoint. Except knives are up close and personal. Makes it easier to inject someone."

"You said Theresa stabbed Detective Leach, though. Why not make that look like an accident?"

"I don't know. Maybe it was a spur of the moment decision. Maybe Leach didn't cooperate. He fought back when she tried to inject him. That way everyone would know he was murdered and didn't kill himself or die of a heart attack."

"Makes sense." Elena flexed her fists. "What now?"

"Where is Dan?"

She checked her phone. "Setai Hotel." She whistled. "That's a fifteen hundred a night room."

"Either the government is paying the tab, or he's a big spender like Theresa." Carver started walking down the sidewalk. "Let's pay him a visit."

"Are we going to use the same trick to find his room number?"

"I don't think we'll need to. It's early. A guy like that isn't going to stay in his room. He's either got more business or he'll go looking for pleasure."

"You sound awfully sure of yourself." Elena pointed out where she'd parked the car. "How do you know?"

"Just a gut feeling." He dropped into the car. Started it. "Where's your motel?"

"Back on the mainland, why?" She buckled in.

"We need a ruse. Something to get him back to his room."

"I have no idea how we'd do that."

"Simple. You're one of my targets."

Elena stared blankly at him. "And?"

"I need to make it look like you're dead."

"Oh, smart." She nodded. "With some creative makeup, I can make it look like you beat me to death or shot me."

"No, it's supposed to look like an accidental or natural death." He shifted the car into gear. "Where's the motel?"

She showed him on the map. He put the phone on the center console and followed directions.

"Um, so how are you going to make it look like either of those?"

"Suicide works too." He stopped at a traffic light. Pulled out his burner phone and ran a search. "Quick stop."

"What are you thinking?"

"Suicide is the easiest. I can make it look more realistic." He turned a few corners. Took the causeway to the mainland. Drove through Little Haiti.

"Explain."

"Gallagher's man never said how she died, did he?"

"No."

"How do you think she did it?"

"How do I think Nicki faked it?" Elena shrugged. "Certainly wasn't a bullet to the head."

"What's her modus operandi?"

"Knives and poisons."

Carver nodded. "So, what do you think?"

"She drugged her." Elena frowned. Thought about it. Snapped her fingers. "I know how she did it."

"Then that's what we're going to do with you." He stopped at a small shop. "Be right back." Carver went inside. Found the guy behind the meat counter. Told him what he wanted. The man nodded and brought back a small container. An American might think the request was strange, but it wasn't strange for an islander.

Carver put it in a bag. Went back to the car and got in. Gave it to Elena. "Don't let it spill."

"You think this will really work?"

"It'll work well enough." They drove to her motel. It was a small, seedy place. Perfect for what was about to happen.

The room stank of stale cigarette smoke despite the no smoking signs inside. The bed was small. A blacklight would make the room look like a crime scene. This was the kind of place that rented by the minute or hour too.

"Let's do it." Carver checked the time. Checked the tracking app. Dan's car was still at the hotel. It was possible he'd taken a taxi somewhere else. But he seemed like the kind of guy to go to the bar.

He turned on the bath faucet. Let it fill. He checked the temperature. Made sure it was warm. Might as well be comfortable while filming a fake suicide scene. The old tub had mineral rings and rusty stains. It might be clean, but it looked filthy.

Elena opened the container from the butcher shop. It was a pint of pig blood. "How are we going to fake the wounds?"

"We don't need to. The bloody water will cover it up."

"Okay."

Carver turned off the water when the tub was almost full. "Get in."

She looked down at herself. "Fully clothed?"

"That's how most people do it. Take off their shoes, get in with the clothes on."

"That's really how most people do it?"

He shrugged. "I don't know. Just from my experience."

"Your experience revolves around killing people."

"Maybe I'm wrong."

"I think so." She grabbed a towel. Left the bathroom. "I don't want blood all over my clothes. I didn't pack a lot."

"Fine with me." Carver waited in the bathroom. Gave some thought about how to stage the scene.

Elena returned with a towel wrapped around her. She stood next to Carver. Looked at the tub. "Want me to just get in?"

He tapped a finger on his chin. "Hold on." He searched for images on his phone. Looked them over.

Elena shivered. "That's sickening."

"Can you make your face look paler? Make your lips a little blue?"

"Yeah. Looks like all that work I did dressing up as a zombie for Halloween is finally going to pay off." She opened a makeup bag. Applied powder to her face. Dabbed on some other colors to make her skin different shades of brown with dark patches under the eyes.

She finished it off with powder on her lips. The final effect was convincing. Elena stuck out her tongue and tilted her head like she was dead.

"Looks good," Carver said.

"It took me countless tutorials to learn how to do that for Halloween." Elena looked at the tub again. "Okay. Let's do this." She removed the towel. Dropped it on the floor. Stepped into the tub. Carefully lowered herself into the water. Rested her head on the back of the tub.

Carver opened the pint of blood.

Elena shivered. "This tub makes me feel so dirty."

"It's a motel tub." Carver carefully poured the blood into the water, lining it up with Elena's arms. The water clouded quickly. Hid her body beneath the water. He took the burner phone. Switched to the camera app.

Elena slumped to the side. Opened her mouth slightly. Kept her eyelids half open.

"You're good at looking dead."

"Shut up and take the pictures."

He took them from all angles. Poured in more blood. Took more pictures. "That's good enough." He reached down and unplugged the tub. "Clean up and let's go." He turned to leave.

Elena rose from the bloody water. "God, look at me, Carver."

He turned. Bloody water sluiced down her naked form. She looked like she'd crawled out of a grave. But she looked damned good doing it.

She held out her hands. Looked at them. "I feel like I'm in a horror movie starring me."

"You are." Carver stepped out of the bathroom. "Shower off. We need to get going." He closed the door.

The shower turned on. Elena came out a few minutes later, hair wet. Towel wrapped around her.

Carver watched the blip on the tracking app. Dan was still at the hotel. That was good. It meant he was probably looking for love at the bar. They had to catch him before he went to his room.

"You might be a killer, but at least you're a gentleman, Carver." Elena was in another set of dark yoga pants and shirt. "You do like women, right?"

"I do." He looked up from the phone. "Within reason."

"Within reason?" She laughed. "What does that mean?"

"Being in a relationship is like being back in the military. Someone else wants to call the shots. Tell me what to do." He shrugged. "I like being my own boss."

"Was Paola bossy?"

Carver shook his head. "She's a good woman. Adventurous. She wanted to travel. See the world."

"And you've already traveled the world. You've seen the worst it has to offer."

"Exactly. She was a cartel slave. Forced to live in a small town. Forced to watch a fat man brutalize women. Forced to sit by while he killed them or lent them out like animals." Carver opened the room door. "She needed to see the good in life. Have some fun."

Elena put a hand on his arm. "Maybe you could use some fun too, Carver."

"That's why I like staying near a beach." He stepped outside. "Sun and fun."

"You don't look like the kind of guy who has fun."

"I can try. I can watch other people have fun." He showed her the pictures on the phone. "What do you think?"

"I think I look dead."

"Good. Let's hope Dan thinks the same thing." Carver got in the car.

Elena slid in and buckled up. "You ever been snow or water skiing? Have you ever sat next to a river in an old European city and enjoyed a bottle of wine?"

"I caroused with Ukrainians at a backwoods pub in the middle of winter." Rhodes had been with him. It had been the first time in a long while that they'd been able to relax between missions. "It was nice."

"Your definition of nice differs greatly from mine." Elena laughed. "I think you enjoy spying more than you do relaxing on the beach."

Carver shook his head. "No. This is just necessary. When something gets in the way of your life, you can either deal with it, go around it, or just stay in place. I'm more of a deal with it kind of guy."

"Obviously. Most people would be scared to death to deal with assassins and corrupt federal agents."

"I wouldn't blame them. There's no right or wrong. You just do what works best for you."

"Understatement of the year." Elena laughed again. "Have you spoken with Paola since the last time you saw her?"

"No reason to." Carver checked the map app and followed the directions to Dan's hotel. The tracking app said his car was still there.

"What do you want me to do while you're meeting with Dan? I can hide somewhere and record you talking to him."

"No." Carver shook his head. "Don't take my picture. Don't record me, okay?"

"But—"

"Promise me, okay?"

She sighed. "Fine. But it's counterproductive. He might say something incriminating."

"Maybe, but your phone won't pick up what he's saying from across the room."

"True. Maybe you could set your phone to record him while you're there."

Carver's plan didn't involve gathering evidence. He wasn't a cop. He wasn't a federal agent. He was just a man who wanted to be left alone. To do that, he had to find out who wanted him dead. He could treat symptoms all day long, but until he rooted out the cause of the problem, he wouldn't know peace.

Hopefully Dan would fall for the ruse. Hopefully, Dan would lead Carver to the source. Or at least provide information leading him there. Carver didn't know much about the man. He might be too perceptive to be fooled. Too smart to give Carver what he wanted.

Carver had dealt with plenty of people like Dan. Go-betweens and messengers who were just pawns in the greater scheme of things. Some were smarter than others. Some had more tactical awareness than others.

Dan was probably a corrupt federal agent. Someone who worked both sides against the middle. He'd become moderately wealthy from his position. That usually made someone cocky. Overconfident. It made them easy pickings for someone like Carver.

In about five minutes, Carver would know what kind of man Dan was. Maybe Dan would pretend to go along with the ruse. Maybe he would turn the tables on Carver. Maybe he already knew Carver wasn't the real assassin and was just playing along.

There were endless possibilities. Rhodes was the kind of person who would sit down and think about everything. Formulate a plan. Create contingencies in case things went sideways. Everyone had a role, a part to play.

Carver wasn't like that. Trying to think through everything just paralyzed him. To know something, he had to see it in action. Deal with it head-on. It wasn't elegant. It wasn't smart. But it worked for him.

The hotel was about what he'd expected from a place that charged fifteen hundred bucks a night. It was more modern than the Betsy. Had more glam and glitter. But like every place, it was run by people. People who were just as fallible as everyone else.

He slowed and pulled into a handicap parking spot on a side road. "Don't go inside. Don't risk letting him see you. There's a coffee shop around the corner. You can wait there."

Elena scowled. "I can buy a ball cap or something to hide my face. I can find a dark corner and watch from there. You might need backup. I promise I won't record anything."

Carver gave it some thought. Whether he said yes or no, she'd do what she wanted. She was a reporter. Someone who risked her life to get a story. He didn't know Elena well. He'd only known her for a few hours.

From the little he knew she was the kind of person you wanted on your side. The kind of person who'd watch your back. She might not be military trained, but she'd do her best to help. If Carver died, she probably wouldn't survive long.

So, as long as she didn't give up the game before it started, there was no sense leaving her out in the cold.

"Why are you staring at me like that? I'm a big girl. I can take care of myself."

"Okay. Just wait outside until I send you a text. I don't want him seeing you."

"Okay." She smiled. "See? It's not so hard working with someone."

Carver turned the car around. Drove it to the valet station. The young guy gave him a ticket and drove the car into the parking garage. Elena walked down the sidewalk away from the front. Carver went inside.

The bar was on the other side of the lobby. It was nice enough for a hotel bar. It was crowded too. There were people dressed casually. Some dressed like they were ready for a night on the town. Others lounging in shorts and flip-flops.

Dan was at the bar. Alone. Drinking a martini. He wasn't talking to anyone. Wasn't looking at anyone. Just staring at his phone screen. Cracking a smile every so often. It wasn't what Carver expected.

He observed the man for a while. Waited to see if Dan would spot him. He was too preoccupied with his phone. That meant he was either cocky or just felt completely safe. Like nothing could get to him.

His safety was an illusion. The moment he'd become involved in this situation, he'd stepped out of normal life and into something completely different.

Carver decided it was time to shatter that illusion completely.

CHAPTER 28

Carver sat down next to Dan.

The other man looked up briefly from his phone. He flinched. "Holy shit, where'd you come from?"

"It's done."

"Which one?"

"Diaz."

Dan nodded. "You have proof?"

"Yep." Carver pulled out his phone. Showed him a photo of Elena playing dead in the tub.

"Suicide? Nice."

"Let's discuss payment."

Dan put his hand over the phone to cover the image. "Not here."

Carver nodded. "Where, then?"

"My room. I'll confirm and authorize payment."

"Let's go." Carver stepped away from the bar while Dan paid. He texted Elena. *Heading to his room in a few minutes.*

She replied. *Wow, sex already? You move fast.*

Carver tucked the phone in a pocket. Dan joined him. They walked to the elevator lobby. Dan punched the up button. An elevator arrived and they stepped in. Carver wasn't surprised when Dan pressed the penthouse button.

"Living the good life?"

Dan nodded. "Enjoy life while you have it."

Carver realized something. Something he should have realized before he got on the elevator. Dan's posture was different now. He looked confident. Like everything was under control. Like a hired assassin hadn't just appeared at his hotel.

He hadn't asked how Carver found him. Hadn't looked worried that Carver knew where he was staying. His demeanor at their first meeting had been assured. Confident. He hadn't seemed like the type of person to blindly stare at a phone.

Dan broke the silence. "How'd you find Diaz?"

Dan realized Carver was thinking. Realized Carver knew something was off. They were two floors from the penthouse. Two heartbeats away from that final stop.

Carver pounded the emergency stop button. The elevator jolted to a halt. He lunged at Dan. Dan dodged sideways. Tugged a gun from behind his back. It was a slim profile Glock. Not great from a distance, but in an elevator, it would work as well as anything else.

Carver threw out an arm. Hit Dan's wrist. He grabbed it. Squeezed. The gun fell from limp fingers. Dan's knee came up fast. Carver turned sideways. Caught the blow on his thigh instead of the groin.

His forearm slammed into Dan's neck. Pinned him to the wall. The emergency stop bell was ringing. They were one floor down from the penthouse. "How many people are waiting up there?"

Dan wheezed. Struggled. "What gave it away?"

Carver shifted. Twisted the other man's arm behind his back. Shoved his face against the wall. He hit the emergency stop button. Pressing it had reset the other buttons, so it wasn't still going to the penthouse. He hit the button for the fourth floor.

Dan tried to move. Groaned in pain. "What are you doing?"

"Taking you somewhere quiet. I have some questions."

"You'll want to reconsider that. We have the reporter."

"You knew I wasn't the assassin you hired from the moment we met. You realized I was one of the targets. There's no way a hired anonymous assassin would have set their hotel as a meeting place."

"I assume you heard me when I said we have the reporter. My people have Elena."

Carver kept talking. "You knew Theresa, or whatever her name was. You knew Nicki too. They're not hired assassins. They're assets. Maybe even agents."

"In case you're deaf, I said—"

Carver slammed Dan's head against the elevator wall. "I'm not deaf. I just don't care." The elevator stopped. The doors slid open. No one was waiting outside so it saved Carver an awkward explanation.

He kept Dan's arm twisted. Stooped down and grabbed the Glock from the floor. Tucked it into his back pocket. Then he shoved Dan into the hallway. Grabbed him by the back of the neck and pushed him forward.

There was a floor diagram on the wall. It showed where the icemaker was. There were vending machines in the same rooms. There was also a small game room. Carver took Dan to the icemaker room. The cooling fans were at full speed. Loud enough to wake the dead. Loud enough to cover up shouts of pain.

He shoved Dan between the machines. Pulled the gun and held it low. "How'd you know I was coming tonight?"

Dan stared at the gun. Moved his eyes up to Carver. "You really don't care about the reporter, do you?"

"All I care about is being left alone. You tell me who wants me dead and why. I'll make a decision. Maybe you live, maybe you die."

"Facial recognition picked up the girl yesterday outside the police station. She looked right at a camera. You didn't. We just saw your size and knew it was you. You followed Flores and Turner. We didn't need to follow you. You came to us. I got a guy to come watch you, then I put in an appearance."

"Flores and Turner are in on this, whatever this is."

Dan laughed. "Hardly. But they're useful to me."

Carver tossed out another question. "Which federal agency are you with?"

Dan bared his teeth. "Carver, you don't have a clue, do you? If you'd just died in Morganville like you were supposed to, we wouldn't have all this collateral damage. Elena Diaz wouldn't have to die." He smiled. Held up his hands in surrender. "I think you care for her. Just a little. After all, you helped that Brazilian woman."

"She benefitted from my actions. It's not the same as helping." Carver took out his phone. There was another text from Elena. *I'm still waiting. When can I go in?* It was from two minutes ago. Maybe they had her, maybe they didn't. He sent her a text.

Dan kept looking confident. He was a good actor. "We have her."

"Keep talking. I think I know how you knew, but I want to hear it from your mouth."

"My guy saw Elena put a tracker on the cars. I knew you'd come to me. I set things up and waited. It was easy."

"What's your relationship to Theresa and Nicki?"

"We can skip all the side talk. Get straight to business." Dan straightened his shoulders. Lowered his hands. "My client wants to ensure all chatter about Morganville is quieted. You are a huge loose end. We need to ensure you're taken off the board."

"I've been off the board. What about the Morganville PD? You plan to kill all of them?"

He shook his head. "They're playing ball. The FBI shut them down and tied up the investigation."

"Okay, so why come after me? I haven't been talking to anyone."

"We decided to let things die down. Figured you'd keep your mouth shut." Dan sighed. "Diaz got nosy. Started asking questions. They were the right questions to make her a blip on the radar."

"That was her making noise, not me."

Dan shrugged. "We decided to let it play out. Maybe she could find you and we could put a nail in this thing. It seemed like a bonus to take you out."

"Efficient and clean. Except you should have left me well enough alone. Now I've got to tie up my own loose ends." Carver backed into the hallway and looked around to make sure no one was coming. He stepped back inside the room. "Who's at the top? Who do I have to kill to make it go away?"

"Oof." Dan blew out a breath. "You pissed off too many people with Morganville, Carver. You might have been better off leaving the country after that."

"You're blowing it out of proportion. Some people aren't happy. Some are irate. Some are mad enough to do what it takes to make me dead." Carver shrugged. "That tier of people is going to be small. Very small. Maybe one or two people, tops. People talk big, but when it comes to taking action, they don't have what it takes."

"You have an interesting way of seeing the world, Carver." Dan shook his head. "Let's go upstairs. Let's talk this out. Maybe we can prevent a lot of bloodshed and end this another way."

Carver shook his head. "Dan, whatever your name is, I'm going to give you one more chance to answer me. If I don't get a straight answer, I'm going to end you. Then I will keep hunting for whoever is behind this and end them. Maybe I'll get killed, maybe I'll succeed. Either way, it's better than listening to you for another minute."

"Fine!" Dan held up his hands in surrender again. "I'm with Breakstone. Theresa and Nicki were sisters also working for Breakstone. It's part of a new initiative. Branching off from Dorsey's vision of a privatized military."

"Only Breakstone and not government agencies?"

Dan nodded. "The new CEO, Leon Fry is the one pushing for it."

Carver's eye twitched. "Fry is the CEO of Breakstone?"

"You know him?"

Carver had served with him. He'd been in Scion with Angel, Menendez, Rocker, Rhodes, Jericho. After Scion had been disbanded, several former squad members went to work for Breakstone.

Rhodes had found out Breakstone was behind the disbanding of the squad. Behind the human trafficking allegations against Carver. Rocker and Menendez had staged it. The military police had done their job. Their special unit had been disbanded.

Menendez found out Rhodes had tracked down the women used to frame Carver. She'd contacted Carver. Told him she needed his help. He'd shown up, but Menendez knew he was coming. He'd worked it into a plan. Kill Rhodes. Frame Carver for her murder.

Carver had been arrested and tossed in the Morganville jail. A corrupt cop and two Breakstone specialists had tried to kill him that night. It hadn't worked out for them. Now Rocker, Menendez, and former CEO, Chad Dorsey, were dead. But Breakstone lived on.

And it seemed Leon Fry had been in on the frame from the get-go. That was disappointing. It was surprising. But it was reality. And Carver had to deal with it.

"Let's make a deal." Dan lowered his hands. Held them out pleadingly. "You go on living your life. We'll release the reporter. Talk things over with Fry. Make him agree to leave you alone."

"If I let you go now, you'll warn him. It'll make things even more difficult." Carver shook his head. "I can't trust him, that's apparent. I can't trust you, either."

"So, you're going to kill me even if I promise to release the reporter?"

"I don't think you have her."

Dan pointed his hand toward a square shape in his front pants pocket. "Can I show you something on my phone?"

"Yes."

Dan slid it out with two fingers. He turned on the screen. Rotated it toward Carver. Elena was in a chair, bound. She didn't look scared. She looked furious. "Carver, we have her. I know you don't care, but if we can come to an agreement, we can all walk away alive."

"Or I can kill you, then go upstairs and kill whoever is up there."

"And make a huge mess. Bodies everywhere. Cops looking for you. Morganville got tied up in a neat little bow. No nationwide manhunt for a vigilante killer." Dan shrugged. "This won't be the same. I can guarantee you that."

He was right. Carver had done his best to avert his face when walking near cameras, but he wasn't perfect. His face had been recorded somewhere. If he left a trail of dead bodies at the hotel, all hell would break loose.

This wasn't a Podunk town with an incompetent police force. This was Miami. They had the resources and the personnel to hunt him down. Somehow, he had to reach a deal with Dan. Figure out a way to put the final nail in the coffin with Breakstone.

Maybe that meant killing Leon Fry. Maybe that meant striking a deal. He didn't have much of a choice in this situation.

Carver made a decision. "Let's go upstairs. First sign of an ambush and you're dead."

"I understand."

"I hope so." Carver walked him to the stairwell. "Let's get some exercise." Dan's people would be watching the elevators. Maybe they wouldn't be watching the stairwells.

Dan sighed. "You really think I won't have anyone watching the stairs?"

"The elevator is a kill box. No way to retreat." Carver prodded him to start climbing.

Dan huffed. Started up the stairs. They reached the top floor. Carver knew the basic layout of the penthouse level. Like the Betsy, it was divided into two penthouses. A single hallway with the elevator lobby ran between them.

Dan's crew would know things hadn't gone to plan. They'd know something was wrong. Since Dan hadn't sent them a text about his situation, they'd assume Carver had him. If they had no hostage, they would've come looking.

But they had a hostage. They could afford to sit and wait. Or so they thought. Carver didn't want Elena to die. Hell, he hadn't wanted Theresa to die. But they all had one thing in common. They compromised his safety.

Some people were willing to die for a cause. Carver had been like that once. He'd believed everything the military spoon fed him. He'd believed that his superiors had the best interests of the nation in mind with every decision they made.

He'd been wrong. Some people were true believers. Most people were just doing a job. Other people were actively enriching themselves on the backs of others. Throwing lives away just for a dollar.

Breakstone was just the latest example. Chad Dorsey had been willing to kill for a profit. Now it seemed Leon Fry was willing to do the same. Carver saw a path. Saw what he had to do to end this.

The trick would be getting Dan to agree with it. If he did, then Elena could walk out of here alive and free. Carver would take care of business. Then everyone could go on living their lives.

Carver paused at the door to the penthouse hallway. "Who sent the assassins after me and the reporters?"

"Leon." Dan stood facing the door. "Why?"

"If he's dead, will the next CEO send more?"

"No. Most of the board was against the move. But Leon said loose ends needed to be tied off."

"How many people on the board?"

"Just four. Used to be Chad Dorsey, Tony Menendez, Sam Rocker, and Leon Fry. Then you killed three of them so Fry became the CEO."

"Who owns the company?"

"Dorsey owned it privately. It was his personal kingdom. In order to get the others to help him realize his vision, he gave them ten percent each with bonuses. There was a lot of complicated succession planning, and that's how Leon inherited the CEO position."

Carver didn't know much about how corporations worked. He didn't really care. "You can guarantee that Breakstone will leave me alone if Fry is out of the picture?"

"I'm not a board member, but I think they would be more than happy to put everything behind them. They want to get back to the basics. Become a normal security contractor again, not a privatized military arm of the United States."

Carver nodded. "Open the door."

Dan slowly opened the door. "Hold fire! It's me!"

The door swung open. Four men were in the hallway. Two were facing them. The others were guarding the elevator and other stairwell door. They wore the same dark military fatigues Carver had seen on Breakstone personnel in Morganville. No badges identifying them. Anonymous private soldiers.

Dan kept his hands high. "Carver and I are trying to come to an understanding. I want everyone to stand down."

The men rose. Kept their weapons at the low and ready position. Not aiming at Carver, but not at ease either. Carver held his ground.

"I want to see Elena."

Dan looked smug. "See? You do care about her."

"No sense in letting her die if I can help it. I've needlessly killed enough people in my life."

Dan looked like he wanted to argue, but he shrugged, conceding the point. "Bring her out, please."

One of the men opened the penthouse door to Carver's right. Another guy pushed a struggling Elena into the hallway. Her wrists were bound together. She was gagged. Like earlier, she looked more angry than afraid.

Carver admired her bravery. She was probably scared out of her mind. Probably figured she wasn't leaving here alive. But she wasn't begging. Wasn't crying. She was fighting to the end. And that was about all you could ask of someone.

If he played his cards right, maybe they could both walk out of here alive.

CHAPTER 29

Carver gripped Dan by the back of his neck.

"I'll trade him for Elena."

"No can do." One of the soldiers stepped forward. "I'm under strict orders not to release her."

Dan straightened his shoulders. "Did Leon tell you that, Blake?"

The other man nodded. "I updated him on the situation. Our orders are to end this at all costs."

"A shootout in a hotel?" Dan sighed. "Come on, man. This won't look good for Breakstone. It'll create a whole new headache for Washington. They might not bail us out this time."

Blake raised his rifle. "I'm sorry. Leon was adamant."

Carver kept Dan between him and the gun. "What if Leon wasn't giving the orders anymore?"

Blake hesitated. "What do you mean?"

"Leon used to be in my squad. He sold me out. Sold out the entire squad so he could push Breakstone's agenda of privatizing special forces and other military operations." Carver let that marinate a moment. "Dorsey, Menendez, and Rocker were part of the conspiracy. Now they're dead. The way I see it, there's just one more to go—Leon. You let Elena walk out of here with me, and I'll let everyone here live."

Blake laughed humorlessly. "You'll let us live?"

Carver nodded, dead serious. "I might die, but all of you will die with me. I promise."

The soldier next to Blake gulped. Glanced uneasily at one of the other soldiers.

"Blake, you saw what Carver did in Morganville." Dan held up his hands in surrender. "Please don't put that to the test now. I've heard you bitch and complain about Leon plenty of times. If he's willing to sacrifice me to kill Carver, then it's only a matter of time before it's one of you."

Blake worked his jaw back and forth. He looked at the other soldiers. "None of us are happy about the current situation. But we have a job to do."

Dan held out his hands pleadingly. "How about this? We let Elena and Carver escape. Carver finds Leon and kills him. Breakstone gets new leadership. Good leadership. Then everybody lives happily ever after?" He looked back and forth from Carver to Blake. "Otherwise, this fine hotel is going to turn into a slaughterhouse."

Elena stared at Carver. Her eyes looked uncertain. Like she didn't think Carver would agree to it.

"Come on, Carver." Dan gave him a pleading look. "Elena is going to die in the crossfire. You say you don't care, but I know you do."

Carver gripped Dan's neck a little tighter. "I want guarantees."

Dan winced. "Blake, buddy, what do you say?"

Blake huddled with the other soldiers. They seemed to be having a heated argument. Two of them got into a pushing match.

"Enough!" Blake roared. "We can go in circles all day."

"I don't like betrayal." One of the soldiers stepped back. "Leon is the leader, like it or not."

"He's betraying us," Dan said. "He said it was okay for you to kill one of your own!"

"Listen to reason, man!" Another soldier shook his head. "It's not betrayal if one of the pack is acting against our best interests."

The reluctant soldier looked at the floor. Jaw worked back and forth. "Fine, since I'm the odd man out. I'll agree, but I don't like it."

Blake stared at him. "You'll keep your mouth shut?"

He nodded. "We're brothers. We fight together, we stick together."

"That's what I like to hear," Dan said. "And Elena has to agree to never report on anything related to Breakstone."

Blake lowered her gag. "Do you agree?"

Elena stretched her jaw. "Yes, I agree."

Dan turned around slowly. "Carver, do we have a deal? You and Elena walk out of here happy and healthy. Then you and I can communicate about how to take care of our mutual problem."

Carver released his neck. "Untie Elena and let her walk over here. Then I'll send Dan over."

"Carver, you have to agree to help us with Leon if you want this to end." Dan faced him. "We can feed you intel and make it happen quick."

"Elena first."

Dan nodded. Looked at Blake. "Send her over."

The reluctant soldier cut the plastic cuffs off her wrists. Removed the gag. Blake took her by the elbow and escorted her away from the other soldiers. Let her go. Elena rubbed her wrists. Glanced back at the soldiers. Walked toward Carver.

She looked Dan up and down. Looked at Carver. Didn't say anything. Just walked behind him and stood there. Carver thought about the situation. About how little he knew Elena. What if she wasn't a reporter? What if she was just bait?

He imagined her pulling a gun behind his back. Aiming at the back of his head. Pulling the trigger. It was the perfect ruse. The perfect trap.

Carver jumped back a step. Put his back toward the corner. Faced her. She was looking at him with wide eyes. Confused.

"What was that about?"

Dan laughed. "Carver, you are the most paranoid SOB I've ever met. It's no wonder you survived so long in the field."

"You thought I was helping them?" Elena's mouth dropped open. "Did you think I was going to shoot you in the back?"

Carver shrugged. "I had some thoughts. Better safe than dead."

"It's no wonder Paola left you. Did you ever pull this on her?"

This wasn't the conversation that needed to happen right now. Carver took Dan's phone. "Unlock it."

Dan unlocked it.

Carver gave the phone to Elena. "Put in this number and text it." He gave her the number to a burner phone.

Elena did it. Handed it back to him. Carver gave it to Dan.

"If I take care of the problem, it better end things. It better mean you leave me alone."

"Breakstone will stay out of your life forever. I promise." Dan tucked his phone in a pocket. He nodded at the stairwell door. "So, go. I'll be in touch."

"Open the door and start walking, Elena." Carver stepped back from Dan.

Carver heard the door open behind him. Heard Elena walking on the stairs. He backed through the door. Closed it. Wished he had a way to block it. Hurried after Elena. He stepped out on the fourth floor. Led her to the elevator. They took it the rest of the way down.

They made it outside. Carver gave his ticket to the valet. The guy brought the car around a moment later. Carver tipped him and then he and Elena got in the car and drove off.

Elena glared at him. "You really thought I was a plant? That maybe I was part of an elaborate plot to engineer a standoff just so I could get behind you and shoot you? That's the craziest thing I ever heard."

"It was just a thought." Carver shrugged. "I'll drop you off at your motel. I suggest you go somewhere safe. Somewhere you don't have any connections. Keep low."

"Until what? Until I see that Leon Fry was murdered and Breakstone has new leadership?" Elena laughed scornfully. "There is no way in hell I'm missing out on this."

"You agreed not to report on it." Carver glanced at her. "All of this has to be kept secret. It means all your Breakstone stories die on the vine. Everything."

"There are ways around that. Besides, they kidnapped me! They broke the law. I can't just let that slide."

"That's your decision."

"You're not going to try to stop me?"

"I trust you to leave me out of it. Not because you promised me you would, but because you don't want me hunted down and arrested or killed." Carver stopped at a redlight. "Or, maybe you don't care at all."

"I do care. But I have instincts, Carver." Elena pounded a fist on the car door. "I don't like being in this situation. The juiciest story ever is dangling right over my head, and I can't touch it."

"Better than being hunted down and killed."

She huffed. "True."

Carver parked outside Elena's motel. "Just go home, okay?"

She shook her head. "I want to see this through. Like it or not, I'm part of this now."

"It's not a good idea."

"Getting out of bed every morning isn't a good idea, but I do it anyway." Elena opened her door. "I can't believe I dunked myself in that nasty bathtub and pig blood for nothing, though. I deserve an upgrade. I want to stay at the Betsy."

Carver figured if she was sticking around, it was better if he could keep an eye on her. "Fine. Get your things."

It didn't take her long to get her suitcase. She tossed it into her car. Followed Carver back to the Betsy. They dropped both cars at the valet and went inside. Up to the penthouse. Elena went into the bedroom. Locked the door and took a long shower.

Carver grabbed a beer. Went to the back deck and leaned on the railing. He listened to the waves crashing in the darkness. For the first time in days, he had a moment of peace. Maybe this would all be over soon.

Leon Fry.

It was hard to believe the idealistic youngest member of the squad had been in league with Menendez and Rocker. Then again, he'd always been a little impressionable. They must have talked him into it.

Leon wasn't that much younger than Carver. He'd seen a lot of action. It was easy to get jaded. Easy to think the world owed you more than it did. Carver still remembered the new kid on the squad. The one who hesitated to pull the trigger on a target. Almost threw an entire mission.

Then dead-scoped a headshot on a moving target from half a mile.

Leon wasn't someone you wanted ready for you. He wasn't a person who would miss if he saw you coming from a mile away. The element of surprise would be vital. Now Carver had an inside man. Inside information. This should be a walk in the park. But it never was.

"Are you brooding?" Elena leaned on the railing next to him. She was in shorts, a t-shirt, and sandals. Long hair in a tight bun. A beer in hand.

"I'm thinking about Leon."

"Will you ever tell me more about yourself? Where you came from? Your military experience?"

"Why should I?"

"Dan was talking about those other men like you knew them from before."

"I did."

"And Leon is one of them."

"Yes."

Elena motioned him to keep talking.

He didn't.

She rubbed her forehead. "Carver, it's not going to kill you to tell me what happened and why all this matters. Please."

Carver pulled up a chair next to the railing. He sat down. Crossed a leg. Motioned for Elena to join him. She slid her own chair across from his. Pulled it so close their knees were almost touching.

"I was in the blackest of black ops. Code named Scion. Off the radar. Secret chain of command. I only knew the first link, Rhodes."

"The police chief who was murdered in Morganville?"

Carver nodded. "Tony Menendez, Sam Rocker, Leon Fry, Jaqueline Rhodes, Jericho, and Angel. Sometimes others would join us. Most often it was just us. Rhodes and I were assigned to gather intel on the next Ukraine mission. We did that for a few days, then I was assigned a dark ride back to the nearest base. That means base security won't search the vehicle. They let it through the gate, no questions asked.

My ride was a military cargo truck. I climbed in back. There were four coffins strapped down inside. The truck drove onto base and into the cargo plane taking us back to the States. When we arrived home, military police raided the plane."

Elena tightened her fist. "Something was being smuggled in the coffins, right?"

"Women. They had oxygen masks. One was dead because her tank failed. The others told the MPs I kidnapped them. That I was involved in human trafficking. The hammer came down on the entire unit. They were all guilty by association. Scion was disbanded.

Rhodes discovered two of those women in Morganville. She was playing a role, gaining their trust. Trying to find out what really happened. She found out that the women were paid to finger me. That Rocker and Menendez had staged it.

"Why would they do that?"

"Because Breakstone was paying them to sabotage Scion. Breakstone was working behind the scenes to get other black ops squads disbanded and the members discharged. That made it easy for Breakstone to hire them. Made it easy for Congress to look at privatizing black operations."

Elena whistled. "That would make Breakstone a new kind of PMC. Who would they be accountable to?"

"Nothing and no one." Carver shrugged. "Or, just a select few individuals. I don't know how it was supposed to work. Breakstone knew about the drug trafficking at Whittaker Paint. Once the bill passed, they were going to carry out an operation against it. Paint it as a shining success of the new PMC bill."

"That bill would have meant Breakstone could break all the laws it wanted in the name of safety." Elena sipped her beer. "And make billions doing it, I'd bet."

"Yep." Carver stared at the darkness. "Rhodes sent me a message. She wanted me to come see what she'd found. Menendez and Rocker found out. They decided to kill her and frame me for the murder. That would have killed two birds with one stone. It didn't work out so well for them."

"It didn't turn out well for a lot of people in Morganville." Elena shook her head. "Please tell me what happened. I want to hear all of it."

Carver considered it. Decided she knew too much already. So he told her the rest of the story.

"Holy shit." Elena was on her third beer when he finished. She swallowed the rest. "So, Leon is the final piece to the conspiracy. He wants Breakstone to become the ultimate PMC." She shook her head. "No, more than a PMC. A private army with full black ops and spy operations. They'd be like the CIA and military rolled into one."

"That about sums it up." Carver raised his beer bottle. "Rest in peace, Rhodes."

"Did you go to her funeral?"

Carver shook his head. "I couldn't stick around. I had to get out of town."

"Makes sense." Elena stared at her empty beer bottle. "I don't know if I should admire you or be scared of you."

Carver stood and stretched. "You don't scare easily. You also don't admire easily. Seems best if you don't go either way." He went inside and tossed the bottle in the trash. Went into the bedroom. Closed the door and locked it. Took a shower.

He was tempted to fill up the jacuzzi tub in the corner. Turn on the bubbles and just soak in it. But he was tired and the tub looked too short. It had been a long day.

Elena knocked. "Carver, my bags are in there. Do you expect me to sleep on the couch?"

He opened the door. "It's a nice couch."

"You're not much of a gentleman."

"You're right."

She opened her suitcase. "Well, I'm not much of a lady. So, I'll sleep in here. You don't snore do you?"

"I don't think so. No promises."

"I'll let you know if you do." She slid under the covers. "Good night, Carver."

"Night." He got in bed. Turned off the lamp. Closed his eyes.

DAN CALLED LEON himself.

He'd huddled with Blake and the others for hours. Made sure everyone had their story straight. Carver took Dan hostage. Threatened a bloodbath. Explosives. Blake had no choice but to cut Elena loose. Trade her for Dan.

Leon wasn't happy. "Sounds like Carver. He's paranoid."

"Yeah, he is. I think he has a sixth sense." Dan sighed. "I don't want this to turn into another Morganville. For a minute, I thought the hotel was going to become a killing floor."

"Carver does what Carver wants," Leon said. "I can't believe you talked him down."

"I've got another plan," Dan said. "I know we can make it work."

"Your cover is burned. Nothing more you can do." Leon sighed. "Pack up and come home. I'll take care of this, no matter what it takes."

CHAPTER 30

Something woke Carver.

Maybe it was Elena's gentle snoring. Maybe it was a random noise in the night. Maybe it was something else. He slipped out of bed and quietly treaded through the darkness. He crouched in the den. Listened. Heard the distant crash of waves. Elena snoring.

He felt alert. Something had woken him. Something had triggered his lizard brain. Told him to wake up or die. Maybe Dan had double-crossed him. Maybe he figured it was better to put Carver at ease. Then kill him in his sleep.

Theresa had been staying here. Breakstone was probably paying for it. Dan knew exactly where to find Carver. Then again, he'd known that already and hadn't moved against him. He'd played along to lure Carver into a trap.

It didn't make sense for Dan to break the deal they'd made. Maybe Dan hadn't. Maybe he'd told Leon that Carver escaped. Leon thought Dan failed. He was pissed. So, he sent someone else to finish the job.

Leon had sent another assassin. They were in the hotel room. Lurking. Hiding. Trying to put a bullet in Carver. Carver couldn't see them or hear them, but he felt that gut-deep sense of unease that told him he was right.

Carver kept low.

He made his way behind the kitchen counter. The vantage gave him a view of the deck and the living space. The ambient light was enough to reveal everything. There were no curtains to hide behind. No walls. It was a minimalist space.

Once he made sure the area was clear, he checked the sliding glass door. It was still locked. He checked the main door. It was locked. The chain was off. He couldn't remember if he'd latched it earlier or not. He locked the deadbolt and the chain. Kept looking.

He checked the bathroom. The bedroom. Elena was the only other person in the suite. She snorted. Sat up. Gasped. "God, Carver, you scared me."

He turned on the lights. Checked the closet, the rooms again. It was all clear.

"Another moment of paranoia?"

Carver nodded. "Something woke me up and it wasn't your snoring."

Elena looked indignant. "I don't snore."

Carver double-checked the locks. The windows didn't open. Only the doors. The suite was secure. He turned off the living space lights. Closed the bedroom door. Locked it. Sat on the bed and stared at the door.

"Carver, you can go to sleep. I'll protect you."

He cracked a smile. "Thanks."

"Are you afraid Dan double-crossed us?"

"I thought about it. Decided he wouldn't. But he probably told Leon we escaped. Leon might have sent someone else to finish the job."

"And we're staying in his assassin's hotel room. Not too bright."

"Nope." Carver kept looking at the door. Like someone might burst in at any moment.

Elena took his hand. Squeezed it. "Maybe we should take my car. Find a little motel somewhere."

"I like this hotel." Carver pulled the sheets over him. Lay down. "We'll be okay."

"You're a strange man, Carver."

"Thanks." He turned out the light. Closed his eyes and went to sleep.

CARVER WAS STILL ALIVE the next morning.

That didn't mean anything. He'd learned to trust his senses. Sometimes they were wrong. Sometimes they saved his life. Like in the elevator with Dan. He'd felt the shift in behavior. The change in demeanor.

Even then, it had almost been too late. The hotel was amazing. Comfortable. A nice, relaxing break from the norm. And it was time to leave. Leaf blowers were humming loudly outside. The gas-powered rigs buzzed and blew. The racket was enough to wake the dead even in the penthouse.

Elena was still sleeping like it was perfectly quiet. He eased out of bed and stretched. Thought about what he wanted for breakfast. Might as well make it expensive since this was the last morning in the Betsy.

Carver went to the bedroom door. Unlocked the deadbolt and the chain. Opened the door. He stepped forward and saw something from the corner of his eye. He dropped to the floor. A gun coughed three times. Bullets thudded into the wall.

Carver rolled. Backed into the bedroom. He grabbed the Glock from the nightstand. Something flashed past the bedroom door. He couldn't get a bead on it. A door slammed open and shut.

He got up. Ran into the hallway. Saw a figure disappear around the corner to the elevator lobby. Carver ran after it. He eased around the corner. The elevator dinged as it arrived. But no one was waiting.

He heard a door close. Ran down the hall. Turned another corner. Found the stairwell entrance. He opened the door. Listened. Heard running footsteps. Carver leaped down the first flight. Grabbed the railing and propelled himself down the next.

He made short work of several flights of stairs, but the shooter was far ahead. He burst out of the bottom stairwell. Ran into the lobby. Saw a feminine figure in athletic clothing run out of the front doors.

She turned the corner and kept running. Carver didn't get a good look at her face. She was five feet five inches. Lean. Black hair. Tanned skin. She was also apparently an Olympic runner. By the time Carver got out of the front door, she was gone.

People were looking at him. He was just wearing shorts. No shirt. It probably wasn't his clothing they were looking at. It was the gun in his hand. His heavy breathing. The fact that he'd run across the lobby like he was chasing someone.

Carver palmed the small gun. Walked over to one of the onlookers. "Did you get a good look at the woman who just ran past?"

The man blinked. "Not really. She was running so fast I didn't get a good look."

Carver asked some others. No one had a good description of her face. They were looking at him suspiciously. Asking what happened. He told them she tried to steal his wife's purse. That stopped the questions.

He returned to the room. Elena was pacing back and forth in the den. "What happened?"

Carver told her. "Pack up. Let's go."

"Leon sent an assassin to kill us in the morning?" Elena looked flummoxed. "Why not during the night?"

"I sure as hell wasn't expecting it. Most attacks come in the dead of night. Around three in the morning is the best."

"Clearly, I'm not a good killer." Elena shivered. "It's crazy!"

"Yeah, it is." Maybe it was smart because it almost worked. Maybe it was the dumbest thing Leon could have done. Maybe the assassin had broad latitude. Maybe she could have done whatever she wanted.

Carver checked the bullet holes. They were small. Twenty-two caliber. Bullets that size wouldn't go through a dozen walls and blow the head off someone three rooms down. It was a thoughtful move on the assassin's part.

Up close, those bullets would do plenty of damage to a person. All it took was one in the skull for lights out. Carver didn't know how he was still standing. She'd had a full second to cap him when he stepped from the room.

That flash of movement in the corner of his eye had saved him.

He looked at the sliding glass door. It was still locked. The killer must have broken in. Maybe used the same method Carver had used to get into Turner's room. Except the front door had been locked and latched.

The coat hanger method wouldn't work with the chain and deadbolt. The only way to unlock the door was with a keycard. Then it was easy enough to use a thin object to push the chain out. Carver closed his eyes and thought back when he'd popped awake during the night.

He'd checked the doors. The chain and deadbolt hadn't been secured. He usually locked everything out of habit. That was why he didn't remember if he'd locked them. But he almost certainly had.

It meant the assassin had tried to get in last night. That had woken Carver. They'd tried again this morning. The leaf blowers had created a steady ambient sound from outside. The assassin had used the noise to cover the infiltration.

They'd had time to get in. Get set up. Turn the living space into a potential kill box. And they'd failed. Breakstone needed to hire new assassins. So far, they were batting zero for three.

At least with the assassin chased off, he had time for breakfast. He called down and ordered a nice spread. Then he took a shower. Got out and opened the door for room service.

Elena watched the food delivery, a confused look on her face. Once the server left, she finally asked what she was thinking. "Why are we still here? Someone just tried to kill us!"

"They won't be coming back here this morning. They'll try to get us later. Might as well enjoy breakfast in the meantime."

Elena put a waffle on a plate and covered it with butter and jelly. "I guess. You're the specialist here, so I'll trust you."

"Once we eat, we're going to have to sneak out somehow. They might recognize your car, so we'll make sure no one is following us when we leave Miami."

"We're leaving Miami? And going where?"

"I don't know yet." Carver sent a text to Dan. *Still waiting on target intel.*

Dan replied. *Target remains in Atlanta. Suggest you travel there. Await specific instructions.*

It was almost like taking orders again. Carver texted back. *Confirmed. Someone tried to kill us in our hotel room this morning.*

Carver polished off a waffle and started on the bacon. Dan's reply arrived two bites in.

It wasn't me. It was Leon. I didn't think we had any more assets in this area. I guess he doesn't tell me everything.

Theresa and Nicky have another sister?

No. Did you get a description?

Carver described her then finished his eggs.

Dan responded. *I don't recognize the description. I also don't know everyone Leon has hired.*

Carver finished breakfast. Packed up the few things he had, including Theresa's assassin case. He hadn't decided how he was going to kill Leon yet. He didn't like poisons. They were sneaky. Deceitful.

That didn't mean he wouldn't use them. There was no such thing as a fair fight, especially with your life on the line. Losing didn't mean you got to go home and lick your wounds. It meant you got buried. Worm food.

If you wanted to live, you'd use every trick in the book. If you had to take out the CEO of a militarized organization, drugs and poison might come in handy. A sniper rifle might be even handier.

The only way he was going to come out on top was if Leon wasn't ready for him. Because if Leon got wind of this, there would be no safe approach. The man had an uncanny knack for baiting his enemies in for the kill.

Carver would die from a bullet to the head just like everyone else. He had to pull this off smoothly. Get in close where he had the upper hand. Tilt the odds in his favor.

He and Elena packed and went downstairs to the valet station. Carver didn't bother checking out. He'd let Breakstone pick up the tab for the extra week he'd added. It was only fair considering the trouble they'd put him through.

The valet pulled up with Elena's car. He looked confused. "Didn't you have an Audi?"

"We're slumming today." Carver gave him a good tip. "You know what, why don't you take the Audi tonight? Drive it around for a few days? We're going to Orlando for a couple of days and then coming back here."

The kid's eyes widened. "You're not serious, are you?"

"I'm dead serious." The Audi came with a valet key that slid out of the main fob. Carver gave him the entire fob. Gave him a little extra cash from the drug dealer's stash. "Take your girl out for a nice night."

"Wow, thanks so much, mister!" The valet beamed. "I hope you have a great time in Orlando!"

Elena hopped in the driver seat while Carver put the bags in the trunk. He eased into the passenger seat and the car seemed to drop by an inch. Elena grinned sheepishly. "I think the shocks are bad."

Carver got situated. The seat was more comfortable than the one in the Audi. It didn't have the bolsters that pinched his back and shoulders. "As long as it gets us to Atlanta."

She pulled out of the circle drive. Headed for the causeway. "That was really nice what you did for the valet."

"It's misdirection. Plus, no sense letting the Audi go to waste."

"Just tactics?" Elena gave him a sideways look. "Or did it make you feel a tiny bit good to make someone's day?"

Carver thought it over. "Yeah, it made me feel a little okay. Maybe a little jealous that the kid's got a nice free life. Nobody hunting him."

"Carver, you're hopeless." Elena burst out laughing. "First of all, that kid is probably twenty."

"He's seventeen. Works weekends. Goes to school in Little Haiti. Lives with his grandmother since his parents died trying to cross the ocean on a raft to reach the US."

Elena gave him a sharp look. "You can't possibly know all that about him. You're just joking, right?"

"I heard him talking with another valet when I was waiting for the car the other day. I asked him some questions. He told me his life story."

"What questions?"

"If he or anyone remembered much about Theresa when she dropped off the vehicle. He said the other valets noticed that you weren't the same woman. They told me I'd upgraded, and they wouldn't tell my wife."

Elena laughed. "Bros before hoes."

"Something like that." Carver kept checking the side mirror. He had to change the angle so he could use it for spotting tails. "If you're going to be somewhere for a few days, it's good to know the regulars."

"I suppose." Elena shook her head. "I never think about stuff like that."

"You shouldn't have to. It's not your job."

"Whose job is it?"

"The job is layered. The military is a shield. Projects strength to keep out invaders. The feds have agencies to prevent international and domestic terrorist threats. The cops try to minimize domestic crime. Layers of shields designed to protect civilians so they can do what they want."

She steered onto the causeway back to the mainland. "I never thought about it that way. People bitch and complain about the military and law enforcement like it's some kind of totalitarian state we live in. But it's more like we live in a womb."

"It's not a perfect design. Bad apples weaken the shield. Bad decisions make people question its usefulness. But if you take away one layer, the entire fabric is weakened. More people die." Carver kept tabs on the vehicles behind them. A white Toyota had been with them since the hotel. He'd seen it pull out of a parking space across the road. Maybe it was following them. Maybe it was coincidence.

"We've seen the effect in big cities," Elena said. "Murder rates are skyrocketing in places where they cut back on the police force."

"Personally, I think it's useful if people don't feel entirely safe." Carver kept watching the Toyota. "Too much safety breeds overconfidence. Breeds contempt for the system that protect you. Makes the populace weak. Easy to control."

"Now you sound like a conspiracy theorist."

"No, just facts. Lots of people talk tough because they have guns. They think they can take on the government. But politicians are soft too. They want power. Money. The same thing everyone else wants. They'll keep the status quo the best they can." Carver studied the other traffic. Spotted another car that had been with them a while. "If one weak link breaks, the system collapses. It's almost happened a few times."

"What are you talking about?"

Carver leaned his seat all the way back. He took off his seatbelt. Low-crawled to the back seat. Raised the monocular just over the edge of the seat and zoomed in on the white Toyota. The darkhaired assassin was driving it.

He looked at the silver Honda a couple cars back from it. A curly haired, middle-aged man was driving it. He had the same dead look in his eyes as the darkhaired woman. It wasn't the same dead look morning commuters had on their way to work. That was more of a hopeless look. A blank stare.

These people had a mission and Carver was the objective.

CHAPTER 31

Two assassins were tailing them.

"You see something?" Elena asked.

"Yep." Carver slid back into his seat. Raised it back to sitting position. "The assassin from this morning and another guy. Act like you don't know they're there."

"Act normal when we have two killers following us?"

He nodded. "Especially when you have two killers following you." He checked his phone and saw a text Dan had sent him earlier.

I received word that two or three assets might be after you. Leon is pulling out all the stops.

Carver typed back. *Leon is still in Atlanta?*

Affirmative.

"Shit." Carver mulled the options. They couldn't go to Atlanta. Couldn't even head in that direction. Leon would know they were coming. They had to pretend they were going somewhere else. That was the only way.

"What now?" Elena stopped a red light. They were about to reach I-95.

The best way to Atlanta was to head north on I95 and cut west on I75. Follow it all the way to the destination. There were plenty of other places to go, but it didn't make sense to drive for hours as a fake out.

"Go south."

"South?" Elena looked at the map. "There's nothing but the Keys and the Everglades south of here."

"We're not going that far south." He traced a finger on the map. "Go into Little Haiti."

She turned onto Biscayne. Drove a few blocks. Took a right into Little Haiti. "What now?"

"Keep driving. I'm thinking." The Toyota and the Honda were still following them. It would be hard losing them. Especially in Elena's car. Misdirection was the only way to go. Only way to make them think they hadn't been noticed.

Carver pointed to a turn. "Go there. Turn right. Pull into this parking lot." They were near the hardware store he'd used before. Right next door was a used car dealership. That was where they were going.

Elena looked concerned "Why are we going to a used car dealership?"

"We're trading down." He checked the other cars. Found a nineteen-seventies Ford that belonged in a museum.

The used car salesman came out of his little building. Smiled wide. "How can I help you?"

Carver tapped the Ford. "How much?"

"I can make you a very good deal. Two thousand dollars with your trade-in."

Carver nodded. "Let's go inside and talk."

The dealer's grin grew wider. He'd found himself a real idiot.

The inside of the office smelled like cheap cigars and bourbon. Carver looked out the window. Saw the Toyota park in the lot across the street. The Honda stopped at a nearby convenience store.

They weren't being aggressive yet. They'd wait for a quiet stretch of highway to make their move. Probably a drive-by shooting, or even run them off the road. There were long stretches of dead space this far south in Florida.

The dealer rubbed his hands together. "Do you owe anything on that car, Miss?"

Elena shook her head. "No, I just paid it off." She turned to Carver. "I'm no car specialist, but are you really going to let this guy rip us off?"

Carver pulled out his wad of cash. "I'll give you five-hundred dollars to let us park that car here and borrow the Ford. We need to drive it to the airport. You can pick it up there later."

The dealer blinked. Disappointed. Confused. "What? I thought you were going to—"

Carver held up a hand. "Does the Ford run?"

"Yes. I cranked it up the other day."

"It's in bad shape. Hardly even worth five hundred. I'm just asking to borrow it for that much."

The dealer thought it over. His greasy smile vanished when he realized he didn't have a couple of chumps in his office. "Fine. Five hundred. Leave that old beater of hers in the parking lot and take the Ford. Why are you doing this? You in some kind of trouble?" His eyes lit up as he sensed another money-making opportunity.

Carver gave him the money. Held out his hands for the key. The dealer reached into a wall cabinet. Pulled a key off the hook.

"Don't scratch the paint."

The paint was chipping and peeling so bad already, Carver didn't think it could get any worse. "I'll leave it in short term parking."

He and Elena took the things from her car. Dumped them into the back seat of the Ford. Carver climbed in. Cranked it up. The old V8 rumbled to life. He revved it. It felt solid. No smoke. No odor. The car looked like hell, but it ran well.

There was no air conditioning, so they rolled down the windows manually.

"What's the point of this charade?" Elena said. "They're watching us switch cars."

"They don't know we know, and them not knowing is half the battle."

"That's not what GI Joe said."

Carver raised an eyebrow. "How would you know?"

He drove past the convenience station where the silver Honda was parked. He drove south to 112, then headed to the airport. The Toyota and Honda followed far behind.

Carver entered short term parking. Long term was easier to hide a car in, but short term was a lot closer to the terminal. They needed to get to the terminal before the killers found a parking spot.

The killers might opt to dump their cars at the curb. They were probably stolen or registered to someone else. No risk to them. The plan hinged on what they did next. Carver watched the rearview mirror. The Honda and Toyota turned onto the road to the parking deck.

Carver drove in circles going up level after level. Most of the parking was taken. He finally found a slot on the top level. Pulled in. They grabbed their things. Hurried to the elevator. The Honda and Toyota reached the top just as the doors closed.

Most people would take the sky bridge on the middle level. Carver had it take them there. If the killers were watching the numbers on the elevator, he didn't want them to see where it really took them.

They hustled out of the elevator. The doors closed. It hummed and started going up. The killers were coming. Carver and Elena took the stairs. They went down. Down some more. All the way to the bottom.

There was another way of finishing this. Carver considered luring the killers somewhere to kill them. But it was risky doing it at an airport. Cameras everywhere. Even in the parking deck. Evasion was better. This way, they'd think Carver and Elena were boarding a plane.

The killers would purchase tickets so they could get past security. They'd rush to the gates. Search the terminals. Not find them. Not know where they went. Then Carver would be free to go to Atlanta without Leon knowing he was coming.

The bottom level was where the taxis were waiting. He and Elena waited in a short line. Got a taxi. Told the driver to take them to the car dealership.

Elena grinned. "That was pretty smart. They'll be running through all the terminals looking for us."

"That's the point."

The taxi pulled onto the road to exit the airport. Traffic was stuck at a redlight. Carver glanced back out of habit. Did a double take. The Honda and Toyota were four cars back. He pulled out the monocular. Zoomed in.

The darkhaired woman was on a cell phone. She was smiling. Laughing. Looking like she didn't have a care in the world. Like she hadn't just been chasing someone.

"What is it, Carver?"

He saw the other driver. The man wasn't laughing or smiling, but he didn't look like he was on company time either. He was relaxed. Had earphones in. Didn't look vigilant.

Carver slumped in the seat to keep out of sight.

Elena grabbed his arm. "Carver, what's wrong?"

"I'm not sure." He didn't know what was going on. Why had the killers given up? Were they under orders to not follow him into the airport? A heartbeat later, he knew the answer. Leon had sent them to follow him. To make sure he was going to Atlanta.

Leon knew Carver would spot the tails. He knew Carver wouldn't want to drive in the middle of nowhere with two killers following him. The logical choice would be to take a flight instead. Leon wanted Carver in Atlanta so he could finish this today.

When the darkhaired woman failed to headshot Carver this morning, Leon had probably been furious. Told her and the other guy to make sure Carver came to him. Leon would take care of business himself.

Carver's plan had been to return to the dealership to get Elena's car. Take it to Atlanta. But now he wasn't so sure. Leon was ready and waiting in Atlanta.

Dan might be helping Carver, but that didn't mean much if Carver let Leon herd him right into a trap. He had to turn things around. Make this happen on his own terms.

"Carver, I can't tell what you're thinking." Elena gripped his arm tighter. "Say something."

Carver didn't want to talk in the taxi. He kept an eye on the Honda and Toyota. They both turned north on I95. Probably headed to Atlanta. It seemed strange they wouldn't fly there. The cars they were driving looked like throwaways. Something didn't jibe.

The taxi dropped them off at the dealership. Carver put their stuff in Elena's car. Elena took the passenger seat. Gave Carver the key fob. He pushed the seat back. Got comfortable. Started the car and pulled onto the road.

Their morning adventure had taken nearly two hours. It was almost lunchtime. He pulled into a small restaurant, and they went inside.

Elena had remained quiet. Probably knew she wouldn't get anything from Carver. "We're not in a hurry to get to Atlanta anymore?"

"I'm thinking about things." Carver ordered a sandwich from the server.

Elena ordered one too. "Okay. Care to share or do I have to keep guessing?"

"Ukraine. Ten years ago. An election year. A middle of the road populist was going up against the president. He was projected to win by a landslide. But the president was friends with powerful people in our government." Carver traced a finger idly on the table. "The CIA started psyops. Spread disinformation about the challenger."

"But, why?" Elena's mouth dropped open. "Was the challenger dangerous or did his friends in our government just want him to win?"

"There was no strategic benefit either way." Carver shrugged. "The psyops didn't swing public sentiment enough. They sent us in six months prior to the election. Had us set up a staged play."

"A staged what?"

"The challenger was going to a popular tavern. One of those events where the politician pretends to be a normal guy having a drink." Carver cracked a smile. "Typical Joe Schmo stuff. We set up as bar patrons. Set up a secret entrance and hiding spot so advance security would think the place was clear. I was normally the trigger on close quarters like this, but we found out one of our old contacts was with security. He'd recognize me right off."

"Sounds like you spent a lot of time in Ukraine."

"It's a hotspot of Russian activity." He glanced around at the other restaurant patrons out of habit. He didn't see anything to be concerned about. "Leon got the assignment. He was the only one of us that the guy wouldn't recognize because he hadn't been with us long. All he had to do was brush past the target and prick him with a needle. The poison would give him a heart attack a few hours later."

Elena looked horrified. "You can do that?"

"Yeah. Modified hemlock compound. Has a time release formula that delays the reaction."

"Hemlock?" She shook her head. "I'm starting to wish I didn't know how easy it was to kill someone."

"It's not that easy especially if the guy is surrounded by security. The needle is extremely slender and short so there's not much of a sensation when it goes in. One mistake and it breaks off under the skin. Leaves a clue."

"And shows up on a metal detector."

"Yeah." Carver rapped his fingers on the table. "Leon refused to do it. He said it was unconscionable. Evil. He said there was no reason to kill the man. No strategic value."

"He was right."

Carver nodded. "He was right. But any of us would have done the job because orders were orders. Even Rhodes, smart as she was, would have pulled the trigger."

"So, the mission didn't go through?"

"Rhodes told Leon to do it or he was out of the military. Dishonorable discharge. That he would be labeled a spy. His entire family would be disgraced."

"God, that's harsh! She would have really done that?"

Carver shook his head. "No, but the SOC, secret operations commander, would have. They were very selective about people in Scion. I don't know how Leon got in, to be honest."

"Did he do it?"

Carver nodded. "He did it. The challenger died. There was a huge wave of sentiment. The challenger's wife took his spot and almost won the election."

Elena grinned. "Damn, that would have been an amazing story if she'd won it."

"That wasn't the only time Leon fought against orders. He even offered his own ideas for targets. He wanted to assassinate dictators in North Korea and Belarus. Free the people." Carver saw the server coming with his sandwich. "I get the feeling that he's compromising some of his beliefs so Breakstone can become a privatized black ops arm of the government. Then he'll be free to do what he wants."

"Killing you, me, reporters and detectives is how he's compromising his values?"

Carver nodded. "He had a soft spot for journalists. He hated it when psyops targeted them. He especially hated it when we had to kill them. One time I thought he was going to rescue a target and run. In the end, he followed orders."

"And this is why you've been so pensive since the airport?"

"I'm trying to figure the angles. Dan says Leon is following Dorsey's path. It seems like that would be counter to Leon's ideals, but I think I see why he's doing it now. He wants to start his own side missions. Kill the people he thinks deserve it."

"And he needs us dead to make sure no one finds out."

"More or less. He must think we know more than we really do. That's not uncommon." Carver bit into his sandwich. "The assassins were just corralling us. Making sure we went to Atlanta so Leon could be ready for us. Which is why we're not going to Atlanta."

"We're not?"

He shook his head. "We're going to make Leon come to us."

CHAPTER 32

Carver knew how he was going to kill Leon.

He texted Dan. *I'm not going to Atlanta. Leon knows I'm coming. I need him to come to me.*

He formulated a plan while he waited for a reply. It was simple. If Leon came to town, he'd survey the island. See that there were multiple high-rise condos. Countless vantage points for sniping. He'd find a location he liked. Have his people try to herd Carver into the kill zone. Take his shot.

Blood would mist from Carver's skull. His body would tumble to the ground. Leon would look away. Close his eyes. Maybe even shed a tear. He'd cried over targets before even if he didn't know them. Maybe Carver was worth a tear or two.

Carver's plan was simple. Dan would tell him where Leon was staying. Carver would infiltrate. Kill Leon and anyone else who got in his way. It would have to be quick, brutal, and efficient. No time for thoughts, only actions.

He finished his sandwich. Ordered coffee. Leaned back in the seat and looked out the window.

"It sucks you have to kill your friend," Elena said. "He doesn't sound like a bad guy."

"He's not. But sometimes idealists turn into fanatics." Carver pressed his lips into a thin line. "I don't have a choice."

"Maybe you can talk to him. Reason with him."

"I don't have his number."

"I do." Elena fished in her bag. Pulled out a notepad. "Good thing I don't keep my entire life on my phone." She found a number. "This is his personal cell."

"How'd you get it?"

"I stood behind his assistant when she was eating lunch. She was sending him a text about the FBI news conference."

"Maybe you should be a spy too."

She grinned. "Yeah. As long as I don't have to kill anyone."

Carver grinned back. "No promises."

"You have a nice smile for a killer."

"I brush my teeth daily." Carver sipped his coffee and his smile faded. "I'll try to talk to Leon."

He entered the number in his burner phone. Sent a text. *Leon, this is Carver. We need to stop the killing and talk.*

"I hope it works," Elena said.

"Yeah." Carver wasn't too hopeful about it. He drank his coffee and thought about where to go after this. Elena's motel or one like it would do.

Dan replied to Carver's earlier text. *I'll see if I can convince him to come to Miami.*

They finished their coffees and left the restaurant. Carver went to his storage unit. Put the duffel bags into the trunk of the car. It was time to clean up the weapons and get ready for business.

He found a motel in Little Havana. It was a nice, clean area. Small houses. Small businesses. Quiet community. It was a short drive to the island but far enough away to feel safe. He unloaded the car and took everything inside.

Then he selected his weapons for the task. One rifle. Three pistols. One of Theresa's knives. Ideally, it would be a CQC operation. He had a suppressor for one of the Glocks. That would keep the noise down, but it wouldn't stop bullets from punching through walls.

If it went down in a hotel, it would get messy. There might be collateral damage. Carver would do his best to avoid that, but all bets were off when it came to completing the objective. Leon might bring a small army of guards, or he might come with just a few. Until Carver knew the specifics, he had to be ready for the worst-case scenario.

There was a small laminate table in the room with a plastic chair. Elena sat and watched him. "That's a lot of guns. Do you take them everywhere you go?"

"I went into Morganville with nothing but bare hands. Came out with all this." He tucked away the AK-47 and one of the Colt carbines. He stripped down the Glock pistols. Checked the springs. The barrels. The firing pins. Put them back together.

He opened a box of 9mm. Picked up an empty magazine. Started loading it.

Elena picked up one and did the same. She was quick and efficient. A cop's daughter. "Well, at least I know this is a magazine and not a clip now."

"You didn't already know that?"

Elena shook her head "A country boy from Morganville corrected me."

Carver examined a firing pin. "Can you strip down a handgun?"

"Yes."

"A rifle?"

"Never tried. Dad took me shooting at the gun range. I shot rifles, shotguns, pistols. To be honest, they scared me."

"Do they still scare you?"

"Not in the same way." Elena shrugged. "They're tools. They do a job. I don't love them or hate them. But I respect them."

"Sounds like your father taught you well."

She nodded. "Yeah, he did. He was the same way. Pragmatic."

"What about your mom?"

"She came from Venezuela. They disarmed the citizens there a long time ago to prevent uprisings. She didn't use guns, but she liked that Dad was good with them. It made her feel secure."

Carver had been to Venezuela a few times. The government had nationalized oil production. Had gone into league with the Russians. Someone in the US government wanted it to stay that way. They'd taken out dissidents of the communist regime. Made sure nothing changed.

"You got that distant look to your eyes, Carver." Elena finished loading her second magazine. Picked up a third. "What are you thinking?"

"We had missions in Venezuela. Propped up the communist dictator a few times to make sure they kept the oil nationalized."

She stopped what she was doing. "But, why?"

"Someone up the chain of command wanted to keep it that way." He shrugged. There weren't any more magazines to load, so he stripped down the Colt M4 carbine. "Rhodes told me she figured an oil company wanted to keep prices high."

"When was this?"

Carver told her the year.

"Domestic oil production was at an all-time low during that period and oil prices were nearing record highs." She finished loading the magazine and set it aside. "I was writing news stories about it, so I remember it vividly. But Trident Oil was still doing business with Venezuela. They were raking in record profits."

Carver shrugged. "I don't recall that name."

"They're a subsidiary of a British company. Zero US ownership." She looked at him as if to drill the point home. "Whoever gave you those orders was aiding a foreign company at the expense of domestic companies."

"Wouldn't surprise me." Carver checked the rifle barrel. Ran a cleaning brush through it. "We did all kinds of missions that seemed bad for the US. Leon was the only one who questioned them. The rest of us did our jobs."

"Mindless soldiers are a nation's worst enemy, Carver." Elena took his hand away from the rifle. Squeezed it. "How could you be like that?"

He let her hold his hand like that while he thought about it. He didn't have a good answer. At the time, he just hadn't cared. Carver had always been somewhere in the middle when it came to things. He was a big kid, but he didn't bully others. He also didn't help anyone who was getting bullied.

His dad had been a soldier. He'd ordered Carver around. Given him a sense of duty at the end of a whip. Done the same to his mom. Nothing serious. Verbal threats. Cursing. The occasional backhand when someone didn't do what he wanted.

He was away on missions most of the time. Carver's mom did what she wanted to do. Left Carver alone to do what he wanted to do. Then two days before his dad was supposed to return from overseas, she vanished. His dad died on a mission the next day.

That left Carver bouncing around between foster homes. Adults told him what to do, he did it. It was just ground into him at that point. Going into the military seemed the natural choice. Once he'd gotten in, he'd done what people told him to do, no questions asked.

It wasn't until his dishonorable discharge that he realized no one else should be ordering him around. Especially not when they betrayed him like they had. Framed him for human trafficking when it was the last thing he'd ever do.

"Is it that hard to answer, Carver?"

He nodded. "It is. I don't think I'm the same person now as I was then."

"I think you're right. I think that's why you made that deal with Dan. Why you saved me."

"No sense in letting you die. There was a way out and I took it."

"No, I think it's more than that." She rubbed his oil-stained hand. "You're developing a conscience."

"It's easier not to have one. Leon always seemed to be in pain. I didn't want to live like that."

Elena laughed softly. "I can't disagree. But you still get points for saving me. For saving Paola."

Carver reclaimed his hand. Put the Colt back together. Checked that there weren't any missing parts. It'd be a bad time to forget the firing pin. Then he wiped down the guns. Set them on the dresser along with the other gear he wanted to take.

He washed his hands. Dried them. Elena took his clean hands in hers. She stood on tiptoes and kissed him on the lips.

"You're not a bad person, Carver."

"I'm not good either."

She kissed him again. "You're better than most."

He kissed her back. She had nice soft lips. The scent of gun oil. He put his hand on the small of her back and drew her in close. Kissed her harder. Then he released her. Let her take a breath and decide if this was what she really wanted to do.

"Why'd you stop?" Her brown eyes grew big.

"Give you a second to think it over. You know what I've done. What I plan to do. The kind of person I am." He put his hands on her hips. Backed her up a step so he could slip past. "Do you want sleeping with me on your conscience?"

Elena stepped in front of him. Put her hands on his chest. Nodded. "Yes. I think I can live with that." She put her arms around his neck. Pulled him down to her. Kissed him.

He put his hands under her legs. Picked her up so she straddled him. They kissed for a while like that. Lips on lips. Lips on necks. Ears. His hands gripping her hair tight. Her fingernails raking down his back. Teeth biting his shoulder.

Women were one of the finer things in life. Strong women were even finer still. Elena was certainly one of those. She'd proven it over and over. She was tough. Ready to fight. Ready to win. And that was the kind of person Carver liked the most.

DAN CALLED LEON.

"He's not going to Atlanta. I still have my people here. We can finish this."

Leon remained quiet for a long time. "No. Best I do this myself. I don't want more collateral damage. We need to keep it quiet and contained."

Dan nodded. "Agreed, sir. Shall I arrange accommodations?"

"Yes. I need to be somewhere high. Somewhere with a good vantage point."

"I know just the place. I'll send you the details."

"Thanks."

Dan made a reservation. Top floor of a condominium high-rise. La Playa. The same one with Club Periclean at the bottom. It seemed fitting to end this right where it had begun.

Leon would arrive. He'd bring his prized rifle with him. The scope was powerful enough for him to see targets from miles away if the weather was right. The man was one of the best shots Dan had ever seen.

The plan would be to lure Carver into the open. Let Leon take the headshot from so far away, the sound of the rifle wouldn't even reach Carver until after he was dead. Except the person in the sights wouldn't be Carver.

Carver would be in the building. Riding the elevator to the top. Coming up behind Leon on the roof. Then it would be over. The company would be free. Dorsey's vision would no longer hold sway.

Dan checked the time. Leon was flying down in the corporate jet. He'd be there by nightfall. Enough time to get all the pieces into position. Get everything ready for the big show.

Tomorrow was going to be a bloody day.

— • —

CHAPTER 33

Carver woke with Elena in his arms.

He'd slept better than usual. Sex usually had that effect on him. He imagined a life without all the violence. A life where going to the grocery store and having sex were the highlights of the day.

Asking someone if they needed something from the store. Picking up bread, milk, eggs. Mowing the lawn. Cleaning the kitchen. Picking up the wife and carrying her to the bedroom.

Carver shivered just thinking about it. He didn't even know why, but domestic life scared him more than assassins. The Navy psychologists hadn't been able to figure him out either.

The shrinks for his black ops unit hadn't tried to figure it out. They'd said it was the reason he was so good at what he did. Carver figured they were right. It was nice being able to do business without it eating away at you.

Leon let everything eat at him. It probably kept him up at night. But once he'd gotten into Scion, that had been it. There was no getting out. He'd adjusted. Done his duty even though he morally opposed it.

It was strange to think he'd become close to Menendez and Rocker. That he'd been fourth in line to become CEO. The succession didn't make sense. Then again, Carver wasn't a company guy. He didn't understand business.

He did understand value. Leon was a crack shot. The best sniper Carver had ever seen. Priceless to a company like Breakstone. They must have made all kinds of promises to Leon. Told him he could do the missions he wanted. That he'd be well paid. That he didn't have to compromise his morals.

Leon had wanted out of Scion so badly he would have done anything. Even if it meant betraying Carver. But Carver didn't think Leon knew about that part. Menendez and Rocker probably told Leon they could get him out of Scion. But he had to promise to become part of their new team.

It had to be something like that. Carver could almost imagine the greasy sales pitch. Menendez patting Leon on the back. Telling Leon he only had to compromise his values one more time to get out.

Carver might ask Leon just before the finale. He wanted to know where things went wrong. Where Leon lost his soul. Maybe he still had it. Maybe he thought he could use Breakstone to right all the wrongs he'd committed.

He smoothed Elena's hair from her face. She looked peaceful. Almost sweet. But the woman had a sharp edge to her. A survival instinct. Claws. Her father had taught her well. Maybe not well enough to keep her alive, but enough all the same.

Carver slid his arm from beneath her. She stirred. Stretched. Opened her eyes and smiled at him. He smiled back. It wasn't a fake smile. It felt authentic. Probably some caveman instinct even Carver couldn't repress.

He got in the shower. Cleaned up. Got dressed. Elena did the same. She wore her usual athletic gear this time with purple tennis shoes. Carver wore cargo shorts. He wouldn't put on his dark fatigues until later.

They went to a diner. It was Cuban, so the breakfast was a bit different. Coffee with milk. Eggs. Toast. Plantains. Rice and beans. It was similar to an Irish breakfast, Carver decided. Almost enough food to last him through lunch.

Dan texted halfway through the meal. *Leon is staying at La Playa Condominiums. Room 30102. His plan is to lure to a location where he'll have a clean shot.*

Carver raised an eyebrow. Texted back. *He chose that place himself? Or did you?*

I chose it. Thought it was fitting.

How does he expect to get me into a specific location?

Dan replied. *I have no idea. He'll arrive at nine tonight.*

"What's wrong?" Elena asked.

"Dan lodged Leon at La Playa. The same condo building where Club Periclean is. Just a few rooms down from the one Nicki Jones took a swan dive."

Her eyes widened. "Sick sense of humor?"

"Don't know. Don't care." His phone buzzed. A text from Leon.

I agree. No more bloodshed. Let's meet at the Fontaine Rooftop Café. 8 AM tomorrow. I'm buying.

Carver checked the map app. Looked from street view. In 3D view. The café was visible from the roof of the La Playa. It was an eight hundred yard shot. Almost half a mile. An easy shot for Leon.

"Damn." Carver sighed. "Damn."

"That's the first time I've seen you remotely upset." Elena rubbed his arm. "What's wrong?"

"Leon doesn't want to talk. He wants me to line up for a kill shot."

Elena sighed. "Shit. That sucks. I was hoping you could get through to him."

"Me too." Carver hated it. But it looked like he was going to have to kill Leon, no questions asked.

Dan was supposed to send a decoy target to a location once they knew what it was. But Carver didn't need that. He had what he needed. A location. Leon was going to get a three AM wakeup call. Except he wouldn't be awake for long.

Leon would be dead long before meeting for breakfast. Carver considered waking him. Asking him what changed him. But that would only give Leon a chance to fight back. It would be safer to end it fast.

"You don't look happy."

"I'm not." Carver couldn't stop thinking about Leon as the kid of the squad. The baby-faced sniper with twenty-three official kills. Two unofficial kills had saved Carver's life. His cover had been blown and he hadn't known it.

Leon was supposed to be aiming for someone else. But he saw that Carver was in danger. Two shots. Two targets dropped. Everyone had been confused at first. Especially Carver. Then he saw that they'd been coming to kill him.

Carver had never had the chance to repay him. Now it looked like he never would. He never could, not if he wanted to keep breathing. It was best to do the job. Be done with it. Put Morganville and Breakstone in the past. Put Leon in the ground.

He went to the La Playa website. Like a lot of condos on the island, they were for rent. Renting was easy. You could choose an oceanside view. You could choose which floor you wanted. It all boiled down to how much you wanted to pay.

Leon's room was the top floor. Just a few rooms down from Nicki Jones' former room. It didn't have an oceanside view. His balcony looked out across town. The Fontaine was right in the line of sight. He wouldn't have to leave the comfort of his condo to take the shot.

Carver looked at the pictures of the specific room. It was spacious. About the same size as the room he'd just left at the Betsy. There were two bedrooms, but the master was much larger.

Elena scooted into the booth next to him. Looked at the images on his phone. "What's that?"

"The room Leon will be staying in."

"What's the plan?"

Carver turned off the phone. Dropped some cash on the table. "Still working on it."

They left the diner. Drove to the La Playa condos. Carver went inside.

The concierge recognized him. "Did you ever find what happened to that poor girl?"

It looked like Leach hadn't told her he wasn't a cop. "Did Detective Leach get all the videos?"

"Yes, I gave him everything." She shook her head sadly. "It's just awful. Do you think that man roofied her?"

"It's possible." Carver nodded toward the elevators. "We think his accomplice might have had a room here as well. Can you get me into room three zero one zero two?"

She typed on the computer. "I don't have a record of anyone staying there that night."

"We think he broke in. I need to take a look around. I'll need to check the neighboring rooms as well."

She didn't look surprised. "These electronic locks aren't as secure as everyone thinks." She gave him a keycard. "That will get you into all the rooms on that floor."

"Thanks." Carver glanced at the security room. "There are no cameras in the rooms, right? Just the hallways?"

The concierge nodded. "Elevators and hallways."

"I'm going to take another look at something." He went into the security room. The cameras only covered the elevators and the elevator lobby. They only saw a small section of the hallway. He still didn't want them recording.

The concierge hadn't followed him into the security room, so Carver clicked on the cameras for the cargo elevator and the thirtieth floor. He disabled recording in the software. If things spilled into the elevators, they wouldn't have Carver on video.

Elena nodded. "Good idea."

They went to the elevator. Carver punched the up button. The doors slid open. He and Elena stepped inside. He hit the button for the top floor. The doors closed. The elevator lurched upward.

"That woman really thinks you're a detective?" Elena frowned. "You're wearing cargo shorts and you're with me. She didn't even ask why."

"Just act like you know what you're doing, and most people will go along with it."

The elevator stopped and they got off. They walked out of the elevator lobby. Carver heard people talking. Men issuing orders. Equipment clanking. Doors opening and shutting. Carver put a finger to his lips. Hurried to the hallway corner. Peered around it.

He saw room 30102. The door was propped open. The neighboring rooms were also propped open. Men in nondescript utility uniforms were working in the rooms. They had ladders. Tools. Computers. Carver saw one of the men put something in the overhead light fixture of Leon's room.

"What are they doing?" Elena whispered.

There was a stack of weapons cases in the room to the left of Leon's. The utility workers were setting up a laptop on a table in the room to the right. It was a lot of hustle and bustle. Were they setting up for Leon's arrival? Why hadn't the concierge mentioned them?

The answer was simple. She didn't even know they were here. They'd hacked the keypads. Now they were putting surveillance equipment in Leon's room. The laptop on the neighboring room was for monitoring. The weapons cases in the left room looked the right size for Colt carbines.

Leon was not going to be the easy target Carver had hoped for. He had an entire advance security detail. They had eyes and ears and muscle. The moment Carver tried to break into Leon's room, they would know. They'd respond instantly.

Carver imagined different approaches. He could get into the room. Punch out Leon's lights in five seconds. If the people watching were still attentive at three in the morning, they'd see Carver the instant he walked in. They'd see him fire a pistol three times.

By then, they'd recover from their stupor. Hit the alarm. The guards in the left room would grab their weapons. Open the door. Burst into the hallway. That gave Carver ten to fifteen seconds. If the watchers were especially alert, he'd have ten seconds.

The guards wouldn't be staged for immediate combat. They'd be in their room keeping busy with something. Maybe playing cards. Maybe sitting at a table drinking coffee. Reading a newspaper.

They were probably former military. They'd follow squad tactics, not rush out singly. That would slow them down. The alarm would sound. They'd grab their weapons near the door. Queue up. Shoulder pat. Burst outside. Engage.

Carver would be gone by then.

If they put a camera in the hallway, that would change things. They'd see him coming. The guards would be up and ready before Carver reached the door. That would make it considerably more difficult.

He kept watching. Moments later, one of the techs affixed something small and black above Leon's doorway. It watched the approach. From this corner to the doorway was a good thirty feet. Even at a dead run, Carver couldn't get in and out in time.

Elena couldn't see what he was seeing. She tried to look around the corner, but he barred her with his arm. It looked like they were finishing up. Getting ready to go. One worker stepped into the hallway with a laptop. His profile was angled away from Carver. It gave Carver a glimpse of the screen.

There were two camera feeds. It was hard to tell what was on the screen, but one was probably the hallway and the other was Leon's room. The man went into the room on the right. Returned a moment later and closed the door behind him.

The other workers exited the other rooms. They were carrying toolboxes. Coming toward the elevators. Carver motioned toward the elevators. He and Elena hit the buttons. Waited. Voices echoed down the hallway. The men were coming. Almost here.

The elevator arrived. They hopped inside. Carver hit the button for the 29th floor. The voices reached the elevator lobby.

"Hey, hold the door!"

The doors closed. The elevator dropped a level. Carver and Elena got off.

Elena looked confused. "What did you see? Why did we get off here?"

Carver told her what he'd seen. He exited the elevator lobby. Found a fire escape diagram on the wall. The elevator lobby was in the center of the building. There was also the cargo elevator at the back.

A hallway bisected the lobby. It intersected two hallways that ran parallel. Those hallways then branched to the sides. At the end of each side was a stairwell. At the end of the southwest branch was the cargo elevator.

Carver walked toward room 29102. It was right below Leon's room. He went left at the end of the hallway. Entered the stairwell. Followed the two flights up to the next floor. He opened the door. Put his monocular to an eye.

The camera above Leon's door was a black dot. Carver didn't see another camera watching this approach. He and Elena edged along the wall. Reached the room to the left of Leon's room. Used the keycode the concierge gave him.

The door opened. He looked around. The furniture in the den had been moved back leaving a large clear space. There were six rifle cases. Carver opened one. Inside was a Colt carbine and a suppressor plus three loaded magazines.

"God, what an arsenal." Elena looked at the other weapon cases. "He travels with six bodyguards?"

"Looks like it." Carver pulled out the rear breakdown pin on the Colt. Flipped it open. Pulled the charging handle. Removed the bolt assembly. It was smooth and easy. The weapons were well maintained. "You have a bobby pin or good fingernails?"

Elena looked in her bag. Pulled out a bobby pin. "What are you doing?"

"Making an adjustment." He bent the bobby out slightly. Used it to pry out a cotter pin. Reached in and drew out the firing pin.

Elena shook her head. "Anyone worth a grain of salt is going to know the firing pin is missing."

"These weapons have been broken down and cleaned. They're in tip-top shape." Carver put the cotter pin back in. Slid the bolt assembly into place. Clicked the rifle back together and put it in the case. "I personally check every weapon. Make sure it works."

"Right. And you think these people won't?"

"They might." He examined the tip of the firing pin. "Let's go to the car."

"Wait, you're only taking one?"

"For now." He closed the case. They left the room, Edged down the wall out of sight of the camera. Took the stairs down a level. Took the elevator the rest of the way.

Carver went to Elena's car. Opened the bag with his cleaning kit and other tools. Inside was just the tool he needed. He tested it and it did the trick. He put the tool in his back pocket.

Elena nodded approvingly. "Okay, now that might work."

"Let's hope." They returned to the room. Carver put the firing pin back in the rifle. He opened the other cases. Repeated the process with the rifles inside. When he was done, they left the room. Carver made Elena wait in the stairwell. Then he edged beneath the camera over the door. Entered the surveillance room.

The laptop was set up on a table. It was open and on. There were three views: the hallway, the inside entrance of Leon's condo, and the master bedroom. The camera in the hallway was angled up slightly to see to the end of the hallway. It couldn't see what was right beneath it.

That was perfect for Carver's needs.

There was an option to start recording whatever the camera saw. It was off for now. There was a case on another table. Inside were more of the micro cameras and tiny adhesive discs for securing them to surfaces.

They were civilian issue. Nothing that couldn't be found online. Carver found the name of the camera app. He downloaded it to his phone. Linked the cameras to the app. He tested one of the cameras. It showed up in the app as a new device.

He added it. The camera remained discoverable to anyone using the app. There was an option to lock it to one device and disable discoverability, so he did. He put the camera in the corner to watch the surveillance room.

Carver checked the laptop. The cameras linked to it were locked to only that device. He couldn't add them into his app. It also meant the laptop was the only device receiving the cameras feeds. The techs weren't watching the live feed from somewhere else.

They couldn't see anything unless they used this laptop. Carver could walk right in front of the cameras now and it wouldn't matter. No one would see the live feed.

Carver connected three more cameras to his app. He put one in the guards' condo. Put two in Leon's condo. Now he was ready.

Leon wouldn't know what hit him.

CHAPTER 34

Six guards arrived an hour before Leon.

Three of them picked up their rifle cases and went to the surveillance room. Carver hadn't expected them to split up, but it made sense. An attacker wouldn't expect it, and it gave them two firing angles down the hallway.

Leon arrived alone. He pulled a suitcase behind him. A long rifle case was slung over his back. His sniper rifle. Leon went straight inside his condo. Didn't stop by the other rooms to talk to the guards. He went to the bedroom. Leaned the rifle case against the wall. Put his suitcase on a dresser.

He sat on the edge of the bed. Looked at his phone. The screen was visible from the camera. The resolution wasn't high enough to read it. Carver took a risk. He sent a text to gauge Leon's body language.

Did you go to Rhodes' funeral?

Leon kept staring at his phone screen. No reaction. He used his thumb to scroll through whatever he was reading. He put the phone down on the bed. Walked toward the bathroom and vanished from view.

"He doesn't look like a killer," Elena said. "He looks so young."

"He's not that young. Just has a baby face." Carver shrugged. His phone buzzed. There was a reply from Leon.

Yes. What happened to her was a travesty.

Elena looked at the reply. "His text seems sincere."

"Looks can be deceiving." Carver looked at the guard rooms. The guards were relaxed. Watching TV. Looking at phones. They didn't look ready to react at a moment's notice. Their weapons were still in the cases, but the cases were open.

Two of them had checked the firing chambers. None of them had stripped down the rifles. So far, they hadn't impressed Carver. Never trust a weapon someone else gives you. Always check it. A bad weapon could get you killed.

Dan texted him. *When will you strike?*

Carver didn't see a reason to tell him exactly. They wouldn't need a decoy. He'd be in and out in seconds. The guards wouldn't even have time to react. Their mutual problem would be solved. Everyone except Leon would live to see another day.

He says he wants to meet for breakfast at 8AM. Fontaine's rooftop. It's to line up a shot from his balcony. I'll come up behind him while he's scoping the target.

Dan replied. *Roger that. We'll have your decoy in place. Just make sure you get him before he takes a shot.*

Carver cracked a smile. *Won't be a problem.*

Leon was back on the bed. Looking at his phone again. Carver watched carefully. Waited to see if he received a text. Dan might double-cross Carver and warn Leon. It was better to be sure. But Leon kept scrolling. No texts arrived.

It looked like Dan was on the straight and narrow. At least just straight enough to be believed.

Elena stared at the live feed. "Do you think they'll really leave us alone after this?"

"Hopefully. I don't want to have to kill more people."

"I never thought I'd have a conversation like this." Elena laughed nervously. "I think I'm ready to go back to my quiet life of reading the news on air."

"No more investigative journalism?"

Her gaze went distant. "I'm not saying that. But clearly I need to know which battles I can win, and which ones will kill me."

"It's hard to tell until it's too late." Carver put a hand on her shoulder. "It's not a crime to keep your head down."

"Yeah, but what would my dad think?"

"Maybe that he raised a smart daughter." Carver didn't like giving advice. It felt contrived. Like it was only to make someone feel better about themselves. He thought about what advice he really thought was useful. What would he tell himself?

"What are you thinking?" Elena took his other hand in hers. "Is it about tonight?"

"I'm thinking that maybe the world is better off with you in it. Maybe you can do what you want whether it's investigative journalism or reading off a cue card. Maybe your dad would be happy as long as you're happy." Carver shrugged. "I don't know what else to say."

Her face brightened. "Amos Carver cares if I live or die? I'm not just potential collateral damage?"

"I think I just said that."

"While still remaining as distant as possible." She rolled her eyes. "I understand. I see why Paola couldn't stay with you. Why I couldn't stay with you even if I wanted to."

Carver understood. "Because I kill people."

She laughed. "No, Carver. I mean, yes, it's a little disconcerting knowing what you did in Morganville. But that's not the problem. The problem is that you dedicated your military career to following orders no matter what. It didn't matter if you thought it was right or wrong. You did what you were told."

She squeezed his hand. "Then you found out it was all a lie. You were just a pawn that was sacrificed as part of a chess game. Now you're playing your own game. Taking no orders or responsibilities. Doing what you need to do to survive. It makes sense. And it's incompatible with a relationship."

"I don't exactly feel emotions like a normal person," Carver said. He stroked her cheek. "That doesn't mean I don't like people. That I don't have some kind of feelings for you or Paola."

"I know. And it's okay." She stood. Pulled him up. Pulled him toward the motel bed. "It's all okay for now."

DAN LET HIS PEOPLE know the plan.

Lance was nervous. He was the guy playing the decoy. "Are you sure Leon won't shoot me?"

"You'll show yourself briefly then stand behind one of the concrete columns on the roof. He won't have a line of sight. By the time you come out, it'll be over."

He nodded. "Okay."

"You're the only guy big enough to look like Carver." Dan clapped his shoulder. "I promise we have your back."

"I watched Leon practicing before. The man can nail a bullseye from a half mile."

Dan picked up his phone. Looked over the texts he'd sent. The other teams had checked in. All was good to go. "Just be in position and listen for my mark."

Lance nodded and left the hotel room.

Dan went to his computer. Read through the work emails. Business was picking up again now that Breakstone had been cleared of all charges. By tomorrow morning, Leon would be out of the picture. The harm he was doing to the company would be stopped.

Dan just hoped Carver could pull it off as easily as he claimed.

CARVER WOKE UP at two AM.

Elena stirred beside him. Rolled over and snored gently.

He took a shower. Put on a black t-shirt and cargo pants. Holstered his pistols. Checked his ammo. It was probably overkill, but he wanted to be safe. There was only one gun that he planned to fire and that was the Glock with the suppressor.

Elena was dressed and waiting. "I'll sit in the car, okay? I just don't want to be left here alone wondering what's happening."

"Sure." Carver gave her the compact Glock. "Hold onto that in case."

They got in her car. Drove to the condos. It was two-thirty in the morning. Club Periclean was still thumping. A long line stretched from the door and into the parking lot. Carver hadn't shown up for work or even called in sick since the incident. He probably didn't have a job there anymore.

Not that it mattered. Tomorrow would be a clean start, provided Dan kept his word. Provided whoever took over Breakstone honored that agreement. Either way, Carver was going to say goodbye to Miami. He wasn't sure where to go next. Maybe it was time to leave Florida altogether.

He checked the camera feeds. Leon had gone to bed at ten. The guards were asleep too. One guy was awake, watching the camera feeds. He was working through a pot of coffee. Trying to keep awake.

So far, he'd gone to the bathroom three times. Carver planned to time his approach with the fourth. It would probably happen around three AM. He wanted to be in position before then. Even if it didn't work out that way, he could still be in and out in seconds.

It would be too late for the guard to do anything. Especially since they were asleep. The only guy in any kind of position to respond was the guy watching the cameras. It was doubtful he'd try to stop Carver alone.

Carver rehearsed the sequence in his head. Take the elevator to the 29th floor. Climb the stairs. Edge along the wall so the camera couldn't see him. Unlock the door. Open the door. Slip inside. Turn on the flashlight to confirm Leon was there. Three shots. Run out.

Back down the stairs. Down the elevator. Into the car out back. Escape. Quick and easy.

Elena was looking at Carver's burner phone. Watching the recorded footage from earlier. Watching Leon climb into bed. Turn off the lamp. "Any chance he moved from the bed?"

Carver shrugged. "I'll check with the flashlight to confirm he's in the bed."

"Why not use those night vision goggles in your bag?"

"They don't work. I keep meaning to get them fixed but it's not a priority."

"They'd be real handy right now."

He nodded. Using the flashlight would blind Leon but also expose Carver. Carver would still have the upper hand.

Elena went back to the start of the recorded footage.

Carver parked behind the condos. He was going in the back entrance. Taking the cargo elevator up. He checked the time. Just past two thirty.

Elena showed him the footage. Leon wasn't on the screen. "I just noticed something."

Carver didn't see anything except the bed and Leon's cell phone lying on it. Elena showed him something else. Showed him the time stamps. She told him what she thought. Carver mulled it over. Agreed with her. Something didn't add up.

"Something else just hit me." She showed him a picture of Chad Dorsey. "Look at it. Now, look at this." She showed him another picture.

Carver stared at them. Noted the differences and similarities.

"What do you think?" Elena asked.

Carver thought back over the past few days. Added up the minor inconsistencies. It was little to nothing to go on. But there was a bigger body of evidence he already possessed. A certain personal knowledge that made him think it might be worth the extra risk.

"I'm not sure." He got out of the car. Entered the service entrance using the keycard the concierge had given him. It was the same kind of keycard the cleaners used to get around.

Carver stepped into the cargo elevator. It was much larger than the main elevator. There was padding on the walls. Tough vinyl flooring. Otherwise, it worked just like any other elevator. He took it to the 29th floor.

He exited the elevator. Walked to the stairwell close to room 29102. Entered the door. Walked up two flights to the next door. He checked the camera feeds. The guy watching the laptop was fidgeting. Almost time for a potty break. He got up fifteen minutes later. Vanished off the screen.

Carver left the stairwell. Edged along the wall. Used the keycard on Leon's door. He closed it quietly. The foyer was marble. He walked slowly. Quietly. There was enough ambient light in the area for the camera to see him. But the watcher was gone for the next minute or so.

The bedroom door was closed. Carver eased it open. Slipped inside. The ambient light spilled into the room. The bed was barely visible. He turned on the flashlight. Aimed the suppressed weapon.

Leon was there. His eyes blinked open. He reached for the pistol on the nightstand. Carver fired. Once. Twice. Three times.

It was over.

CHAPTER 35

Leon lay on the bed.

There was no blood. Just chips of wood and fluff from the pillows. He was still alive and blinded by the flashlight shining into his eyes.

"Get up go to the bathroom. Hurry."

"Carver?"

"Do it now. Take your phone."

Leon grabbed his phone. Walked into the bathroom. Carver followed him. They were out of sight of the bedroom camera, but the guard might have been back at his station. He might have seen what happened.

Carver closed the bathroom door. Turned on the light. "Turn on your phone. Unlock it. Then open the texts and toss the phone to me."

Leon looked just as baby-faced as ever. But there was a hardness in his eyes. A distrust. "Why?"

"Just do it."

Leon did it. Turned the phone toward Carver. Carver stayed well back from him. Waited for him to toss it. Waited to see if he might try something. Leon tossed it. He didn't try anything. He knew Carver. Knew what he was capable of. Close quarters combat was Carver's strength.

Carver caught the phone with his free hand. He looked at the texts. Confirmed Elena's suspicions and his. "You never got my texts, did you?"

Leon looked confused. "What texts? When?"

"Yesterday. Today. Elena noticed that you'd left your phone on the bed and somehow replied to one of my texts earlier."

"You bugged my room? How in the hell did you know I was here?"

"Does a man named Dan work for Breakstone?"

"A lot of people work for Breakstone. I don't know all their names."

"Does Chad Dorsey have a close relative you know?"

Leon frowned. "What does that have to do with anything?"

Carver was almost positive he was right. He knew why he thought Dan looked familiar. "Who got you this room? Who have you communicated with in the past twenty-four hours?"

"That would be Trevor." Leon's eyes darkened. "Trevor Dorsey."

Elena had shown Carver a picture of Chad. She'd shown him a picture of Dan. The similarities had been too close for coincidence. But Dan was too old to be Chad's son. "Trevor is Chad's brother."

Leon nodded.

"Did you come here to kill me, Leon?"

"I came here to find out what really happened in Morganville and why you're trying to kill me."

"I think we've both been set up." Carver motioned with the Glock. "Can I put this away?"

Leon nodded. "We were brothers in arms, Carver."

Carver holstered the pistol. Leaned against the bathroom counter. "How did you get caught up in Breakstone?"

"I didn't get caught up." Leon closed the toilet seat and sat down. "Tony and Sam inspired me to join. They said I could be a part of a company with civilian oversight. No more blindly following political orders. I would always know who we were targeting and why. And the money would be enough for me to start a family."

"Just like you always wanted."

He nodded. "Yeah. Just like I always wanted. They told me there was a way out of Scion. Once we were out, we'd join Breakstone together. I told them I'd only agree if I had part ownership of the company. I wanted to be my own boss. So, they drew up the papers. The shares were private. If anyone left the company, the shares reverted equally to the other partners."

"That's how you became CEO. You were the last man standing."

Leon nodded. "I didn't even know about Morganville. There were a lot of operations I didn't know about. They sent me all over the world taking out what seemed like really bad people. The same kind of people I'd wanted to target in Scion. But when I found out about Morganville I started digging. I found out that most of the dossiers were falsified."

"Did you know about Breakstone's private assassin division?"

"I knew of it, yes, but not until very recently. Trevor told me that you were out to kill me. That he'd tracked you to Miami. I asked one of my trusted local assets to verify the information, but to only communicate with me. He ended up dead."

"Was his name Desmond Price?"

"Yes."

"How was he your asset? I thought he was in the DEA."

"He was in the DEA. I've been recruiting people from various domestic agencies to liaison with me under the table. It's not exactly legal, but it gives me eyes and ears on the ground." He shook his head sadly. "Desmond was thinking of leaving the DEA to work for me. He had some ideas for reforming the way law enforcement goes after drug dealers and I was onboard."

"How did he know your assassins?"

"I told him they were looking for you. That he should make sure they didn't find you before I had a chance to talk to you."

"He went above and beyond, apparently. Tossed one of them over a balcony."

"I don't know why he would. I think something else happened."

"Maybe it did. We may never know." Carver thought of another question. "What happens if the last partner of Breakstone dies?"

"Since I'm the only person holding shares, it would mean Dorsey's next of kin would inherit them. Chad had no wife or kids. It would have gone to Trevor."

"Did you know there are armed men in the neighboring condos?"

"No."

"I thought they were your guards. They bugged your condo too."

Leon pressed his lips into a thin line. "How many men?"

"Three in each room. Most are asleep. One is watching the cameras from a laptop."

"How do you know all of that?"

Carver showed him the phone. The live feed. The guard watching the laptop was staring blankly at the screen. He hadn't seen Carver wake Leon and take him to the bathroom.

"Just as clever as ever, Carver." Leon grinned. "You've always been good at turning enemy assets against them."

Carver tucked the phone away. "It seems obvious what Trevor wants."

Leon nodded. "Trevor wants you to take me out. Then the guards he put in the rooms to either side take you out. They'll tell law enforcement they were just guarding me. Trevor will take over the company and all the loose ends will be tied up."

"Yep. What happens if Trevor runs the company?"

"Trevor fought my direction. He wanted to follow in Chad's footsteps. Turn Breakstone into a fully functioning black ops PMC both domestically and internationally."

"Isn't Breakstone almost there already? I thought Congress passed a law."

"They did. The President has to sign it, but he shelved it."

"Probably waiting for Trevor to take control."

Leon nodded. "I wouldn't doubt it."

"You're in charge of this operation, Leon. No politicians or secret commanders in the way." Carver folded his arms over his chest. "Tell me what you want to do."

Leon shook his head. "What do you suggest, Carver? You're better at improvising. I'm better at long term planning."

Carver told him what he thought. He figured it would be the fastest way to handle things.

Leon made a call. Spoke to someone. Ended the call. "Thirty minutes."

"Easy enough." Carver texted Elena. Told her what to do.

You're serious? She replied. *That's insane.*

She was probably right.

"Okay, let's go." Leon turned off the bathroom light. He opened the door. Slid back into bed.

Carver stuck to the edge of the living room. Followed the wall to the door. Eased it open and slid out beneath the camera. He reached the stairwell and made his way down to the 29th. Elena was waiting there.

"Carver, are you sure this is the best way?"

"No, but I think it'll work." He checked the time. Fifteen minutes. "You can handle your part?"

"Yes." She steeled herself. "I can."

The time ticked down to zero. Carver received a text. It was go time.

He and Elena took the elevator to the 30th floor. Carver drew a pistol. Looked at the live feed on his phone. Stepped into the hallway and walked toward Leon's door.

The guard watching the camera feed on the laptop flinched out of his tired stupor. He grabbed a radio. Started talking. There was no audio on the cameras, but it was clear what he was saying. *Target is here! Get to your positions!*

Lights flared on in the other condo. The three guards tossed on body armor. Grabbed their rifles. The three guards in the other condo were doing the same. Carver opened the door to Leon's condo. He watched the six guards staging inside their rooms. Like they were doing door-to-door searches in a warzone.

The guy watching the laptop was talking into the radio. Probably waiting to give the order. Carver fired three rounds into the bed. The muzzle flash lit the room. He turned on the bedside lamp.

Leon lay face down. A red stain spread on his pillow. The man watching the camera spoke on the radio. The guards exited their rooms. Carver couldn't see them, but he imagined them staging right outside the door.

No one was watching the camera feed on the laptop. Carver snapped his fingers.

Leon got up. Looked at the stain on the bed. "Water and ketchup was the best I could do."

"Looked convincing enough for the guy watching the camera."

Leon opened his rifle case. A shiny Barret fifty caliber was nestled in the foam inside. Two Sig pistols were also inside. He pulled them out. Loaded the magazines. "Why haven't they come inside yet?"

"They want me to open the door. Then they'll light me up." Carver shrugged. "That's what I'd do."

"Not ideal."

"I'm not worried." Carver walked toward the door.

"Wait! Are you crazy?" Leon took cover near the kitchen counter.

"If I did my job right, I don't need to be worried." Carver checked the live feed on his phone. He could see the laptop screen. Could see that the six guards outside were brandishing their Colt M4s.

He opened the door. The guards were lined up outside. One of them grinned. "Chad Dorsey sends his regards."

"So do all our buddies in Morganville," another said.

Carver shrugged. "The dead don't talk."

Triggers clicked. Firing pins inside the firing chambers sprang toward primers on bullets. The gunpowder would ignite. The slugs would rocket from the gun barrels and turn Carver into Swiss cheese.

But the firing pins stopped short of the primers. Carver had clipped a few millimeters off the ends. Instead of primers, the firing pins hit empty air. The guards kept pulling triggers as if expecting a different outcome.

Carver grabbed the nearest guy. Kneed him in the gut. Threw him to the floor. Leon came around the corner, Sig P365 aimed at the others. Carver brought up the Glocks, one in either hand.

"Unless you want to be sending your regards from the grave, I suggest you drop the rifles and get on your knees."

"Fuck you!" The one who'd grinned at Carver reached for a sidearm.

A red dot blossomed on his forehead just below where the helmet protected it. He slumped. Dropped to the floor. The gunshot echoed loudly in the hallway. Leon aimed at the others. "Unless I'm mistaken, I'm still the CEO of this lawless company. Get on your damned knees or I'll drop every last one of you."

The others dropped their rifles. Carver frisked them. Took their sidearms and knives. Four people appeared down the hallway. They hurried toward Carver and the others.

Detective Flores and Agent Turner led the pack. The third guy was Leach's former partner, Maynard Hughes. Elena was behind them, phone camera recording everything.

Flores and the others cuffed the guards. Dragged them inside the condo.

"Damn it, Carver." Maynard looked him up and down. "I told Leach to stay away from this business. It was too dangerous. And it got him killed."

"He was doing his job." Carver shrugged. "Can't blame a man for doing that."

Flores turned to Leon. "Explain what's going on right now."

Leon set his pistol on the kitchen counter. He sat in a stool. "Long story short, Chad Dorsey's brother, Trevor, was trying to have me killed so he could inherit Breakstone. To do that, he manipulated a lot of chess pieces and got some good people killed. One of them was Desmond Price. Another was Detective Leach."

Agent Turner sighed grimly. "He was a good man. I still don't understand what happened to him."

"Assassins happened," Carver said.

Leon explained the situation. Told them how Desmond was looking for Carver to keep the killers from reaching him first. Nicki Jones apparently tried to drug Desmond. He managed to turn it on her. Then he took her to her condo so he could get her out of the way and call Leon. Something happened. A fight, maybe. Somehow, Nicki went over the balcony. Rang the dumpster like a dinner bell.

"Then Theresa took revenge for Desmond killing her sister," Carver said. "That was why she gutted him like a fish instead of making it look like an accident. Then she saw that Leach was helping me and took him out."

Hughes frowned. "And how did Theresa die?"

Carver shrugged. "Natural causes, I guess."

Flores laughed. "That's your answer?"

"It's the one I'm going with," Carver said.

Flores looked at Elena who was recording everything. "She told us she's a news reporter from Atlanta. How did she get mixed up in this?"

"The killers were after her too," Leon said. "It all goes back to Morganville."

"There's a lot to unpack. Too much." Carver nodded toward the guards. "Better to finish this first. Talk later."

"Finish it how?" Flores asked.

Carver walked to the coffee table. Picked up the cell phone lying there. It belonged to the guy who'd been watching the laptop. The others hadn't been carrying phones. He held it up to the laptop guy. "Unlock it."

"I'm not doing anything until I see my lawyer."

Carver nodded. "You have a better chance of seeing the parking lot before you see your lawyer."

The man frowned. "That doesn't make any sense."

"Sure, it does." Carver hauled him off the floor. Dragged him to the balcony. Leaned him over the railing. "That's the parking lot down there."

"You can't scare me. The cops won't let you do it, especially not in front of witnesses."

Flores put a hand on Carver's back. "He's right. If he didn't have his pals in there, I might let you do it."

The laptop guy sneered. "Told ya."

Carver shoved him over. He screamed. Carver grabbed his belt before he fell. "Last chance."

"Help!" Laptop guy screamed. "You can't let him do this!"

Elena grabbed Carver's elbow. "Carver, I got it handled."

"How?"

"Get him inside and I'll tell you."

Carver dragged the guy back over the railing. Most people would have crapped their pants. The laptop guy was former military. Maybe special forces. He looked more pissed than scared. Carver dumped him next to his buddies.

Elena had the laptop from next door. She put it on the kitchen counter. Put the cell phone on the counter. Set the leech next to it. It was finished in a few seconds. She plugged it into the laptop. A folder with the contents appeared.

She scrolled down. Opened a folder called *Security*. Inside was a file with a six-digit number. "Most phones don't encrypt the PIN."

"That's it?" Carver said.

"We need his fingerprint too." She turned on the cell phone screen. It prompted for a fingerprint.

Carver walked over to the laptop guy. "Tell me which finger or I'll break them all until I get it."

"This is against the law! I want my lawyer!"

The man's hands were bound behind his back. Carver spun him around. Pressed the man's right thumb to the screen. It unlocked and asked for the PIN. Elena entered it. They were in.

Now it was time to catch the big fish.

— · —

CHAPTER 36

Carver opened the texts on the laptop guy's phone.

There was one to Trevor just before the guards tried to kill Carver. *Target is approaching Leon's room. Will let you know when mission is complete.*

Trevor had replied. *I thought he was going at 6AM.*

The laptop guy texted back. *Must have changed his plans.*

I'm fifteen minutes away. Send me pics of the bodies when it's done. Then I want to come up and kick Leon's lifeless body in the face.

"Trevor really hates Leon," Elena said.

Leon smiled. "I'm not surprised."

Carver looked at the pool of blood where the dead man's body had been left. He gave the phone to Elena. "Take a good shot, okay?" He hefted the body. Dragged it to the side.

"I'm surprised none of the neighbors reported my gunshot," Leon said.

"Someone did. We told dispatch we were handling it," Hughes said.

Carver stained the back of his shirt with the dead man's blood. Then he lay on his stomach. Head turned sideways in the blood. Eyes open and lifeless.

Elena took two pictures. "Okay."

Carver got the pillow from the bedroom. Soaked it in the blood. Put it back on the bed. "Your turn, Leon."

Leon played dead. Elena took pictures.

"Send him a text."

She sent Trevor the pics. *They're dead.*

Trevor replied. *ETA 5 minutes.*

"Coward." Leon laughed. "Won't even come up until after he's sure I'm dead."

"Let's have some fun," Carver said. "Elena, find a good spot to record from."

Flores looked concerned "What are you doing? This is a crime scene!"

"We're baiting the biggest fish in for the catch." Carver went into the guest room. There were six pillows on the bed. He stripped the pillowcases. Gagged the laptop guy with one. Silenced the other four guards. Dragged them into the guest room and closed the door.

Leon stripped the dead guy and swapped clothes with him. He laid the corpse face down on the floor. Carver went prone on the cold tile in the puddle of blood.

"You're way too comfortable doing that," Elena said. "It's gross."

It wasn't the first time Carver had played dead in another man's blood. Playing dead was a good way to stay alive.

Hughes, Flores, and Turner positioned themselves in the guest room to stay out of sight. Leon held one of the M4 carbines and stood in the doorway. Without the firing pin it was useless, but this was just for show. The elevator dinged in the distance.

"He's coming." Leon faced away from the door.

"I should've known Carver would go against the script." Trevor laughed as he walked inside. "Did he go down fast?"

"Dropped like a rag doll," Leon said mimicking the voice of the laptop guy.

"Good." Trevor stepped around the blood.

Carver saw his feet. Trevor was probably looking at the bodies. Not even looking at Leon. He stepped to the side. There were three thuds. Trevor kicking the body.

"Die, you goody two-shoes asshole!" Trevor gasped. "What the hell?"

"Surprise, mother fucker!" There was another thud. Trevor hit the floor.

Carver rose, coagulating blood oozing down his face. He looked down at Trevor. Grinned. "Hey, Lieutenant Dan."

Trevor pushed woozily to his knees. "What the fuck?" He looked up at Leon. "You're dead!"

"Not quite."

Trevor lunged. Leon fought him off easily. Grabbed his arm. Spun him around and pinned it behind his back. "Wow, Trevor. You did a lot of bad things. Using assassins to kill a DEA agent? Trying to kill me so you could take over the company?"

"You'll never prove it!" Trevor grimaced in pain. "I have powerful people in government on my side."

"Yeah? I doubt it."

"I do!" Trevor struggled. "Just wait until they step in."

"Give me some names," Carver said.

"I'll wait for my lawyer." Trevor clammed up.

Carver grabbed him by the throat. "Should I just dump him over the railing?"

"That would probably be safer," Leon said. "I don't want him coming after me later. Plus it would have nice symmetry, you know? Maybe land him in the same dumpster as his assassin."

"Sounds good to me." Carver grabbed Trevor by the back of the neck. Opened the French doors to the balcony.

"Stop! Stop!" Trevor screamed and struggled. "I'll tell you anything!"

Leon got in his face. "Tell me who your government contacts are."

"I don't know their real names." Trevor sobbed. "I never even met them. They'd send anonymous messages and people to meet with me. They told me they wanted me as CEO. They're the ones who sent me the assassins to help."

"I don't believe you." Leon rapped his knuckles on the railing. "Carver, do the honors."

"I'm telling the truth!" Trevor shook with sobs. "Go to my hotel room. Turn on my laptop." He rattled off a long password. "Everything is on there. I promise."

Elena walked up behind them still recording. She lowered the phone. Punched Trevor in the face. "That's for trying to have me killed, asshole."

Carver dragged Trevor inside. Dumped him on the couch. Knocked on the guest room door. "Okay, he's all yours."

Flores and the others stepped out.

Trevor's eyes flared. "You've been here all this time? He violated my due process!"

"Did he?" Flores looked confused. "I didn't hear or see anything."

Hughes cuffed Trevor. Read him his rights. "You're lucky I don't throw you over the balcony for killing my partner."

"I want my lawyer," Trevor said. "I'm not saying another word."

Agent Turner stepped in front of Elena. Held out his hand. "We'll need your cell phone for evidence."

"I'll be happy to give it to you once I've had a chance to make a copy."

"We can't let any of that get on the news until we go through it."

Carver stepped between them. "Let her make a copy first."

"I don't think so."

"Turner is right." Flores put a hand on Carver's chest. "None of this gets out until we can get things sorted."

"So you can let the FBI, DEA, and other federal agencies cover it up like they did Morganville?" Elena shook her head. "I don't think so."

"We're not giving you a choice. Hand it over or we'll arrest you."

Leon snatched the phone from Elena. Gave it to Turner. "Here. We don't want any trouble."

"What in the hell?" Elena lunged at Leon. He dodged. Gripped her wrist and spun her like he was dancing. Then he dragged her out of the condo and into the hallway.

Carver glared at Flores and Turner. It was in his best interests to keep things quiet. As long as Trevor and his conspirators went to jail, he didn't care. The last thing he wanted was to get tangled up in a federal investigation.

He turned and walked away.

Leon was talking to Elena. She looked mollified. He turned to Carver. "Let's go right now."

"Go where?"

"To get Trevor's laptop."

Carver shook his head. "I'm out. Best if you keep me out of all the investigations to come too."

Leon frowned. "You don't want to get to the bottom of this?"

"We did get to the bottom of it. Case closed. I just want to put it all behind me."

Carver got into the elevator. The others got in after him. They went to the lobby. Carver was still covered in sticky dead man's blood. No one was at the concierge station. Club Periclean had gone quiet next door. It was five in the morning and everything was closed.

Leon looked around. "I don't have a car here."

"I do." Elena pointed to the side. "It's around back."

"Let's go."

Carver stopped and watched. "You two are going to get the laptop?"

Elena nodded.

"The cops took the burner phone. Do you even remember the password?"

"I do," Leon said. He held up the leech. "And I made a copy of the phone before I gave it to the police. Everything is here."

Carver stared at them. Part of him wanted to go with them. But the bigger part told him it was time to go. The threat was over. The biggest threat now was law enforcement. He needed to go. Put some distance between them.

Elena took his hand. "You're not coming, are you?"

He shook his head.

"You're leaving town?"

He nodded.

"Carver, don't go." Elena gripped his hand tighter. "Stay and help. We can bring down the powerful people behind Breakstone."

"That's your calling not mine." Carver kissed her forehead. It left a bloody mark. "It's not mine."

"What's yours Carver?" She jerked her hands away. "Being alone? Is that what you're best at?"

"It's what I want."

She wiped tears from her cheeks. "No, you just want to walk away from responsibility."

"That's not what I'm doing. This is finished for me. It's done." He looked at Leon. "Right?"

Leon nodded. "As long as I'm around, Breakstone isn't coming for you. I'm going to root out everything rotten and rebuild."

"And you can report on it, Elena." Carver backed away. "I think your dad would be proud."

Elena wrapped her arms around his neck. Pulled him down. Kissed him fiercely. Came up for air. "I know what Paola saw in you, Carver. And I know why she left you. I know why you'll always be alone." She kissed him again. Stepped back. "Good luck."

Carver blinked a few times. Her words stung. It was a new sensation for him. Words had stopped bothering him when he was a kid. So, why did hers get to him?

It didn't matter. He nodded. Turned away. Started walking.

ELENA WATCHED CARVER go.

Leon put a hand on her shoulder. "Don't try to figure him out. None of us ever could."

"He's always been like that?"

He nodded. "Maybe that's what made him so good at what we did. We killed for nameless, faceless manipulators. People who wanted to shape the course of history. Those same people were helping Trevor. They still want Breakstone."

"Why Breakstone? Why not start over with another company?"

"Because they intentionally destroyed the darkest, blackest special operations forces the government had. And Chad Dorsey hired most of the displaced personnel at Breakstone. He created multiple secret divisions. Left behind an organizational maze that I've barely started to unravel."

"Maybe Carver isn't out of the woods yet. Maybe those people will go after him again."

"Doubtful. They don't have a reason to do it anymore. It was personal for Trevor. It's not personal for the people he hired."

"Maybe Carver made it personal for them." Elena smiled to herself. "He has a way of doing that without meaning to."

Leon shrugged. "Let's go get that laptop."

Elena watched Carver disappear down the sidewalk. She bit her lower lip. Nodded. "Yeah. Let's go."

CARVER WALKED BACK to the Betsy.

He found the valet he'd lent the Audi to. "Have fun?"

"I had the best times of my life, sir." The young guy couldn't stop grinning. "I'll get it for you."

"Thanks."

The kid brought the car around. Carver tipped him. He'd left his weapons stash in Elena's car. All he had were his pistols. That seemed like enough. With Breakstone off his back, maybe things would quiet down.

He wasn't sure where to go, though. There were beaches on the west coast. Maybe it was time to give them a visit. Maybe he could go down to the Keys or hit the other side of the Gulf of Mexico. There were still options. Still places to go.

He crammed himself into the Audi. Revved the engine. Pulled out on the road. Headed across the causeway. Got on the interstate. Drove until he had to make a choice. North, or west? Carver made a decision.

He hoped this time it was the right one.

Epilogue

Elena stared at the computer screen. At the four words.

Who is Amos Carver?

She knew who he was now. Knew what he'd done. A part of her missed him. Maybe not him so much as the security she felt when she was with him. He had a surety of purpose that made her jealous.

She opened a video. A news segment she'd created and edited all by herself. It seemed safer that way. This one was just ten minutes long. It had interviews. It had live footage of the events at La Playa condos. It had screen captures from Trevor's laptop. It had footage from the trail cam at the Granby Mine.

Charlie had even let her interview him. She thought it was too dangerous for him, but he insisted. He tried to get Holly Robinson to talk to her, but she wouldn't do it. Even with Breakstone no longer a threat, she was still scared.

Despite that, it was a bombshell of a report.

Elena had edited out several things. Carver was nowhere in the footage. Never even mentioned. That was the way things had to be. He wanted his privacy. As far as her news story was concerned, he didn't exist.

She would talk to her manager tomorrow. Convince them to let her make this special report. Otherwise, she'd take it to another major news outlet. Once they got a whiff of what was on the video, she didn't think there would be much resistance.

Elena switched back to the text document.

Who is Amos Carver?

She deleted the text. Filled the space with something else.

Best just to leave him alone.

She closed the program. Deleted the document. Emptied the trash. Then she closed her laptop. A tear rolled down her cheek. "Goodbye Carver."

About the Author

John Corwin is the bestselling author of the Amos Carver Thrillers, Overworld Chronicles, and Chronicles of Cain. He enjoys long walks on the beach and is a firm believer in puppies and kittens.

After years of getting into trouble thanks to his overactive imagination, John abandoned his male modeling career to write books.

He resides in Atlanta.

https://www.facebook.com/groups/overworldconclave

Join the Overworld Conclave for all the news, memes and tentacles you could ever desire!

https://www.facebook.com/groups/overworldconclave

Or get your fix via email: www.johncorwin.net

Fan page: https://www.facebook.com/johncorwinauthor

BOOKS BY JOHN CORWIN-

Books by John Corwin
Want more? Never miss an update by joining my email list and following me on social media!
Join my Facebook group at https://www.facebook.com/groups/overworldconclave
Join my email list: www.johncorwin.net
Fan page: https://www.facebook.com/johncorwinauthor

PSYCHOLOGICAL THRILLERS
The Family Business
AMOS CARVER THRILLERS
Dead Before Dawn
Dead List
Dead and Buried
Dead Man Walking
Dead by the Dozen
Dead Run
Dead Weather Days
Dead to Rights
Dead But Not Forgotten
CHRONICLES OF CAIN
To Kill a Unicorn
Enter Oblivion
Throne of Lies
At The Forest of Madness
The Dead Never Die
Shadow of Cthulhu
Cabal of Chaos
Monster Squad

No Darker Fate
The Next Thing I Knew
Outsourced
Seventh

Printed in Dunstable, United Kingdom